Maggie's scream expired in a gasp that sucked the filmy substance into her mouth. Bees swarmed in her head. Fire burst through her lungs.

Blinded, with one eyelid plastered shut, the other eye blurred, she arched her back. Clawed. Slapped. Her fingers brushed a nose. She rammed it with the heel of her hand.

Her assailant grunted and withdrew far enough that Maggie could pinwheel her arms.

Her fists connected, flew open, and shoved against shoulders clad in a napped fabric until she freed herself. Clawing the covering off her face, Maggie flung herself upright, gasping, coughing deep, raspy hacks. Heart pounding, she fought against the darkness, flinging her arms lest her attacker come at her again. Only when she heard the faint snick of a door latch did she sink back onto her pillow in exhaustion.

Sweat-soaked, she lay panting until the room stopped spinning. Finally, she slipped off the bed and crawled over to lock the door. There she sat until the last bee in her head buzzed away.

Mental clarity brought fresh terror and more questions and self-doubt than Maggie wanted to consider. Had the intruder been male, or female? She remembered the texture of the attacker's clothing. Corduroy? Chenille? A loosely knit ribbed sweater? And how had her attacker gotten into her room? Try as she might, she couldn't remember locking the door when she came back to her room after dinner. But she surely had, after living in L.A. where locking up was automatic.

Praise for Raymona Marie Anderson

"An actress returns to her hometown determined to ease the burden of old wrongs. Her arrival triggers murder and she needs every bit of her courage to face down not only her past but the dangerous present. A page turner."
~Carolyn Hart, author

~*~

"Not even a growing reputation in Hollywood can bury the pain of having been left at the age of eleven in the care of a predator. After nineteen years of resentment, Maggie Simpson returns home to confront her sister for betraying her. Against the national trauma of the Kennedy assassination, Maggie uncovers secrets within secrets in this complex tale of murder, lies, and redemption."

~Maeve Maddox, author

Bitter Pills and Deadly Potions

by

Raymona Marie Anderson

This is a work of fiction. Names, characters, places, and incidents are either the product of the author's imagination or are used fictitiously, and any resemblance to actual persons living or dead, business establishments, events, or locales, is entirely coincidental.

Bitter Pills and Deadly Potions

COPYRIGHT © 2019 by Raymona Marie Anderson

All rights reserved. No part of this book may be used or reproduced in any manner whatsoever without written permission of the author or The Wild Rose Press, Inc. except in the case of brief quotations embodied in critical articles or reviews.
Contact Information: info@thewildrosepress.com

Cover Art by *Kim Mendoza*

The Wild Rose Press, Inc.
PO Box 708
Adams Basin, NY 14410-0708
Visit us at www.thewildrosepress.com

Publishing History
First Vintage Rose Edition, 2019
Print ISBN 978-1-5092-2865-2
Digital ISBN 978-1-5092-2866-9

Published in the United States of America

Dedication

In memory of my parents,
Raymond and Halley Roberts,
who always kept me safe

Chapter 1

November 25, 1963

Charmaine Dorsey stepped from the cross-country bus to a welcoming committee of one. A red leash secured the raccoon to the handlebars of a bicycle parked within the Morning Glory Hotel's arched front gallery. Neither someone's choice of a pet nor the fact that the hotel's coffee shop still doubled as the bus station surprised an Alden native like Charmaine.

The critter eyed her with the avid interest she longed to see in a crowd of adoring fans. Fans without the adoration would be good too.

She swept a fallen lock of hair into place under her pillbox hat and met the critter's x-ray gaze. Could the animal see past her Hollywood persona into the thudding heart of Maggie Simpson, the eleven-year-old who left town almost nineteen years ago and grew up to become Charmaine Dorsey?

The animal looked past her to the bus driver and scuttled toward him the length of its leash. Laughing, the man withdrew a peppermint stick from his pocket. The raccoon held up its paws. The driver glanced up. "Jefferson Davis does like his sweets."

Rejected again, this time for a cheap treat, Charmaine twisted her lips into a wry smile. As for the desired reunion, she wished now that she had phoned ahead. Could being told not to come have been worse than the fear of being turned away? At the least she'd have saved the price of the bus ticket.

She tipped the driver, picked up her suitcase and cosmetic case, and squared her shoulders. No one else got off the bus, and no one came out to board, so she let herself into the coffee shop—and stepped into the past.

The aroma of freshly baked pumpkin pie wafted from the kitchen. Two old men at the counter sat just as they might have in 1943, when Charmaine came with her sister Doreen to see Doreen's husband off to fight the Nazis. Back then it would have been war news the old-timers listened to from a radio above the pass-through to the kitchen.

Today, bagpipes skirling and drums rattling a somber cadence riveted their attention to the television set shelved there. Absorbed in the drama of President Kennedy's funeral cortege, neither man turned to see that the bus had left behind a slender blonde in a green suit whose jacket copied the short, semi-fitted ones the first lady favored. *Former first lady*. Still hard to imagine all the changes wrought by President Kennedy's assassination.

Events in Dallas the past few days held the whole world hostage, it seemed. She'd never known national tragedy covered minute by minute in such a way, bonding families, binding them to their TV sets. Commentary suggesting that divisiveness in the country lay at the root of events in Dallas, and that all Americans shared the blame, had brought her to this moment.

She couldn't fix the country, but she meant to cleanse herself.

Eagerness to get past the awkward first contact spun through her. Navigating among tables draped in linen only slightly less snowy than Charmaine remembered them as a child, she cleared her throat loudly. "Excuse me?"

One man at the counter and then the other swiveled around on stools whose ball bearings squealed protest. One pair of eyes, old-denim blue, looked out under white brows on a lean, no-nonsense face that appeared at odds with several peppermint sticks visible in his striped overalls' bib pocket. The raccoon's owner, no doubt.

The other old-timer appraised Charmaine through dark eyes behind spectacles framed in black. He wore brown wool trousers. Elastic bands caught his white shirt sleeves above the elbow.

Once, she'd probably known both individuals. Names eluded her now. "I'm Charmaine Dorsey—" she began, careful not to lift her voice in a way that begged recognition. She hadn't lowered herself to that.

Mr. Overalls pursed his lips. His plump companion nodded politely.

"Maybe you saw me in *The Pioneer's Daughter*," Charmaine offered. "I played the daughter's cousin."

Spectacle-rimmed dark eyes widened. "In the movies, you mean?"

She nodded, checked the other man's reaction. Blue eyes encompassed her in a long shot before panning from black-veiled hat down to black suede pumps and up again. What might have been a flicker of recognition vanished so quickly that she credited it to wishful thinking.

He extended his hand. "Forgive me. I don't see

many movies."

She accepted the courtesy in what she hoped would be a brief gesture and eased out a sigh when he quickly let go.

"I'm Fate Halperin," he said. "Welcome to our little town, Miss Dorsey, isn't it?"

Charmaine responded with a smile while the name Halperin whispered prompts from her memory. Fate—odd name she'd forgotten, but Charmaine would never forget the man's sister, Folly.

"Halperin doesn't watch much television either," the other man at the counter put in. "Too busy reading *The Rise and Fall of the Roman Empire* or some old encyclopedia."

Next thing she knew, his hand engulfed hers, clung. She scarcely registered his name for wanting him to let go. "…the local pill roller."

Pharmacist, Charmaine interpreted. Ed something he'd introduced himself. Danby maybe? Should she remember him?

He held fast, pumping her hand until her palm moistened inside her cloth glove. The more she tried to disengage, the more tightly he clung. Blessedly then, the swinging doors to the kitchen *whumped* open around a shapely behind whose owner carried two pies. Her yellow uniform skirt swished around her knees.

The druggist gaped. His grip loosened enough for Charmaine to free her hand.

Turning, the waitress smiled at her. "Sorry, ma'am. I didn't see you come in. Be with you in a jiffy."

The druggist inclined his head in her direction. "Now Joan here, takes in every movie that comes to Alden. Isn't that right, Joan?"

Clearly skilled at dealing with chatty old men, the young woman nodded without looking up while she cut the pies.

He tilted his head toward Charmaine. "This is Miss Charmaine Dorsey. She's an actress. You might have seen her in…" Hesitant, he glanced at her. "*The Pioneer's Daughter?*"

Joan snapped to, her dark eyes wide. "I did see that movie." She sounded short of breath. "Charmaine Dorsey, you say?"

"She played the daughter's friend," he added.

"Cousin," Charmaine corrected him. "A minor part."

As all her roles had been and would always be unless she relented and took the plum her agent currently dangled by its repulsive casting couch strings.

She felt diminished by her lack of fame, and as embarrassed as the young woman appeared for failing to recognize her. To Charmaine's relief, the television commentator said something about a horse that drew everyone's attention. Onscreen, a magnificent black stallion pranced and sidled alongside his handler behind the caisson that bore Kennedy's flag-draped casket toward Arlington National Cemetery.

The empty saddle and the cavalry boots reversed in the stirrups held a touch of theater. Charmaine found it totally in keeping with the ache in her heart. What a wonderful job Jackie had done, planning this day. How courageous she'd been through it all.

Fresh pangs of loneliness swept through Charmaine. She smoothed aside her bangs and stood taller. "Maybe one of you gentlemen will remember me as Maggie Simpson. Doreen Rice's little sister."

Slack-jawed, Danby gasped, "Maggie?" His eyes busied themselves trying to reconcile the child with auburn pigtails she'd once been with the strawberry blonde in front of him now. He elbowed his companion. "You hear that, Halperin? This little gal and her sis grew up on the farm right next to yours. Mildred Simpson's granddaughters. Took them in when their folks went to find work during the Great Depression."

And never returned for their children. That first abandonment in Charmaine's life.

The druggist shook his head as if contemplating a miracle. "You were a skinny little thing in rolled-up bib overalls last time I saw you, Maggie."

"Going on twelve years old." She glanced at Halperin, about to inquire about his younger sister, Folly, when he spoke.

"Maggie, is it?" He shook his head, frowned. "I should have known."

Why he'd say that when she bore no likeness to the child, Maggie, might have given her more pause if she'd been less concerned about how easily the men fell back on her given name. Everyone who knew her then would probably use it too.

The realization heightened her anxiety. Dare she go by Maggie, this near the Missouri border? Not far beyond, folks in Springfield could hold long memories about her past.

She sighed. "Yes, the same Maggie who ran wild through the woods between your farm and ours and pestered you for rides in your old buckboard."

She'd hoped the memory might soften him. No dice. Charmaine welcomed the waitress's smiling approach.

"Well, I think it's exciting," the young woman bubbled. "Someone from Alden related to a movie star." She proffered a menu. "You might like to sit over there." The table overlooked the winter-bare garden.

The anticipation and anxiety churning in Charmaine's stomach left no room for food. She shook her head. "Maybe later."

The druggist narrowed his gaze. "How is your sister, anyway? I hope things worked out okay for her."

As if time had stopped, and her heart with it, Charmaine felt adrift. Always, she'd pictured Doreen and Johnny on the farm the sisters inherited when their grandmother died in 1940. "Doreen and Johnny moved away?" She barely got the words out.

"Oh, Johnny lives here yet," Halperin put in quickly. "No one has heard from your sister since the two of you left town with that traveling medicine show while Johnny served his country."

Her thoughts reeling, Charmaine couldn't speak. Only she, then just Maggie, left town with the *Health and Happiness Revue*. Doreen had promised to fetch her before her birthday the next week.

Doreen never came.

Chapter 2

*Doreen...Doreen...Doreen...*Maggie's high heels struck her sister's name from the sidewalk in brisk cadence along Main Street. She'd left the coffee shop in a state near shock after declining the druggist's offer of a ride to Johnny's new house in town. The composure she'd hoped to regain as she walked refused to return. She should have known she'd be Maggie to everyone here. But how could she have guessed that the sister she'd pictured in this town for eighteen years had neither been seen nor heard from in all that time?

Where had Doreen gone? And why?

The leaden sky did nothing to lift her spirits, nor did the view to the south. There Mainstreet crossed South Boundary Road onto the graveled road past Fate Halperin's place to Maggie's childhood farm home. There, she'd hoped to come to an understanding with, and find forgiveness for her sister—and herself. A wooded area separated the two properties. A wind gust bathed her in scents of fallen leaves and blew a tattered newspaper along the sidewalk. She grabbed her hat. The paper wrapped around her leg. She kicked free and picked up her pace.

Doreen...Doreen...Doreen—physically absent yet overwhelmingly near as Maggie passed the drugstore whose window displayed a boxed set of Evening in Paris toiletries among the more modern offerings of

Tabu and Windsong. Tears stung her eyes at the memory of Doreen dabbing on scent from the little blue bottle with its tassel when she dressed up to go out.

A fly on the lam from winter buzzed against the inside of the pane in frantic starts and stops that mirrored Maggie's confused thoughts.

Facts and lies had chased one another around in her head since Fate Halperin had said back in the coffee shop that she and Doreen both went with the medicine show. Protest had died on her lips when a younger man stepped in, nodded at her politely, and then greeted the old men.

Danby glanced at his pocket watch. "You're running late today, Deputy Warner."

"It was either chop firewood or get by with the bathroom heater tonight." The deputy pulled off his knitted cap and raked splayed fingers through his rust-colored hair. An errant strand in the crown sprang immediately back to attention. He smoothed it down.

The druggist's chuckle loosened the constriction in Maggie's throat. "But my sister didn't go with the medicine show," she blurted, apropos of nothing at the moment and drawing a puzzled glance from the deputy.

Rather than explaining, Halperin said, "Of course she did. She left a note." Furrows snaked across his forehead. "I milked her cows morning and night until Johnny came home from the war two months later."

Danby nodded. "I remember plain as yesterday. Johnny looked everywhere for you and your sister that fall." One of the old man's shaggy brows tented above his spectacles. "Where in the world did that medicine show go from here, anyway?"

Vaguely, Maggie heard someone ask the waitress

to bring him the meatloaf special before she felt the room tilt. She stood near enough to one of the tables to grasp the back of a chair.

Danby sprang from his stool, but the deputy reached her first. He caught her by the arm. "You all right? You're pale as death."

Her nodded reply sent the room spinning.

Halperin stood. "Ralph is at the hotel's registration desk today. Please, if I may speak to him in your behalf?" Not awaiting her reply, the old man headed for the archway between the coffee shop and the hotel lobby. "I feel sure Ralph will be more than happy to provide a place for you to rest a few hours before you catch the bus on to Tulsa tonight."

She'd sat down with the deputy's help, but the idea of being hustled out of town cleared her head. "I came prepared to stay a while. Nothing here suggests I shouldn't do exactly that. If you'll be so kind you can take my suitcase in for the desk clerk to watch until I come back."

Whether he or someone else had done what she asked, Maggie couldn't be sure. Nor did she remember much about the conversation that followed except the directions to Johnny's house.

Now, moving away from the drugstore and past the post office, she saw one change on Main Street. Ahead, an auto parts store sat where traveling entertainers had pitched their tents on a vacant corner lot. Maggie had waited in line to audition for one of the children's parts in the *Health and Happiness Revue*'s five-day stand in Alden. She won the role.

Later, she learned how much using local children for bit parts boosted sales of the cure-alls Dr. Xavier's supposed wife hawked between acts. The two belonged to a dying breed of hucksters that dated to horse and buggy days. They stayed in business during wartime rationing only by trading alcohol-laced patent medicines for ration stamps to keep them in gasoline and tires.

Doreen...Doreen...Doreen... Maggie's heels quickened their tempo past the auto parts store where she crossed to walk west on Elm Street toward a showdown with Doreen's husband. The two questions that roiled in her mind, demanded answers.

****

Folly Halperin would have skipped doing the Rice house on this day of national mourning if she hadn't had five others to clean before Thanksgiving less than three days away. Upstairs in Marti's room, she was smoothing fresh sheets on the bed when the phone rang.

She flipped the frilly pink bedspread into place. Six rings later she decided Johnny must be too absorbed in watching Kennedy's funeral to take the call. She scurried across the hall to the extension in the master bedroom.

"Rice residence," she said in the proper tone from what she considered an impressive repertoire. "Miss Folly Halperin speaking."

"Sister?"

Her brother, Fate's voice on the other end of the line caused Folly to catch a breath. He hadn't called her here since their brother, Chance, had a falling out with Johnny last summer. "What's wrong?" Weak-kneed, she broke a house rule by plunking down on the edge of a freshly made bed. "Has something happened to Chance, or to one of the children? I told him that boy has no business with one of those motor scooters."

"The children are fine," Fate said. "However, I sense serious trouble in the offing for our brother."

Folly frowned. "You mean in the senatorial race?"

Silence.

"Fate? Are you still there?"

"Yes. You need to tell your boss that Maggie Simpson is back in town."

Heart fluttering, Folly leaned forward and clasped her hand to her chest. "Maggie Simpson? Doreen's little sister?"

A wry chuckle came over the line. "That Maggie indeed. But no longer so little. When she learns what is going on with her grandmother's place, and how it came about, the word trouble does not begin to describe the difficulties ahead."

Mouse feet skittered through Folly's stomach. "She'll get Doreen here on it too, you think?"

"No." Another long pause. "Maggie came looking for Doreen. It appears the two lost touch some years ago. Warn Rice. Tell him to prepare some acceptable answers, some way to put out that fire before it blazes out of control."

****

Chance Halperin retreated from his living room to the kitchen for a break from the televised events in D.C. While he mourned what had befallen his country, he hadn't shared Kennedy's political views. The liberal media's canonization of the man annoyed him. He opened the refrigerator door. On the wall beside it, the phone jangled.

He closed the fridge to answer. "Halperin residence."

"John Rice here."

The curt greeting could signify anger, or reluctant capitulation. Preferring the latter, Halperin felt a smile tug at his lips. "Good to hear from you, Johnny. I hope this means you've come to your senses about the easement."

"Forget the damned easement. I need legal advice."

The smile slid away. "I thought you relied on that high-dollar attorney from Oklahoma City these days."

"He went to Maine for Thanksgiving."

"Surely your legal problem can wait until his return."

"My problem could be walking up my front sidewalk even as we speak, you bastard. Your brother called. He said my first wife's sister is back after all these years."

Halperin sucked in a sharp breath, released it in ragged spurts. "Maggie?" He tried to imagine her face as an adult, leaned against the refrigerator, and shook his head to clear the vision. Silent too long, he heard a sharp "Halperin" in his ear.

"I'm listening. But I think you'd have considerably more to worry about if Doreen appeared on your doorstep, fella."

"So would you, I guess."

Chance's knuckles turned white on the receiver. "My reputation at the bar is spotless."

"That's your trouble, Halperin; you're so goddamn cocky. Just because your walls are papered with all those degrees and commendations—"

"Hold it a minute, Rice. Despite what you or anyone else might think, I worked hard to get where I am today. Go welcome your sister-in-law back to town.

We have nothing to discuss where Doreen and Maggie are concerned."

"Dammit, Chance. Don't hang up on me. Am I in the clear on this thing with the farm their grandmother left the girls?"

"What you're asking in fact, is whether I know my job. Go to hell, Rice." The attorney slammed the receiver onto the hook. Staring blankly at the calendar above the phone, he reflected on the last time he'd seen either Doreen or Maggie. Both had been truly dead in his mind for so long he could scarcely comprehend otherwise.

Little Maggie of the auburn braids. Such an innocent memory to surface again as harbinger of trouble. Could he hope to prevent its spread into his senatorial campaign?

He opened the fridge again, but the shelves loaded with fruit breads and other treats ready for Thanksgiving no longer offered enticement. He reached for a beer, paused, remembering how hard he'd worked to lose a few pounds, and shut the refrigerator door.

The need for diversion pushed him out to the back porch closet and into a jacket. He set out for the archery range behind his hunting lodge north and a little west of the house. Later, he'd have a chat with his older brother. Although Chance would never admit it to Johnny Rice, he'd never kidded himself about how much credit for his success he owed his siblings. Folly's hard work as a domestic, Fate's farm and later his junk store in town had helped finance Chance's early years in college. He meant to honor the family name by winning a seat in the Oklahoma Senate, Doreen and Maggie be damned.

Chapter 3

"Well, well, Johnny—how you have prospered," Maggie muttered at first sight of his Tudor style home against its wooded backdrop. If memory served, he'd owned nothing but an old jalopy when Doreen hired him on at the farm. They'd married shortly after.

Maggie surveyed concrete cherubs scattered among hollies and yellow chrysanthemums, the crisscross lace curtains in an upstairs window. No one in the coffee shop had mentioned a second Mrs. Rice.

She guessed there must be one.

In the driveway, a new red pickup bore the logo, *Rice Construction.*

Neck rigid, Maggie crossed the front terrace. She pressed the door chime button four times. It had taken all four rings for her to remind herself she'd returned to Alden to make peace, not war, and that honey draws more flies than vinegar.

The carved oak door swung open on a man taller and more muscular than the Johnny she remembered, but unquestionably the man she sought. His John Wayne sincerity might have disarmed her completely had his brown eyes been less apprehensive.

"Maggie?" He did a double take. "What a surprise."

He might have won a role in a grade B western at best. Unable to suppress a grin, she said, "I'd forgotten the efficiency of the small-town gossip mill. Who called you?"

Laughter bellowed, but he didn't reply, instead stepped aside and swung back his arm in welcome. "Come in this house, darlin' little girl."

Once upon a time she'd liked his pet name for her. Now it held a false note, but his stevedore build against a backdrop of French provincial furniture on gleaming hardwood floors squelched any possible retort. What looked like Daum Nancy figurines surrounded an ornately gilded clock on the fireplace mantel. Impressionist prints graced the walls.

The clear plastic covers that protected upholstered pieces in blue and gold damask, infused the room with a faintly oily essence.

Johnny's intense gaze drew hers away from the scene.

"My wife is a decorator at heart." He sounded defensive. As if on cue, a vacuum sweeper roared to life upstairs. Risers curved upward from the hallway that bisected the house front to rear. Maggie glanced up to the second-floor landing. "Your wife must work tirelessly to keep everything so immaculate."

Some of his defensiveness evaporated. "I said she decorates. Folly Halperin cleans. Surely you remember her?"

Indeed. Older than Maggie by at least fifteen years, Folly had nonetheless encouraged a child's dreams of Hollywood stardom.

Johnny spoke. "Folly's still Alden's most coveted housekeeper." He strode to the bottom of the curved stairway. "She thought you were a talented little girl— you'll want to say hello, I'm sure."

"Not yet." The proverbial elephant in the room had made itself known—its name Doreen. "Folly can wait. Where can we talk privately?"

Resignation bracketed his mouth. "My office is down the hall. He gestured toward the back of the house. "It's pretty much off-limits, even to Mrs. Clean." He led the way and ushered her into a room thick with cigarette smoke. Big game trophy heads stared down from paneled walls—deer, elk, even a moose, their antlers draped with dust-coated cobwebs.

Maggie's grimace drew a humble pie look from Johnny that resembled the one Maureen O'Hara always managed to wrest from Duke Wayne at some point in the fray. He tilted his head toward two leather club chairs in front of three casement windows at the rear of the room. "Have a seat. I'll open a window."

The drum table between the chairs drew her attention, more specifically the crystal decanter and accessories thereon. A shaft of sunlight had escaped the clouds, jeweling the decanter's amber contents and what remained in a glass beside it.

Air swooshed from the other chair's cushions as Johnny settled in. She felt his appraisal.

Could he read her correctly? Would he take advantage of her weakness?

In the periphery of her vision, the decanter loomed. She refused to look at it—she could, she would, get through this stressful day without a drink. Half-turned, looking past him, past the table, she stared out into the flawless yard cloistered within a tall picket fence. On one of the poplars that bordered the spacious corner lot on the south, a single yellow leaf still clung. Long past time to let go in autumn's scheme of things, the bit of gold reinforced her determination.

"Bourbon?" Rice asked as if aware of her thoughts. Trying to find her weakness?

No thanks rose to her lips, but he was already pouring.

After refilling his glass, he picked up ice tongs. "On the rocks?"

Too dry-mouthed to speak, Maggie watched him add a couple of cubes. She accepted the drink, but left it untasted, instead watched Johnny savor the aroma from his.

The yellow leaf's tenacity held her thoughts. Resist.

He quaffed his drink, and then remarked, "I must say, you do look great." His dark eyes took in how she'd styled her hair.

What might he figure out if her bangs had escaped the veil? They needed a trim, but hair stylists in Hollywood charged a fortune. She fought the urge to tuck any stray locks under her hat. "We aren't discussing me, here," she reminded him stiffly.

"I would never have thought of you as a blonde."

Had he thought of her at all? Maggie sat forward abruptly. "I'm ready for some answers, Johnny."

"I haven't heard the questions." He refilled his glass, flicked a glance at her untasted drink.

Now, the elephant in the room trumpeted for attention. She heaved it into the conversation by its trunk. "For starters," she said, "I want the truth behind the gossip you started about Doreen all those years ago."

His eyebrows gathered above his nose. "You mean that she left me for some other man?"

Maggie shook her head. "I'm not so sure she did. Mostly, I want to know why you didn't squelch the false rumor that she and I both went with the medicine show."

"I don't know the story wasn't true."

"And that, Johnny Rice, is a bald-faced lie." Maggie plunked her glass onto the table. Bourbon sloshed over the rim. The sweet smell caught at her throat.

She clutched her handbag's handles more tightly. "I saw you in the audience that night in Baxter Springs. You knew Doreen wasn't with the medicine show. Never had been."

Again, Rice affected the humility he did so well. "You saw me that night?"

Her gaze drifted past him again, taking in the backyard, the hazy sky. Memory projected images onto the gray, visuals forced aside for years. "I was onstage holding strings of popcorn while Linette and the local boys who played my brothers decorated a Christmas tree that kept falling over. Dr. Xavier grew angry waiting for his entrance cue."

"But you looked happy."

Had selfishness blinded him to the logical reason for that? She faced him. "Happy? Sure. Happy to see you seated on the back row. I thought Doreen had sent you to bring me home, as promised."

His regard sharpened. "What about Doreen's promise?"

"My birthday," she began, "on the Fourth of July, you know. I turned twelve that year. Doreen would bring me home to celebrate. She'd saved ration stamps for sugar to make ice cream—" the words lodged in

Maggie's throat.

Oh God—just one drink. But, no. "Doreen never came. I never saw her again."

No response.

The silence expanded, deepened until Maggie could scarcely breathe for wondering if he might find a single word of apology for leaving her that night with no explanation for anything.

Ghost images of regret in his dark eyes weren't enough.

"Mind if I smoke?" He didn't wait for a reply. Lighting a cigarette from the box on the table, he held the lighter in unsteady hands.

"I always believed my sister sent you to persuade Xavier to keep me with him," Maggie ventured.

Vigorous puffs veiled his features with smoke. He removed the cigarette with two fingers, held it aside. "What gave you that notion?"

All Maggie knew was what she'd been told and fervently hoped wasn't quite true. "So you and Doreen could have time alone."

He barked humorless laughter. "I expected to find her there with you, Maggie. Her note said—"

She leaned forward, gripping her purse. "Damn the note—if it even existed. Only I—"

"There *was* a note."

"—went with the medicine show."

Another smoke cloud billowed before he said around the cigarette, "The old man told me how you kept at Doreen until she agreed to let you go."

How many more lies? "Actually, I'd given up on going. Out of the blue, Doreen changed her mind."

His brow arched, settled, knotted. "But you must

have been thrilled."

Was his astonishment feigned? She watched a reflective smile dance into his eyes.

"I remember how you always played dress-up and movie star."

The breath flew from her lungs, hot, angry, as she reached for her glass. She meant to toss its contents into his face, but the aroma paralyzed her beneath a flashback of Dr. Xavier's breath, sharp with his Golden Elixir cure-all. Out of that past, his plump, white hand fell onto her shoulder. "Of course, you saw your brother-in-law out there. He's just back from the war in Europe. He and your sister need some time alone together." His whisper fell on her again, wrenched from shuttered memories.

Although barely twelve years old, Maggie had caught his meaning exactly—thanks to Xavier's depredations.

She forced herself to the present, lowered the glass to the table while Johnny's eyes questioned the repulsion she couldn't hide. "Dr. Xavier," she quavered, "told me you paid him to keep me with him for the rest of that summer."

Red-faced, Johnny sprang from his chair. "Damned liar! I had just enough money to get back to Alden. It took months to save enough to go looking for Doreen again." He crossed to the gun cabinet near the hallway door where he stared through the glass panes that enclosed his collection.

Fear scratched at Maggie's insides. Might he seek easy relief from her pressing questions? "Johnny?"

He faced her, his eyes imploring. "How could I have taken care of you, a little girl, alone? Xavier had his wife to help."

Not wife, she wanted to say, but didn't. "You could have come for me later, looked everywhere, the way you told it around Alden. The medicine show headquartered in Springfield, not all that far from here. I matured fast, Johnny."

Hands out, palms up, he shrugged. "What can I say now, except I'm sorry?"

Shame kept her from revealing exactly how sorry he should be. The barrage of lies she'd heard in the past hour pounded at her temples. She rubbed the ache and then smoothed aside her bangs. "This business about Doreen leaving you a note…didn't you find it strange she'd run away then tell you where to come looking?"

"I guess I didn't want to accept the truth." Deep lines bracketed his mouth. "What's the truth? Where *did* she go?"

"You surely checked with the sheriff about that? You didn't just look around at the farm she left and see a way to better yourself?"

He worked his jaw in silence for a moment then shook his head. "You're dead wrong, Maggie. I adored your sister. Doreen had a wonderful sense of humor and was beautiful to boot."

Maggie frowned in her effort to summon images that might confirm his remark but drew a different picture of her sister. "I remember her as plump, always sunburned from so much farm work."

Contradiction hardened his features. "Not skin and bones like you. Definitely not plump." Head tilted, he narrowed his eyes in appraisal. "Look in the mirror, Maggie," he said softly. "You'll see Doreen…especially now that you've bleached your hair."

Taken aback, she asked, "Do you have a snapshot?"

He made a huffing sound. "Would I keep a picture of someone who dumped me?" Furrows crept across his forehead. "Besides, Paula wouldn't like it."

The wife. The perfectionist. She'd certainly want no clutter from his first marriage. "Paula's a jewel," he continued, "beautiful from the inside out. Today, when a president we both helped elect is being laid to rest, she went as usual to her volunteer job at Wellington School for the Retarded in Tulsa." Sadness had crept into his tone. "Our only child attended classes there until she died last year."

Maggie felt sorry for him in spite of herself.

After clearing his throat several times, he asked, "Will you be in Alden long?"

Had she a real answer to that? Until reconciliation with Doreen became impossible, she hadn't realized how far beyond desperate her need for it had gone. "I intend to stay as long as it takes to learn the truth about my sister."

He narrowed his eyes. "Why now? What brought you back after so many years of silence?"

"When someone on television said that we are all at fault for the horrors in Dallas last Friday—the divisiveness that breeds violence—I realized that change begins with the individual. I needed to make peace with you and Doreen." Her hope to understand and forgive them for abandoning her, and the need to forgive herself for what followed, Maggie found too personal to share.

He paced the room. "Well, that punk, Oswald, got

what he had coming."

"You misunderstand me, Johnny. If Oswald did shoot the president—and how can we be sure of that?—didn't he deserve his day in court? And why was he denied it?" She uttered a harsh laugh. "Because some other punk with a chip on his shoulder decided vengeance was his."

At the windows now, Johnny stared out, silent.

Maggie joined him. "I heard how some school children cheered at the news of Kennedy's death." Her hand settled on Johnny's shoulder, pressed him to look at her. "Their president, Johnny. They cheered because he'd been shot."

He waved aside her distress. "You know how kids are."

"I haven't had the privilege of motherhood," she said, "but I know about monkey see, monkey do. Children usually reflect attitudes they see at home." The way he tightened his jaw told her he thought she sounded like a street corner evangelist.

So be it. She'd found the implications of those children's remarks reprehensible.

"Our culture has grown so hardened to resentment and hatred that there's no compassion for those with whom we disagree," she continued. "What can anyone of us do to change that, without changing ourselves?"

He looked at her, his eyes bright with pain. "You hated Doreen and me so much?"

That state of affairs and its cause she'd meant to talk over with her sister. No one else.

He crooked his finger under her chin so she couldn't look away. "Maggie, you must believe I'm truly sorry for any wrong I've done you. But Xavier told me you loved every minute of your life on the road."

Ice hardened around Maggie's heart. "And Linette, Xavier's so-called wife? What did she say?"

"Saw nothing of her. Off packing costumes, I think."

Unable to stand another moment of it, Maggie turned to go, remembered her mission. She paused in the doorway. "Let's try to put the past behind, Johnny. That's why I came."

He approached, smiling.

"About the farm," she said. "It'll be all right if I stay there a while I guess."

"Well..." His gaze slid past her shoulder to the nearby gun cabinet. "I'm afraid the house isn't available."

"You rented the place?"

His eyes darted everywhere. "No. I'm developing the property. There's a dam going in on the Arkansas River near here. A new law disallows lakeside homes, but retirees will want quiet places near good fishing."

Noting how quickly he assumed the humble pie expression, Maggie's pulse quickened. He needed watching. "We should both profit," she said carefully.

He spent some time with his cigarette.

She stepped away from the pungent smoke. "Johnny?"

"Sorry, Maggie. You no longer hold legal interest in the property."

Of all she'd imagined, this had never entered her mind. The shock that rippled through her body left her barely enough breath to gasp, "What...what...do you mean?"

"Both you and Doreen have been declared dead."

Maggie grasped the door facing for support while he, without a glance her way crossed to his desk where he withdrew a folder from the top drawer. "These court documents make it official."

Cold, then hot, she said through gritted teeth. "I'll get an attorney. We'll see how dead I am."

"Sorry Maggie, the legalities are solid. I've already discussed it with my attorney."

"And that would be?"

"Folly Halperin's brother, Chance."

It took a moment for the name to register. She tried to picture a third Halperin. How could she have forgotten Chance among three siblings named Fate, Folly, and Chance? Suddenly, she knew why the older brother had tried to hurry her out of Alden. "Fate Halperin warned you I was in town, didn't he?" Eyes narrowed, Maggie twisted her mouth around her suspicions. "Maybe losing Doreen wasn't as traumatic as you had everyone believe. Once you'd located and abandoned me, you controlled a nice little acreage, didn't you?"

"Don't give me that 'I'm miserable' expression, John Rice. I'll bet it was a mortgage-free acreage at that."

"You're dead wrong, Maggie."

"No more than I am dead and out of the rosy little dream you've built for yourself and your 'beautiful inside' new wife."

Chin thrust forward, he took a few steps toward Maggie. "You leave Paula out of this."

She held ground. "I mean to learn the truth about Doreen, Paula be damned. I owe my sister that much for saddling her with all the blame for so long"

He grasped her upper arm. "Let's talk about this."

Her effort to pull away tightened his grip, the pain drawing a gasp. Released abruptly, she staggered against the gun case. The glass panes rattled.

She brushed away his attempt to steady her, instead, stared at a snub-nosed revolver in the case. "Many times in my life I wanted to see you dead, Johnny. Until now, I thought I'd outgrown such feelings."

"You wouldn't stoop to murder," he scoffed, but added a laugh as false as the excuses he'd made about why he left her with the medicine show.

Maggie bolted from the room and collided with someone standing just outside the door. A woman cried out. An object fell at Maggie's feet. Glancing down, she kicked the feather duster aside and fled to the slate-paved entryway and out the door.

On the front terrace, she paused, realized she'd almost toppled none other than her old friend, Folly Halperin.

Courtesy and regret told her to go back and apologize.

Her feet wouldn't listen, instead carried her down the walkway and out to the street where her heels resumed their earlier cadence, repeating her sister's name.

Doreen…Doreen…Doreen…

Why did the repetitions sound ominous now? Nothing Johnny said suggested her sister had come to harm. Maggie remembered the note he'd mentioned.

Had Doreen meant for Johnny to find and bring me home as she'd promised?

Or had someone besides Doreen written the note? If so, who? And why?

Chapter 4

"Hey there, Mr. Halperin, sir." Sheriff Randall Turkeson tipped his Stetson at the old man headed out of the coffee shop as the sheriff entered. From his counter stool, Deputy Guy Warner watched the two shake hands, then turned back to the funeral proceedings on television.

The commentary got lost in a bellow at the old man from Turkeson, better known as the Turk. "That coon of yours is getting mighty antsy out there. Runnin' back and forth on the end of his leash. I'm fresh out of peppermints, but after he got over the surprise of a lemon drop, he seemed happy enough for the moment."

"Jefferson is a bit on the impatient side when it comes to his meals," came the reply. "Normally, I feed him immediately after I finish eating. That is always around twelve-thirty. Today, I found it hard to walk away from coverage of the president's funeral."

At that, the deputy quirked an eyebrow. The old man had disappeared into the lobby *tout de suite* after the woman named Maggie had sailed from the coffee shop like a destroyer under full steam. He'd returned within minutes but spent the rest of his long lunch hour trying to find a comfortable spot on his stool. Its squeak and squawk had set Guy's teeth on edge while he tried to follow events unfolding in Arlington and eat at the same time. Not an easy task at best with the old men dropping sporadic remarks about the woman into the mix. Despite his normal dislike of small-town gossip, today's topic had poked the deputy's curiosity button.

The Turk's back and forth with Halperin in the doorway finished, he made his way to the counter. He settled on the end stool beside Danby. To their left, Guy slathered butter on another hot roll fragrant with yeast.

He nodded at his boss. "Afternoon, Turk. Things quiet over at the office, I suppose."

"A mausoleum."

Guy had requested an extra day off in anticipation of such a situation—not that much in Alden required his attention anyway. Except for an occasional crackdown on midnight drag racers on Main Street, directing traffic out of the football stadium on game nights pretty well summed up the deputy's job description.

At the opposite end of the counter, Joan, the waitress, and Lila, the cook, sat over a late lunch. Both looking tearful, they stared at the television screen.

The Turk, leaning forward to see around his companions, *tisked tisked* the cook. "Lila. Lila. No wonder you're fat. I hope you saved some of that meatloaf for me."

Guy doubted the woman would tip the scale at a hundred pounds unless she filled both apron pockets with a load of the Turk's bull.

Her failure to jump up immediately didn't typify the service in the Morning Glory, but reflected the sense of the world out of joint since the assassination. Even Guy had abandoned his radio in the groundkeeper's cabin out at Chance Halperin's hunting lodge to find a television set. The likelihood that somewhere his ex-wife and son watched too, eased somewhat the sorrow of national loss.

In her own good time, Lila fetched the Turk's lunch.

The funeral procession reaches its destination. A band plays. Bagpipes lament. Jets roar low in the missing man formation.

Guy tuned out his companions through the final tributes, heard only the bugler playing *Taps*, the gunfire in salute.

The widow lit the eternal flame that signaled Kennedy's enduring spirit, but the end of America's Camelot.

A collective exhalation whispered in the coffee shop. Deputy Warner sensed a wider response—life stirring beneath grief. As much as the flame marked John Kennedy's place in history, it symbolized freedom's continuity. The new president stood among the mourners, cowboy hat in his hands.

Guy tugged his railroad watch from its pocket. Fifteen minutes past two. An hour later in Washington.

The cook picked up her plate and headed for the kitchen.

The waitress topped off coffee cups all around and began clearing the counter.

Predictably, Ed Danby launched into a recap of the nearer drama: The return to Alden of a woman called Maggie. A genuine, though obscure Hollywood actress, no less. Trouble for John Rice, of all people—war hero, paragon of civic progress.

While the exact nature of that Trouble remained vague, the story clearly involved Johnny Rice's first wife, Maggie's guardian sister. Gossip claimed she took the child and ran off with some itinerant patent medicine hustler near the end of the second world war.

Only two years a small-town resident, Guy tried to take the advice Chance Halperin had offered. "You want to offer a comment once in a while in Alden's endless speculations about each other's business. Otherwise you'll be considered uppity."

Guy's gossip skills remained stunted, however. In this case, he felt qualified to do little more than nod agreement with the assessment that Chance Halperin certainly knew the lawyering business, and if the two women in question had been legally declared dead, Rice had no worries.

The sheriff, a relative newcomer in town as well, jumped onto Pending Trouble with both feet. His deputy recognized the move as his way to introduce a personal take on current events—how the lawmen in Dallas bungled the job of protecting President Kennedy's accused assassin.

"Like I said," the Turk declared for possibly the hundredth time within earshot of his deputy since the Oswald shooting. "If I'd-a had Oswald in *my* jail, he wouldn'-a gone outta there without I'd-a damn sure locked up that courthouse basement secure as Fort Knox."

"If you ask me," Ed Danby put in, although no one had asked, "Oswald is clear proof our culture is on the collapse. His parents divorced, I heard, or never married. I'm not sure which. And there's getting to be more of that all the time. No wonder kids today are so messed up. Mothers off somewhere working. I hate to say it, but I have to agree with folks who say we're all to blame for letting our country come to this."

Guy didn't agree. Doing so he'd have to feel guilty for choosing to help pursue justice at the cost of a normal life with his wife and son. Sometimes, right decisions turn to crap no matter what. "I think you overgeneralize," he told Danby.

Open-mouthed at the notion anyone would question Great Truths as analyzed by Television, Danby puffed up visibly. Guy didn't give him space to argue. "Whether Oswald is guilty or not, you can't blame his mother."

"Well...I wasn't exactly—"

"Hell," Turkeson said. "It's beginning to look like Oswald was a commie pinko at the very least. Never should-a let him back in the country with that Russian wife of his."

Agreement murmured along the counter. Guy didn't add to it, too busy assessing the freshly baked pies. "Joan..." He crooked his finger at the waitress, busy rolling knives and forks into clean napkins at the end of the counter. "How about a piece of that chocolate pie, then?"

She flashed a grin. "How about now, instead of then?"

Accustomed to teasing about the upper midwestern idiom he sometimes let slip, he grinned back at the waitress. "Now is fine, then."

"Like I always said," the Turk informed anyone willing to listen, "strong law enforcement is our only hope of lowering the crime rate in this country. I say that means anticipating the worst and seeing it doesn't happen."

Through the steam rising from his thick, white coffee mug, the Turk leaned forward to peer around

Danby. "That's why I asked the commissioners for a deputy here in Alden; ain't that right, Guy?"

A nod sufficed, Warner figured, forking into pie crust that fell into flakes, gratitude swelling his heart for cooks like Lila Lewis. Crumbs clung to filling so dark and buttery the sight and aroma tweaked his taste buds before the chocolate melted sweet over his tongue.

Actually, Chance Halperin had planted the idea of a deputy in the Turk's mind and then assured Guy that in that role in Alden, he'd attract no outside notice. Halperin, after all, had facilitated Frank Jackson's metamorphosis into Guy Warner, and knew his friend's need to remain invisible to the larger world.

When, as the town's new deputy, he had pinned on the badge that made him part of a justice system he'd learned to distrust, Guy had found the idea laughable. It no longer amused him.

What began as a temporary retreat from the city life he knew and loved, felt more like a prison sentence since Kennedy's death. He'd heard talk of a need for a program that would protect government witnesses in federal trials. Figuring it for a Kennedy kind of thing, he doubted President Johnson and the late president's brother, Attorney General Robert Kennedy, were on good enough terms to accomplish much of anything.

Glumly focused on personal concerns, Guy came slowly to the awareness of a dead silence around him. Attention had shifted to the coffee shop's street entrance where the woman supposedly bent on causing Johnny Rice trouble, stood hesitant, surveying the room.

All the talk he'd heard over the past hour had sharpened his interest. He'd noticed the heart-shaped face earlier, but whatever had transpired in less than an hour had left the even features pinched and pale. He resisted the impulse to order the skinny creature a Super Glory Burger with a side of fries, a chocolate malt, and two pieces of pie.

In the brief time it took him to make those observations, she visibly regrouped, negotiating her sinuous way among the tables toward the counter as if on stage. Chin up, boxy handbag hung over her wrist, she placed one foot on its black high heeled pump exactly in front of the other without so much as a wobble. The result transformed the deputy from breast man to leg man in a heartbeat.

He felt like a splay-toed, gnome-eared, knobby-elbowed ninth grader and despised himself for it. To compensate, he leaned back onto his elbows and focused on what he sensed she wouldn't like him to see behind her confident step and smile.

Namely, he eyed the high color outside the boundaries of artfully applied rouge. Miss Hollywood had come away from Rice's house deeply shaken and ready to fight the whole town if need be.

The Turk, of course, levitated from his stool in an absolute froth to captain Alden's troops. His deputy offered a silent prayer of thanks for the promised anonymity of his role as chief latrine digger. If the woman's so-called missing sister act was a ploy to gain publicity to boost a sagging career, Guy needed to stay as far from her as possible.

Oddly, she dismissed him, and the sheriff, in one glance. Danby, she clearly preferred.

"Mr. Danby," she said, the husky voice that had surprised Guy when he first heard it intriguing now. He heard a rasp of anger she quickly tucked behind a warm smile for the old man. "I'm so glad to find you here yet, sir."

"Yes...well..." Danby bolted from his stool as if suddenly remembering he'd left water running in the bathtub at home.

****

Startled by the old druggist's quick response to what she considered a pleasant greeting, Maggie soon realized he hadn't moved out of eagerness to please, but to escape. She also knew that once word of her clash with Johnny spread, sympathetic ears would be as scarce in Alden as stretch limos. She trailed Danby to the door. "I'd hoped to catch your friend, Fate, before he left," she said. "I need to locate his brother, the attorney."

"Umm...uh," the old man hedged. "You'd likely find Chance at home today." Tilting his head toward the man whose hazel eyes had stripped her naked in a glance, the druggist said, "The deputy there, looks after things at Halperin's hunting lodge. That's the property next to your grandma's old—" he broke off, the ruddy stain in his cheeks deepening. "I mean, Chance lives hardly a mile from the lodge, maybe the deputy saw him sometime today."

The younger law officer shook his head. "Sorry." He settled more comfortably into the pose of one content to let others slay the dragons.

Unaccountably, Maggie felt an emotional pull toward him she didn't like.

She appealed to Danby again. "My business with Attorney Halperin involves my grandmother's farm place—Doreen's and mine by right. He should know that his client misled him about some facts in the case."

No one spoke for a moment, then the tall, slump-shouldered man with a sheriff's badge on his tan uniform's Eisenhower style jacket stepped forward. "I'm Randall Turkeson, ma'am. As county sheriff I'm the most qualified to help you." A valiant effort to straighten his shoulders failed. "My office is just over a block. Ride with me so we can talk about this in private."

His intense dark eyes called to mind those of the medicine show owner, Dr. Xavier, and jellied her insides. She heard the door wheeze shut behind the departing druggist. Fortified with a deep breath, she turned to the deputy, whose gray-green eyes tried to play sleepy coonhound but leaked bird-dog intelligence.

She decided intelligence could forgive a man for a bit of ogling.

The sheriff, she spared a mere glance. "If your deputy lives near Chance Halperin," she said, "he might give me a lift there."

The big man's smile stiffened. His hand settled onto her shoulder. "I'm sure Guy would be happy to do that," he said, "but since you feel there's been some injustice done to you here in Alden, I really should be briefed on the details."

Maggie pivoted free of his grasp. The movement put her near enough to the deputy that she could smell Aqua-Velva shaving lotion mingled with wood smoke. She glanced out into the street where Danby backed away from the curb in a white car. Of the two vehicles left there, one was an official looking black and white sedan with a red spotlight, the other an old green Studebaker.

She considered the latter vehicle's showroom shine, the buffed, chrome nose and turned to the deputy. "I guess that Studebaker out there belongs to you. Airplane front, did they call that style? I don't know that I've ever ridden in one."

"Commander Model. Nineteen fifty." Pride slipped in under the clipped accent of more northern climes. "The hood on the Champion is a little shorter."

Maggie nodded, settled onto the stool Danby had vacated. Any moment she expected the weight of the sheriff's hand on her shoulder again. She plunked her handbag down onto the counter, patted the wrinkles from her skirt, all the while picking up on vibes of interest from the deputy while he feigned indifference. Break a leg, she told herself and plunged right in.

"Your wife shares your interest in old cars, I hope." She allowed a breathy laugh to hang in the silence for a moment or two. "My first husband owned several, drove one of them often—an old Austin Healey." Maggie laughed again, lightly. "I'm afraid I wasn't always really happy about the time he spent tinkering with that car."

She interpreted his tiny shrug as his only response until he finally said, "I haven't much else to do in my free time except tinker."

The sheriff huffed explosively and slumped his way toward the front of the coffee shop.

Although his deputy didn't crack a smile, green lights danced in his eyes. "I wouldn't bet old Beetlebomb out there against the likelihood you'll hear more from the Turk."

It took Maggie a moment to identify Beetlebomb as the Studebaker. Laughing, she felt the knot in her chest pop a few threads. "Wasn't Beetlebomb the horse that always crossed the finish line last in that old Spike Jones song?"

"I'm in no hurry to get anywhere." He lifted his cup for the waitress to refill, then appraised Maggie. "Maybe you'd like some lunch, then?"

She hadn't eaten since the previous night. Smells from the kitchen certainly teased her nose, but she remained too on edge to eat. She rested her hand lightly on the deputy's plaid sleeve, the gray and green flannel soft beneath her fingers. "Please," she said. "Couldn't you just take me to see Chance Halperin? I really need to talk to him today."

"You'll be going back to California tomorrow, then?"

The glance he flicked at her tightened her chest again. Why was everyone in such a damn hurry to get her out of Alden? She affected a Kate Hepburn tilt of the head. "I don't plan to leave until I've made people in this town as uncomfortable with my questions about Doreen as they make me feel for asking them."

The deputy shrugged. "Folks hereabouts are curious, that's all. It does strike me odd, however, how hot you are for a reunion after what I take must be most of your lifetime out of touch. You could have called before you came. Saved yourself a long bus ride."

"I don't see my relationship with my sister as your concern, Deputy."

"Yet I should get all excited about helping you learn what you could have found out years ago, had you taken the trouble." He stated rather than questioned, his smile wry. "Of course," he added, "I'm sure you've been busy becoming a famous actress."

The remark hit her jugular, not by accident she suspected. Stage presence saved her with a cool expression. "Not that you care but this was the worst possible time for me to leave Hollywood. I've been offered a role my agent thinks could win me an Oscar nomination." No need for him to know she had no intention of accepting the part with its strings to a tumble on the casting couch with the director. Better this joker believe she coveted the opportunity.

"And so, a little publicity would be nice, wouldn't it, Miss Dorsey? Or whoever you are at the moment." The bitterness in his tone segued into disgust. "I figure you knew your sister wouldn't be here. Stirring up controversy for the television cameras is the name of the game these days, isn't it?" He lifted his coffee mug in a mock toast.

Her fingers itched to snatch the cup from him. A scalding mouthful of the dark brew might quench the thirst that had consumed her since turning down Johnny's bourbon. The headache she'd tried to ignore all afternoon swelled from annoyance to debilitation, a percussion section at double-fortissimo inside her skull. She sprang from her stool, staggered a few steps to her right before regaining her balance and her pride.

Her trembling legs carried her halfway to the door before they buckled.

Chapter 5

Maggie fell against a table, clutched the edge, and then slid to her knees.

Strong hands lifted her into a chair. "Either that performance had Oscar written all over it," said the deputy, "or you've cut more calories than even a body as unaccustomed to nourishment as yours obviously is, can function on."

"My body is no concern of yours." Maggie struggled to her feet.

He promptly seated her again.

A middle-aged woman emerged from the kitchen.

"Lila," the deputy said. "Just the gal we need. Would you please fix Miss Dorsey a tray? I'll check her into the hotel."

For all her desire to slam her fist on the table in protest, Maggie lacked the strength to lift a finger.

Alone in her room twenty minutes later, she sat on the edge of her sway-backed bed and studied the tray in her lap. How had she eaten every scrap it had held? The little green enameled coffee pot sat empty as well. Only a crumb of crust and smear of chocolate marred the saucer that once held pie piled with meringue.

Until now, she hadn't noticed the odors of stale tobacco smoke and old wallpaper paste in the room. Earlier, she'd been certain she couldn't keep down a bite of anything but sipped a spoonful from the bowl of clear broth. Soon she'd torn off chunks of fragrant yeast roll, dipping into the savory liquid, slurping dribbles.

After a crisp salad dressed with vinaigrette, she had considered the roast beef, mashed potatoes, and carrots, all of which refused to lay there untasted. All gone now. Uttering a soft groan, she patted her stomach and leaned back onto the lumpy mattress. Her eyelids weighed about ten pounds apiece. Down they slid. She forced them open.

No time for sleep—strategy to plan.

The deputy's goodbyes had resonated with finality. She had heard echoes of the faint mockery in his repeated use of her stage name, as if he considered her fainting spell an act. So much for expecting any moral support from that quarter.

Thus far in Alden, nothing had turned out as hoped. But had she ever let that stop her from moving on?

Surveying her room, Maggie wondered if it had seen new furnishings since the hotel opened shortly after the turn of the century. On the yellowed wallpaper, florid bouquets transferred from someone's nightmare vision of a rose garden, bloomed in endless array. Vines clung to trellises yellowed with age. The faded paper smelled depressingly of pages from an old book.

Overhead, a bare bulb struggled against gloom cast by shadows from the cedar tree that towered outside her second-floor window. Restless branches scratched the screen, talons denied opportunity to snatch away the room's struggling light, sending shivers along Maggie's spine.

She huffed a dry laugh to chase away the megrims, thankful for the warmth that wheezed around her with every clank of the ancient steam radiator. Her gaze roamed through the open bathroom door, lingered on the claw-foot tub.

After two days on a bus, the prospect of a bath offered sheer heaven. But first, she had a phone call to make. The telephone dated to the forties at least, a sullen black monster on the dressing table beside the door. She pushed herself upright and got from the bed to the phone when she felt unable to move a single step. She dialed the hotel operator.

"Switchboard." The voice sounded like that of the desk clerk. Morning Glory Hotel in its golden years a one-man operation?

He rang up the number in L. A.

After an interminable delay, Scaff Russell's gruff, "Hello," crackled in her ear. She heard voices in the background, something about a reception ongoing at the White House. Television created the sound effects in everyone's life today.

Odd, she thought, how everything so paramount in her thoughts since Friday exited stage left behind news of Doreen's disappearing act.

"Hello?" Russell repeated, impatient now.

Even irritated, her agent's nasal greeting brought the sting of tears into her eyes. "It's Maggie," she quavered.

A pause. "Who?"

"Charmaine."

"Well, it's about time you called. Do you have any idea of the position I'm in out here? High and dry with this damned unsigned contract on my desk while you gallivant off God knows where."

She sighed. "Just once, Scaff, will you forget

business? I have a problem here."

"Yeah?"

"My sister...the one I came to see? She isn't here."

Silence.

"Scaff?"

"So, what's the problem? You said you two were estranged anyway. Come on back, let's get this contract ironed out."

"Nothing to iron. I don't like the strings attached."

She could almost hear him boiling inside.

The eruption came as no surprise. "Ten years, I've waited for this kind of commission off you."

Maggie examined a chip in her coral nail polish while he ranted on. "Ten years I've stuck with you through bit parts, no parts, abusive men, even crapper-cleaner commercials. Stuck because you got talent if you could ever quit playing Miss Icicle. Get past that stiff-necked refusal to play ball with—"

"Ball, you mean," she interjected. "Ball the sleaze balls who call the shots in Hollywood." She slapped the top of the vanity dresser. "Forget the deal. Find someone else for the role."

"The hell I will. What's the difference between trading a favor for a favor, and marrying some guy you don't care about?"

Her thoughts spun around guilty fears he might be right. No time for that. "I cared," she replied through tight lips. "But if I'm as right for that part as you think, that producer will meet my terms."

"Not if you don't quit playing family reunion and get back here where your business is."

"That's why I called." Maggie closed her eyes, hoped the request she was about to make didn't anger him to the point of hanging up on her. "I packed some of my things in a trunk in case I decided to stay a while," she said in a rush. "The trunk is ready to ship. Would you please take care of that for me?"

"Oh sure." His tone sneered. "And I'll dance *Swan Lake* at the Hollywood Bowl as soon as wardrobe comes up with a tutu that reaches around my gut." Silence. She waited it out and as she'd hoped, he asked, "Where shall I send the damned trunk?"

Maggie stared at her hollow-eyed image in the vanity mirror and realized she had no address. She shrugged at her reflection. "The hotel, I guess. Morning Glory Hotel."

"Address, I said."

"Alden is a one hotel town." Thickness invaded her throat. She tried to swallow without success, said huskily, "This thing about my sister not being here? Everyone insists she and I left town together."

"And?"

"We didn't. I don't think anyone has seen her since." Maggie recounted the day's events, feeling the weight ease as she shared her side of the story. He listened in silence until she got to the part about Johnny taking away the farm.

"Hot damn, Lady," he said then. "You hang in there for a while. I'll see what I can do about this contract. You're talking some good publicity there, whether you realize it or not."

Her headache pounded back, full throttle. What would Scaff think if he knew how little she cared about publicity? The idea of people digging around in her past scared her to death. She rummaged through her makeup kit for the small envelope that held her headache powder, retrieved a tumbler from a shelf in the bathroom. Water clotted with bits of rust ran from the tap, stirring the powder, but didn't dissolve it completely. Maggie chugged down the mixture.

She made short work of unpacking. The old formulary that held her recipes for cosmetics, and had been meant to show Doreen, she left in the suitcase. Minutes later she sat in the pink and gold silk kimono left over from the better days of her first marriage, a towel draped over her shoulders. Staring into the vanity mirror, she gave her face its first thorough cleansing since the bus left California Saturday morning.

The small alabaster jar that held her face cream contained only an application or two. Without the fresh ingredients in her trunk she'd have to visit the drugstore. She preferred to make her own cosmetics, and shared cold cream, herbal mask, and cheek and lip color with friends in the acting community. Formulas, she kept to herself.

The cleansing ritual eased the ache in her neck and shoulders. Her face slathered with moisturizer, she ran bathwater and settled into the cosseting warmth with a sigh.

Oddly, the deputy popped into her mind. She scolded herself for not knowing how to handle him, told herself she'd be more tactful in future.

Meanwhile, after a nap, she'd find and apologize to Folly Halperin for almost bowling her over in the hallway outside Johnny's office. No telling how many people she'd already told about Maggie's argument with Johnny. The woman needed to know Maggie had no intention of harming anyone, ever again.

The hotel's towels were thin and rough, but

whoever did the laundry hung the sheets outside to dry—the coarse fabric smelled of sunshine and fresh air. Her last waking thought centered on the deputy, and how she might yet enlist his aid.

She awoke headache free and recharged. After slipping into gray wool slacks and a black sweater set, she made do with a light powdering of her nose and a bit of lip color from the tiny artist-palette she kept in a box that once held a triple strand of dime store pearls. The bluish stain beneath her eyes needed time and the skills she'd learned as a makeup artist's apprentice when she first arrived in Hollywood. Or eight hours of sleep. She shot her image a look askance, lifted and finger-combed her hair, and called it a wrap.

Folly, she'd been told, occupied a ground floor apartment at the rear of the hotel. There, Maggie knocked lightly on a door glossy with layer upon layer of varnish. Waited. Rapped again. No sound came from within. Disappointed, she turned away but had gone only a few steps when a latch snicked behind her. She turned to see the door open a crack.

Retracing her steps with a smile on her lips, she said, "Folly?"

The crack disappeared.

Maggie rapped again. "It's Maggie Simpson." An ear cocked to the door, she listened, heard nothing. "Please, could we talk about this afternoon? I owe you an apology. And it's important you understand how upset I am about my sister."

The door remained tightly shut.

"Folly? I'm afraid something bad happened to Doreen all those years ago. That's why I didn't come back and apologize after I ran into you. I couldn't think of anything except my sister."

The door swung open abruptly on a woman in a yellow poodle skirt topped by a blue corduroy jacket. Folly's impossibly maroon hair frizzed out from under a felt pillbox the identical red of a croc bag straight out of wardrobe for a forty's movie.

Maggie sucked in her breath, and frozen by eyes transparent blue and cold as a glacier, managed not to laugh.

As if a moment's delay cost too much, Folly remained in the doorway. "Your sister," she declared, "did a good job of looking after herself, don't you worry." Even in anger, she spoke in the well-modulated tone Maggie remembered.

"Doreen also did a good job of looking after me—until the last. Do you have any idea what changed her?"

"The war."

"I'm not buying that until I hear a plausible reason she'd abandon every responsibility she'd previously embraced."

Deep lines settled around the older woman's thin lips. "Johnny went off to the war and left her to take care of the farm without a man. Doreen liked having a man around."

The remark suggested things Maggie didn't want to hear. "Doreen looked after the farm just fine after Johnny left. She bragged about his bravery, enlisting when he could have requested a farm deferment."

Folly nodded emphatically. "A brave man indeed."

"After today," Maggie said, thinking about his perfect wife and home, "I can't help wondering if he also wanted to learn what other opportunities the world might hold. He obviously found out."

"If you expect me to take your side against Johnny, you've come to the wrong person. I heard you threaten him. I will swear that in court."

Her animosity gnawed at the fond image Maggie had carried of the woman so many years. "Surely you realize you heard a fit of temper, nothing more. I'd never hurt Johnny. It's only that no one will help me…" she paused for a beat before adding, "I thought for old times' sake you might arrange for me to meet with your brother, Chance."

Wide-eyed and stiff-backed, Folly said, "You leave Chance out of this," before she retreated. The door about to close in her face, Maggie stepped inside. It took a minute to find her voice in a room bulging with knickknacks, antiques, books, crocheted doilies, and photographs. On two walls, ceiling to floor bookshelves sagged beneath their burden.

Despite the quantity, order reigned. Not a magazine lay tossed carelessly aside. The odor of lemon oil permeated the air.

All welcoming, except the hostility in her old friend's eyes.

In search of a pathway through it, back to the days when common interests bonded an unlikely pair of friends, Maggie spotted a familiar title on one of the bookshelves. She walked over and took down the leather-bound volume, expecting Folly to object. She didn't.

"You still have the old Elizabeth Barrett Browning," Maggie said, rewarded at seeing softness creep across Folly's features.

"I loved how you read it aloud." She offered her the book—open on "The Lost Bower."

Emotions warred on Folly's features. Her red handbag slid down from the crook of her arm into her hand. Finally, heaving a sigh she dropped the purse into a chair and reached for the slender volume of poetry.

Blue eyes no longer cool, lost focus as if she followed Maggie's thoughts back to the woods between the Simpson and Halperin farms where, by turns, she and Maggie played audience and performer. The Halperins were all hungry readers.

Folly had recited verse. The star-struck child parroted favorite lines from Shirley Temple movies. They applauded each other. Could anyone in the current atmosphere of friction between generations understand such a friendship? Doubting it, Maggie closed her eyes to listen:

"…Years have vanished since, as wholly
As the little bower did then;
And you call it tender folly
That such thoughts should come again?
Ah, I cannot change this sighing for your
smiling, brother men!"

Maggie hadn't understood the poem as a child. Since, she'd read it often. She joined in:

"For this loss it did prefigure
Other loss of better good,
When my soul, in spirit-vigor
And in ripened womanhood,
Fell from visions of more beauty than an
arbor in a wood…"

Folly choked down, the remaining verses an echo in the memories the two shared. Wind howled around the window sash, scattering golden moments to the past. Folly closed the book.

Maggie touched her arm. "Is the amphitheater there yet, in the woods? Or have Johnny's bulldozers obliterated it as cleanly as he tried to erase Doreen and me from Alden's memory?"

Folly returned the book to its shelf. "The hollow remains unchanged." She retrieved her handbag. "Go away Maggie. I can't imagine why you chose to come back now, when there's nothing left for you here."

"I came to make peace with Doreen"

Seeing too many unanswerable questions about her relationship with Doreen in the blue gaze holding hers, Maggie shrugged. "Don't you see? Without Doreen, I have no one."

For a tenuous moment Folly appeared ready to capitulate. Instead, she opened the door and drew the curtain behind her eyes. "Johnny searched everywhere for your sister. Chance handled the case, and my brother is as meticulous about his work as Doreen proved irresponsible about hers at the last." She tilted her head, chin high. "He'll win that senate seat—you'll see."

Her meaning soaked in slowly. "You're afraid my inquiries will reflect badly on your brother."

Folly stepped out into the hallway. "I have errands."

Maggie stayed at her heels. "You were…are a fixture in homes all over Alden, Folly. If Doreen cheated on Johnny, you'd have known."

The thin lips quivered.

"I remember how kind you always were."

From the hotel lobby down the hall, laughter cut through the tension that separated the two women.

Folly's shoulders drooped. "Among your sister's

things—" Her voice rose as she edged toward the hotel's rear exit. "Johnny found a roll of exposed film."

Before Maggie could speak, the woman skedaddled in a flash of yellow skirt, pausing at the door to fling back, "I found snapshots of some man. A stranger."

Chapter 6

The sun hung low in the trees when the deputy returned to his cabin for the second time since lunch. There, on the archery range behind the lodge he found the man he'd looked for all afternoon. Chance Halperin held his bowstring taut, his focus the bullseye downrange. Guy stood silent lest he spoil the attorney's aim.

The bow twanged. The arrow overshot the mark and thuncked into a tree. Halperin swore.

"And you've always told me the Halperins would've starved during the great depression if you hadn't all been crack shots with a bow and arrow," said Guy, unable to resist needling him a bit.

Chance turned, a sheep's grin on his lips. "I once performed considerably better at many things. You may ask Beth how really good I used to be."

"Whoa." Guy waved his hands, palms out. "I'll not touch that one with a ten-foot pole." He knew that Elizabeth Halperin, daughter of a respected judge and married to an influential man, took herself much too seriously to even be considered open to a suggestive remark. Especially not one that involved her personal life.

He waited while the attorney retrieved his arrow and then joined him on the path.

"Believe it or not," said Chance, "I focused so hard

on the shot that I didn't hear you drive in."

"I keep telling you Beetlebomb's got the smoothest engine in Alden."

"Should purr, considering the time you spend stroking her various parts."

"Gotta stroke something besides my five-o'clock shadow since you gave me such hell for whittling away my lonely hours." The deputy referred to the miniature cars and trucks he carved on cold nights beside the fire. Indicating the wooden, recurve bow his friend favored, he said, "As for your hobby old man, maybe you need to spend a bit more time at it."

"Old man?" Chance struck a bodybuilder pose. "What's ten years—"

"Twelve years, you have on me."

Chance's silvery blonde brows quirked. "I concede. However, let me point out that it isn't years, but muscle tone that counts. Endurance."

Laughing with him again, Guy noticed his friend's amusement didn't touch the famed Halperin baby-blues. It didn't require a degree in psychology to ken the real reason behind the man's lack of focus—he'd heard about the actress and her troubles with Johnny. "You weren't here when I came looking earlier," he said, setting out for the cabin.

"I hiked over to the farm." Chance fell into step beside him.

"Your brother told you about the woman, then."

"Fate wasn't home."

"I didn't find him there either. Nor at his store." Guy had gone both places looking for his attorney friend. "I'd called your house, but Beth said you'd gone out. She didn't know where. I thought you should know that I'd had a run-in with the woman. She's after you next."

Dusk edged into the blue of Halperin's eyes. "Johnny Rice phoned to warn me."

"Yeah, from what I saw of Miss Charmaine Dorsey—or Maggie—to everyone here, I'd say she and Rice locked horns. Even so, she means to take you on the first chance she gets."

The attorney kicked a small stone off the pathway and heaved a sigh. Lines deepened across his brow. Guy tilted his head toward the lodge.

"Put away your gear. I'll boil up some java."

He watched the man go away, concerned by his uncharacteristic heavy tread and the weary way he lifted off his quiver before entering the building.

The cabin sat nearby, the cats waiting on the front stoop. Guy hallooed them by name, then realized the calico and the new troublemaker in town shared monikers—*Maggie*. Laughing, he bent over to greet the female as she came running. She wrapped herself around his ankles. Jiggs, the yellow tom, emitted a gruff growl.

He stroked Maggie's back. Aloud, he wondered, "Why do you suppose a lawyer as skilled as our friend, Chance would worry about a challenge he could swat down like a pesky fly?"

The cat meowed her indecipherable reply.

He finally managed to disengage from the feline's enthusiastic greeting. Once inside, he stoked up the coals in the old iron stove that centered the main living area, and added wood. The propane heater in the bathroom, and the kitchen range kept the water pipes from freezing when he was out, but it took Old

Firebelly to warm a man's bones. The chill had left the room, and the coffee ready by the time Chance came in.

Shivering in his jacket's upturned collar, Halperin warmed his hands over the stove. "Feels cold enough to snow out there."

"Not supposed to." Guy had listened to the radio long enough to hear the weather forecast and catch up on the latest in Washington, DC. Mostly a rehash of the president's funeral that morning.

Chance shed his jacket and tossed it on the wooden rocking chair beside the stove. "Coffee smells good."

"Come sit, then." He'd set out the coffee and what doughnuts remained in a package he'd bought a few days earlier.

Chance pulled out one of the dinette's yellow-padded chairs, sat, and reached for the mug.

"Sinkers are a bit stale." Guy scooted the plate over before settling in.

"Never too stale. Good for dunking."

More about the friction between Johnny Rice and the new woman in town was an itch Guy needed to scratch but didn't want to appear too curious. Ten minutes and a couple of doughnuts got them through obligatory remarks on the weather—typically Oklahoma, changing with scant notice from unseasonably mild to frigid. Silence fell. Guy sipped coffee while his friend stared into his mug, shifting it in tiny half-circles on the table top. Finally, he glanced up. "I guess Johnny found himself in a world of hurt this afternoon."

"Seems so, but I think the woman came off with some wounds too."

"How's that?"

"I saw her in the coffee shop when she came back from the Rice place. Pale as a ghost." He went on to tell the rest. "I kind of appreciated how she gave Turkeson the cold shoulder—but that didn't turn out so well for me after all."

"How so?"

"She'd stiff-necked me at first but then tried to mollycoddle me into driving her over to your house." Guy did an eyeroll. "Quite an actress, that one. She claims your client treated her and her sister unfairly. Says maybe you weren't as careful about learning the truth about their whereabouts as you could have been."

Red crept into Chance's neck. "Rice stands square on *terra firma*." His mellifluous courtroom tone frayed a bit on the declaration. "No one had heard a peep from either sister in years."

"So I understand. I talked to Turkeson a while ago—Rice called him this afternoon. According to the Turk, the man sounded damned well shook up."

"I can imagine." The words held a bitter edge. "Rice is accustomed to having things go his way."

"Actually, he's afraid of getting shot."

His coffee cup stalled halfway to his lips, Chance asked, "Little Maggie's carrying a gun?"

"Not carrying. But Rice said she talked like she'd find one from his collection mighty handy if she could get at it." He hitched up one eyebrow. "Little Maggie, is it?"

"That's how I remember her. She lived on the farm next to ours, roamed the woods between.

Expecting him to launch into talk of those good old days, Guy waited through a long silence while Chance wore a faraway look that suggested troubling thoughts.

Interruption seemed in order. "Your little Maggie turned into a knockout. Skinny as a rat, but great gams." Unsought, the image clarified in the deputy's memory. "Fair skin, almost translucent. Green eyes, assessing every minute. The only warmth I saw was in her hair."

"Chestnut brown pigtails with red highlights," Chance reflected aloud.

Guy snorted. "So even the strawberry blonde hair is fake."

"Strawberry blonde, you say?" A wistful smile played across Halperin's lips. "Last I saw Maggie was around Easter during my second year of law school at the University of Oklahoma. Mostly Beth and I visited her father in Oklahoma City."

Guy hooked another doughnut, dunked it, and shook off the excess liquid. "What do you think about Maggie's claim that she left Alden with the medicine show?"

His question remained unanswered, his companion staring off into space again. After a moment he blinked. "How's that, you say?"

"Do you think Maggie is really the only one who went away with that medicine show?"

"Her story flies in the face of local history, for certain." Chance pushed back from the table and fetched the coffee pot. He refilled their mugs. "So, does Maggie have any idea where her sister actually might have gone?"

"Apparently that's what she pinned Johnny down to find out. Her theory is that he bamboozled everyone in order to have the sisters declared dead and claim the property their grandmother left them."

"Really? And Rice's response to that assertion?"

"He insists he had a good lawyer on the deal."

"Damn!" Chance, the coffee pot in hand, began to pace. "Rice swore he'd neither seen nor heard of either woman in almost twenty years."

"He lied, you think?"

At the far end of the combination living room and kitchen, Chance stopped in front of the shelf that held the miniature wooden vehicles Guy created with his pocketknife. "Damn good job on old Beetlebomb," he said, tilting his head toward the tiny Studebaker.

"Thanks." He got up to go tend the fire. *No need to mention that he meant the miniatures for the son he might never get to see again.* He grabbed a sizeable chunk of wood from the box beside the stove and shoved it into the firebox, then motioned with the poker. "You can put that coffee pot on Old Firebelly here."

Chance looked down at the pot he still held, shrugged, and came over. "Won't it boil again?"

"Push it to the back." After a last poke at the fire, he closed Old Firebelly's door. "I guess you think Johnny is lying when he claims he never saw either his wife or his sister again."

"I believe that Maggie Simpson is a better actress than her lack of fame as Charmaine Dorsey would suggest. I consider it likely the actress learned somehow about the property transfer, and that the sister search is a ploy to come stir up trouble." He sat down at the table and hooked another doughnut.

Joining him, Guy felt the doubts he'd wrestled with all afternoon flare strong, souring the coffee in his stomach. "I'm more worried that she came here with that missing sister story in order to generate publicity for a flagging career."

"In which case, Deputy Warner, I strongly advise you to leave it to your boss to investigate the woman's claims."

"You got it, friend." He alone privy to his friend's need to live unnoticed beyond Alden's borders, Chance Halperin certainly knew how getting caught up in some publicity stunt that made news could destroy Guy's safe haven.

Trouble was, the woman had zeroed in on him, not Sheriff Turkeson for help. "The Turk is so hooked up with wondering how his wife spends her lonely nights when he's on duty that I doubt he'll show much interest in the actress after the way she cold-shouldered him this afternoon."

"Personally, I'd gladly help her out of town."

****

The deputy reflected on that statement while he sat whittling beside the fire later that evening. His usually unruffled attorney friend had left abruptly after the remark. Why? Hard to believe that someone of Chance's sterling reputation as a lawyer would fret over a simple property transfer after two people were declared dead.

A crackle from the stove interrupted his musings. He glanced down at the miniature fire truck he'd been whittling and saw how deeply into his thoughts he'd strayed. If anything, the object resembled a foreshortened delivery van.

He tossed the dud into the wood box and put away his pocketknife. Cleaning the kitchen area, he listened to Walter Cronkite wrap up the afternoon's events in

DC.

Cronkite soon lost out to the day's happenings in Alden. He rehashed them over the dishpan, lamented having found Fate Halperin's junk store closed that afternoon—the place was a gold mine for the Zane Grey novels Guy collected—and finally, sat down to read *Thunder Mountain* for the third time. He didn't make it much past "One night when the afterglow of sunset..." near the bottom of page one, before the mental image of Maggie Simpson as a little girl with pigtails coaxed him from the story.

Odd that Chance remembered her so clearly as that child. Admittedly, the man had brains—one of a remarkable trio orphaned young and left to fend on their own by older siblings who sought their fortunes elsewhere. If the rest of the clan was as eccentric as Fate and Folly Halperin, it came hard to imagine how they fared in the wider world.

In Alden, the mainstream swept the two along in its current, Folly in her garish ensembles of cast-offs from closets in houses she cleaned, her elder brother crisp in overalls and shirts ironed by that same, devoted, baby sister. Astonishingly, both commanded vocabularies Guy secretly envied.

More remarkable, their middle sibling, Chance, entered college on savings the three had scraped together from meager farm and domestic labor incomes. To their credit, neither Fate nor Folly would accept any part of the easy life their successful brother offered now, nor did he show the slightest embarrassment over his siblings' lifestyles. Old Fate shared quarters, probably slept with, the pet raccoon he called Jefferson Davis and took almost everywhere. The skill with which the animal scurried ahead of the old man's bicycle at the perfect pace to avoid the front wheel without pulling the leash too tight always made the deputy wish he might develop the same sense of timing as a misfit in Alden. He needed to fit in, but feared letting some of his past slip out in some casual sharing of experiences.

The phone rang. It sat on the wide arm of a school chair beside the front door. He picked up the receiver to hear the sheriff's blunt, "You there?"

Hello to you, too. "What's up, then?"

"More trouble for Johnny Rice."

"As in Maggie Simpson?" Guy squirmed inwardly because she'd remained that close to his thoughts.

"Yeah." The Turk sounded pooped out. "Paula Rice called. The actress phoned Johnny to apologize. She's goin' over there tonight, and Paula has to be out. She's nervous about leaving him alone with that woman. Thinks maybe someone could watch them through the office windows out back and not intrude but would be there if the hatchet the woman wants to bury is aimed at Johnny's head."

The image earned an eyeroll. "Paula Rice is nervous about everything."

"Yeah. Well, someone at the Morning Glory overheard the tail end of a fuss the Simpson woman had with Folly Halperin late this afternoon. A while before Simpson phoned Johnny." Silence hung on the line for a couple of beats before Turkeson continued. "Don't make sense how she'd stir up trouble one minute and the next be all mealy mouthed with apologies for her dust-up with Johnny earlier."

Undeniably odd. But then, the woman *is* an actress,

he reminded himself on his way to the Rice home five minutes later.

****

Maggie approached her second meeting with Rice with nerves taut as the skin on a bongo drum. So much depended upon her ability to avoid another argument with the only person she knew who might tell her about the snapshot Folly had mentioned.

Although the petite blonde who responded to the doorbell this time around wore a courteous smile, looking into her eyes was like looking at gray marbles. The delicate hand she extended in greeting scarcely appeared able to support the weight of the multi-carat diamond dinner ring that graced it. The bejeweled hand snatched Maggie's purse before she could say hello.

Paula Rice put the purse on a shelf in the coat closet beside the door. "In case you came prepared to carry out your threats against my husband," she snapped.

Maggie slipped off the tweed topper she wore over her black sweater and gray wool slacks. She handed it to Paula. "Don't worry, Mrs. Rice. I'm not carrying a gun in my purse or a knife up my sleeve. There's quite enough violence in the world these days without my contribution."

Some of the hardness left Paula's eyes. "You know, I'd almost forgotten for a moment—and I thought that I never would." Her voice broke on a sob that brought a lump of shared sorrow into Maggie's throat.

"We all thought nothing could ever take precedence over those last few terrible days, didn't we, Mrs. Rice?"

Hanging up Maggie's coat, the petite woman nodded. "Someone has been at prayer in our church since the moment we heard about the president's assassination last Friday. I'm due there now." She took a black cashmere jacket from the closet.

Maggie helped her into it, the satin lining sibilant against the woman's blue silk blouse. Not long ago, Maggie had sold a coat as fine from her dwindling wardrobe of rich-last-husband finery. Such losses were trivial in the wider course of her life. And today, this—

"You'll find Johnny back there in his office." Paula stepped to the front door. "Sheriff Turkeson knows you were expected." She hurried out into the night, casting over her shoulder one worried last glance.

****

The Rice home stood at the edge of the woods, a stockade fence in back. Deputy Warner followed the narrow trail between the trees and the fence and let himself in the gate. Ahead, light streamed from three casement windows on the rear of the house. Inside, Rice sat in one of two club chairs. He stood, a drink in hand, and disappeared from the room.

Outside in the darkness, Warner watched in the shadows of a large cedar tree near the windows. The actress accompanied Rice when he came back. She settled onto the edge of one of the chairs. Johnny refreshed his drink before sitting down.

He spoke, but not loud enough for the deputy to catch. He stepped closer and into something slick and smelly. "Crap," he muttered, meaning it literally. *How the hell had a dog found its way into this fortress of a yard?* The Rice's surely didn't own a pet—Paula's allergy to animal dander was famous in Alden.

He glanced around uneasily, lest the canine intruder still be somewhere about and leap out in a flurry of barking. After a moment he shrugged, wiped the sole of his shoe in the grass, and entertained dark thoughts about the sheriff in his warm car on a side street. As if the man could be of any help from that distance if the actress threatened Johnny some way.

Damned stakeout is a farce. Rice's behavior appeared more erratic than Maggie's. Already about three sheets to the wind, he'd poured a drink for the woman, then worked steadily on his fresh one while she held hers on the chair arm. Guy glimpsed one coral-tipped finger rubbing the glass as she asked something about a photograph, the soft husk in her June Allyson voice registered too low to carry well.

He inched forward again, careful to avoid the dog poop and the rectangle of light cast out the window.

The woman's voice rose on an insistent note. "But why would Folly make up something like that?"

One too many drinks rendered Rice's reply unintelligible. Maggie apparently hadn't quite gotten it either. She leaned toward him, her classic features pale in the lamplight as she harped on the idea that Rice had some photograph of her sister. Despite Guy's resolve to remain indifferent to the woman's situation, his curiosity mounted by the moment. And wasn't it odd that the sister would have kited off with another man when she owned property here? He'd like a look himself at the mysterious Doreen Rice.

A breeze worried the tree. Guy shivered and stifled the urge to yell out at Rice—*Give the woman the damned photograph.*

"Surely there's something among her things that

would help me, Johnny." Her voice quavered.

Rice sprang from the chair, staggered bit, and then steadied himself. "I told you, Maggie, I gave Fate Halperin everything in return for clearing the old farm place."

"You gave away everything?" Disbelief rang in her voice.

"Damned if I didn't. Why won't you hear—"

"What are you so afraid to tell me, Johnny?"

"Nothing! I swear to you—I have no information for you." He threw back the last of his drink and plunked down the glass. "I adored your sister. If I'd found her with some other man, at least I'd know she was still alive somewhere."

Features crumpled, voice timorous, the woman asked, "Do you really think Doreen might be…dead?"

"I don't know what to think, Maggie." Swaying, Rice enunciated carefully. "Stayed in that farmhouse for years, all her stuff exactly where she'd left it. Brooded myself sick looking for answers where there were none."

His genuine distress sent a pang through Guy's chest.

"Then I met Paula," Rice went on.

"You're afraid if I find Doreen you'll lose Paula."

Rice nodded, his chin low. Maggie stepped back, still clutching her drink. "If you worshiped Doreen's memory for as long as you claim, I find it hard to believe you didn't keep so much as a photograph of her."

The big man sagged into himself.

"Please Johnny. Doreen was—is all the family I have. If you do have a picture of my sister, or of the man Folly mentioned, please let me have it. If I find Doreen, I'll see that she doesn't make any trouble for you over the land. And I promise the same."

Reeling, the man palmed his forehead for a moment before looking up to say, "If Folly mentioned such a photograph, she made it up."

"She wouldn't do that."

"I know she treated you special as a little girl. But don't think Folly isn't above a little white lie if it benefits her family. Those Halperins hang together."

"Maybe so, but she sure came to bat for you."

"Yes, and you'd been asking her about Chance. He's running for public office. Any hint he helped me claim the Shimpson..." The man shook his head at the slurred word and repeated, "Simpson property through illegal means won't shet well with the voters."

It seemed doubtful that either one of them would remain standing much longer. She trembled visibly; Rice kept righting himself as if his knees had buckled.

"So, you never found a roll of undeveloped film among my sister's things."

Rice furrowed his brow. "Maybe...if I did so during my breakdown. Nothing about those months are clear now. All I do remember seeing is a scrapbook Doreen kept since high school."

"Yes!" Maggie clasped one hand to what Guy considered an admirable bosom for a woman so slight. "Doreen's scrapbook has a green cover. She put a handkerchief in it, one you sent her from the place you trained for the army."

The man shook his head. "The scrapbook went with the stuff I gave Fate. But I still...have—" He balanced himself and lurched toward the door to the hallway. She started after him. He flapped his hand at her. "I'll bring them."

"Them?"

No reply.

Deputy Warner, his feet numb with the cold, shivered under his collar and wiggled his toes inside his boots. And waited, cursing his boss, the Turk, under his breath.

Chapter 7

Through the open window, frigid night air poured over Maggie. She shivered in her chair, yet welcomed the chill against her flushed awareness of the drink she couldn't seem to put aside. She glanced at her watch. Johnny had been gone thirty minutes. What kept him?

Words from an old folk song fleeted through her mind: *Oh dear, what can the matter be. Johnny's so long at the fair.* That long-ago Johnny had promised to bring his waiting lady a bunch of blue ribbons. All Maggie wanted was a simple photograph.

She crossed, uncrossed her legs. At the same time, she longed for the bourbon's warmth on her tongue but drew incredible power from her ability to resist. Tiny ripples in the liquor betrayed her inner turmoil, the day's endless disappointments.

Precariously near the edge of a wagon she dared not tumble off lest it crush her beneath its wheels, she carefully placed the glass on the table beside the decanter then forced herself to look elsewhere. The amber liquid seduced her gaze back into its spell.

"Be damned!" Springing from her chair, she snatched up the glass and whirling, cast its contents through the open casement window behind her. Something moved in the shadows cast by the big evergreen tree.

She retreated a step or two before remembering

how far she'd come from city dangers and moved forward again. The only movement discernable was the cedar's branches worried by the slight breeze that lofted resinous fragrance into the room.

"Silly goose." She laughed outright, sitting down again, placing the glass firmly onto the table. She crossed her legs. Uncrossed them. Smoothed aside her bangs. Crossed her legs again. Jiggled her foot, every nerve in her body playing a fanfare for what might come next. Her gaze drifted to the doorway through which Johnny Rice had disappeared, slithered back to the decanter.

Five hundred and one days she'd resisted.

Prickles at the base of her neck tugged her attention back to the windows before she decided her sense of being watched came from Johnny's big game trophies.

She met the elk's glassy stare. "Five hundred two days," she promised herself.

Her patience, however, had reached its limit. She flung herself from the chair.

Out she marched into the hallway, toward the living room and into silence broken only by the gilded mantel clock's loud tick. A lamp cast rose and blue rays through its leaded glass shade onto a fruitwood table that held only a white telephone. Nearby, the brocade couch with its plastic cushion covers might never have felt the weight of a backside.

The only other illumination fell from a wall sconce at the head of the stairs. She started up the risers. "Johnny?"

Silence from above. From below, the clock's *tick, tick, tick* lent an eerie Alfred Hitchcock atmosphere. Illusion, of course, nonetheless, the sense that skeletal fingers pattered along her spine propelled her to the second-floor landing. There, dragging in breaths, she paused. To her left along a passageway, a sliver of light fell through a door ajar, drawing her there. She knocked lightly.

"Johnny? Are you there?"

An agonized groan lifted the hair at the nape of her neck. She pushed open the door and peered into the room. Mingled stenches of vomit and feces brought her hands to her mouth.

Johnny lay in a fetal curl beside an open footlocker.

Groaning again, he writhed in such agony that her heart thudded in alarm. She knelt at his side, saw skin gray as wet putty. Sweat beaded his forehead. Maggie touched his shoulder. "What's wrong? What can I do?"

He convulsed, clutching his stomach with both hands, revealing a crumpled sheet of blue paper he'd held. In the open trunk Maggie could see several airmail envelopes and the brown shoelace that had probably secured them.

"Doreen's letters?" Only his agony kept her from snatching them up. A comforting hand on his shoulder, she said, "Just hang on. Hang on. I'll get help."

Shouldn't his wife be home any minute? Maggie had no idea. He'd kept Doreen's letters. He really loved her. Racked with guilt for misjudging him, she dashed out into the hallway.

"Maggie," his weak cry drew her back to kneel beside him. He pressed the crumpled piece of stationery into her hand and motioned at the letters in the trunk. She'd just picked them up when he vomited explosively.

Retching, she fled. "Doctor...you need doctor..." Words failed, snared in her throat by the memory of another man so ill. His smaller hands plump, soft, his eyes black onyx.

She whimpered beneath his phantom touch and backing away stopped at the hallway's wall behind her. Her hand clasped over her mouth, she felt the gorge rising into her throat and leaned for support, wallowing in guilt. Another heart-rending cry from Johnny sent her fleeing down the stairs and into the living room to phone for help. Receiver in hand, she stared at it stupefied. *Whom to call?*

Nothing in the picture-perfect living room looked as useful or mundane as a telephone directory. Desperate, she dialed "0" for the operator.

The woman's assurances that an ambulance would soon be on its way from a hospital in a nearby town unlocked the nervous tension that had held Maggie together. Her knees folded, spilling her onto the couch where she dropped the telephone receiver and buried her face in her hands.

At a snail's pace, lucidity crept past her confusion, and with it the realization she'd dropped Doreen's letters. She found them scattered up the stairway. Light-headed for want of air pounded from her lungs by her thundering heart, she crawled up the risers, gathering the envelopes one by one.

Get out of town, Panic demanded.

Where? How?

The image of a red pickup shifted into focus. She'd seen it parked out front when she arrived earlier. Had Paula Rice driven it to the church? Hard to imagine so prissy a woman behind the wheel of a truck.

Would the keys be in the ignition? Dare Maggie take the vehicle to the hotel to collect her things? She remembered Fate Halperin mentioning an eastbound bus. Had he mentioned the hour of departure?

Only when she heard the click of her heels on the foyer's slate floor did Maggie realize she'd moved forward while those questions spun through her mind. Already, she grasped the knob on the closet door to retrieve her jacket and handbag. Those in hand, she jammed the letters into her coat pocket. Movement in her peripheral vision drew her attention to the end of the central passageway.

Someone stood in the shadows at the far end of the hallway.

She didn't give the figure a second glance but fled, out across the front terrace, down the driveway.

While sanity urged her to stop, her ratcheting nerves drove her forward. She opened the door to the truck. Light poured from the overhead lamp. She jumped into the driver's seat and slammed the door shut while she fumbled for the ignition key.

"Yes," she exulted.

The engine caught on her first try, purred, whined as she backed from the driveway. Taking side streets remembered from childhood, she found her way to the hotel. Parked in the back alleyway, she finally drew a breath that held odors of new leather upholstery and the last cigarette Johnny smoked in his shiny red Ford. God, don't let it be his last, she prayed, getting out of the truck.

The sole visible light in the hotel leaked around the edges of closed window shades in Folly Halperin's ground floor apartment. Outside, an unshaded bulb lighted the rear entrance. A low stone wall surrounded the rear gardens. Once inside the gate, Maggie paused among the tangled vines that draped a curved trellis over the slate pathway. When her eyes had adjusted to the darkness enough to make out a flagstone pathway, she picked her way along it to the circle of light around the back porch. Once inside the hotel's central hallway, she paused to be sure no one had heard the door open and close.

She heard laughter from the coffee shop and the clink of china. On tiptoe she made her way to the central stairway, which rose just beyond view of the desk clerk. Ascending, she breathed in strangled spurts and fought down the urge to take the risers by twos. In the upstairs corridor, she hastened to her room, looking neither to the right nor to the left until safely inside. Leaned against the closed door, Maggie listened for footsteps in the hallway before turning on the light.

Bathroom pipes clanked from deep inside the building.

She crept to the bed and perched tense on the edge of the sagging mattress.

Her first rational thought materialized on Doreen's letters. Johnny clearly believed they held a clue to her whereabouts. In her pocket, she found the one he'd crumpled in his hand. She tried to read the slanting script but could only see the image of her brother-in-law's ashen face as he writhed in agony. Fresh guilt washed over her, bringing with it the certainty that Paula Rice had already returned home to find Johnny deathly ill and her, Maggie, gone.

Or maybe it had been Paula she saw in the shadowed hallway outside Johnny's office rather than some man. Maybe Paula had already phoned the sheriff.

Every wisp of common sense she possessed taunted Maggie for running scared. Head tilted, she listened for sirens that might indicate an ambulance screaming to Johnny's aid or a patrol car rushing to the hotel.

Blood rushed in her ears, blocking out any other sound. In the vacuum, her thoughts ricocheted to the eastbound bus. Could she hope to disappear into Tulsa's back streets long enough to formulate a plan?

Plan? The thought turned on her, cold water dashed in her face. She'd done nothing to harm Johnny Rice. He'd probably drunk himself to death. So why behave like a serial killer pursued by baying bloodhounds?

And why this compulsion to retrieve her suitcase from under the bed? Something it held screamed for attention. She knelt to see what—

A crash resounded behind her.

She leaped to her feet, gaped at the door as it swung inward. There, smiling his crooked smile stood the sheriff, his black eyes impaling her.

Maggie screamed and fell back across the bed. There she curled into a ball and found escape in darkness.

Chapter 8

As of two o'clock Wednesday afternoon, Guy Warner considered himself redundant in the John Rice case. Nursing a can of root beer, he stood inside the open bay of Bob's Service station while the station's owner put new tires on the Studebaker.

The air wrench's decisive whine lifted the deputy's spirits by the minute. He'd interviewed John Rice's widow and had searched the property and Maggie Simpson's hotel room. That did it for him.

Should he decide to flee the whirlpool that was sucking him into the actress's troubles with the law, Beetlebomb would be ready.

Across the street from the station, two women got out of a white sedan nosed to the curb outside Fate Halperin's second-hand store. Otherwise, Guy would've gone over to check the old man's bookshelves. He'd had enough of nosy Aldenites pumping him for gossip.

Only Maggie appeared immune to the endless speculation that swept the town. Sheriff Turkeson complained that any time he approached her cell she burrowed into the blankets on her cot and fell asleep.

But yesterday, when Guy delivered her lunch tray, she'd clutched his arm with slender fingers strong as railcar couplings.

"Please," she whispered. Desperation glittered in

her eyes—green fire that burned straight through the door he'd thought firmly closed on his belief that the search for truth and justice should prevail over all else.

Defense shattered, he'd mumbled praises of Chance Halperin's legal skill and made his escape. He still had to remind himself regularly he couldn't afford to empathize with her.

"Well," boomed a voice at his back. "That about does it."

Trapped in the memory of Maggie's plaintive expression when he left the jail, Guy hadn't noticed the silence from the mechanic's stall or the man rolling two tires toward him. He swallowed the last of the root beer and tossed the empty can into a barrel beside the front door.

The tires turned out to show enough tread to have some value. Bob lifted them onto a rack of used tires and flipped a red grease rag from his hip pocket to wipe his hands.

Guy gestured at the rack. "You can give me a little better in exchange, then."

The other man glanced out into the street, a grin intercepting the grease smudge on his cheek. "Can do. Here comes an almost certain buyer."

Fate Halperin's pet raccoon hightailed it toward the station, his owner hard at his heels.

Guy chuckled. "Old Jeff must have made a break for it when those two women left the store."

The white sedan was just pulling away.

"Jeff's pretty good at that," the station owner said. "Knows I keep a jar of peppermint sticks by the cash register. You watch now."

Sure enough, the critter scampered straight through

the service bay into the adjacent customer service area where he propped himself upright against the candy case. He peered around at Bob. Fate puffed past the two men, nodding as he passed. Bob fell in behind him.

"Such a rascal, that Jefferson," Fate muttered, "runs off at every opportunity." He scooped the animal into his arms. "You are about to get yourself grounded again, my friend."

Bob reached into the jar of peppermint sticks near the cash register. He handed over one of the candies. Halperin appeared a bit sheepish accepting it, but the raccoon went after it like one who knew his due in the world.

The old man fussed at his pet. "It being Thanksgiving tomorrow, I might take you to Chance and Elizabeth's with me. But Friday, you must remain at home all day and consider your transgressions."

"Give old Jeff a break." Guy nodded toward the tire rack. "He got you here just in time to make a real deal on some good used tires."

The raccoon tucked into the crook of his arm, the old man ambled over to inspect the merchandise.

Guy asked, "You wouldn't happen to have a new Zane Grey on hand?"

"Nothing on the shelves. However, I have yet to unpack several boxed lots from that auction over at Regier's place last Saturday. Perhaps something will turn up." He fished his wallet from a pocket in the bib of his overalls, counted twenty one's into Bob's hand. Glancing at the Studebaker, he said, "Four new tires. Do you plan a trip?"

"I might move on. Alden gets on my nerves a bit, if you must know. Too much hearsay to deal with all the time."

The driveway service bell jangled as a yellow Volkswagen pulled up to the pumps. The deputy grinned at Bob. "You'd best hurry for that one, then. Peggy might not need to gas up again until after Christmas."

Halperin spared the car a glance before looking down to watch Jefferson Davis lick the last of the sweet-smelling stickiness from his paws. Chuckling merrily, the coon settled more snugly into the crook of his owner's arm. The old man smiled down at his pet, stroked his furry back. "I have wondered how long a man bred to the diversions of big city life could endure the stultifying speculation of one another's affairs with which we in rural America occupy ourselves."

Well aware his urban background must be as obvious to someone of Fate's intelligence as the starched crease ironed into the man's overalls, Guy hoped word of his home city hadn't gotten around town. Choosing silence as the best way to change the subject, he watched the old man scratch the raccoon fondly behind one pointed ear. The animal lifted beady eyes to peer up through the furry bandit mask that so well fit his character.

"It must be difficult," Fate observed, "to conduct an objective investigation for a popular murder victim when the perpetrator's identity is so obvious."

Guy wondered how the old coot sensed so much of what Guy preferred to avoid. He sighed inwardly. "Actually, I have nothing to compare this investigation to. It's my first. And I don't plan to involve myself much further in this one."

Pungent gas fumes drifted from the pumps. Bob

wiped a spill from around the Volkswagen's gas tank and screwed on the cap.

If the tableau diverted Halperin, he wasted no time with it. The deputy felt his gaze, sharp with speculation. It seemed wise to insert a make-do response. "I hired on to keep reckless drivers in line and help the dispatcher hold down the office when the Turk is out."

"From what I gather," Halperin surmised, a bulldog at the other end of his owner's argyle sock, "little investigation is required. Folly can testify to the bad blood between Rice and the actress."

"Folly is an indisputable witness, all right. Thing is—she didn't witness what went on in that room before Johnny went upstairs."

Fate nodded. "I understand you witnessed the second meeting, unobserved. The fact that the woman threw out her share of the poisoned bourbon without tasting it should attest to her guilt."

At that, a hot thickness invaded Guy's chest. Supposedly, only his boss, Turk Turkeson knew details of his deputy's surveillance. Damn the diarrhea-mouthed bastard. "I don't know where you got your information. As for the poison, that is pure ginned-up speculation after someone got a look at my report. Far as I know, the only crime the woman is known to have committed is taking Johnny's pickup. Turk saw her drive away in it. The cause of Johnny's death is undetermined."

The garage owner came in from the gas pumps, flushed and out of breath. "Deputy, you'd better get on over to the office. I just talked to Peggy out there. She said there's some folks pretty upset about the way the Turk is handling the investigation into Johnny's death."

"I'm not involved in that."

"Evonne Callahan, Peggy, and Peggy's uncle, Case Murray, are headed over to give the Turk an ultimatum," the man went on without a pause.

****

Odors of damp cement and dusty woolen blankets penetrated Maggie's sleep. Her eyes flew open. Full awareness rode in on static-garbled call numbers from the two-way radio she'd seen on the sheriff's desk the night he brought her in.

From earlier, brief awakenings she knew Johnny Rice had died, and that she occupied a cell in what could have been Sheriff Taylor's office in Mayberry, USA. Only there was no affable Andy Griffith. The man seated beyond the waist-high room divider that separated her cell from his desk specialized in bluster and threats. Any time he came near, she escaped his piercing gaze the way she long ago reacted to Dr. Xavier's approach. She withdrew from reality.

Another burst of static from the two-way recaptured Maggie's attention, followed by, "That you, Warner?"

The radio distorted the reply, but Turkeson obviously had no trouble understanding him. "The hell you say! On their way here?"

More garbled words drew his boastful, "Nah. I can handle it."

That same moment, a clamor arose outside the door, burst through it.

Instinct drove Maggie back under the covers.

The ruckus merged into one voice—strident, female. "That murderess—"

"Sit down, Evonne," the sheriff barked. "Show

some respect for this office before I throw the lot of you into that other cell back yonder."

Silence. Maggie caught herself holding her breath. After a moment, chair legs scraped against the concrete floor. She peeked from beneath the scratchy blanket, then driven by curiosity, sat up. Beyond the room divider Turkeson sat hunched forward, facing the hurricane winds of dissent from two women and a man seated in front of his desk.

"All right, Evonne," Turkeson said after a moment. "You had something to say?"

The brunette sat taller, her pillbox hat the same mustard-crust yellow as her coat. "Damned right, sheriff. You've held that murderess almost two days, and what have you done about getting justice for Johnny?"

No one could have gotten in a word edgewise before she added, "You've done nothing, that's what."

"I'm not runnin' a torture chamber here you know. Miss Dorsey's too tired and strung out to make a coherent statement yet."

"Miss Dorsey my patootie. If she wasn't a Hollywood actress, you wouldn't have wasted one min—"

"I haven't wasted a minute. Me and my deputy have gone over the Rice place, and her hotel room with a fine-toothed comb. We've talked to everyone in this town the woman so much as said 'boo' to. We believe Johnny ingested something that caused his death."

Maggie felt the blood drain from her face. Thank God and Alcoholics Anonymous she hadn't tasted that bourbon.

"All's left to find out," the sheriff continued, "is if

what he'd been drinking had been tampered with, and, if so, how the woman might have managed to do the job in the few hours between their meetings."

But I didn't, Maggie wanted to scream.

"Meantime," Turkeson was saying, "your Maggie Simpson, or rather Hollywood's, Miss Charmaine Dorsey, is *my* business, no one else's."

"But sheriff." The younger woman sat forward, her hands clutched to her chest. "What if she escapes somehow? I'd be scared for Vicky to walk to school or play outside."

The man spoke, a bullhorn demanding attention. "Unless you lawmen and judges make the criminal element sit up and take notice there won't be no future at all for kids like Peggy's little girl, anyway. Just look at what happened in Dallas!"

Turkeson gained a couple inches in height, his shoulders square now. "Don't throw what happened at Dallas on me."

"Sure, you're to blame. All of us are to blame. What happened down there don't hold a candle to what's ahead for this country. Mark my word, Turk."

"I'm trying—"

"Hell, you are!" the man shouted. "You have a responsibility to the citizens of this town, Turk. No one else will do for Alden what Johnny Rice has done. The swimming pool dug for free with his equipment. The cement he donated."

Maggie covered her ears, unable to bear any more praise for the man she felt sure would be alive had she not come back to Alden. Propelled to her feet by guilt and regret, she sprang across the cell and gripped the bars. "Make these people leave!" Her knuckles whitened around corroded iron. "I did Johnny no harm. You've no right to hold me here."

Shocked silence swooped down for a split-second before the woman named Evonne popped up from her chair. Through lips twisted with scorn, she said, "You don't look as tired and strung-out as the sheriff said a while ago."

Her remark released the invisible lock that had bound the others to their chairs. They faced her, the young mother pale, as though she confronted the serpent-haired Medusa.

Maggie glared at the sheriff. "You run some jail here to allow this kind of sideshow."

His dark eyes skewered Maggie. "Now don't go high and mighty on me, Miss Fancy Lady. I know what I'm about and neither me, or you, or any of these good citizens of Alden will interfere with due process while I'm sheriff of this town."

"And we'll see about that," blustered the man Maggie would have sworn by his voice, stood eight feet tall. Shorter than Maggie's five foot eight, he stared at her through shrimp-like eyes.

Maggie dismissed him with a knife-edged glance at the sheriff. "You talk about due process." She chose a tone calculated to wither his manhood. "You've held me two days, filed no charges, and you have the gall to talk about due process?"

"You want charges, lady?" He shook his finger at her. "How about larceny of a vehicle? Does that sound highfalutin enough to suit your big city fancy?"

Momentarily struck dumb, she stammered, "I...I...I just borrowed that pickup."

Protest rose among the detractors, prompting the

sheriff to gesture skyward with sharp thrusts of his forefinger as if firing a sidearm to control a mob. The trio's angry chirping did stop.

But there was no relief for Maggie, who caught his next salvo, "You, Miss Dorsey, shut up." Then, under silent fire by turn: "You, Evonne. You, Peggy. You, Murray. Clear out now, all of you. I've had enough of this crap."

Mr. Shrimpy squared his jaw to the degree possible for a man lacking a discernable chin. "Not until we hear what real charges you mean to file," he thundered. "I won't budge one step. Your larceny of a vehicle charge won't hold her no time."

Turkeson curled his lip. "When I'm damned good and ready, you'll know what charges I intend to file." He pointed at the door. "Now go. The kit and caboodle of you, before I lock you up for staging an unauthorized demonstration on city property."

They went.

Before Maggie could heave a sigh of relief, she found herself back in the line of fire.

"And you," Turkeson said. "You'd best thank your lucky stars I've kept you out of reach of people like Case Murray. Bastard turned his pit bulls loose on some neighborhood kids when they turned over his outhouse last Halloween. They'd likely be dead if they hadn't been good at climbing trees."

Shuddering involuntarily, Maggie considered a reply, decided on a position of strength. "I've looked out for myself since I turned thirteen. I can look out for myself now."

He barked an ugly laugh.

She cast disdain in a glance past the wood-paneled

divider between the office and the cells, took in scarred metal filing cabinets against the far wall, and around the corner of the room, the front door. A green window shade on the door hung askew about six inches down from the roller. "You just want me in this Podunk Junction excuse for a jail so I can't find out for myself who poisoned Johnny, and why that person wanted him silenced."

Scarcely had she spoken when Maggie realized her mistake. Her knees turned to liquid. Gripping the cell bars to stay upright, she saw a "gotcha" look spring into the sheriff's eyes.

He said nothing but stalked over to the filing cabinets. A drawer screeched. Paper rustled. He turned and pushing through the divider's half-gate held up the old medical formulary handed down to Dr. Xavier by his father, a for-real physician on the American frontier.

Turkeson leaned so close to the bars she could smell the mouthwash he'd used that morning. "If you know for sure John Rice was poisoned," he said too softly, "you're ahead of me. The toxicology report isn't in yet." Lifting the slender book in its age-worn blue cloth binding, he added, "And maybe you'd care to explain what use you have for this? Some of these recipes are mighty odd."

"If you'll bother to look, there are also formulas for things as common as face cream. I make my own. Besides, many of the poisonous ingredients in those old medicines are harmful only in specific amounts." Although she knew she babbled, Maggie couldn't stop.

"Women used to eat little wafers laced with arsenic because they thought it gave their complexion a delicate appearance." She paused to suck in a breath. "Anyway,

I doubt some of those concoctions are any more dangerous than the stuff in modern medicine."

"Modern medicine doesn't concern me. I'm asking why you felt the need to tote along this book when you stopped over in Alden for a so-called reunion with someone who hasn't lived here for better than eighteen years."

Maggie grasped her forehead in an effort to slow her thoughts. "I demand my right to call an attorney."

That widened his eyes. After sputtering a while, he said, "Chance Halperin's the only lawyer in Alden. Today's Wednesday. He's in his Tulsa office on Wednesdays."

"I'll choose my own counsel, if you don't mind."

The big man shrugged. "So, who do you want me to get?"

"I'll make the call."

She could hear him swearing under his breath. He hoisted the formulary into an armpit while he fiddled with his keys. He fumbled around with the lock. The minute the door creaked open, he grasped her arm.

Maggie jerked free. "Where would I run to?"

Despite his scowl, he didn't touch her again.

When she sat down at his desk to pick up the phone, she went totally blank. Who did she know with connections in the business world except her ex-husbands and her theatrical agent, Scaff Russell? Tears blurred her vision, but with a trembling forefinger she made it through the numbers on the dial.

Would Scaff take her call seriously? Or would he see her predicament as a publicity windfall?

Ten rings. No answer.

Turkeson returned the book to the file drawer and

came back to hover over her right shoulder. She glanced up. "I need to try another number."

He nodded, his sharp features steel.

She dialed. Rose Abbot picked up on the second ring. "Rose?" The lump in Maggie's throat threatened to break out into a sob. "This is Maggie," she said hurriedly, then remembering that no one in Hollywood knew her by that name, bleated a tremulous laugh. "Charmaine, I mean."

"Char!" Her friend's greeting bubbled. "How are you? You should see these cats of yours. They're so cute. They run to the door every time the bell rings, thinking it's—"

"Rose," she broke in. "I'm in trouble. Could you please get hold of my agent? Ask him to locate a good attorney in Tulsa or Oklahoma City. Tell him to contact—" Maggie cast a wild gaze around the office. A second desk held scattered papers, a two-way radio, and a name plate. She read aloud: "Deputy Guy Warner. Tell Scaff to get the rest of the details from Guy Warner at the sheriff's office in Alden."

Turkeson's hand heavy on her shoulder, she added, "And Rose? I asked Scaff to ship my trunk. Tell him to hold up on that."

With a silent prayer that her last request would reach her agent in time, she cradled the receiver. Some mementos her trunk held could appear more damning than the formulary.

Turkeson herded her back to her cell, the front one in a row of three. "I'm afraid my deputy won't have time to handle your messages."

"He can decide that for himself." Maggie shrugged away from his grasp and marched into her prison with her chin high.

The barred door clanked shut. "I plan to keep Warner on the case until we learn all there is to know about you and that arsenic in Johnny's bourbon—if arsenic it was."

Her heart pounding so hard she could scarcely breathe, Maggie said hurriedly, "I tell you, I know nothing about any arsenic."

"But that's what you say killed him."

Unable to bear his appraisal, she flung out the first scenario that popped into her head. "I once saw a dog die of arsenic poisoning. Johnny's sickness reminded me of that. That's all."

Turkeson's key grated in the lock. "And you just happened to toss your drink out the window by coincidence?"

Maggie inhaled sharply.

Grinning, Turkeson hitched up his gun belt with his thumbs. "My deputy had you under surveillance."

It took her a couple of beats to remember the movement she thought she'd seen in Johnny's backyard that night and relate it to the shadowy form she'd seen later at the end of the hallway. "If the man did his job well," she said, "he can tell you I never touched that decanter."

"You had no shortage of opportunities to do that earlier that afternoon. No one in Alden ever locks a door. You could've slipped into the back while the Rices were upstairs."

"Or maybe someone else did that very thing."

The lawman blew air through his nose. "Who in Alden would want Johnny dead?"

When she gave that a moment's thought, a chill

trickled along her spine. "Maybe that someone hoped to kill two birds with one stone. Could be someone doesn't want me to learn what became of Doreen." She paused, considered. "Or," she said slowly, "maybe Johnny poisoned that bourbon himself."

Lines etched the sheriff's forehead. "Why would Johnny do such a stupid thing? The man had everything in the world going for him."

"Maybe because what happened to my sister held no mystery for him after all. Suicide might have been more attractive to a town hero than being exposed as a killer."

"You've seen too many movies."

"For all we know," she snapped, "Johnny might have found Doreen living with another man. He could have killed them both in a fit of jealous rage."

Turkeson pivoted and walked away.

A stealthy image of Harvey Oswald's face drifted across Maggie's mental screen. Might he too have been innocent? Or someone's pawn?" She grasped the bars again. "You're just desperate for a scapegoat."

The sheriff spun around, taut faced. "I want to see justice done."

"Then get off my back. You won't even consider the possibility that his death is related to my sister's strange disappearance. Learn the truth about Doreen. You'll find your justice."

He stalked back to her cell and thrust his face close to the bars. "Where did you get the arsenic you put in Johnny's bourbon, and where did you discard the container that held it?"

"I brought no arsenic to Alden."

"Then why did you run?"

She retreated, taking in her surroundings with outflung arms. "You've kept me in this stinkhole two days without offering me a shower, or even a toothbrush, much less filing a charge. And you ask why I fled the scene?

"Don't talk to me about justice, Sheriff. File your silly larceny of a vehicle charge and get me a hearing so I can get out and help find whoever killed Johnny. I'll bet in the process I can learn something someone doesn't want me to know about Doreen's whereabouts."

Unreadable dark eyes held Maggie's so long her head began to buzz, but he finally walked away. She heard him key the mike to the dispatcher's radio. He reeled off a series of numbers.

After a static-filled response, he said, "Nah. I took care of that. What I want you to do is talk to Paula Rice again. Use some tact, dammit, but find out if there's any chance Johnny did himself in."

The radio exploded into garbled protest.

"I don't give a damn if you've talked to her sixteen times and told me twice as often you want off the case—talk to Paula again."

Glowering at Maggie, he lifted the telephone receiver. She heard him dial.

"Even if you sweet-talk the D. A. into lettin' you outta here," he said, jabbing a finger at her again, "I mean to scour this town for something solid to haul you back in on a murder charge. Meanwhile. you're not to meddle in this investigation. *Comprende?*"

Maggie nodded, her fingers crossed behind her back.

"What's more," Turkeson continued, "I'll not take responsibility if some hothead like Case Murray takes a pot shot at you for the trouble you've brought to Alden."

Chapter 9

What kind of fool would choose the agony of poison over a quick death by Colt, Magnum, or Mauser? Surveying the small arsenal in Johnny Rice's gun cabinet, Guy Warner considered the idea that the man had killed himself less plausible by the minute.

The death throes he'd witnessed when he went upstairs that night still haunted his dreams. None of it made sense. Why would Maggie Simpson kill her sole link to her missing sister?

On the other hand, he couldn't forget the woman's determined effort not to drink from the decanter. And in that glimpse of her face before she fled, he'd seen guilt, especially after she glanced down the hall at him midflight.

Yet, she'd called the ambulance before fleeing.

Guy turned his back on the firearms. If he'd seen any hint of anger between the woman and Rice that night, he'd more easily accept the circumstantial evidence against her.

Everything about the case grated on his nerves, not the least of it the prospect of dredging through Paula Rice's grief with questions about suicide. Furthermore, women bearing casseroles to feed relatives who had yet to show up had forced a delay that left him too much time to dwell on his shortcomings as an investigator. His one piece of real detective work for the railroad had backfired, the racketeers free while Guy served a life sentence of exile from all he held dear.

Longing for one of the flannel shirts he'd traded in for the uniform, he tugged at his starched collar and went to open one of the casement windows. He took several deep breaths while he studied the backyard. Rice had built as close to the woods as he could get and still be in town. A padlock secured the gate he'd found open the night of the murder. No telling who else walked right in.

Guy studied the big evergreen that had sheltered him that night, then the manicured lawn, frost-bleached, and finally the in-ground pool with its blue cover. Some anomaly he'd experienced amid that perfection nipped at the heels of his memory, yapped, circled, and when he almost grasped it, bounded away.

The yard held enough shrubs and ornamental trees to provide cover for someone with mischief in mind. Guy hooked his thumbs into his gun belt and narrowed his eyes. The heck was, if Johnny Rice counted an enemy among his acquaintances, it remained Alden's only well-kept secret.

Seemed like no one could heap enough praise on the man for his altruistic nature or his devotion to Paula—Johnny the rugged native cedar and she the hothouse flower, opposites successfully entwined—the house, the yard, all monuments to a man's love for his wife. Rice's only space, it appeared, was this room where he could smoke, admire his big game trophies, and enjoy the bourbon that likely provided passage to a very messy death. Something about that nagged at the deputy, skirted the light, and left him frowning.

"Deputy Warner?"

Softly spoken, the words boomed into his reverie. He spun around.

The widow Rice held a lacy linen square over her nose and mouth—against the room's allergens, he supposed. Gray eyes queried his thoughts and glanced past him. "What is it? What troubles you?"

He wished he could figure that out. Grasping the first reply that presented itself, he said, "I was thinking what a waste, such a nice pool and no one to enjoy it."

Surprisingly, smile crinkles appeared around the edges of the hanky. "You've probably heard that Johnny built it for our daughter, Marti. And my, how she did love it, and for me to swim with her." The pleasant expression faded. "I'm not really the outdoor type. Allergies you know. But my husband didn't swim, and Marti needed someone with her." A thoughtful silence passed before she added, "I suppose we should have filled in the pool long ago."

No longer able to bear her sad expression, he looked away, tugging at his collar, wishing he could explain that he, too, understood the loss of a child. But she'd know oranges and apples when she saw them, her Marti gone forever, his son somewhere alive and well—if beyond his father's reach.

Paula Rice spoke into the silence. "In that pool our daughter gained equality with any child her age." She drew away from the past, her eyes bright. "That's why I want to build a camp on the Simpson property. A safe and appropriate place for others like Marti."

A beat passed before her words registered. Had he heard her correctly? "You aren't going ahead with the retirement community, then." The whole town had been talking about Johnny's plans for such a place.

She fluttered dismissive fingers. "That was strictly Johnny's project. He's gone now. What better monument could I build to him?" Enthusiasm brightened her eyes. "City children especially love the freedom of outdoor recreation, whatever their...their...*achoo*." She caught the sneeze in her handkerchief, sneezed twice more, and then uncovered an apologetic smile that saved him from having to comment on disabled children. Blessedly, he had no experience there.

Another sneeze drew another apologetic smile. "Excuse me," she said, waving her hand around the room's array of big game heads staring their fixed stares. "Animal dander is my worst enemy, worse even than cigarette smoke." Shadows robbed her eyes of their sparkle. "That's one regret of mine. Little Marti begged for a puppy. I couldn't let her have one."

At her suggestion they moved to the living room where she indicated he sit on the brocade sofa. He settled in. Air whooshed from the cushions, pushing a faint oily smell from their protective plastic covers. Paula Rice perched on the edge of a museum-quality chair whose spindly wooden arms and legs Guy wouldn't trust to support a poodle. Twice more she sneezed. He watched the flimsy square of fabric in her hands wilt beneath her allergic rampage. When her hands finally fluttered to rest in her lap, her fingers kept picking at the delicate lace edge.

Her vulnerability ignited a spark of anger he directed away from his unpleasant task as interrogator, onto the lack of relatives surrounding her to lend comfort.

"You shouldn't be alone at such a time, Mrs.

Rice."

She twisted the handkerchief into a rope. "My parents were traveling in Europe. I expect them in later today. My husband's parents are deceased."

Mentally scourging his boss for sending him to rip the scabs off her grief with pointed questions about private agonies and hidden discords as motives for suicide, Guy struggled to begin.

Leaning forward, she arched sharply penciled eyebrows. "I don't believe I understand what more you need to know from me about the night of John's death."

"Er, ah…" He cleared his throat. "Actually, I have a few questions about your husband's state of mind the last time the two of you spoke."

The lines that deepened across her forehead told him when she got his meaning. He cleared his throat again. "Had your husband seemed despondent?"

"Despondent?" Chin up, she revealed a rabbit-like quiver in her nostrils. Pink lacquered fingertips picked more unforgivingly at the lace on her handkerchief, a wad now. "Of course Johnny felt a bit down that night. Wouldn't you be upset if someone you believed long dead appeared on your doorstep to accuse you of unfairly taking a piece of property you'd spent years paying taxes on?"

Upset hardly described what the deputy would have felt under such circumstances. "And before that your husband hadn't seemed depressed at all?"

"You didn't know Johnny well, did you? The busier he stayed, the happier he was." Twin splotches of red blossomed in her cheeks, and she sat very straight. "If you're suggesting suicide, you're as crazy as that woman who came here pretending she didn't know where to find her sister."

Methinks the lady doth protest too much. Guy took care not to reveal the thought. "Your husband and your daughter were extremely close I suppose."

White crept around her bright pink lips. "Johnny made as much time for her as he could with all his business interests—"

An edge in her tone put to rest the local myth of a threesome shattered by the child's untimely death. Feeling lower than a lizard's ass for opening that package of stink-bait, the deputy was about to apologize when Paula Rice stood, wringing her hands.

"My husband was a brave man. He saved three comrades by drawing fire while they escaped an enemy ambush. Almost got killed himself. He was a wonderful husband and father, and I refuse to sit here while you suggest he had the slightest reason to choose a coward's death." That said, she marched to the foyer.

Guy remained on the sofa. "But surely you see why we need to eliminate any false premises."

She stepped from view. He heard a door open. She reappeared, his Stetson in hand. "You waste your time here, Deputy Warner. You should spend it tracing Maggie Simpson's movements late Monday. What poison did she use? Where did she get it? When did she put it into the decanter?"

Newly amazed by the local grapevine's reach, he asked, "Why are you so sure the actress is guilty?" *Or that he was poisoned?*

"Because my husband told me how she stood right there at his gun cabinet and told him he deserved to be shot down with one of his own weapons. The woman is a bitch."

The gutter word spewed from cupid's-bow lips trapped Guy's breath in his throat and readjusted his earlier reluctance to explore her private life. "Nothing I saw in the exchange between your husband and Maggie Simpson that night suggested he hadn't accepted her apology in full or that she harbored a grudge over his acquisition of the Simpson farm."

Lips carved marble, Paula Rice stood in the doorway to the foyer with his hat lifted toward him.

He settled deeper into the couch. "The actress seemed less concerned by the property issue than by her sister's possible whereabouts."

"I think that whole business about wanting to reconcile with Doreen is an act."

"She wouldn't have come here prepared to make trouble unless she knew about the property transfer, and how could that be?"

"Why don't you ask your buddy Chance Halperin?"

An uppercut to his chin wouldn't have surprised the deputy more than her insinuation that Chance had conspired with Maggie Simpson. "Would you care to elaborate, then?" *No doubt about that*.

"My husband's refusal to grant Halperin an easement across the Simpson place blew a nasty hole in his plans to develop those lands back near Wild Turkey Creek into a retirement community. This close to Tulsa, demand is growing. Everyone expects it to increase after the lake backs up from that dam going in on the Arkansas River."

Guy shrugged. "I'd think there should be plenty of ideal spots around here for such a project."

"Except Johnny had the idea first. And he wanted

to attract a more middle-class buyer. Halperin's mansions would make Johnny's houses look like cracker boxes by comparison."

That it was all about whose is bigger here, as everywhere else, made as much sense as anything in Guy Warner's life the past few years. Her expectant expression drew the only reply he could muster. "I'd think Halperin could gain access somewhere other than across the Simpson place."

"Surely you've been around here long enough to know Halperin land is surrounded by some rough country." Frost stiffened her smile. "Our property is the only way in."

Time to go. Enough is enough. He stood and shrugged to loosen the back of his shirt where he'd perspired against the couch's plastic cover. Guy reclaimed his hat. "Would Chance Halperin have expected you to continue with the retirement homes after Johnny died?" Outside, he turned to add, "Or would he expect you to sell the property?"

"You'll have to ask Chance Halperin about that." The door swung shut.

Lingering on the flagstone terrace, Guy surveyed the well-laid-out flower beds with their cherubs. "False advertising," he muttered, and then filled his lungs with fresh air and wished fervently he'd never taken the deputy's job. Through all the long conversations he and Chance Halperin had shared, why had his friend never mentioned the retirement community?

Not that it didn't sound like a good idea, with so much of the country surrounding the proposed lake set aside as public lands. It simply didn't seem possible the attorney would resort to murder to carry out his plans.

The deputy looked out at his Studebaker in the driveway. Maybe a quiet drive with cold air blowing through the car's open windows would erase the thought that Mrs. Rice might find her camp for the disabled worth murder. Guy took the steps down by twos.

In lieu of providing a cruiser, the county provided upkeep for his car and paid to install a two-way radio. He liked the arrangement. Beetlebomb represented stability in his life. His sole tangible asset, she came from a salvage yard in Iowa and proved roadworthy enough to get him to Alden. He devoted his first winter here to giving her a new motor and a fresh coat of paint. She never wanted for gas in her tank or a tune-up in case he needed to get out of town quick.

Now, he patted her front fender in passing and used his handkerchief to wipe away the smudge his finger left. Ritual completed, he climbed in, backed into the street, and pointed the car's airplane nose toward Boundary Drive to the south. At the corner he headed east to Main, passing a wooded area and old man Halperin's alfalfa field. A right turn there took him to Rice's construction site on the old Simpson property. Dirt work was already underway.

A few weeks earlier, Johnny had posted a round-the-clock guard. Guy, thinking coffee and a chat with the watchman might clear up some details Paula Rice had glossed over, turned in. Johnny's death had put a stop to work on the site. A dozer stood idle beside a large pile of dirt, and not far away sat a dump truck, a cement mixer, and a small tractor equipped with a scoop. In back, a long-neglected field verged into woods.

Fred Steed's green Chevy truck sat near one of three corrugated metal shacks. Warner honked Beetlebomb's horn and braced himself for a cup of well-boiled coffee.

Wood smoke scented the air. Man and a mug of hot brew met him at the door. "Thanks, Fred." Eye-watering emissions from the mug rivaled any pollutant in Toledo's industrial district, but one didn't quibble when questions needed answers.

The watchman indicated an upturned nail keg near the stove. "Have a seat," he said, settling into a rickety kitchen chair beside the keg.

From somewhere on the grounds, Fred had obviously seen company coming. Red-cheeked, he still wore a blue and black plaid mackinaw and matching hunter's cap. Each sip from his mug intensified the moisture that fogged his glasses. Guy hazarded a swallow from his own. His tongue turned to brass.

"Jeez, Fred." He raised his brows. "You make this today, then? Or last week?"

Steed chuckled. "Well, it's hot, isn't it?"

"It's hot."

"And free."

Both men laughed and then chatted awhile before the deputy took up the business at hand. "Mind if I have a look around outside?"

"It's about the murder?" Steed's brown eyes appeared owl-like through his bifocals.

"If the accused managed to slip poison into Rice's bourbon decanter, her familiarity with the lay of the land might have led her here to dispose of what had held the stuff.

"You do think it's the actress who did it?"

Already on the edge of the old, slippery slope of needing to see justice done, Guy backtracked into the safety of popular opinion. "She had motive," he said, ashamed before the words expired in the shack's stuffy atmosphere. *Did Chance Halperin have as much or more reason to want Rice dead?* The deputy had to admit to himself that he preferred the actress as suspect. "Maggie had opportunity. No one saw her between the time she phoned Johnny to apologize, and eight o'clock when she went to his house. She claims she went for a walk in the woods."

Eyes narrowed, Steed paused, then nodded. "Come to think of it, I did see someone on the country road past here just before dark that night. A man, I thought at the time."

Not what Deputy Warner wanted to hear. "The excavations around here would be a good place to hide something forever."

Steed got up. "What say we have a look around?"

While they walked, Guy scanned the location. "Pretty wild country all around here."

"Yep. Except for a little valley tucked into the woods about a mile to the southwest. Chance Halperin owns it. There's a rough trail in. I've gone fishing back there a time or two."

Guy's nod indicated that he got the picture, but the Simpson property clearly offered best access for the attorney's development.

His attention turned onto the ditches that would have held foundations; he moseyed along one, then another, peering into them for anything out of place.

Fred Steed turned up the collar on his mackinaw. "Me and the night man watch things pretty close, but I suppose someone knowing her way around could sneak in with no trouble."

"Did you know the actress as a child?"

"We were in fourth grade together. I had a little part in that medicine show she and her sister went off with. The girl seemed pretty stage-struck."

"It strikes me odd that no one gives credence to Maggie's claim that only she went with the traveling man." At a quizzical look from Steed, he added, "I thought small town folk always stood behind their own."

"She don't belong here."

"It's her hometown."

"And she never looked back after she left, I'll wager, 'til she heard she might be missing out on some money."

"When Rice took over her property, you mean."

Steed nodded.

"You don't even know if she came for the money in the first place." Shocked by his defensive tone, Guy wished he could take back the remark.

Steed grinned. "Say, you're mighty concerned about the lady, aren't you?" He winked. "Couldn't be you got the hots for that strawberry blonde?"

Not about to dignify the remark with a denial, Guy said, "You've gotten a peek at her too, I take it."

The watchman cackled and said nothing more until they rounded the back of the site and approached two storage sheds.

"What's in the sheds?"

"Cement, in this first one here."

A thorough search bore up the claim. A heavy padlock secured the second shed. "Tool shed?" the deputy guessed.

"No way to stow anything in there. Kept buttoned up tight as your Aunt Tilly's corset. Johnny was crabby about that after the trouble here."

Radar pinging, Guy stopped in his tracks. Steed's expression suggested regret.

"Tell me about the break-in, then."

Steed looked down, kicked at a clod of dirt, then shrugged. "Happened a few weeks back. Johnny didn't report it at the time and gave us strict orders to keep mum."

"Time for loyalties is past." Out of respect for the man's feelings toward his former boss, the deputy spoke softly. "Anything you might be able to tell me about Johnny and his personal relationships could help bring a killer to justice." He stepped over to the locked shed's door. "You can talk while I have a look in here."

"Well…yeah, I guess we need to do that." He fished a key from the side pocket on his overalls. "But if it was Maggie looking for a place to hide something here, I can't see how she'd have gotten the door open."

"How about we consider that someone else might have wanted Johnny dead. The construction boss, for instance, would have a key."

"But why would he—"

Guy's upheld palm cut short the man's argument. Steed didn't hand over the key but unlocked the door himself.

Guy whistled when he stepped inside. "The guy responsible for this must be obsessive-compulsive." He'd never seen a storage area so well organized. Shovels, rakes, and other long-handled tools hung upside down along one wall. Pegboard and hooks across the back wall held all manner of hand tools. Power saws and crowbars and tools he couldn't identify had their places. Boxes on the shelves that covered one wall were labeled as to contents. In the middle of the room, a worktable held a vise and an anvil, big pencils with thick lead, and a variety of small items rowed up neatly.

"Seems almost a crime to touch anything lest I leave it out of place," he remarked, but started looking into the boxes. To Steed he said, "Tell me about the trouble you mentioned."

"Yeah, well. Someone vandalized some of the equipment one night. Sugared the fuel tanks in a backhoe and one of the dump trucks. Cost Johnny two expensive engine overhauls."

Guy moved a box of nails aside to check behind. A Daddy Longlegs spider made a run for it. "Got any idea who did the damage?"

"Happened a few days before Halloween. Johnny passed it off as kids warming up for the big night."

"Passed it off?"

"I think Johnny didn't really believe that theory himself. A gawdawful wind a-blowing rain out of the north that night didn't make for conditions you'd think kids would like."

"Why do you suppose Johnny wanted to hush up the incident?" On his knees in front of the shelves, Guy asked "Got a flashlight?"

Steed handed one down. "I think Johnny kept the trouble quiet because he didn't want anyone to think he might have an enemy or two. Took pride in his reputation."

Shone under the bottom shelf, the light revealed a

couple of nails and a pair of pliers that had gotten kicked back out of sight.

"That's all I know about the trouble." Steed lit a cigarette. He smoked while Guy examined all along the floor at the shed's corners and gave the worktable a thorough going over. He declared the place clean and handed back the flashlight.

Outside again, he poked through a pile of dirt near a bulldozer and found nothing but rusted tin cans. "That's about it," he said. They started for the watchman's shack. "I sure thank you for your time, Fred."

"Welcome. Like I said, it'd be hard for anyone to get in here and dump something without being noticed."

"But not impossible—that's what happened with the equipment vandals."

"Yeah. We watch closer now."

Guy drove away from the construction site with mixed feelings. Like the watchman, he didn't see the vandalism as a juvenile prank and from what he knew of Chance Halperin, he couldn't imagine the attorney stooping that low over a right-of-way issue. Halperin had money, and money talks.

Guy reined in his musings with a self-deprecatory chuckle. Scarcely an hour earlier, he'd halfway convinced himself that his friend, Chance, could be a killer.

"You're losing it, buddy," he muttered, pointing the Studebaker toward the sheriff's office to write up his report.

He found Sam the dispatcher on duty, the Turk not yet back from Maggie's meeting with the D. A. Curious about the outcome, he weighed the idea of hanging around awhile, against the prospect of listening to Sam's catalogue of ailments, and headed home.

On the way he picked up fresh milk to make potato soup. Well into that project thirty minutes later, he stopped to answer the phone. Expecting the Turk's blunt greeting, he was taken aback by a sandpaper voice that asked if he might be Deputy Warner. His inability to identify a regional inflection lifted the hair at the nape of his neck. *Someone had found him.*

He affected a down-home drawl. "Yep, you've sure nuff got the man."

The caller identified himself as Charmaine Dorsey's theatrical agent. Guy took a beat to substitute Maggie's name for the stage moniker. The agent broke in, "Scaff Russell is the name."

Relief weakened the deputy's knees. He stared down at the initials carved on the chair-desk's wooden arm while he tried to regroup.

The agent growled, "You still there?"

"How did you get my number?"

"Charmaine left word for me to call you. Guy named Sam at the sheriff's office gave me your number."

Anger knotted Guy's insides. So much for the safety of an unlisted number. He started to hang up.

"What's going on back there? Her friend told me Charmaine's in some kind of trouble."

Russell got the briefest of rundowns, after which he loosed a spate of gutter language and then asked, "Did she ice the brother-in-law? What d'ya think?"

"I think she needs a good lawyer with more faith in his client than you show. There are a couple of other possible suspects, but most folks here consider your client their choice."

"Hot damn! Manna from heaven."

Guy clenched his jaw.

"So, Deputy...what about press on this missing sister thing? Have the Tulsa papers picked up on it yet?"

At mention of the press, Guy Warner muttered words under his breath that reduced the other man's earlier obscenity to a quaint colloquialism. Russell was still taking when the deputy hung up. He last caught "...worth a million, that kind of publicity."

Appetite gone, Guy turned the burner off under the soup. Beside Old Firebelly he sat, staring at nothing while the room darkened. Why should he feel drawn and quartered because she'd contacted her agent? Why *wouldn't* she milk every possible ounce of publicity out of her situation? Hadn't his subconscious forewarned him?

More than any time since his ex-wife and son left Toledo for parts unknown and before Guy testified against Ed Moroni, the deputy felt adrift and alone.

Although it galled him to admit it, learning that his attorney friend had been on the outs with the dead man compromised the trust Guy had placed in him. At eight o'clock he began clearing the kitchen of perishables. He packed the canned goods into a sturdy cardboard box. Those things accomplished, he turned to personal possessions. The miniature vehicles he'd carved on long, lonely nights, he wrapped individually in newspaper. Doing so, he glimpsed one line in a letter to the editor that gave him pause.

"...in retrospect...perhaps the tragedy in Dallas

will awaken America to stop the disrespect for law and order we have witnessed in recent years." He shook his head and heaved a sigh. *And here in Alden America, Deputy Guy Warner, sworn to uphold the law, is scampering away from his duties like a scared mouse.* Too emotionally weary to feel shame, he packed the miniatures into a wooden box.

Innocent or guilty, Maggie Simpson as Charmaine Dorsey, could draw news crews and their cameras to Alden. If charged in Rice's death, she'd stand trial. As local deputy, he'd wind up in the spotlight with her. Eventually the mob's tentacles would reach him.

Ed Moroni's brand of justice didn't include a trial by jury.

Chapter 10

"The D. A. ordered you not to leave town, savvy?"

Maggie nodded as she scooted out the passenger side of the sheriff's patrol car. Turkeson handed over the brown paper bag that held the few personal items she'd been allowed in the cell.

"And if I was you," he called after her as she passed under the hotel veranda's Moorish arches, "anytime I stepped outta my room, I'd watch over my shoulder for the likes of Case Murray."

She hurried through evening shadows brooding under the veranda's tiled roof. In the lobby, she steeled her empty stomach against the savory aroma of meat on the grill in the adjacent coffee shop's kitchen. Curious eyes, some hostile, watched from the dining area while she passed the wide, open doorway.

Possibly, some of those people had known her as a child. Aching to see one smile, hear one word of encouragement, she held her head high and approached the desk clerk. He handed over her room key without a word of greeting.

Climbing the stairs opposite his desk, Maggie imagined herself as Joan Crawford in a vintage forties suit whose shoulder pads spoke the final word of defiance. Once in the upstairs hallway, however, she scurried to her room like a cockroach caught in sudden light.

The lock Turkeson had broken when he entered her room Monday night had been repaired but looked barely secure enough to slow down a ten-year-old boy. But fear would not be her master. She focused on the prospect of privacy and a hot bath.

A steamy welcome hissed from the ancient radiator. The moist heat also leached the jailhouse stink of concrete and old woolen blankets from her clothes and skin. She locked the door and stripped. The last tumbler on the lock that had bound her spirit since being jailed didn't fall into place until she'd bathed and slipped between the sheets. The threadbare cotton whispered over her bare flesh, soft as a lover's caress. A long sigh of contentment escaped her throat, then a giggle.

Had it been that long since she felt a man's loving touch?

But the canary had escaped the cage. Her musings fluttered to the deputy with the soft hazel eyes. Despite his obvious attempts to remain aloof the few times she'd seen him, she'd caught flashes of empathy in his manner.

From somewhere in her memories of jail, she remembered seeing him in a tan uniform. He'd looked pretty good. How he might look out of it stirred the wings of her imagination.

He might even be persuaded to smuggle Doreen's letters from the evidence file so she could have a look at them. She doubted the files were all that secure in Turkeson's office. Maggie snorted away such fantasies and snuggled deeper under the covers. The reconstruction of her life that began with acceptance of her dependency on alcohol had strengthened her self-image. She couldn't bring herself to dishonor herself or the deputy in such a way.

What she couldn't squelch was the hope that he'd help her some way. Having surveilled her meeting with Johnny the night he died, he'd surely heard about Doreen's scrapbook. Had he checked with Fate Halperin about Johnny's claim he'd given everything to Fate for tearing down the old farmhouse?

The uncertainties gnawing at her transformed the sheets into prickly burlap. Hunger growled through her stomach. Eyelids lowered, she painted on their dark curtains the image of an American Beauty rose, and so found a quiet place. There, on the twilight edge of sleep, she lingered until a clawing sound at the window above her head jerked her full awake.

Heart pounding, she sat bolt upright. After several seconds she realized the sound kept rhythm with the shadow of a wind-tossed tree limb on the opposite wall.

"Silly goose," she muttered, sinking back onto her pillow. After all, where could one escape when fear was the enemy? She glanced at the luminous dial on her wristwatch. Only *eight fifteen?* Fully awake now, she heaved a sigh and got up.

Ten minutes later, clad in her green suit skirt and black sweater set, she descended the stairs. At the doorway to the coffee shop, she paused to smooth aside her bangs before entering center stage, head high.

Two couples at one of the linen-covered tables looked up from their dessert plates. Forks hovered midair. Silence crashed down. Smiling, Maggie tilted her head in greeting on her way to a table under the bay window. No one smiled back. Seated, she glanced out into the garden's winter landscape. A light wind shifted limbs and branches, allowing glimpses of lights at the distant railroad crossing. Between boxcars, warning lights gleamed red, disappeared and reappeared, and finally went dark.

The dark-haired waitress she remembered as Joan, ambled over, *sans* the friendly smile she'd given Maggie when they first met. "We're getting ready to close."

Maggie gestured at the notice posted behind the counter. *Open daily 7 a.m. to 10 p.m.*

Sighing, the young woman walked away and brought back a menu.

For all Maggie's studied nonchalance, she couldn't deny the anxiety churning in her stomach. Steak no longer sounded good. She ordered chicken consommé and a Cobb salad, and as the other diners succumbed to their need to exchange what were likely scathing observations about her, decided to enjoy her role as Typhoid Mary.

She cast occasional smiles over her teacup until her food arrived, then bolstered by the delicately seasoned broth and the crisp greens, lingered over cherry cobbler and a fresh pot of tea. Clearly disappointed by her refusal to be intimidated, her detractors left before finishing their pie.

The waitress approached. "Anything else?"

"A glass of warm milk to take upstairs would be nice," Maggie said.

On her way through the lobby, she picked up a magazine from a table beside one of several overstuffed chairs. The desk clerk had already retired, the placard on his counter advising latecomers to ring a bell for service. Alden, it seemed, had little need for security.

Maggie locked her door and kicked off her suede pumps. The rejection downstairs had hurt, but she'd showed her mettle, and tonight had a real bed to sleep on, lumps and all. What more could she ask?

The milk and a magazine article about how to create a table-top Christmas tree out of three dozen empty toilet paper cylinders, lulled her toward sleep. She'd reached the instructions for decorating it with silver spray paint and glued-on cranberries when her eyelids closed. The familiar old nightmare became her next reality.

Onstage with a USO show for an audience of Marines in the South Pacific, she struggled through a dance routine accompanied by a sousaphone that pumped out *Singing in the Rain*. Gene Kelly danced circles around her, kicking and leaping while she slogged along beneath the weight of an ankle-length yellow slicker and a huge, black umbrella.

Maggie cried out in dread of what came next, but rather than the familiar portly figure standing in the audience to record her humiliation with his bulky old camera, Johnny Rice sprang up, pointing an accusatory finger.

New, too, the chill breeze that rattled the palm fronds drooped over the stage. Hunched deeper into the raincoat, she lowered the umbrella against the draft. Whipped inside out, the fabric plastered her face. Clung.

She clawed at the filmy substance. It resisted her fingers. Every breath she tried to draw seared her lungs. Her eyes flew open, focused on a shadowy form bent over her. *No dream, real!* She struck, tugged at the intruder's gloved hands. Tried to scream.

Chapter 11

Maggie's scream expired in a gasp that sucked the filmy substance into her mouth. Bees swarmed in her head. Fire burst through her lungs.

Blinded, with one eyelid plastered shut, the other eye blurred, she arched her back. Clawed. Slapped. Her fingers brushed a nose. She rammed it with the heel of her hand.

Her assailant grunted and withdrew far enough that Maggie could pinwheel her arms.

Her fists connected, flew open, and shoved against shoulders clad in a napped fabric until she freed herself. Clawing the covering off her face, Maggie flung herself upright, gasping, coughing deep, raspy hacks. Heart pounding, she fought against the darkness, flinging her arms lest her attacker come at her again. Only when she heard the faint snick of a door latch did she sink back onto her pillow in exhaustion.

Sweat-soaked, she lay panting until the room stopped spinning. Finally, she slipped off the bed and crawled across the room to lock the door. There she sat until the last bee in her head buzzed away.

Mental clarity brought fresh terror and more questions and self-doubt than Maggie wanted to consider. Had the intruder been male or female? She remembered the texture of the attacker's clothing. Corduroy? Chenille? A loosely knit ribbed sweater?

And how had her attacker gotten into her room? Try as she might, she couldn't remember locking the door when she came back to her room after dinner. But she surely had after living in L.A. where locking up was automatic.

Shaking with cold as much as fear, she knew she couldn't sit in front of the door until morning. The phone sat on the vanity dresser beside the door. She reached up for it, but her fingers caught in the cord and jerked the thing to the floor. The resounding crash made her jump, but she didn't care about the noise—let whomever might still lurk out there know she took action.

She scrabbled around for the receiver and then listened for a dial tone. Even in her terror, she couldn't bear the thought of that sheriff invading her space again, so she dialed the front desk to have the clerk call the deputy. After several rings went unanswered, she remembered that no one had been on duty downstairs. Someone could have walked in off the street, found her name in the registration book, and taken the extra room key from its cubby hole. Even tiny Alden was no longer safe.

She reviewed the attack, and in the end discounted rancorous citizens like those she'd heard in the sheriff's office. With Johnny dead, who but she still cared why Doreen had disappeared? More importantly, why did that person want her questions about her sister to go away?

Fury spurred her to her feet. She snatched her kimono off the chair beside the bed and walked into her pink satin mules on her way out into the corridor. She dashed down the hallway, losing one slipper, kicking off the other before descending the stairs.

At the lower landing, she paused to reconnoiter.

Light from a phone booth near the lobby's front door and a lamp on the registration desk illuminated the room. Uncertainty and then fear burned through her earlier bravado. Shadows lurked behind overstuffed chairs, around potted palms, and in far corners. Beyond the archway open to the coffee shop, a neon sign in the eatery's front window cast an eerie red glow over the white linen tables. No warm smells from the oven now, only stale cigarette smoke from the lobby.

Her breathing rasped in the silence while she examined various shades of gray around her and imagined standing spotlighted in the phone booth while she searched the directory for the deputy's home number. The thought drew a shaky laugh—in the first place, she'd forgotten his name. Secondly, she had no dime for the pay phone.

On feet numb with the cold, she crossed to the registration counter. There, the sign advising guests to use the public phone drew a snort as she looked behind the counter at a desk piled with papers. A directory lay atop a pile of magazines. She retrieved it, found the number, and dialed the sheriff's office. It took five rings before someone drawled, "Sam Baker here."

****

On what Guy expected to be his last night in the groundskeeper's cabin, he'd hit the sack shortly after ten o'clock. At midnight, he still lay awake trying to decide where to go and sweating out the gut feeling that he owed something to the pursuit of justice where Johnny Rice's death was concerned. He'd been brave enough to help seek justice in Toledo, but he'd been spooked by that theatrical agent's focus on gaining publicity for Maggie through the investigation. If mob retaliation found him, would he live to see his son again?

Exhaustion denied him a reply.

A fire alarm jerked him awake. No—the phone in the cabin's front room. Groaning, Guy considered ignoring the summons. Who but the Turk would call at such an ungodly hour? Warner had called him earlier to resign as deputy. At first light he would drop off his uniforms and his report on the afternoon's interviews and then point the Studebaker toward Alden's city limits.

He fell back onto the bed, jerking the covers over his head and willing the phone to stop ringing. No such luck. And what if Chance Halperin was calling instead of the Turk? When Guy had told Halperin of his plan to leave, the attorney had agreed that might be a wise move. The touchy business of Halperin's possible motive in the Rice murder had been part of Guy's report. He hadn't mentioned it to his friend when the two said goodbye.

If the sheriff had already spoken to Halperin about it, he deserved to know that Guy believed in his innocence.

He threw back the covers and hopped across the cold wood floor into the living room. Scrunched into the chair-desk's snug confines, he picked up the receiver.

The caller spoke before Guy could say hello.

"Deputy?" Her husky whisper identified the last person he wanted to talk to. The fear he heard kept the receiver to his ear.

"Yes." He mentally condemned the unknown ancestor who'd burdened him with the caretaker instinct.

"This is Charmaine Dorsey."

As if he hadn't figured that out.

"Maggie Simpson," she said quickly, and then before he could respond, "forgive me for calling so late, but the sheriff's dispatcher told me it would be all right."

Warner rolled his eyes. Did the man demand a bribe every time he gave out the cabin's unlisted number? It took effort not to snap at the woman. "Sorry. I'm no longer with the sheriff's department."

"Sam said you'd be on the roster until midnight."

"Its five minutes past."

"Someone just tried to kill me," she blurted. In a rush, she told how she'd been dreaming about being wrapped in an umbrella blown backward and woke to find someone holding a plastic bag over her face. If she faked terror that well the woman would have to be a world-renowned actress.

It took him less than ten minutes to call Sheriff Turkeson, dress, and get to the hotel. His possessions already in the Studebaker, he planned to leave town as soon as Turkeson got to the hotel. Stepping from the car, Guy shivered in the cold wind and chuckled at the thought of the sheriff being routed from his warm bed for a change. If the man's bed was all that warm, considering the gossip about Turkeson's wife.

Maggie stood behind the glass panel on the lobby's front door. She opened the door, relief flooding her face. He tensed, instinct stabbing him with distrust again, half-suspecting a publicity stunt—someone with a camera in the shadowy room.

Seeing only a woman alone, white-faced, he suspected she tottered on the edge of a nervous breakdown.

Guy felt like a man going down for the third time in a rough sea.

Would he have the strength to turn her over to the Turk's relentless suspicions?

****

The compassion staring at Maggie from under his seaman's watch cap weakened her already rubbery knees. She swayed forward but stopped herself a split-second before leaning against him lest she appear as wimpy as she felt.

"Thank you for coming," she said, and in a rush added details to her earlier account of the attack. Her words crackled with nervous tension, leaping, twisting like electric current freed from a broken power line.

Wide-eyed in alarm, he reached out, as if afraid she might fly to pieces. His wild gesture toppled the potted palm beside the door. Tree and brass pot crashed to the floor, flinging soil.

A stunned silence followed. Then, Maggie heard a door open somewhere behind her. Slippered feet slapped the tiled floor. She glanced around. The desk clerk bore down on them, every step jostling his black hairpiece lower over one ear. His scowl scourged first Maggie, then the deputy, busy scooping dirt back into the righted urn with one hand while he supported the tree with the other.

"What the Sam Hill is going on here?" Purple crept up the clerk's neck. He wagged his finger. "I don't condone this kind of disturbance in my hotel!"

She sputtered a few times and then propped her hands on her hips. "How dare you speak to me in that tone? I could be dead for all you'd care, no security locks, no—"

Silenced by a gentle hand on her upper arm, she felt warmth spread through her kimono's sleeve. The deputy's hazel eyes cautioned her and then skewered the desk clerk. "Someone gained access to Miss Dorsey's room tonight," he put in before she could speak again. "That someone tried to smother her."

The clerk huffed up. "No one here would—"

The deputy shook his head. "Sheriff Turkeson is on his way. I'm sure he'll want a full statement from you regarding the Morning Glory's inadequate security."

The clerk held his bulldog look for another beat or two, then snorted. He swung his arm toward the stairs, forefinger stiff. "Get her back to her room. I want her out of here at daylight."

Maggie stayed put. The deputy's hand on her upper arm urged her toward the stairway. She shot a look at the clerk. "If the law says I'm to remain in Alden while Johnny's death is investigated, the only hotel in town should be obligated to rent me a room." She cut a glance at Guy. "Isn't that so? You tell him."

Gently but firmly he propelled her up the stairs but spoke to the clerk in passing. "The hotel might hold some liability for tonight's incident."

The man opened and closed his mouth a few times.

"Furthermore," the deputy said, "no one is to leave the building. Sheriff Turkeson will require interviews."

When they reached her room, the deputy examined the latch before they went in. "You're sure you locked up when you returned to your room after dinner, then?"

"I can't imagine not doing so."

Once inside the room, the way he looked everything over reassured Maggie until he said, "If you pulled the plastic bag off your face, where is it?"

Her mind a total blank, she stared at him. "I don't know." Thoughts tumbled in then—replaying the attack; the person drawing away; the feel of the plastic, soft, pliant as she jerked it away.

"Did the man take it then?" the deputy asked.

"All I remember is sitting up, muddle-headed, fighting to breathe." The tremor she had finally overcome while waiting for Warner to get to the hotel, slipped back. "I…I…I'm not even sure it was a man."

He eyed her askance. "A woman your size against a man of any build—"

"Have you ever fought for your life?' Maggie cut in, her hands on her hips. "If there's no bag here, then whoever tried to kill me still has it. And furthermore—"

"Whoa. Whoa. Okay." He crossed to the window beside the bed. "A slight woman might have slipped through here," he said, then examined the latch. "You did say you felt cold before you were attacked?"

"In my dream, yes." The umbrella blown inside out had been different, otherwise it had been a recurrent dream about which she wanted to say nothing

He opened the window and peered out into the big cedar tree's prickly branches. "Only a monkey could climb that maze."

"So, either I forgot to lock the door, or someone had a key." Chilled beneath the resinous breeze, she clutched the front of her kimono more tightly and shivered. He closed the window and turned back to her, meeting her gaze for a moment. As he did so, she noticed the dark smudges under his eyes and wondered if he had slept badly—and why he had resigned as deputy.

He quirked a rusty-red eyebrow at her. "Is it possible the incident happened in your dream?"

Disbelief stiffened Maggie for a beat before she flung her arms wide in frustration. "What is it with you people in this town? Why won't anyone believe a word I say?"

He trapped one of her arms mid-swing, then the other, holding them at the wrists. "I find it hard to believe you could fight off a determined hummingbird, much less someone with murder on the mind."

A come-back on her tongue, Maggie heard footsteps in the hallway and fell silent. The deputy released her.

Sheriff Turkeson stalked in, uniform rumpled, his expression faulting Maggie for every inconvenience in his life. His brow beetled. "Want to tell me what happened here? Couldn't get nothing from old Ralph downstairs except some disjointed tale about someone attacking Miss Dorsey in her sleep."

"And didn't want me alive to tell the tale," she snapped. "That someone tried to smother me with something plastic—a dry cleaner's bag maybe." She recounted the story again.

"And didn't I warn you?" the sheriff said when she'd finished. Open-mouthed with surprise that he believed the attack was real, she let him bluster on. "From what I hear, you were downstairs bold as brass for supper tonight." He shook his head. "How the hell can I convince you that some folks in this town figure it would save the state a heap of money if someone eliminated the bother of a trial?"

The deputy moved close enough to her that Maggie felt his warmth at her right shoulder. Unspoken support? She didn't look away from Turkeson's accusatory eyes and her reply gave him no ground. "I'll grant you, I'm probably a target right now. But for different reasons than you choose to acknowledge."

His eyes shifted almost imperceptibly. "Only one person in this town threatened Johnny."

She sensed tension growing in the deputy and waited for him to defend her. Wind-tossed branches scratched the unscreened windowpane. Neither man spoke.

Maggie flung up her hands in despair and waved both law officers toward the door.

"Don't let me waste your time, either of you. I'll find out on my own who wants to shut me up."

"You stay out of this case, Miss Dorsey or Maggie Simpson whoever you are other than trouble." He pointed at the deputy. "And you," he declared. "you take her to your cabin and keep her out of sight until I say different."

"Wait a damned minute. I resigned, remember?"

"Without proper notice. No soap."

"I'm packed. The Studebaker is on idle."

"Not now, it isn't."

Unable to keep up with their back and forth, Maggie grasped the only positive note in her situation. Turkeson was unwittingly putting her exactly where she might be able to persuade the deputy to help her find the killer, and without a doubt, her theory that Johnny died because of her questions about Doreen had piqued the man's interest. Why he kept trying to escape the matter she meant to find out.

"You can't quit," she told Warner. "You witnessed my meeting with Johnny that night. You know I harbored no grudge against him at the last."

The deputy's eyes under his watch cap's cuff appealed to the sheriff. Turkeson stared back, unrelenting until Warner heaved a sigh. He turned to Maggie.

"Tell me about Monday night, then. You've never given a satisfactory reason for tossing out your drink."

"I told the sheriff. I don't drink."

"Huh—I saw how you looked at that glass. You were practically licking your lips."

As often as she'd repeated the words at AA meetings, she'd always resisted admitting weakness in front of those who had no problem with alcohol. Try as she might, she saw no way to avoid the hazel eyes that probed her self-disgust.

"I'm a recovering alcoholic. Five hundred and one days sober when I arrived in Alden. I struggled to refuse that bourbon."

Turkeson swore, a man who'd clearly counted on that tossed-away bourbon to help make his case against her. He looked like someone wondering how to plug a sudden leak in his rowboat. "Get her outta here," he snarled at the deputy. "I want her alive while I figure out if she's a damn drunk or a damned good liar."

As for the deputy, he clearly wrestled with some private demon a few beats before he began to count: "five hundred two, five hundred three, five hundred four," he paused. "Going on five hundred four days sober, then." A shrug dismissed any lingering problem. "Get your things together before I change my mind."

It didn't take Maggie long to dress and get downstairs. When he helped her into the car a few minutes later, she saw how much stuff he had moved around to make room for her luggage and realized how close she had come to being totally abandoned in hostile territory.

"You really were leaving town for good."

He started the engine. "Funny thing about courage," he replied. "It can be contagious."

Mulling that over while he backed the car away from the curb, she gave free rein to her curiosity about the man. At the outset she'd tagged him as arrogant with a voyeuristic bent, then recognized intelligence in his roving eyes. Turned out he hid a gentle streak as well, and now this—good thing he isn't handsome to boot. Maggie had had enough of handsome men.

"Thanks for staying," she said as the Studebaker pulled away from the curb.

"Don't count on a long reprieve, and nothing more than protection. I can't afford to get involved with your problems."

****

At the cabin, they took her things in first, pausing on the front stoop while he petted the cat that materialized out of the darkness. Its rusty cogwheel of a meow brought a wistful smile to Maggie's lips. "You like cats too. I have a Siamese and an old calico."

Warmth sounded in his chuckle as he gently toed the cat out of the way. "Later, Jiggs." He opened the door and reached in and flicked a light switch before making way for Maggie. After setting her luggage inside, he headed back to the car he'd left with the lights on in a graveled parking lot beside a big log building a short distance away.

Listening to his footsteps crunch away on the winding path, she surveyed her new quarters. His masculine scent of wood smoke belonged to the room as well, its source a pot-bellied stove. Around it sat an antique rocker, two ladder-backed chairs, a side-table, and an empty magazine rack.

One end of the room held kitchen cabinets, a gas range, and a chrome dinette with a yellow Formica top. The same cheery color padded the chairs' upper backs and seats. On the wall behind the heating stove a door opened onto a square hallway. Folding closet doors filled the rest of the room's back wall. An easy chair, floor lamp, and bookcases completed the furnishings.

The deputy was a reader. Maggie liked that. Beside her near the front door, a one-armed school desk held a phone. Aside from the bookcase, the room offered no other clues to his character, except that he knew how to clean a place before moving out—the lifeless space a fresh reminder that she'd almost been left alone against the sheriff's obsession to prove she'd killed Johnny. The problem of how to make Warner an ally rather than simply her caretaker chilled her to the bone. Shivering, she wrapped her arms around herself and moved close to the stove only to find it as cold as she felt.

Her keeper returned with a large carton of food staples. He glanced at her. "There's firewood in the box." He carried the carton to the chrome dinette and began transferring cans onto shelves under the kitchen counter.

Whether he considered it a given that she possessed what for him must be such a basic skill as building a fire, or suspected she had no clue and wanted to embarrass her, Maggie didn't debate. She bent to the task she'd witnessed countless times in her childhood on the farm. She selected an armload of wood and stacked it in the firebox. "You have matches, I suppose. Or do I rub two sticks together?"

Amusement glinted in his eyes when he handed her a box of matches. She struck one on a leg of the stove. The flame and sulphur-tainted smoke held her gaze. Once, long ago, a rodeo cowboy who lit matches on the heel of his boot had saved her life. The memory unsteadied her hand. Transfixed until the flame seared her fingertips and burned down into a black coil, she finally dropped the stub. "Damn."

The deputy stood watching, a can of tomatoes in his hand. "You'll need some kindling."

"I know that," she said, and hoped her nose didn't suddenly take on a growth spurt. "I didn't see anything to use."

That part was true.

To her further humiliation, he came over and dug around in the wood box. He produced shavings and an old newspaper. Kneeling beside her, he took the firewood from the stove and stacked it on the floor. "Unpack your things," he said, "I'll see to the stove."

"I can do it. Just hand me the newspaper."

He elbowed her arm aside. "You'll find a closet back there in the hall." He nodded at the open doorway behind the stove.

By now racked with tremors instead of merely feeling a chill, Maggie stood with her hands on her hips. "You don't really intend to keep me cooped up out here in the woods, do you?"

He stuffed crumpled paper into the stove.

"So how are we supposed to learn who really killed Johnny Rice?"

He tented wood scraps around the paper, used his thumbnail to light a match. Odors of sulphur and paper drifted upward. Flame licked the larger kindling, caught.

How could she not be grateful for the warmth that crept out? "Umm. Feels good," she said. "Thanks."

He didn't look up. "My pleasure."

She wouldn't have bet the farm on any truth in that, had Johnny not already claimed the only farm she'd always thought of as home. "I *have* dealt with a potbelly stove in my day. Could do again, given time."

An iron poker lay on the metal stove mat. Crouched, he prodded the fire with the tool until flames danced into the updraft while Maggie stared, captivated by the reds, golds, and blues. Soaking the warmth into her bones, she watched him stand, brush sawdust and broken bark from the front of his trousers. When he looked at her, she felt an unsettling sense that a long journey had ended, and not understanding or wanting him to see it, averted her gaze. "Where did you say I could put my things?"

"Empty closet in the hall." He pivoted and went out the front door.

Maggie found the closet, which took up all the hallway's back wall except for what looked like an outside door. To her left she saw a bedroom, to her right a door stood open on the bathroom. She busied herself hanging up her clothes and finished as Warner returned with a large tin suitcase. He brushed past her in the hall and carried the monster into the bedroom.

He heaved the suitcase onto his bare mattress,

shucked his coat, and peeled off his cap, which released a reddish-brown cowlick at his crown. He slapped down the errant lock. Up it sprang again.

Maggie would have laughed if it hadn't just sunk in that the one bedroom was it. Too busy before to think about it, she wondered aloud, "Which of us gets to sleep in the bathtub?"

Chapter 12

Turned out that the closet doors in the front room opened on a fold-down bed. Maggie watched the deputy take fresh sheets and a blanket from a narrow closet on the same wall, and then start to make up the bed. She pitched in, appreciating the fresh-air scent that lingered in sheets dried on a clothesline.

After freshening up in the bathroom, she slipped into her gown and kimono, wishing she'd brought flannel pajamas for the cold Oklahoma nights. Actually, not much night remained, and she wasn't sure she could doze, much less fall asleep. Every muscle in her body yearned for rest, but her brain screamed for action.

How had she imagined that a small town would be exempt from evil? Out there among the butchers, the bakers, and the candlestick-makers, some Sunday-go-to-meetin' Christian held a secret that her return to Alden threatened to expose. She marched from the bathroom, determined not to twiddle her thumbs while the sheriff looked for some way to pin Johnny Rice's murder on her.

His deputy obviously considered her a thorn in his backside. She found him in the kitchen unloading the carton he'd left on the table earlier. Glancing up, he looked like a man who contemplated a year in the Everglades with a single can of insect repellent.

Did he consider her situation a stroll along Rodeo

Drive? "You surely don't expect me to stay here doing nothing while that half-assed sheriff contrives some way to get me back into his stinking jail." To phrase it as a question hadn't been an option.

"You can do something." He flung a gesture at the carton on the table. "Hand me the rest of that stuff." Crouched, he started shelving canned goods under the counter.

Two boxes of macaroni and cheese and a bottle of Jack Daniel's remained in the carton. The bottle held two ways to escape—she could break it over his head and run, which his attitude invited, or she could find oblivion in the contents. However, bad choices had never worked out well for her, so she handed him the mac and cheese.

"As for Sheriff Turkeson," he said, stowing the box. "He's not so dumb—self-important, but smart enough."

Maggie offered no argument to the deputy's characterization of his boss. All she could do was hope that when it came to the sheriff's smarts, he had enough of them to find the real killer. She no longer doubted that Rice had been murdered—not after tonight. She handed Warner the Jack Daniel's. "I hope I'm not the only one here who can't handle this stuff."

A fractional shift in his mood revealed itself in his eyes. *Concern*? "Want me to pour it out?"

"Not for my sake."

He stashed the liquor in the bottom shelf's deepest corner. Maggie picked up the empty grocery box. "Where shall I put this?"

"Out on the front step for now."

She complied and was startled by a gruff meow

from the big tomcat she'd seen earlier. He crept into the rectangle of light from the open door, sniffed at the box, and meowed again. "Hello Jiggs." When she knelt to stroke his back, the cat shot off into the night.

Warner, watching from the doorway said, "Sorry about that," and blessed her with one of his rare, warm smiles. "Old Jiggs is as inhospitable as I am. The female is more visitor-friendly, but she must be somewhere on the hunt."

"My cats are Miss Kitty and Cleocatra," Maggie said.

He blinked, then laughed. "Miss Kitty? Cleocatra? Those must be really uptown, Hollywood pussies, then."

If he intended a double entendre, he didn't show it. Maggie ducked her head to hide a smile, and still kneeling, extended her hand and tried to coax the cat from hiding. "Here kitty, kitty. Here Jiggs." Once she'd regained her composure, she glanced up. "It's almost morning. Maybe he's hungry."

"He's mostly a mouser. But how about you?"

She stood. "Well, I'm definitely not a mouser. But if you're asking if I could eat a bite, the answer is yes."

Back in the kitchen, she washed her hands at the sink while he retrieved a couple of cans from below the counter and took some bread from a drawer. "I hope you like apricots and deviled ham," he said.

"Not together in a sandwich."

The last of his discomfiture dissolved into hearty laughter that lightened her heart in a way Maggie wouldn't have thought possible an hour earlier.

"Sounds like some kind of fancy Hollywood *hors d'ourve?*" Rolling his eyes heavenward, he had butchered the French term into *whores devors*.

"Actually, I eat about anything." Survival had demanded that from the time Maggie turned thirteen.

He gave her a slow, critical head-to-toe look.

She waved her hand at him and nodded. "Okay, so I could use a few more pounds here and there. It isn't for lack of a healthy appetite." No need for him to know how tough finding food had been the past year. She went to the cupboard next to the sink and took down two plates. "As for playing detective," she said, "my investigative talents might not impress you, but I definitely got someone's attention. As Johnny is my witness."

"You're sure of a link between your questions about your sister and Rice's death, then."

"I'd bet my last nickel." Watching him slather mayonnaise on a slice of brown bread, she admitted to herself that being in protective custody would save her a few precious nickels. That didn't mean she meant to molder away in this cabin. "I intend to find out exactly what the link is between my arrival in town and Johnny's death."

The deputy's square jaw flexed. "Sorry, but you'll stay right here as Turkeson ordered."

"We'll see about that."

He slammed down the knife, flinging mayonnaise globs across the gray countertop. "Dammit, woman!"

Male temper tantrums had ceased to move her during her first marriage to the famous actor who'd wanted her only as eye candy. Calmly, she reached for the roll of paper towels that stood on end to the left of the sink.

He retrieved the knife and scooped up the mayo in

a single motion before she could wipe the counter. "This is no damned Hollywood whodunnit you're mixed up in." He jerked the paper towel from her hand and swiped the knife clean. "The Turk wasn't kidding back at the hotel when he said half the people in this town would like to see you hanged from the yardarm. You must have heard him as we left—grilling the desk clerk for not locking up the extra room keys after hours."

She arched her brow. "You're absolutely certain the clerk himself is above suspicion?"

"He's more of a newcomer in Alden than I am. Probably didn't know Johnny Rice well enough to be all that concerned over who did him in."

"Maybe not. But the man sure doesn't like me for some reason."

"General principles. He doesn't care much for women."

"Oh."

"You're lucky the Turk is concerned enough about your safety to hustle you out of sight." Warner arranged the sandwiches on the plates, added dill pickles, and some potato chips.

While she set the food on the table, he pulled out a chair for her, then one for himself. The terror she'd felt when that plastic bag shrouded her face remained fresh enough that Maggie didn't *pooh pooh* Warner's remark about her good luck. Nonetheless, she couldn't quite buy the sheriff's outward concern for her safety. "I still think your boss is mostly afraid I'll interfere while he tries to prove my guilt."

"He believes in the criminal justice system." The deputy bit into his sandwich. Chewing, he looked thoughtful for a moment, then swallowed. "It hit the Turk hard, seeing Oswald shot down right under the nose of men sworn to protect him until he could stand trial."

With nothing to say to that, Maggie bit into her sandwich, wondering why a meal shared with someone else always tasted better.

After a few moments, he spoke again. "I think the Turk is afraid something like what Jack Ruby did in Dallas could happen here. After tonight, I tend to agree."

"Is that why you didn't leave town?"

The food on his plate appeared to lose its appeal. Or was his obvious distaste directed at her? Unaccountably, she felt hollowed out. "What is it? What's wrong?"

Cold eyes delved into hers. "You can count me out on your little games, Miss Dorsey."

"Games?"

"I talked to your agent this afternoon."

Maggie's pulse leaped. "Scaff contacted you?" Leaning forward in excitement and then deflated by his hard expression, she sat back again. "Why didn't you tell me?" She reached across the table to touch his wrist "Tell me he's sending an attorney—"

Silenced by his icy glare, she slumped in her chair.

"Am I supposed to believe it's really the attorney who interests you?"

She frowned. "Of course! What else—"

"How about publicity?" he broke in. "I know the importance of good press in an acting career. And don't think I don't realize how much attention you might squeeze from your troubles here."

"Publicity is the least of my concerns." She pushed aside her plate. "I don't know what your problem is, but I get the impression that if your mother sent you a box of homemade cookies, you'd have them analyzed for ground glass."

"A box of cookies from my mother would certainly be a cause for suspicion, Miss Dorsey. She and my dad are both dead."

Despite the absence of emotion in his tone, his eyes betrayed loss. Beyond that, Maggie saw the isolation of a man for whom close ties had been severed. Hadn't she seen the same pain in her mirror often enough to recognize it?

****

The deputy's expression haunted her long after they had decided to try and sleep a while before full morning. Listening to him pace his room, she ached to lend comfort. If he truly had no close family relationships as he'd claimed after she apologized for her remark about his mother and the cookies, where had he planned to go when he packed to leave town earlier? And why in the middle of the night?

A shiver slithered up her spine. Might the deputy himself have had a reason to want John Rice dead?

She hid her head under the covers, trembling, yet disgusted with herself for her suspicions. Would every moment of her search for Doreen be a struggle between paranoia and the need to find someone in Alden to trust?

After a moment's reflection, she decided she'd seen a bit of paranoia on the deputy's part too when he mentioned Scaff Russell's call. Mystery upon mystery, she'd stumbled into. Maggie thought back to remarks she overheard between the D. A. and the sheriff, who'd mentioned how well Warner had shaped up as an investigator. She'd figured out that Chance Halperin had recommended him for the deputy's job.

So, were they old acquaintances? Client and attorney perhaps? Did Warner shun publicity because of some close brush with the law elsewhere?

More than ever, Maggie wanted to talk to the attorney but had no idea how to do so without the deputy's cooperation. Her head buzzed with fatigue and conflicting emotions, but when she tried to quiet them, the terror pushed aside by the activities that followed the attack on her crept back in. The evil she'd felt in her room struck her now like a composite of the hostile stares she'd faced at dinner in the coffee shop. Who dare she trust?

What if the deputy slipped away while she slept, leaving her at the mercy of the same evil? Or another, yet to reveal its presence?

Chill bumps crept down her arms. She burrowed more deeply under the covers and lying alert, listened lest the deputy try to leave.

Overtaken by fatigue, she fell asleep and awoke suffocating again, fighting the bedcovers the way she'd fought her assailant. Heart knocking her ribs, she finally freed herself and sat bolt upright. Only then did she hear bacon sizzling in the pan and smell its savory aroma.

Deputy Warner stood at the opposite end of the room, ostensibly tending breakfast at the gas range, in fact ogling what her flimsy nightgown didn't quite hide.

Relief pushed away the night's terrors even as she jerked the blanket up beneath her chin and watched him decide whether to pretend nonchalance or look away.

He did neither, instead shrugged. "I rather enjoyed the view." A smile played around his lips. "Breakfast in two, three, or five minutes, depending on how you prefer your eggs."

"Flat and hard with brown lace edges." She retrieved her kimono from across the foot of the bed. "Cooked exactly the length of time it takes to shower."

He snorted. "I never knew a woman who could shower in five minutes."

Wondering exactly how many women he'd timed, Maggie raced to the challenge. When she emerged from the bathroom, a clock visible inside his bedroom at the opposite side of the hallway showed she'd met the challenge. "Five minutes on the dot," she said on her way to the table.

He tented his eyebrows and plied his spatula in the skillet. The two eggs he slid onto a plate looked perfect, and so did the bacon.

Maggie had cheated the time clock a bit by wrapping her wet hair in a towel to dry later and slipping her kimono on over her underwear instead of taking time to dress.

He didn't seem to mind.

Over breakfast she caught him sneaking frequent glances at various points of interest on her anatomy. Familiar from adolescence, those glances. Unfortunately, her talent hadn't quite lived up to her physical assets, thus the problems she had encountered with casting directors who expected sexual favors in exchange for plum movie roles.

Despite her pride for sticking to the word "no," Warner's continued appraisal unleashed a notion that maybe she could relax her policy. Would he, with the right kind of persuasion, find some enthusiasm for helping her learn the truth about her sister's whereabouts?

About her height, and lean, the man had a sinewy toughness about him that suggested a rugged outdoorsman. A smattering of freckles and the intelligence she'd seen in his eyes at their first meeting in the coffee shop four days earlier added to his appeal.

Lest those intelligent eyes ferret out her thoughts, Maggie busied herself with a second slice of toast, slathering it with butter. Foolish thoughts they'd been, acting on them likely to wreck any chance of developing a real friendship that might achieve her ends without betraying her hard-won principles.

"A penny for your thoughts."

Startled, Maggie almost dropped the piece of toast. She recovered soon enough to come up with a reply near enough the truth to sound plausible. "I was thinking how good it feels to sit here normal as anyone after that awful cell and that awful man," she said.

Warner fetched the coffee pot and refilled their cups. "Sheriff Turkeson isn't so bad."

The perfectly brewed dark roast left just enough bite on her tongue to beg more. Turkeson's character she didn't want to discuss. She looked away from the deputy, assessing his Spartan quarters. Surely the place would seem more homelike after he unpacked the rest of the boxes stacked in one corner of the room. "Have you lived here long?"

"Long enough to get too accustomed to my own company for my own good." Again, that bit of a smile. "Confession time. I have to admit present company is a hell of a whole lot preferred over breakfast with the Turk at the Morning Glory."

"Thanks." She arched an eyebrow. "I think."

From there the conversation flowed easily to his work and hers, the differences between city and small-town life.

He'd grown up in Toledo. Married. Divorced. One son. The way he spoke of the boy made her wonder why he'd moved so far away. His only explanation was he needed a change of scenery after failing at marriage.

If Hollywood had taught Maggie anything, it was how few divorces are so cut and dried. Moreover, her matrimonial mishaps had shown her that new surroundings alone didn't heal the scars, but she didn't press him on the matter. He might want her to reciprocate with details of her love life and earlier travels with the medicine show and how she escaped.

Consequently, their get-acquainted scenario took on a celluloid quality, idealized, all the bloopers left scattered on the cutting room floor.

After stacking the breakfast dishes to wash later, they settled in beside the iron stove he referred to as Old Firebelly. There, Maggie unwound the towel turban and started drying her hair. He watched.

A moment passed. "This being Thanksgiving, I plan to loaf the day away without apology." He selected a small piece of wood from the box beside the stove and took out his pocketknife. Whittling, he didn't look up. "Unless, of course, you insist I go out and shoot a turkey for you to stuff and put in the oven."

Thanksgiving? Maggie hadn't given it a thought. "Forget the turkey." Her most ambitious culinary undertaking involved a beef roast with potatoes and carrots. "After the week I just survived, I'm just thankful for a quiet place to warm my feet and regroup. She wiggled her toes inside her satin slippers. Contentment seeped in with the warmth.

Was this how it felt living happily ever after in story books?

The uncharacteristic sentimentality made her laugh.

"In today's episode," she sing-songed in response to her companion's questioning glance, "Ward and June Cleaver toast their tootsies while the turkey roasts and the boys play touch football out back."

He stopped whittling, glanced up. "More likely, Wally just threw a baseball through the neighbor's window, and the Beaver is on his way into the house to tattle."

Laughing with him at the scenario from the television show, the glance became a long search among one another's thoughts. The tiny cabin closed in on what she sensed were two people on the same page emotionally. Lonely, hungry for more than a clean-cut Ward and June moment.

The fire crackled, flames roared up the stovepipe. They both jumped. Warner reddened, put aside his pocketknife and the vehicle that had been taking shape in his hands. Silent, he went into his bedroom.

The radio there came on. Christmas carols, already.

When he reappeared, he avoided her eyes as he sat down and resumed whittling.

Neither that nor *Here Comes Santa Claus* sung merrily from the bedroom closed the door on what looking into one another's souls had unlocked. Nothing in the sexual tension in the atmosphere had had anything to do with her earlier thoughts about seducing him. The mutual need had been unmistakable.

She summoned nonchalance. "What are you carving?"

"A miniature."

"Miniature what?"

"Log-truck, I think it'll be."

"For your son?"

He whittled more vigorously. Wood shavings rained onto the newspaper at his feet.

Guilt niggled at Maggie, as it had the night before. "Did bringing me here upset plans to go visit him?"

"No."

For want of a safe retreat from intimacy she'd built a wall, but now the isolation weighed her down. A chill raked her, from still-damp hair, down her arms, but the need burned hotter, drawing her forward, arms wrapped together as if she could crush desire. Her kimono slid open over her knees. She closed it, but he had noticed and stopped whittling.

How long since she'd wanted a man this much?

She couldn't. She mustn't let it go any farther. As she had reasoned away her previous impulsive idea to gain his help with her body, Maggie tried to reason away her body's genuine response to a man she found attractive despite his lack of leading-man features. If she gave in, he'd never help her learn the truth about Doreen.

His slow grin banished any thought of her sister. He stood, arms open.

Maggie found them as warm and safe as she'd imagined. Her only nontactile awareness during what followed became the radio beside his bed, voices merrily in chorus: *Jingle Bells.*

Later, snuggled in his embrace she listened to his heartbeat grow calmer along with hers and remembered to be afraid again.

Why couldn't their intimacy have been merely physical—a few moments shared by two people starved for affection? She'd long practiced the act of love as stage art. What about this man changed that? What in her had changed?

Sickened by what he'd think when she asked him to disobey his boss and help her learn who killed Johnny and what it might have had to do with Doreen, she hid her face in the curve of his arm, only to find that his woodsy smelling skin triggered a fresh jolt of desire. What she had to ask cooled the moment she drew a deep breath to speak.

"Warner?"

He laughed softly, nuzzled the top of her head. "Don't you think you could call me Guy, now?"

Impossible not to smile at that, but his heart pounding against hers made it hard for her to remember what she must say. "Guy," she began, "there's something I must ask—"

Distracted by his hand following the curve of her arm, over onto her breast, she moved against him. "I...I hardly know where to—" she meant to say, "start," but before the word found its way to her tongue, his mouth closed over hers.

The time to ask what she wanted of him besides warmth and breath-stealing crescendos of desire never felt appropriate until much, much later.

They'd finally gotten around to cleaning up the breakfast dishes. She washed. He dried.

"You know," she said, sloshing a green plate through the rinse water, "there must have been something in Doreen's letters to Johnny he thought would help me." She handed him the plate. "If only I could get a look at them."

"No chance. The Turk won't release those until the investigation is closed."

"But you could get at them, couldn't you?"

He wiped the last pearl of water from the plate and stacked it atop the others in the cupboard, and said nothing.

She rinsed a cup, gave it to him. "Knowing what Doreen wrote could mean so much to me, Guy. I don't know how I'll ever clear myself, or learn what happened to her without your help."

"Tampering with the evidence file could get me in serious trouble." His voice had tightened. "Make things worse for you, as well."

"But I thought—" she faltered, warned by the comprehension growing on his face.

His towel lashed the cup, poked, turned, whipped aside. "I get it. This morning was all about softening me up." He slammed the cup inside another in the cabinet.

Shame seared Maggie's cheeks. How could she begin to explain what she'd really felt when she scarcely dared admit those feelings to herself? "I *am* an actress, after all."

The words clearly had their intended effect. He recovered quickly. "Using a man takes no talent."

The need to defend herself burst free. "Why shouldn't I do whatever is necessary to get what I want? God knows I've been used in that way often enough."

A pause. He stood holding the towel, his eyes

probing vulnerabilities Maggie hated. He said, "I suppose you'll explain that remark."

"Ask my first husband. You'll find him at the poshest party in Beverly Hills with another beautiful woman on his arm to impress the world with his manly appeal. But be warned. Carl will only have eyes for you."

Warner appeared too taken aback to reply.

"Then Maurice came along," she said. "That marriage blew to pieces when he asked me to sleep with the casting director so he'd favor Maurice for a plum role in a big movie."

"You refused, then?"

"Damned right. I also lost a few career plums I could have plucked for myself after a little roll on the casting couch."

Although the deputy's lips softened perceptibly, his chin jutted as sharply as ever. "Admirable principles. I'm sorry they proved so costly in the past." He hung the drying towel on a wall rack. "I'm even sorrier you find me insignificant enough that you managed making love to me in the hope I'd abandon my principles on your whim."

"Guy—" She pleaded with her eyes for a beat or two before looking down at the platter she held in a death grip above the sudsy water. She sloshed it in. "This morning wasn't the way you think."

A moment passed. "How was it, then?"

The desire to tell him what he deserved to hear pierced her heart. She couldn't risk the intimacy. Maggie put the platter into the rinse water. "I'm honestly sorry I disappoint you, Guy. That's all I can say."

Shrugging, he pivoted.

She watched him out the door, appealing with a gesture at the last minute.

He didn't spare a backward glance.

****

The day's unseasonable warmth did little to melt the ice in Guy's chest. The cats came running. Seated on the top step, he murmured greetings and stroked their sleek fur.

"Rowwr," came from Jiggs, looking up as if he sensed something amiss.

"Rowwr, yourself." He rubbed the feline's head playfully. Guy believed the woman truly felt regret for using him. Why did he want more than apology, and why wasn't he sure exactly what that *more* should be?

Might he have as much to apologize for as she?

He'd recognized seduction when he saw it but had gone along, thinking of her as a warm body in a world that grew colder, more impersonal, by the day. Shockingly then, she'd breached his emotions. Some of his anger afterward he owned for letting her do that. How had he convinced himself she'd gotten something more from it than a few seemingly earth-shattering climaxes?

From somewhere in the snake's nest of confusion she'd made of his insides, Guy dragged out forgiveness. He gave Jiggs a last, fond pat on the head, then went back inside.

Still at the dishpan, she didn't look around until he spoke.

"How about we start fresh from right now. You and me." He extended a hand. "Friends."

She exhaled a great whoosh and gripped his

fingers. Soap suds slid off her hand and around his wrists.

"Oh Lord," she said in that marvelously husky, breathy little voice of hers, bursting into a nervous giggle. She grabbed the tea towel off the rack and dabbed off the suds.

The rest of the day didn't go at all badly, in Guy's view of things. Chance called to find out if he'd really left town and ended up inviting him for Thanksgiving dinner.

Guy thought he'd convinced himself Chance had nothing against Maggie, until out of his mouth fell the all-purpose excuse of a colicky virus to turn down the invitation. Shame rushed through him for the lingering doubt that kept him from revealing her presence in the cabin.

She watched from the doorway opening onto the hall, her face slathered with some kind of white goop. When he hung up, she frowned. "You should have gone. Don't you trust me here alone?"

Unsure whom to trust, least of all himself, when she came over, smelling of almonds or whatever the heck perfumed her face cream, he went over to stoke up the fire. "I'm under strict orders to keep you under wraps, remember? What's in that stuff on your face, anyway?"

She had told him she made most of her own cosmetics.

"Secret." Her expression brought to mind Maggie the cat when he caught her with a feather between her claws.

"And speaking of secrets," this Maggie of the green eyes continued, "your buddy, Chance Halperin, will figure out I'm here soon enough."

Glum, Guy nodded.

She tilted her head, bird-like in thought while she wiped off the cream with a tissue. "Is he a smallish man?"

"He's probably six feet tall, has to watch his weight."

"Then if we can rule out the desk clerk as the one in my room last night, we can check your attorney friend off the list as well. My assailant was slight."

She spoke with conviction.

More and more, the case intrigued Warner. He decided a little fresh air might drive such dangerous thoughts from his head.

"How's about a walk in the woods, then?"

Surprise and delight paraded through her eyes, their glow matching that of her freshly cleansed skin. "I'll put on slacks."

Chapter 13

When Guy locked the door behind them before they set out for their walk, Maggie wondered about his caution. Who would bother anything on Thanksgiving? And out here in the boondocks? Elation burst through her with the next breath, the joy of freedom overwhelming everything else. She sprang down the steps ahead of him, flinging her arms wide, exulting in the open air fragrant with damp tree bark and fallen leaves. Gathering sun-spangled dust-shafts in her arms, she clutched them to her heart and laughing, broke into a run.

Behind her on the leaf-strewn path, Guy's footsteps quickened. He touched her elbow. "Shush, Maggie."

She spun around in alarm to see him scanning the woods, his brow tight above his nose.

Blood ticking in her ears, she asked, "What?" Only the rustic log hunting lodge and two small sheds stood among the trees.

When their eyes met again, he said, "I doubt anyone will be out and around on Thanksgiving. But archery is a popular sport hereabouts." He nodded toward the target downrange. "I'd hate to see you end up with an arrow in your rear."

"Are you insinuating someone might mistake my backside for one of those big, round targets?"

"Not even with a bullseye painted on." The banter

had eased the tension from his face. "The thing is, if someone sees us the whole town will hear about it before dark. I don't think you want your whereabouts known any more than I do."

Her nod added an unspoken amen. "Archery is a big sport around here?" That had changed since her childhood. Warnings to avoid the woods in autumn were always about hunters careless with their rifles.

Moving forward again, Guy said, "Chance built and maintains the place for family. Others pay a small membership fee."

They fell into step. "All the Halperins are archers?" Maggie chuckled at the thought of the woman in her poodle skirt, sighting on a target, the bowstring drawn.

"Chance's wife, Beth, doesn't participate," Guy said in response to her question and added, "Their teenage son and daughter do well in competitions. Last year the guest of honor at the annual venison feed was the four-point buck Folly bagged over on Wild Turkey Creek."

Before Maggie could comment, the yellow tomcat appeared from a clump of brush beside the path and inserted himself on the path in front of them. A sinuous calico followed. Both greeted Guy with much switching of tails and meowing. While they rubbed around and between his ankles, he stroked each in turn, after which the calico padded over to Maggie.

She knelt to scratch the feline's head. "What's her name?"

Mischief sparkled in the deputy's eyes. "I'd been reluctant to tell you—she's a Maggie too."

She laughed. "To go with Jiggs, of course."

"You remember the old comic strip characters,

then."

Nostalgia for those simpler times twisted through her. Farm life demanded much, but she and Doreen, and Johnny before he enlisted, always read what they called the "funnies" in the Sunday paper. Every childhood memory increased her belief that Doreen, who treasured the lifestyle handed down by their grandmother, would never have left it willingly.

But hadn't she, Maggie, pushed aside those same values? How precious now.

Guy spoke up. "Penny for your thoughts."

"Just wishing I could turn back the clock."

He stopped again, staring off at nothing. "Don't we all sometimes wish for do-overs in life?"

"We do." Again, she added a silent "amen," thinking her main do-over would have been to stay right here in Alden and forget chasing the dream that left her with nightmares.

They resumed walking. After trotting along for a while, the cats dashed ahead and off toward the lodge where they disappeared around a corner of the building. A pathway from the lodge joined theirs to continue to the archery range. Passing the targets, Maggie asked, "How did the Halperins get so excited about the sport?"

"Actually, bow hunting was family tradition. The Halperins came west after the First World War. Lived off the land, pretty much."

Maggie did remember Fate and Folly selling produce from their big garden every summer. Folly sometimes mentioned the hard work when she happened on Maggie in the natural amphitheater in the woods. For a little while the smooth rocky outcrop at the bottom of the bowl-like depression would become a stage upon which Maggie sang and danced, and Folly recited the poetry she loved.

Out of those childhood memories, Maggie mused aloud. "For some reason I don't remember much about Chance Halperin at all."

Guy looked thoughtful, then shrugged. "Off to college, maybe?" A few steps along the pathway later, he added, "Chance Halperin did well for himself. He's wealthy, powerful, and ambitious. But he's definitely hewn from pioneer stock. Makes for an odd marriage."

"Odd in what way?"

"Elizabeth Halperin grew up rich. Her husband has simpler tastes. I expect that's why he built the lodge. He likes to prop his feet up in front of the fireplace with a good book and a can of brew."

"I remember the Halperins as hardscrabble farmers. How could he afford law school?"

"Fate and Folly put in nickels as they could. I figure Chance got help from his father-in-law, as well. I'm told that Old Judge Avery presided over the district court here for years, later held the bench in central Oklahoma. Elizabeth Halperin inherited the piece of ground that Chance turned into a hunting lodge."

Unable to dredge up the Avery name, Maggie did recall hearing about the extended Halperin family. Most died or moved away before her time. "Folly once reeled off her family names for me. Most have slipped my mind, but I do recall how funny they sounded at the time."

"You mean you wouldn't want to name your firstborn, 'Blessing'?" Guy kicked at a pile of russet leaves.

"The way things look for my immediate future, I'd

hardly consider having a child a blessing."

"I don't know. Motherhood might engender sympathy with a jury." His droll humor segued quickly into an apologetic expression. "Sorry. I discounted how serious things are for you."

She waved away his concern. "I got over being sensitive a long time ago, Guy."

They skirted a small ravine. "Before I tried that smart remark, I meant to ask you how Deliverance strikes you as a moniker. The Halperins had one of those too."

"You're joking." She stopped dead in her tracks.

He crossed his heart. "Chance says that's the moniker his parents hung on what they considered their last offspring, after Blessing, Joy, Pleasant and Thankful—and finally, they thought—Fate."

The past rushed in then, bringing laughter as she recounted the rest of what she remembered. "It was Fate when they produced another, then Chance."

A lopsided grin slid up to Guy's right ear. "Chance loves to tell how he was conceived years later on the family's trip west in a boxcar with all the Halperin belongings.

"Quite by chance, I'm sure," Maggie offered. "And poor little Folly? Imagine going through life saddled with such a name and knowing how literally her parents meant it."

"She shows little sign of emotional damage, unless her haphazard fashion sense is a symptom of some sort."

****

Chance Halperin stepped from the kitchen's mouth-watering smells of roasting turkey, into the dining room. Beth, arranging grapes and yellow chrysanthemums in a tall epergne on the table's snowy linen, shot him a harried glance. A lock of chestnut hair straggled over her forehead.

She blew at it and smoothed her brown slacks and tan sweater, both already sleek as melted caramel. "I'm a mess, and it's almost time for company."

He planted a kiss on her powder-scented cheek. "You look impeccable as always. And you know it."

She'd deny it of course, but before she could do so, the doorbell's Westminster chimes sounded. "That will be Fate and Folly." She glanced out double windows that overlooked the side yard, the woods beyond. "Kent and Linda Sue have gone off somewhere. I suppose we'll have to wait for them. Honestly, Chance, I don't know why those two can't—"

Headed for the front door, Chance readied a smile of approval for however his sister had costumed herself for today's occasion. The approval held as he took in her green plaid skirt teamed with a slightly tired, blue fox jacket. Like most of her outfits, the display bespoke the cornucopia of hand-me-downs available from Alden's more prosperous women.

"Happy Thanksgiving, Sis." She got a one-armed hug before he helped her out of the coat. He hung the fur in the hall closet. "You're looking mighty festive today."

Fate, still on the front porch, rolled his eyes without comment. Chance gave him a smile. "You're looking sharp too, Brother." He wore new overalls, a white shirt, and the blue paisley tie Linda Sue had given him for his sixty-eighth birthday in August. As for his pet raccoon, at the moment straining at his red leash to come inside, Chance issued a reminder, "Outside at mealtime, Jeff—Beth's rules."

He stepped outside then, and kneeling, scratched the coon behind its ear while his brother secured the leash to a nearby crape myrtle. "I'm so glad you're here," Chance told Fate as they joined their sister in the hallway. Thinking of the deputy at home alone and feeling ill, he added, "What would Thanksgiving be without family?"

Folly's blue eyes saddened, and she shook her head. "I can't even imagine." She perked up immediately, sniffing the air as she handed him her red handbag. "Do I smell chestnut dressing?"

"You're good, Sis." He placed the handbag on the coat closet shelf, wondering if it looked familiar because it might have belonged to his wife at one time.

Fate came in, closed the door, and handed over his tweed jacket. Chance said, "Shame about Jeff tied up out there. Why don't you just shut him in the backyard?"

"I am afraid not. Jefferson has been restless lately. Yesterday, he ran off into the woods down near the barn. I searched for hours."

Folly winked. "Maybe the old rascal has a lady friend."

Their laughter drew Beth from the dining room. And nothing to do for Folly but show off the coat. She took it from the closet and stroked a sleeve's molting fur. "Is the color not marvelous? I came across it in Doc Whitsett's spare room. It had hung there, untouched I suppose, since Mrs. Whitsett died. Lord how many years ago now?" Folly shook her head at the obvious waste of a desirable fashion statement. "Doc insisted I have it."

Beth felt the fur and nodded her approval. "I remember Irene wearing this." Chance noticed that his wife had the good grace not to mention how far in the past that might have been. "Good quality skins," she said. The smile the two women exchanged bespoke their affection for one another. Beth touched Folly's arm. "Do come with me to the kitchen, now. I smell that pan of stuffing getting brown."

The brothers followed them to the back of the house.

"I suppose," said Beth, "that Chance told you two he's received endorsements from two more newspapers, and about the five-thousand-dollar campaign contribution from Alvin Oil and Associates?"

Chance had in fact discussed AOA's offer with his older brother before accepting support from a company comprised of so many oilfield service companies. Unsavory business practices by any one of them could damage his credibility if things grew nasty during the senatorial campaign.

A commotion at the back door drew a sigh of relief from his wife. Chance patted her shoulder. "Sounds like the young people are home."

The two clattered into the kitchen just as the adults got there. Cheeks pink, eyes round, both tried to talk at once.

"Guess what!" Linda pushed in front of her brother. "We just saw that murderess over at the lodge." The siblings exchanged glances.

"And," Kent said, waggling his eyebrows suggestively, "she was with the deputy."

Chance felt accusation radiating from his wife as

she turned on him. "You knew this, didn't you?"

He lifted his hands, palms out. "All I picked off the courthouse grapevine was that the sheriff had released the actress and that she caused some trouble over at the hotel. She claimed to have been attacked in her room."

"I certainly would question that," Fate said, to which Folly nodded and said, "I've lived at the Morning Glory all my adult life and feel as safe there as I would in church."

Fate's expression chided her. "And what favorite citizen have you poisoned?"

Laughing with the others at that, Chance fretted inwardly over Guy Warner's change of heart about leaving Alden. He could guess why now. "That damn fool Turkeson probably palmed the woman off on Guy."

"Sheriff Turkeson will fool around until the same thing happens here that happened to Oswald," Fate predicted.

"You mean vigilante justice?" Chance shook his head with stern glances at Kent and Linda Sue. "Keep what you saw this afternoon to yourselves. Hear?"

Folly snorted. "Maggie should never have come back here, stirring up trouble over that place of her grandmother's after all these years. She will cost you that senate seat yet, Chance."

He said nothing, wishing his sister hadn't said anything in front of Kent and Linda Sue. Hustling the two and his brother into the family room, Chance turned the conversation to the high school football playoffs coming up the following week.

The troublesome woman didn't reenter the conversation until after dinner when Fate went to take

Jefferson for a walk. Heading out, he told Chance, "You will be wise to get that killer off your property. The sooner, the better."

****

The telephone beside Sheriff Turkeson's easy chair shrilled again. He ignored it. After ten calls from citizens irate about the actress being out of jail, he couldn't stomach another cussing out. The strident jangle continued until his wife flounced off the couch where she'd been trying to take a nap. Skewering him with a glare, she jerked up the receiver. "Turkeson residence."

She listened a moment, then heaving a sigh held out the receiver. "It's for you again."

"I'm not home."

"You're the sheriff. And you're on call."

He slid lower into the overstuffed chair. "I'm still not at home."

"I'll not fib for you, Randall Turkeson."

Had he not been so stressed out, he'd have laughed aloud. Wouldn't fib for him? If he read the signs right—that she had a new man on the side—she sure didn't mind fibbing *to* her husband. He flung himself to his feet, stalked to the door.

"Then don't lie, damn it!" Snatching his Stetson and jacket from the coat rack near the front door, he left her to answer the next ten calls.

Heavy inside with discouragement, he drove through streets all but abandoned to Thanksgiving's post-feast stupor. Activity amounted to a carload of teenagers, no doubt fleeing the attentions of aunts and grandmothers.

When he finally hazarded an appearance at the

office, the relief dispatcher's face lit up like the Christmas lights set to come on downtown at dusk. He looked like he expected Turkeson to come in with five striptease dancers and a keg of beer. "Say, you're a sight for sore eyes," Sam said through his nose. "I wouldn't have agreed to sit in for you this afternoon if I'd known every joker in town—"

Cut short by the phone, he made a face and flapped his hand at the instrument. "You can get it yourself, this time."

"I'm not here," Turkeson replied, en route to the file cabinet in the back room to remove the evidence file on the Rice case. He sat at a small table, reading Doreen Rice's wartime letters to her husband. Mostly she wrote about staying busy with the farm in her husband's absence and fretted about her little sister's fantasies about becoming a Hollywood star. She mentioned friends, some of the male gender.

None of the names sounded familiar. But reading between the lines in the light of recent gossip, the sheriff thought she wrote like a woman struggling with a problem of some kind. The case file also included an envelope from the actress's makeup case. Danby had told him the substance inside was an old-fashioned headache powder. As always when Turkeson shuffled through the pile, he found the old book most bothersome. The yellowed pages did contain recipes for the face creams and such that she claimed to use, but the medicinal formulas troubled him. He'd discussed some of them with Danby.

"If she said it belonged to the medicine show man, I doubt it," the druggist had commented over a cup of coffee at the Morning Glory a couple of days earlier.

"The real old-timers pushed mostly old Indian herbal remedies and horse liniment. The last of the breed bought patent medicines by the gallon and bottled small quantities under their own labels to sell at jacked-up prices." Danby had laughed. "Mostly alcohol, I'd wager, which accounted for their popularity."

Now, leafing through the formulary's brittle pages, the sheriff shook his head in amazement over ingredients that ranged from dried leaves of camellias to mixtures of oil and tar. The occasional preparation that called for small quantities of arsenic or strychnine, he pondered at length.

Maggie Simpson certainly knew plenty about poisons. Why should he doubt she'd use them to kill? He also questioned the so-called attack in her hotel room. He'd found no evidence that she hadn't concocted the story to send him off on a wild goose chase. The need to prove she'd arrived in Alden with prior knowledge of Rice's land grab ate at his gut like chili reheated too often.

Somewhere between that hotel and the Rice home she'd discarded the evidence, and he meant to find it. No highfalutin actress would make a fool of Randall Turkeson—not with the whole town watching.

****

The ruin Johnny Rice's construction crew made of the farm Maggie had loved as a child, pained less with the deputy at her side than when she visited it the day she returned to Alden. Sharing memories with someone made all the difference. She pointed out the gnarled oak near where the barn once stood. "See that knothole about halfway up? My friend Nina Belle and I hid secret messages in it when we played Nancy Drew."

Guy Warner's eyes sparkled with inspiration. "Maybe if your friend is still around, she can give us a lead to your sister's whereabouts."

Caught up in hope, Maggie grasped his arm. "Does that mean you've reconsidered?"

He kicked at a scattering of pebbles. "Let's say I'm considering reconsidering."

She clapped her hands. "That's what I meant to wish for at the wishing well."

At his quizzical glance, she grabbed his wrist. "Come along. You'll see."

Abandoned long before her time, the hole was covered with heavy planks that extended over the cement apron. Shot through with disappointment, she watched him scoot aside the boards and a sheet of metal to reveal an accumulation of rusted tin cans, beer bottles, grease-caked auto parts, and other trash.

"There didn't used to be so much junk in there," she murmured. "We called it our wishing well." As if sensing her disappointment, Guy rested his arm around her waist.

He said, "Too big to be a well. Probably a cistern, don't you think?"

"Maybe. But Nina and I tossed in pennies and made wishes." Maggie made a wry face and laughed. "We even threw in what was probably a valuable old Indian head penny from over there." She motioned at a house foundation beside a row of cedars.

"Did your wishes come true?"

"I believed so when Dr. Xavier asked me to travel with the *Health and Happiness Revue*." Pausing, she felt the old familiar shame clog her throat, saw questions in Guy Warner's eyes for which she dared give no details. She made do with, "You've heard that old adage, be careful what you wish for."

His arm tightened around her waist. "What's wrong, Maggie? You're trembling."

Over the past few hours, she'd felt the rebirth of trust between them. Once she began explaining her experiences with Xavier, where could she stop and how long would trust survive? She stepped away from him and pulled her light jacket together with both hands. "I'm fine. Just chilled."

"Actually," he said, undoing a few buttons on his flannel shirt, "it's warm for November. You lived too long in California, I guess."

"I guess." Her voice sounded so unsteady that she hurried off toward the old homestead to distract him. "Just beyond those trees is one of my favorite childhood haunts."

Despite the leaves that hid the trail, Maggie's feet knew the way. When she pushed through a low-hanging branch onto the natural amphitheater's rim, that first glimpse of the rock-strewn bowl in the earth in eighteen years quickened her heartbeat. She held the branch aside so her companion could see too. "Folly was right," she said. "It looks just like it always did, except it appeared bigger to a little girl."

A thousand happy moments in this place sprang back to life when her gaze settled on the sandstone outcrop low on the opposite slope. "There. That's the stage."

"Complete with built-in audience seating," he observed, indicating stones exposed near the foot and around the ledge. He grasped her hand. "Come on, then."

They hurried down the path and over to the wide ledge. He plopped down on a boulder in front of it and motioned. "Climb up there. Show me your best song and dance routine."

Inexplicably, her cheeks warmed, and she hung back.

"Surely you're not bashful."

"Bashful?" She shook her head, considering. "I think for the first time I'm wondering if Doreen might have been right when she laughed at my fantasies of stardom. She fussed about how much time I spent here, playacting." At his questioning frown, she said, "What—"

"I'm wondering why she let you go with the medicine show."

"I begged her to let me go. Besides, she thought Linette and Dr. Xavier were husband and wife. At the time I thought so too."

"Linette?"

"Dr. Xavier's companion. Doreen kept insisting they just asked me along to hand out the potions he hawked from the stage."

Silence, broken finally by a statement rather than a question. "That wasn't exactly the truth, then."

Lest meeting his gaze reveal things better left a mystery, Maggie started up the amphitheater's slope in a different direction than they'd taken down. He caught up, and she felt his hand on her shoulder. Hollowed out, she turned.

He said, "Everyone in Alden seems so sure your sister ran off with that medicine huckster—you're certain that isn't so?"

For days she'd tried to remember witnessing any

exchange between them while the show was in town but came up with nothing other than discussions about her possibly accompanying the Xaviers for a few days. She shook her head. "I had stars-in-her-eyes stage blindness the moment he gave me three lines to speak in one of his little plays. I left with him. Doreen didn't, nor have I laid eyes on her since."

They reached the rim. Ahead, tree after tree bore the initials of passers-by, hunters, lovers—some carved so long ago that they had healed into blackened relief.

She paused at D. S. + B. K., and a bit farther along, D. S + J. H.

She felt Guy's scrutiny. "Doreen Simpson?" he guessed.

"My sister married young, but she apparently never lacked for boyfriends before that."

"Maybe," he mused aloud, "all those boyfriends weren't before her marriage." His eyes narrowed in thought. "Maybe Doreen objected to your visits to the hollow because she considered it her special place, too—especially after her husband went off to war."

"I don't think so." Even Maggie heard the self-denial in her tone. Far better to believe that Doreen had cheated on her husband than to admit something bad might have befallen her.

"How much do you remember about the weeks and months before you left Alden?'

Maggie paused on the trail, eyes closed while she conjured images—sunshine, dust between her bare toes on the road into town when there was an extra nickel for an ice cream cone; plump, round peas rolling over her thumb and out of the pod while she still felt sweaty from picking them. "Warm," she said, "early summer days. Doreen so busy, never had time to listen to me. Moody, missing Johnny, I think. Bright and sparkly one day, weepy other times, or cross with me over every little thing." Maggie opened her eyes to see the deputy looking at her thoughtfully. She glanced back toward the hollow. "Those days, the fantasy world I found here became even more important to me."

His nod encouraged more.

"As an adult, I'm amazed that Folly Halperin, of all people, enjoyed performing on that rock stage as much as I did. She emotes poetry like you wouldn't believe."

Guy made a little sound in his throat, his eyes dancing. "Her flair for drama extends beyond wardrobe, then." Abruptly sober, he asked, "When Dr. Xavier and Linette asked you to travel with them was Doreen in a happy mood or a snarly one?"

Feeling cold to her bones, Maggie started ahead, Guy falling into step. "She was weepy. I heard her crying in her room the night before she finally told me I could go." She'd started to go comfort Doreen but found her bedroom door closed. She knew not to go in or even knock. Doreen had been cranky about that. "She moped around the next morning," she told Guy, "but sang while packing my things later that day."

"Maybe missing her husband, wishing she had someone to help her with those tough decisions?"

"I don't know."

"Maybe she received a letter from him, or a visitor—someone that cheered her up."

"Not that I remember."

"You can't recall exactly when her mood changed?"

Eyelids lowered once more, Maggie searched the

darkness behind them for further glimpses of that day. Her eyes flew open. "After the phone call."

"And you have no idea who phoned?"

Lips pursed, Maggie shook her head, feeling all at once too vulnerable. In an automatic motion, her right hand smoothed her bangs aside, then came down over her forehead, her eyes, pressing them shut. "Must we talk about this?"

"So how do you expect to learn what happened to Doreen as long as you refuse to face the past?" The frustration in his question triggered the bright, hot core of pain she'd kept banked in her chest for days.

Pivoting, she knotted her fists at her sides. "What do you want to know?"

Startled back on his heels, he raised his eyebrows, then frowned. "Anything that might help us figure out some reason she'd decide to let you go off with strangers like that. I think it holds the key to this whole mystery, Maggie."

"I have no clue what changed her mind. Don't you get that? Do you want to hear how many nights I laid awake bawling my eyes out after she didn't come for me on my birthday like she promised—" A sob clawed up through Maggie's throat, tore from her lips. "Must you hear how—"

She bit back the rest.

His gaze locked with hers, he rested his hands lightly on her shoulders. "I want to know what, or who, changed Doreen's mind about what I suspect had initially been a wise decision about her little sister's welfare."

That he hadn't condemned her sister out of hand softened Maggie's heart. Her eyes burned with tears she refused to shed. Whatever the truth, she had come home to forgive Doreen and Johnny and find peace within herself at last. Maggie turned away and walked quickly ahead lest he see her cry.

He overtook her moments later. "Doreen obviously held doubts about letting you go off somewhere with virtual strangers. Once we learn why she cast those concerns aside, we might be on our way to some answers in this riddle."

"We?" Little beyond the word registered. She grasped his hand, warm in hers. "You'll help me after all?"

"Not help." Although he spoke sternly, he didn't let go of her hand. "You're to stay at the cabin. I'll snoop around on my own."

Letting others look out for her wasn't written in Maggie's history, but she murmured agreement and hid her lack of resolve in a warm hug. His heartbeat quickened against hers, and she felt his lips brush her forehead.

A twig snapped, not near but loud enough to jerk them apart. Heart bounding now, she glanced into the woods. They both turned toward the sound.

Nothing there but winter-bare branches limned by the lowering sun, beneath them deep shadows.

"A deer, then," he said.

He sounded like a man whistling in the dark, but laughed. "We're a couple of silly gooses, aren't we?'

"Geese," he corrected, laughing more easily than before.

The lyrics of a children's song popped into Maggie's head. "Or maybe it was the Teddy bears we heard. They might be gathering for their picnic."

"Come again?"

"You mean you don't know about the big shindig all the local Teddy bears throw out in the woods from time to time?" Eyes wide, she touched her lips in a cautionary gesture before singing the first line of the song.

A chuckle interrupted her, and he began to sing the second verse off-key.

The rest of it got lost in their laughter. When she could catch her breath, Maggie exclaimed, "You watch kids' programs on TV."

"Billy sat glued to them every morning when I came in from work."

Seeing how quickly the merriment fled his face, Maggie guessed, "Billy is the son you lost to divorce?"

Silence.

"Mightn't it be good if you talk about it?"

His diffident shrug didn't match the self-recrimination in his eyes. "I lost my son after I made some unfortunate decisions on my last job."

"You were in law enforcement?" Purely a guess based on his current job.

"Not exactly." Gently he moved her aside, indicated with a gesture a spot where the woods appeared less dense. "We'd best get back to the cabin, then. Don't want to get caught out here after dark. He struck out in the lead. "You asked about my work. I was a cinder dick."

Open-mouthed, she stopped in her tracks, then hurried to catch up. "You were a what?"

"Cinder dick. The term dates to coal-fired steam locomotives. There were cinders and ashes aplenty around the tracks and in the yards. Truth is, I worked as a glorified night watchman for the Northern States and Central Railroad."

Maggie hooked her arm into his, hurried to match his long stride. "What's to watch in a rail yard?"

"Mostly drifters trying to steal a ride. More and more though, cinder dicks deal with vandals who've nothing better to do than smash out the windows of luxury sedans on their way out of the factory. Thieves of every ilk."

"How in the world did you end up in a burg like Alden?"

Instead of answering, he started whistling the Teddy bears' tune. Maggie guessed that his thoughts were on Billy again and left them to him. Oddly, though, as they neared the hunting lodge, he cast frequent glances into the bushes on either side of the pathway as if he still suspected a watcher in the woods from earlier—someone who followed them.

She looked over her shoulder. "Are you sure no one saw us leave the cabin earlier?"

The lack of assurance in his nodded reply made it hard for Maggie to keep from breaking into a run.

That night, she lay awake a long while, wondering if the sleeplessness that had plagued her since coming back to Alden would become the norm. Was he wakeful too? Dare she call out, invite Guy into her bed again?

Better judgment sealed her lips.

Chapter 14

Deputy Warner felt worse driving away from Chance Halperin's home Friday morning than when he had arrived. He'd slept poorly, spooked by the sense he and Maggie had been followed in the woods earlier in the day. If word of her whereabouts leaked, could reporters with cameras be far behind? Worse, his wakeful mind had found reasons he couldn't discount his attorney friend as a suspect in Johnny Rice's murder. After talking to the man's widow, Guy had rejected the suicide theory he'd never believed anyway.

Consequently, he had arrived on Chance Halperin's doorstep torn between the desire to see justice done and his disillusionment with the legal system in general. The man's office occupied a separate wing of the house. Rehearsing the questions Guy couldn't avoid asking his friend, he rang the doorbell.

Chance, casual in chinos and a cobalt-blue polo shirt, had welcomed him with his usual smile, but then glanced at his watch. "Can we make it short? I'm going to Johnny's funeral at eleven. After that I have a full afternoon's work here."

The blizzard of papers on the attorney's mahogany desk bore out the statement. Logs turning to embers in the fieldstone fireplace testified to the man's early start on the day.

In a room in which Guy normally felt right at

home, he settled into one of two wingback chairs in front of the fireplace as usual. Normally, Chance would sit in the other chair. This morning he remained standing, his smile frayed at the edges.

He took a poker from its stand on the hearth and jabbed the embers back to life. Pitch scented the air. Flames red as newly spilled blood shed embers into the updraft. The attorney lifted a sardonic eyebrow. "You've made a miraculous recovery from your flu bug, I see. Good nurse, is she?"

So, word had leaked out as Guy had feared. No surprise there, but why had the man who had offered him, a perfect stranger then, sanctuary from the mob, now have his shorts in a knot over Maggie's presence on his property?

"Never mind Maggie," Guy countered, as if that were really possible. "Why hadn't you told me you were at odds with Johnny Rice?"

"And as much as you dislike doing so, you're now going to ask what I did between four and seven o'clock the evening Rice died." Chance dropped the poker into its holder, the clang decisive as he turned to Guy.

"That's about it, then," Guy said, trapping the man's guileless blue gaze. "You won't mind telling me where you went after you and I had our conversation about Maggie the afternoon she hit town." *The timeline to plan and execute murder would have been tight, but everything could have been in place, the opportunity seized when Chance learned of the dust-up between Maggie and John Rice.*

Chance waved a dismissive gesture and finally settled into his usual chair. "Let's not discuss my alibi just now. I'd like to hear more about that so-called attack on Maggie."

"That damned Turkeson." Guy slammed a fist into his palm. "How the hell am I to protect her when a sheriff blabs everything he knows around town?"

"Don't shortchange your boss. Actually, I went to him with questions after Kent and Linda saw you with the woman yesterday."

"Then I'm sure you know all there is to know about the situation. Except I don't believe that Maggie had anything to do with Rice's death, and I feel bound to keep her from harm if possible."

"At what cost to your safety?"

"I can get out of town fast if need be. Meanwhile, I have a few ideas that might help her."

With eyes chilled blue as glacial ice, Chance shook his head. "I fear you have your work cut out for you in this town, Guy. The mood out there is as dark as the inside of a rat's belly."

The way he let the warning dangle sent blood rushing into Guy's head. Nevertheless, he had to make sure the talk wouldn't spread from Halperin lips. The family held a lot of respect in Alden. "Surely you warned Kent and Linda Sue not to tell anyone else they saw us on your property, then."

"They need no warning. None of us wants that kind of attention drawn to our family."

"Beth knows, too?"

"And Sis and Fate. Don't look so gut-shot, Guy. This is one story even Folly won't relish telling around town. Both she and my brother are afraid that a suspected murderer sheltered at the lodge will have a negative effect on my senatorial campaign."

The self-interest in his remark came rarely from

Halperin. Red crept up Chance's neck as he grabbed the poker again and launched a fresh assault on the logs. He spoke to the fire. "I should have expected you would ask my permission before bringing her onto my property."

"To be perfectly truthful," Guy countered, "Maggie doesn't know who she can trust, and neither do I."

"You and Maggie don't know who to trust?" He straightened, barking a humorless laugh. "Wednesday night you were hot to leave Alden and the publicity she might bring here. Now you and she stand shoulder to shoulder against the foe. What little favors is she handing out in return for your change of heart?"

"We're discussing other matters, here." Guy's protest couldn't tamp the heat he felt in his face. *Better to soldier on.* "Namely, I want to hear you tell me where you went after leaving my house Monday afternoon."

"I came home. I phoned a client. We talked about the president's assassination—doesn't everyone now? And then I discussed the client's case, after which I hung up and ate a bowl of tomato soup, after which I worked up some briefs for a trial in Tulsa."

Before Guy could ask the logical next question, Chance added, "And no, I can submit no proof of any of that. Conversations with clients are confidential. Kent and Linda Sue were out while I worked on the briefs. Beth slept off a migraine upstairs. She didn't come down until after nine o'clock."

"Are you sure it wasn't Fate you phoned when you got home that day, rather than a client? You told me you'd looked for him earlier, had no luck. Maybe you two discussed how Maggie's return could affect her status as legally dead, and your spotless reputation as a legal eagle." He glanced at the poker in his hand and dropped it into the holder with a clang.

"You can be sure, *Deputy* Warner, that I didn't seek my brother's advice on how to eliminate Johnny Rice and make Maggie the scapegoat."

A politician's nonanswer to the question. "So, you don't plan to start pressuring Johnny's widow for that easement, now that he is dead?"

The slight twitch of a silvery eyebrow indicated a direct hit on the man's conscience, but rather than flaming into angry rebuttal, he appraised Guy with frank admiration "Small wonder you got yourself in trouble with those hoods up North. All the while you've argued your lack of investigatory skill. By God, you've got the instincts of a federal agent."

"Hardly," Guy said, the denial swallowed by a burst of laughter from the other man.

"The easement?" Halperin went on. "Hell, Guy, trying to get through that camp Paula will build for those special children of hers now that Johnny's out of the way would be futile as proposing a truck route across the White House lawn."

The remark confirmed the deputy's earlier assessment of the woman. "She *is* a tiger in a housecat's fur all right."

Halperin nodded, walking over to his desk where he fiddled with a miniature anchor that served as a paperweight. "Johnny promised Paula the Simpson place for that camp and then reneged. Folly cleaned their house that day and heard a knock-down-drag-out between the two over Johnny's betrayal."

Something in Chance's movements suggested

dismissal. Guy said quickly, "The widow's theory is that after Johnny refused you the easement, you called in Maggie to make trouble over the Simpson estate."

Chance's hand holding the paperweight crashed down onto the desk. "Rather than listening to the widow Rice's theories, you should have searched her garage for rat poison, insecticide, maybe weed killer."

Guy silently damned the man for being right, and double-damned himself because the man spoke truth. "That I can't argue, Chance, but to presume Paula's guilt you have to believe that the minute she heard about the blowup between her husband and the actress, she saw an opportunity to get her way the Simpson tract and place blame elsewhere. That's a stretch."

Turning, Chance nodded. "Point taken. But is it not a stretch, as well, to assume someone else acted as quickly?" He returned to the fireplace, stared into the flames. "On the other hand, arsenic—and all the symptoms your friend, Maggie described in her statement indicate arsenic—can be administered over a long period to bring on illness and eventual death."

"I'm not following you, Chance."

"What I'm thinking is that maybe the actress happened into town at exactly the right time for Paula to stop the construction on the Simpson place while it could still become a children's camp instead of an adult resort. Maybe the plan for a slow death got scrapped for a timelier demise." He faced Guy. "You should check with Dr. Whitsitt to see if Johnny had complained of intestinal problems recently."

A tap on the door to Halperin's study drew both men's attention. Beth Halperin had stepped in, greeting Guy and then reminding her husband that it was soon time to leave for Rice's funeral.

Guy had made his goodbyes and now driving away, reflected on Halperin's parting words: "Find somewhere else to play house with this Simpson woman. I don't want her on my property."

Despite all of Chance Halperin's praise for Guy's investigatory skills, the attorney had boxed him in with Paula Rice as the prime suspect in her husband's death.

And what about the coincidence of so much trouble erupting only after Maggie's return and the questions it raised about Doreen's whereabouts?

Folly had hinted about something awry when she told Maggie about the photograph of an unfamiliar man among her sister's things. Yet when Guy asked the woman about it the day after the murder, she offered an airy disavowal, saying she'd thought it over and decided the man was a cousin of Doreen's that Folly had met once, years earlier. She had also brushed off questions about Doreen's scrapbook.

Obviously, the time had come for another chat with the supposed recipient of Doreen's abandoned belongings. Guy drove onto the neat farmstead to find Fate Halperin transferring boxed goods from his rattletrap van to a small white shed—no doubt auction lots that would eventually find their way onto the shelves in his resale shop. This morning his pet raccoon supervised, running to and fro at the man's ankles.

Guy, summoned by a wave, fetched a peppermint stick from the Studebaker's glove compartment and unwrapped it as he approached the animal. The critter met him halfway and rose on his hind legs to receive the treat. The candy disappeared in a few peppermint-scented crunches.

The old man extended his hand in welcome. "Deputy," he said. "What brings you to the poor farm?"

No Oklahoma drawl about Halperin. He spoke as briskly as he moved, and despite the clouded blue of his eyes, the look he gave Guy dug deep.

"I'm hoping you can help me track down a killer."

"I thought Turkeson had his man" A cool smile skimmed Fate's thin face, adjusted wrinkles in passing. "Pardon me—his woman."

"As I mentioned the other day when we talked at the garage, questions remain as to her guilt."

The old man shrugged. "While I have no idea how I might be of assistance, I will certainly try. Allow me to finish here, then we can go to the house."

Guy nodded, took a box from the van, and walked alongside Halperin to the shed where he peered around without any real hope he'd know anything of Doreen's if he saw it. The sheer amount of stuff that greeted his eyes staggered his imagination. No different on their return trip to the van, but he poked half-heartedly through a box of odds and ends on the passenger side of the front seat in case he might find a Zane Grey novel he hadn't read.

He found only spatulas, paring knives, can openers, and other kitchen oddments. Hefting a rolling pin, he wondered if Maggie could manage a pie crust. "How much?" he asked the old man.

"Six bits."

Guy handed over three quarters, which Halperin dropped into the side pocket of his striped overalls. After putting his purchase into the Studebaker, he helped finish unloading the van and then the two headed for the house, Jefferson Davis scampering along ahead.

The square frame bungalow blazed white with fresh paint. Halperin's bicycle on the front porch drew the raccoon for a sniff at its wheels before the old man opened the door. His pet scampered in ahead of Guy.

The clutter inside, compared to the farmstead's overall public face, took the deputy aback. He wrinkled his nose at the mingled smells of old clothes, dust, and bacon grease. Cartons lined the walls, all overflowing with faded draperies and what looked like bedspreads and blankets.

His host motioned him toward the couch, where a collection of mismatched cushions clung sidesaddle over broken springs. Despite the care Guy took in choosing a seat, something sharp poked in his lower back. The coon scrambled up onto a heap of newspapers and magazines at the opposite end of the couch.

Meanwhile, Halperin had emptied a platform rocker of a jumble of books and was stacking them into a neat column beside the chair.

Indicating the books, Guy said, "I see you've been burning the midnight oil again."

"Insomnia. And as I see it, to waste good reading time is criminal. There is so much a man can know, and so little time to learn."

Lest the old geezer launch into the theory of relativity or a discussion of the historical background of events leading to the recent clash between the Turks and the Greeks on Cyprus, Guy put in quickly, "Chance tells me you love to egg him into a political debate—and usually win."

The remark triggered the indulgent look the man

usually reserved for Jefferson Davis. "What my brother failed to reveal, I feel sure, is how astutely he allows me to best him."

"He says you can be counted on for some pretty sound advice."

"Chance is an idealist, often to the point he becomes myopic. Occasionally I can help him see both sides of a situation."

"Was it such a case the two of you discussed over the phone late Monday afternoon?"

Noting a quiver of tension in the old man's Adam's apple, Guy felt a surge of self-confidence. "Chance called you late Monday, I understand."

"When you mentioned needing my assistance in your case, I assumed you meant against the actress."

It wasn't hard to miss his emphasis on her profession, or his displeasure, to which the deputy let a nod suffice and left a silence he hoped the old man would fill.

After a few moments, Halperin leaned forward in the rocker "Let me assure you that my discussion with Chance late Monday afternoon had nothing to do with John Rice's death,"

"Maybe you talked about Maggie Simpson, then. After all, she grew up close to your farm here. Must have been quite a shock to see her again."

The smile that played around the old man's lips suggested that his questioner played out of his league. "Had Chance considered it pertinent to your investigation, he would have told you exactly what we discussed."

"Maggie's anger over her property being channeled into Johnny's hands isn't pertinent, then?"

"Were I you, young man, I would watch my back around that woman." Dark humor livened his normally careful expression. "Further, I would be quite mindful about what I ate as long as she's in your care."

"I've no reason to fear her." *Except for the publicity getting involved in her case could bring.*

"Nonetheless, only a fool would trust her. She had no right to come here and cause difficulty over the transfer of the Simpson property. That was a proper, legal action."

As Guy kept hearing. "How much do you know about the squabbles already going on over that property before Maggie showed up?" he asked to keep the conversation going.

Fate's shrunken neck settled deeper into his blue work shirt's crisp collar and he leaned back, his chair's worn mechanism complaining at each millimeter of change. "How much do you know?" An old gossip, begging more.

After Guy related what he knew about the discord behind the picture-perfect façade of the Rice home on Elm Street, the old man shrugged. "You know as much as I do."

"Your brother thinks the widow is a woman capable of murdering her husband and terrorizing Maggie Simpson."

A gnarled hand traced dismissal in a wave. "I told you, Brother can be myopic. The Simpson woman is the underdog, and Chance is a pushover for underdogs."

Were they talking about the same man? "I hardly call ordering me to get her off his property a show of sympathy for the underdog."

Fate Halperin bristled like a wild pig in a crate.

"Why should he risk a promising political future by protecting a woman half the town wants as guest of honor at a necktie party?"

"In my view, Maggie doesn't need protection from half the town. She needs protection from that one person who is trying to scapegoat her for Rice's murder."

"You are too smart to believe that, Deputy. Presuming the Simpson woman was indeed set up, as you call it, logic questions why the killer would then attempt to kill his scapegoat." A loud snort underlined his statement. "The attack on her, if indeed such occurred—"

"It happened," Guy said as emphatically.

"If indeed so," Fate persisted, "the incident only served to suggest the existence of some mysterious manipulator—"

"You're exactly right." Guy leaned forward. "And you're the very person to help me reveal that person's identity."

"And how might I be of assistance doing that?" No cooperation hinted at there.

Guy explained his growing belief that Rice's death had more to do with Maggie's questions about Doreen's whereabouts than it did with disposition of the Simpson property. "Doreen kept a scrapbook. Did you find it among the things Rice gave you for tearing down the old house? It might contain photographs or other mementos that could lead us to some friend of hers with information about where she went, and with whom."

"Sad to say, such items have little resale value. If such a scrapbook existed, I would have burned it along with other refuse from the house."

****

On Main Street, largely deserted at eleven a.m., Maggie passed the church where, judging by the number of vehicles, most Aldenites gathered for Johnny's last rites. Organ music swelled from the white frame structure—tearful wail of pipe and reed: *Beyond the Sunset—"oh joyful morning"*—echoed from her childhood, filling her eyes with tears. If only she hadn't come nosing around, Johnny Rice would still be alive.

She blinked and wiped moisture from her cheek with the back of her gloved hand, the coarse leather rough, but the only gloves she'd found in Guy's closet. She hastened her steps toward the one business she hoped to find open this morning. An idea had come to her while she had lain sleepless after yesterday's walk in the woods, and she needed to check it out while her keeper was gone. With most of the town at the funeral, she felt safe out on the streets.

The guilt that prickled over breaking her promise to stay in the cabin caused her to shrink more deeply into the upturned collar of the deputy's plaid mackinaw. The coat teamed with a pair of his jeans and cinched with a belt, altered her shape. His faded feed cap covered her hair, which she'd darkened with ashes from the wood stove. Wet coffee grounds rubbed on her face darkened her complexion. Applying those measures, she'd given thanks for her first job in Hollywood as a makeup artist's gofer.

Increasingly over the past few days, she'd come to believe Rice's claim that Doreen had left him a note. Some clue to where she went instead of with the medicine show might turn up in newspapers from the 1940s—if the local publisher kept them on file. The folksy news accounts of those simpler days could reveal some of her sister's social activities and maybe name some special friends still in town.

As deputy, Guy could have done the looking, of course, but only she could connect the dots as one name mentioned stirred memories of another.

The newspaper office stood across the street and a few doors south from Danby's Drugstore. Beneath gilt-edged lettering that identified *The Alden Sentinel*, the front window displayed an Open sign. Maggie entered to the clatter and clack of the same old typesetting machines she'd watched in awe as a child. Black iron monsters, they were—wheels that turned, arms that lifted and lowered, forming hot lead into lines of type for the printing press. The odor of ink on cheap paper permeated the room, a smell she'd forgotten until now.

At one of the machines, a gray-haired woman typed on a large keyboard. Unnoticed, Maggie relived the weekly trip here to buy each new issue—her main interest had been the movie calendar. Doreen preferred the war news and social columns.

Maggie cleared her throat before calling out above the rattle and clatter, "Hello, there!"

The typesetter started and glanced up. Round-faced and pleasant, she rolled her chair back from the machine, stood a moment, then walked stiffly to the front counter. "How may I help you?" Her eyes pecked Maggie from head to toe as if she were trying to put a name with her face.

Settled deeper into her coat collar, Maggie said, "I reckon you don't know me. I'm Roberta Lewis. My husband, Bill and I just bought a hundred sixty acres over by Roseville."

A gray eyebrow twitched, and above it, a faint line creased the woman's forehead. Finally, she nodded and wiped her hands on a red apron already stained black from some process in the typesetting, Maggie guessed. The woman reached under the counter. "You want to take out a subscription, I suppose. We're the only newspaper in the county."

Without a penny on her, much less the price of a subscription, Maggie patted each coat pocket and feigned dismay. "I guess I forgot to bring my checkbook."

The woman handed her a pencil and pad. "Write down your name and address. You can come back. I'm just filling in for the regular linotype operator who went to the funeral. She was a friend of the man who was murdered by that Hollywood actress."

"Oh my goodness. An actress from Hollywood here?" Maggie displayed her best version of small-town shocked disbelief, a hand to her chest. A gasp. "And she killed someone?" Holding the pose, she listened to an account of Johnny's so-called murder astonishingly short on fact. Maggie put in, "So scary. But I'm keeping you from your work. I did want a subscription, but I also hope to look at some of your old editions. My mom's people, we just found out, lived here back in the forties." Fingers crossed inside her coat pockets, she threw out a name and prayed it would be unfamiliar. "The Randolphs?"

The typesetter shook her head.

Maggie shot a glance at the old school-type clock on the wall and felt a rush of anxiety. Almost 11:30. She hoped the preacher was long-winded and the eulogies were many and long. "If you could just show me where to find the issues from that time, I can look for births and deaths and the like. My aunt back in Iowa, she's workin' up the family tree."

"Well—" The woman pursed her lips. "I'm not clear on the policy here."

"I'll handle the papers real careful and put them away when I'm done."

A lifted shoulder signaled compliance. "You'll find what you need in that metal cabinet." She gestured toward the back of the room. "Issues are probably bound six months to a volume. At least that's how we stored them where I used to work over in Sand Springs. There's a table you can work on if you finish before afternoon. We go to press then."

Maggie meant to be gone within the hour. She pocketed her gloves and started going through the issues from 1945, crudely bound and yellowed, but easily readable. One headline touted a donkey basketball game, sharing the front page with "Revival Starts at First Baptist Church," and "Lion's Club Names Sullivan Pres."

Leafing hurriedly through the pages, she noticed dresses with Joan-Crawford-size shoulder pads priced under twenty dollars. Entertaining, if the pulse drumming in her ears weren't a constant reminder that she needed to get out of the place before the funeral ended.

She skipped to the personal news columns. These she perused, running her forefinger down each page in search of Doreen's name. If her sister had attended a wedding shower, a card party, or even a church social, others present would be listed. Maybe one of those people still lived here and might know something of the man in the photograph Folly had mentioned.

Here and there a familiar name brought a smile to Maggie's lips. "Mrs. Ben Whitsitt returned last week from Kansas City where she attended an enclave of the Central States Poetry Society. Her poem, "To a Water Lily" was selected for publication in the *CSPS* Anthology—"

Another item chronicled Chance and Elizabeth Halperin's visit with home folks over Easter, another told of Ed Danby's son, Mike coming to help Danby in the drugstore while Mike awaited results of his pharmaceutical licensing exam.

If Doreen made any news in Alden, she'd occupied too low a rung on the social ladder to warrant space in the *Sentinel*. Maggie sighed, checked the time, and sucked in her breath. Almost noon? Hurriedly, she put away the papers as carefully as possible while keeping an eye on the traffic passing on the street. The funeral procession moved slowly on its way to the cemetery.

On her way out, she thanked the typesetter.

"Happy to be of help. Any luck?"

Maggie shook her head.

"But Joe will be back any minute now," the woman added. "He can be lots of help. Knows all the old names. He's a Reist, one of the oldest families—"

Already out the door, Maggie closed it behind her. Heart racing, she ducked her head and walked away as fast as she dared without drawing attention. Every step echoed her regret for not following the deputy's order to stay put in the cabin. Even if she went unchallenged, someone could follow her to the lodge grounds. Then where would she feel safe?

After the last car of the procession passed, she

crossed to the drugstore, rounded the corner, and dashed for the alleyway. Empty boxes stamped with a pharmaceutical company's logo identified the drugstore's rear entrance.

Footsteps sounded behind her.

She sprinted forward.

Someone grasped her elbow.

Crying out, she twisted around to try and free herself. Blindly, she pummeled her captor with both fists.

Chapter 15

A big hand stifled Maggie's cry. She thrust a knee into her assailant's groin.

"Uhh." His grunt verified a well-placed blow. Half a second later, she realized she'd just kneed the one person in Alden she could trust.

"Ohmigod," she cried, flinging her arms wide.

Clutching his groin, his face twisted in pain, Guy cut her a glance that revealed more green shards than mist gray in his hazel eyes. "You do play dirty pool, don't you?"

"And you," she flung back, "don't mind scaring the beejezus out of a person."

He straightened. "You think my nerves didn't go shot to hell when I got home and found you gone? For all I knew, the bastard who tried to throttle you the other night had tracked you down to finish the job."

Maggie felt as if she'd just been scolded by her mother in those long-ago days before her parents went away for good. "I do owe you an apology, I guess." Lingering shock drained the apology of too much substance, and she knew it.

Even so his eyes softened. "I've searched everywhere—just caught a glimpse of my coat as you disappeared around the corner." He retreated a step, frowning. "What the deuce have you been up to in that getup, then?"

"Self-preservation. It's hard for me to sit and wait for someone else's help when I'm not sure it's forthcoming. I know a few makeup tricks. They passed the test until you came along."

"Dare I ask where?"

"The newspaper office." She launched into a brief rundown of her search there. "I didn't find anything that justified my efforts."

"Maggie…Maggie…you've lived too long in the land of make-believe. In real life, ordinary citizens don't go around solving murders. Although in this case, your so-called deputy hasn't done too well himself."

Just that small hint of self-deprecation offered a much-needed straw to grasp. Maybe he'd just stepped across the chasm into her camp.

"So," she hazarded, "until I hear your story line how do we decide who gets the Oscar for Worst Amateur in a Detective Role?"

Sure enough, his revelations sounded about as discouraging as her report. He'd talked to the Halperin brothers, came up empty-handed on all counts, and discovered that the older sibling's personal surroundings were as foreign to his outward appearance as a pigpen to a hospital's surgery suite.

She was trying to superimpose the packrat image over that of the crisp old man in the coffee shop when Guy spoke again. "So, what do you propose to do next?"

Sizing up the stack of empty cardboard boxes around the freight entrance, she grabbed Guy's hand and started for the door.

He pulled back. "Danby?"

"Why not?"

His rust-colored eyebrows drew together. "You think he can be trusted, then?"

She was already banging the metal door with her first.

The door remained closed, so she banged again, louder, keeping it up until the door swung open. Danby peered out, his puzzled expression reminding Maggie how drastically she'd altered her appearance.

"Maggie Simpson," she said.

He shot Guy a glance, then started to close the door. Guy's booted foot kept it open wide enough to push back until the druggist gave way.

"I have customers I'll never see again if word gets out that you were here." His regard flicked from Maggie to the double doors that separated the storeroom from retail. Visible through the glass-enclosed prescription area to their right, a woman browsed the cosmetics display.

"You might be the only person who can help us learn who really killed Johnny and what it might have to do with my sister's disappearance, Mr. Danby." She tilted her head, pleading with her eyes until he opened the door wider and stepped aside.

"We'll talk over there." He indicated a worktable in a dim corner where she could see bottled pharmaceuticals and a couple of unopened cartons. She'd been ready to ask him if he knew any of Doreen's friends back in 1945, but the plump old man against a backdrop of medicine bottles knotted her stomach with the memory of Dr. Xavier and the cure-alls he hawked from *The Health and Happiness Revue's* stage on show nights.

The glance she shot Guy begged support.

His eyes questioned her, but he stepped closer.

Danby arched an eyebrow. "So that's the way the wind blows." Chuckling, he leaned against the worktable, arms folded across his belly. "I hear a lot of speculation about where you're holed up, Maggie. Seems I've heard at least one correct assumption." A waiting silence invited comment. Neither she nor Guy responded.

The druggist's expression tightened. "If neither of you gets how deep feelings run against Maggie in this town, you'd best wake up and smell the coffee. They nailed the Turk to the carpet down at City Hall last night. On Thanksgiving, mind you, and there's talk of a petition to force his resignation. You're a fool, Warner, taking up with an accused murderer."

Maggie lifted both hands, palms out. "And if you'd stop playing Judge Roy Bean for a minute and listen, you might help me learn the truth about Doreen, and how Johnny ended up dead after I started asking questions about her."

"What am I supposed to remember after twenty years?"

"Eighteen years going on nineteen," Maggie corrected, "and when I came into the bus station the other day and introduced myself, you remembered soon enough what I'd looked like as a child. You knew a lot about Grandma Simpson. The first time you'd seen me in all those years, but you did better at recall than Fate Halperin did, and he'd been our nearest neighbor."

Danby snorted. "Old Halperin probably had his mind on some book he'd left half read back at the house."

"Maybe so, but his sister hinted that Doreen had a

gentleman friend while Johnny served overseas." A flashback from one of the old newspaper items freed the sixth sense that had drawn her to the druggist's door. The item had concerned Danby's son.

Her eyes trapped the old man's. "But Folly backed off in a hurry. Now I wonder if she regretted a slip of tongue. Could it be she wanted to protect Mike?"

The old man made like a fish with his mouth, sputtered a few times, then burst out laughing while Guy looked at her like she'd lost her mind. When the two had stopped exchanging what-is-going-on glances, she explained, "I'm talking about your son, Mr. Danby. I know that Mike worked here that summer. If my sister, a married woman, came in often and hung around the prescription counter, you'd remember well, I think."

The druggist's relaxed manner changed to a stiff expression. "Don't try to drag Mike's name through your mud puddle." He pointed at the door. "Now, scat."

Not hardly. "I'm not out to make trouble for anyone except those who know more about Doreen than they're telling. I'd just like to talk to Mike about her, if you could see your way clear to tell me where I might contact him."

"He's with a pharmaceuticals firm in New Jersey, and that's all you need know except he's about to become CEO. Besides, Doreen must have been three months along before Mike came home that summer."

A couple of beats passed before his remark soaked in. "Three months gone?" Disbelief and belief spun through her head until Guy's arm settled around her waist—unspoken empathy that released the words stuck in her throat. "My sister was pregnant?"

"She came asking for something she could take to get rid of it."

"Did you—"

He stood away from the table, military review straight. "I'll have you know, I don't," he sputtered, "Never have. Would not."

"She asked your son for something, then?" Guy put in.

"It was Mike she asked at the outset." Danby's quivery chin settled into a firm line. "He turned her down."

"And she was three months along?" Maggie asked.

"Almost four, before she came looking for help. I have no idea who fathered the child. My son didn't come home once between Christmas and his graduation in June."

Speechless, Maggie sagged against Guy's shoulder. He asked Danby, "How long after she came to you did Doreen drop out of sight?"

"A week or so," he said after some hemming and hawing, and then to Maggie, "You and she left at the same time, when that phony potion pusher left town. I always figured he gave Doreen what she wanted in more ways than one. Maybe that's why she went off with him."

Anger boiled hot, fire in her chest. "Doreen did *not* go with that medicine show." How many times did she have to say that?

Danby shrugged.

After a silent count to ten, Maggie asked, "You're sure no one else in Alden would have helped Doreen?" A horrible possibility sneaked into her mind. "A back-alley abortion, maybe?"

Frown lines gathered above the druggist's nose. "There *was* someone," came the reluctant reply. "Even Doc Whitsitt could never learn who, and he patched up more than one bungled job, let me tell you." His tone closed the topic.

"Don't let the door catch your heels when you go out."

They found Dr. Whitsitt in his home office on a street where women still hung their sheets on a clothesline and gossiped over the backyard fence.

His tiny waiting room offered the usual chrome and plastic furniture and outdated magazines. Smiling from the cover of one were the long-haired British boys who called themselves the Beatles.

A voice from the inner office invited them inside. The pungent aroma of Bengay pain ointment suggested that Whitsitt's most loyal patients were folks in his age group.

Studying the elderly doctor's face, she imagined how Tony Randall might look at eighty. The red-tipped cane propped beside him explained why Guy hadn't argued against coming here.

The worst she need fear from Whitsitt would be a whack from his walking stick, if he could guess where to aim. He used the stick to indicate they sit down, but neither did.

After asking the doctor what, if anything, he knew about her sister's pregnancy, Maggie waited for some off-putting remark about patient-doctor confidentiality. Instead he apologized for office clutter he could see barely see—if at all.

"Folly missed coming to clean this morning. First time in more than ten years of Fridays. I should have gone to Johnny's funeral myself. Carol, my assistant, offered to take me." Whitsitt flashed a wry smile. "Funerals remind me how little my medical degree means when Death is determined to call." He settled deeper into his chair, a wooden-armed veteran of so many patient consultations that vertical cracks marched around the edge of the black leather seat.

"A lifetime spent trying to fight off Death," he ruminated aloud, "then, by God, he sneaks in where you're not looking." The last trace of affability had vanished. How he knew exactly where to focus on her, Maggie couldn't imagine, yet his empty gaze stabbed into her eyes and straight down to her heart. "John Rice was a damned fine man. They say you fed him poison."

"They're wrong," she said, unable to control the quaver in her denial.

Whitsitt cocked his head as if trying to identify a distant bird call. "You claim innocence, yet trouble and pain radiate from you like the sickness of guilt. I feel it. I hear it in the low pitch of your voice."

Maggie's breath hitched in her throat—blind, he saw what she most sought to hide. "Whatever sins I must answer for," she declared, "poisoning Johnny isn't among them."

She reached down, touching the doctor's wrinkled hand. "Help me prove someone is framing me. Tell me what you remember about Doreen and her pregnancy—any little thing that might help me find the truth about what happened to her."

Hands tented, the old gentleman leaned back and stared at nothing. "So many years over which to recall one pregnancy from so many."

"Different situation with my sister, Doc. She hadn't

been with her husband in more than a year."

"And was desperate to terminate." His empty gaze shifted down, as if seeking hers.

Once again, she felt an overwhelming sense of guilt.

"You're quizzing the wrong person about your sister's troubles, Maggie. Learn who in this town preyed on her kind of desperation back then. Learn, if you're smarter than I, if your sister numbered among those who bled out."

Maggie felt the blood drain from her face. "Died, you mean?"

A nod.

"So, you think that's what happened to Doreen?"

Chapter 16

The doctor finally spoke. "Assuming your innocence in Johnny's death, it seems likely your prying around about Doreen threatened someone in Alden or nearby."

Maggie nodded, and Guy reached over to clasp her hand in his. "Still threatens someone," he said, and told the doctor about the attempt on her life.

Clearly shocked, Dr. Whitsitt considered a moment. "Doreen was such a lovely young woman. I miss seeing beauty. Other things I see more clearly since the accident that took my sight. For instance, I recognize how wrongly I turned away desperate young women when I possessed the skill to save them from themselves."

Maggie wanted to pat his shoulder.

Sighing, he shook his head and then added, "Half a dozen girls or more came here after bungled abortions. I patched up one uterus so badly perforated I could have used it to strain tea."

Taken aback by the seemingly inappropriate remark, Maggie reminded herself that people in the medical field often used humor to help make the terrible things they witnessed more bearable. She listened with horror as he described the girl's death. Anger flared when he told how the mother insisted he fabricate a story about a burst appendix.

"You'd think she'd have wanted the butcher hung by the thumbs," Maggie said hotly.

Whitsitt's expression softened. "To speak the truth would have revealed the girl's shame," he said. "A family's shame in this small town, Maggie. It amazed me what kind of accidents they dreamed up to explain the damage done to them."

"How many do you think actually died?" Guy asked.

"Two, I suspect." After a pause he frowned. "Make it three." He frowned. "Although I'd never counted Doreen, that seems likely now. I never swallowed that hogwash about going away with the medicine show. She didn't seem to want an abortion as desperately as she wanted to marry the baby's father. I convinced myself that she and her lover went off together and lived happily ever after."

Nodding, Guy said, "That would have meant some local guy turned up missing at the same time as Doreen. In Alden someone would have noticed."

Whitsitt scratched his chin, twitched his mustache. "I always thought the man lived in another town. Tulsa, maybe." Pondering, the lines in his forehead deepened. "You and your theories have jolted me. I pegged the abortionist as female, a woman I know who has moved away. But if recent events are an indication, Maggie's snooping scares the hell out of someone still living here. Maybe someone who still practices his or her ugly business."

The doctor sighed again, and seeing fatigue settle around his mouth, Maggie glanced at Guy. "We should go."

They thanked the old man and saw themselves out.

Stepping into a day bright with sunshine, Maggie shivered beneath the mackinaw's upturned collar. A tow-headed boy in pursuit of a yapping rat terrier streaked past. Clad in ragged jeans and a short-sleeved T-shirt, he wore the joy of Indian Summer on his freckled face. A few steps farther along he paused and turned, staring.

Guy steered Maggie away from the curious eyes. "You should return to the cabin."

Unable to speak for thinking of the bloodied teenager Whitsitt had described, she imagined Doreen suffering in such a way and shivered again.

She felt herself pushed gently in the direction of the lodge grounds. "You need to go. Have something hot to drink and a bowl of soup. There's some chicken noodle under the kitchen counter." His grin warmed her more than the prospect of chicken soup, and when he added, "I'll try to get a look at that evidence file," a weight lifted from her shoulders.

Out of concern for him, she said, "Make sure you can do it without being seen. I don't want you to get into trouble with the Turk over me." As if he weren't already up to his neck in that, a fact his expression made clear.

"And you," he replied, "go directly home. Do not pass Go and do not collect two hundred dollars."

The bubble of contentment that rose in her chest at his reference to the cabin as her home as well as his, hastened her footsteps down back alleyways toward the cabin. Once in the woods, however, she realized how easily she could slip over to Fate Halperin's farm unseen. Fate had told Guy that he didn't have the scrapbook, but Maggie figured it could be there without him knowing it.

The sun past midday persuaded her the old man would be at his store in town. On pathways familiar from childhood, she reached his farm in good time, her heart thumping with excitement and a dollop of fear. At the edge of Fate's corrals, a sudden attack of guilt held her behind a clump of leggy Johnson grass. The slight breeze smudged the air with the scent of ripened seed heads.

All around her, silence. Even the old cow in the lot stopped munching her cud.

She saw no sign of Fate Halperin's old van, or of his bicycle, for that matter. One quick, bolstering breath, then Maggie dashed into the open. She squeezed through horizontal pipes that enclosed the corral and stumbled through pulverized hay and manure that lofted earthy smells familiar from childhood. The cow resumed munching. Maggie left her behind and headed for the storage shed, where she paused in its shadow to catch her breath. The entrance faced away from the house. An industrial-sized padlock secured the stout door.

She stepped up and jiggled the lock, muttering in frustration. The shed's windows looked out on the barnyard, and to her relief she found that they opened easily. She clambered in and down into the unsteady footing of a box filled with old coats. Once she had regained her balance, she stepped to the floor. As her eyes adjusted to the gloom, she felt her heart sink down to the boot tops of the old Wellingtons she'd found in Guy's closet.

How could a space smaller than the average Hollywood bathroom contain so many lamps, garden tools, portable radios, lint-laden oscillating fans, tables, chairs, and general paraphernalia? The combined odors brought to mind the overfilled bag of a vacuum sweeper.

No wonder the old man couldn't find the scrapbook. What sane person would willingly search through such a mess for a specific item? Maggie set to work.

The shelves yielded nothing recognizable from her grandmother's house. About to give up, she spotted a chalk statuette of Snow White in a box. Awash with nostalgia, she remembered tossing a coin into a milk bottle to win such a prize at a school carnival. Leaving behind this one, if indeed it once belonged to her, pushed her endurance about as much as when she'd refused the temptation of Johnny Rice's bourbon a few days earlier.

After resisting the chalk figurine, Maggie sifted through more reminders of her childhood in the carton and left them be. When she saw out the window how the afternoon had waned, a sense of urgency ticked in her pulse. Fate Halperin could return home any minute, but she didn't want to give up on the scrapbook. She searched frantically.

Her elbow struck a spindly-legged stand table. Old issues of *Life* magazine slid into the corner under a shelf. Bent to retrieve them, Maggie spotted an open shoebox in the corner.

Among its contents a glittery object caught her eye. Crying out, she rooted for the powder compact with its familiar, gold-plated lattice-weave over red enamel. She clutched it to her heart before opening it, knowing it would smell sweetly of Coty's finely spun face powder—the only brand Doreen used, and that the mirror would be cracked.

As punishment for playing with something of Doreen's without permission, and damaging it to boot, Doreen had denied Maggie the Saturday matinee for three weeks running.

She opened the compact to the expected details. Unexpected—her grandmother's pearl ear studs nestled atop the powder puff. Cradling the treasure in her sweat-damp palm, she remembered that Doreen had worn the heirloom earrings everywhere. Only when she peroxided her hair did she remove them.

Hot tears stung Maggie's eyes, rolled down, and dripped from her chin. Succumbing to grief, she almost missed the sound of tires bumping on the washboard dirt road. She dropped the compact into her coat pocket. She grabbed several items of clothing from the big box under the windows, climbed out, and ran for the corral fence. She shinnied through the two lower bars without a backward glance and dashed across the lot, thankful the soft earth muffled her steps. Out the other fence, and into the woods she went, bent low, heedless of twigs that grabbed her coat sleeves, but clutching the bundle of old clothing for dear life. It held great possibilities for disguise. She reached the path and slackened her pace before realizing the foolishness of her panicked flight.

What could old Fate do to hurt her, anyway? He'd be mad as hell that she snooped in his shed, but he'd known her since childhood. Why would he object if she took something that had belonged to her sister?

Anyway, he hadn't been among the protestors who came to the sheriff's office, rattling verbal sabers while she cowered in her cell.

So preoccupied was she that Maggie belatedly realized she'd wandered off the main path. Nothing around her looked familiar. Shadows thrust dark fingers through woods still as death. She stopped, rooted, blood drumming in her ears while she looked for a pathway that had disappeared. Directly ahead, the leaf-strewn ground dipped into a rocky, dry stream bed.

A rustle behind her spun Maggie around. Dark wings fluttered in her stomach. Her gaze darted, probed, but found nothing amiss. After a moment she uttered a shaky laugh. There, in the fallen leaves a disturbance marked her passage. She retraced her steps until closer observation revealed the rift as a trick of late afternoon sunlight among shadows.

She plunked herself down onto a large rock, the bundle of old clothing across her knees. Her elbows pillowed on the bundle, she cradled her head in both hands and splayed her fingers against her temples to still her reeling thoughts.

Instead of solutions to her problem, her mind insinuated old tales of four-footed predators that slunk from these woods to raid chicken houses at night. She glanced up and around, grasping the bundle, ready to protect her head and neck if need be.

After a moment, she thought how ridiculous she must look

"Well horsefeathers and be damned," she shouted at the silent trees. Hadn't she practically lived in these woods as a child? *Though not at night*, came the whisper she chose to ignore. "Use your head, Maggie." Surveying the cottonwoods, sweet gums, and other native trees, she narrowed focus to the moss that coated one particular trunk and sprang off the rock in a rush of confidence.

She must have headed south some way. The cabin would be to her west and north. If she paid attention to the heaviest growth of the shade-loving lichen, she should be okay.

The going proved slow. Dusk fell before she spotted shadowy landmarks near the amphitheater. A short while later, tall cedars marked the abandoned homestead near her grandmother's old home place. Skirting the dark shapes, she caught their fragrance and remembered how on the night Johnny died she had stood staring out his office window into the cedar. And how she might have been in time to save him had she known he'd fallen ill upstairs.

An involuntary shiver compelled her toward the cabin on flying feet. Her toe struck something solid. She pitched forward. Dropped her bundle. Hands down to break her fall, her palm struck wood. A sliver bit into her flesh.

Two thoughts came in tandem. She'd left her gloves back in the storage shed, and what she tripped over were the weathered planks that covered the old trash pit she'd called her wishing well so long ago. Her wish now—that she'd taken Guy's advice and gone straight from town to the cabin.

Chapter 17

"Once upon a time," Deputy Warner told himself, "you had good sense." Two hours after sending Maggie to the cabin, he knelt behind a dumpster in the alley near the sheriff's office and waited until Turkeson left for his afternoon coffee break. The corn on the little toe of Guy's right foot throbbed. He'd inhaled enough rotten potato smells from the grocery store's trash to spoil his appetite for a week.

All this for a chance to break into the evidence file on Johnny Rice's death, for which he could wind up in a heap of trouble.

How had he come to such a pass, anyway?

The answer had green eyes, of course. Guy swore under his breath.

A one-eared rat terrier trotted past, paused, backtracked to sniff the cuff on Guy's chinos.

"Yeah," he sneered down at the dog. "I own cats. What do you want to make of it?"

The mutt barked a retort, then continued toward the upper end of the alley to the parked Studebaker. He lifted a leg and peed on a rear tire. "That's it, then," Guy vowed. "Enough." He ran toward the car, stamping his feet in a threatening manner. The dog hightailed it across the street. Sharp pains stabbed the corn on Guy's little toe.

He drove toward home with visions of warm

companionship and a soothing foot-soak dancing in his head.

He found the cabin empty, the door unlocked. A glance around the lodge grounds jellied his insides. Had Maggie made a wrong turn on the woods path? Did she wander lost and afraid in the gathering darkness?

At that thought, laughter burst from his throat. Firstly, he couldn't imagine her being afraid of anything. Secondly, gut instinct told him she stayed out somewhere playing detective.

He headed back to town, drove the streets for more than an hour, inquired at the few places he dared. Ed Danby at the drugstore hadn't seen her since their interview earlier in the day. Chance Halperin, leaving the grocery store with a loaf of bread in hand, remarked on how bad pennies always return, then repeated his warning against further involvement with the woman.

Folly, in her apartment, let it be known she expected Ralph Jones any minute. Didn't want to miss the start of the movie. She was too busy looking for a misplaced handbag to listen to Guy's concerns about the missing actress. He trailed her from room to room, wondering how anything larger than a quarter-inch screw could be misplaced in such immaculate surroundings. Suspected the errant purse might be a ploy to distract him.

As if the red polka-dotted skirt and blue checkered blouse she wore, and his sore toe weren't distractions enough.

"I carried that bag to the funeral, just this morning," Folly muttered, feeling down beside the cushions on her overstuffed sofa. Coming up empty-handed, she flitted toward the back of the apartment.

Guy followed.

He tried a new tack. "I'm surprised you kept working for Johnny Rice after he and Chance fell out."

Folly snapped her fingers.

Guy envisioned a light bulb clicking on above her head and limped after her toward the bathroom, watching from the doorway.

"I might have left that purse in here." She checked behind the door. "After helping serve the family dinner at the church, I came straight home—drank too much coffee."

Her backside in the polka-dotted skirt loomed large while she peered into a cranny beside the lavatory, and then into the tub enclosure. He glimpsed pink flamingos dancing on the shower curtain and coughed to cover a smile. Cleared his throat. "Chance told me Rice and his wife quarreled over plans for the Simpson property." A pause for effect. "Strange you didn't mention that when we talked the other day."

"Oh?" Folly stood, hand to cheek. "I thought I did tell you." She fluttered her fingers. "But everything got so mixed up those first few terrible hours. I suppose it slipped my mind." She cocked her head. "Is that someone at the door?" She tapped Guy on the shoulder so he'd step aside.

He fell in behind her again in the hope she might yet toss him a bone of truth.

They passed the kitchen. She flung a gesture. "Look over there, will you? I might have put that handbag on the counter. Paula sent a pie home with me. You never saw as much food as neighbors carried in."

Guy blew air through his nose in exasperation. Without preamble, he asked, "Was Doreen Rice's pregnancy widely known about town?"

Folly had gone deaf. She opened the apartment door to an eloquent greeting in romantic verse from a tweed-suited giant of a man who belatedly spied her companion and reddened to the roots of all three hairs on his scalp.

The deputy sighed and slumped his way back to the Studebaker. The anxiety in his gut had churned itself into nausea. Cold and darkness had leached loneliness from his bones unlike any he'd felt since his early days in Alden. He headed home for a dose of Alka-Seltzer.

He arrived to see lights ablaze in every window. Sore toe forgotten, he sprinted from the parking area and flew into the cabin on wings of relief.

Maggie stood huddled near Old Firebelly, whose ashes were long since dead and cold. Still wearing the garb she'd taken from his closet that morning, she held an armload of kindling. Her bloodied knee showed through a rip in her jeans. Dingy red-blond hair straggled from under his Alden Feed & Seed cap. Emeralds set in hollowed eye sockets lacked focus. Her teeth chattered.

He tamped down the urge to sweep her into his arms and kiss some color back into her parchment lips. "Well," he said, struggling to keep a level tone, "it's about time you came home, then."

"So cold—" she said brokenly, "can't manage—" A stick of kindling slithered from her hands.

Guy retrieved it. "I don't know what perverse pleasure you get from making my life miserable," he said, his jaws so tight the words pained him. "But I'm sick of playing nursemaid only to be rewarded with a kick in the ass."

Firewood fell in measured thuds to the floor around her feet. She knotted her hands against her chest. "Please. I'm fr-fr-freezing."

Taut-lipped, he knelt to work on the fire. Prodding ashes piled deep with neglect since he'd become too involved in Maggie's troubles to keep up with chores, he heard the poker clink against a hard surface. He reached down and brought out a small jar.

Maggie grasped his shoulder. "Guy," she said, her normally burred voice a rusty hinge. "I think know where to find Doreen."

"Jeez, but you're a single-minded, unbelievable piece of aggravation." He held the jar up to the light. One glimpse of the amber contents set his pulse thumping in his ears.

"She's dead, Guy. Doreen is dead. I'm sure of it."

He nodded, but the sweat popping out above his upper lip had nothing to do with Doreen.

Not sparing the jar a glance, Maggie withdrew something from a pocket on her coat. "Doreen's compact." Light gleamed on the gold that trimmed the red-enameled oval in her open palm. "I found it in old man Halperin's storage building."

"Yeah?" Guy's fingers shook unscrewing the jar's lid. The sharp smell confirmed his fears. He clapped the lid back into place.

"She's in the well—" Maggie's voice broke. "Doreen's in the well, I just know it." She paused, sniffed the air. Her thinly plucked eyebrows soared, then gathered above her nose. "Gasoline?"

"Thank God you never earned a campfire badge in Girl Scouts, Maggie. You'd have blown yourself sky high here." He screwed the lid tight and set it on the floor near the front door.

Maggie collapsed into the rocking chair beside the stove. "Who—?" Her voice failed, but her eyes registered horror, gradually replaced by self-recrimination. "Oh Guy. It's my fault. I don't remember locking the door when I left here this morning. And Johnny's killer is watching us."

Guy's thoughts roamed elsewhere to his personal demon, Ed Moroni. Although crude by mob standards, the booby-trap smacked of their methods—a second threat Maggie didn't need to know about.

"I found the cabin locked up tight when I came here looking for you this afternoon." The little white lie brought relief to her expression as he'd hoped it would, but then she glanced down at the compact in her open palm and shivered.

The memento clattered to the floor. The lid sprang open. Out tumbled a pair of ear studs.

"Doreen's," she whispered. "Our grandmother's. My sister wore them everywhere."

****

Guy drew her from the chair and into his arms, holding her close until her tremors lessened. "I'm sorry I spoke so harshly a while ago," he murmured, releasing her. "Let me get a fire going while you tell me about finding the compact and why you think your sister's remains might be in the trash pit."

Nodding, Maggie retrieved the fallen items and returned them to her coat pocket. Then, hunkered around the chill in her heart, she stood near the cold stove and began at the beginning, omitting mention of the possible disguise she'd stashed in her empty luggage upon reaching the cabin. She concluded her account with the tumble over the planks that covered the pit.

"It hit me then that everyone knows about that place. If she died at the hands of an abortionist, the killer might have thought to hide—"

The words, "a dead body," clogged her throat. She choked out, "To hide her guilt under all that trash."

Guy closed the door on the stove. "You think a woman is responsible?"

"Maybe—but on the other hand, the attacks on me in the hotel, and this booby trap don't have the feel of woman's work, do they?"

He shook his head and returned the poker to its stand. "But you could be onto something about your so-called wishing well. It wouldn't be a bad idea to check it out."

"Ohhh," she cried, her face crumpled, her hands clutched over her heart. "How can I bear to see what we might find?"

"The sheriff and I can take care of it."

"But I have to be there." More moan than protest, she repeated, "I have to be. For Doreen." Her eyes pleaded. "But can't we just tell the sheriff if we find her? If he's there and we don't find anything, he'll make everything worse for us."

Guy restrained a sigh of relief. "Keeping him out of the loop goes against protocol, but hell, he's more interested in pinning Johnny's murder on you than he is on finding the truth anyway." Gently, he clasped her hands in his and drew her closer to the stove. "Warm up now while I heat a can of soup." He started for the kitchen, but turned. "Do you really think Fate tried to chase you down this afternoon?"

"I'm almost sure he did, and if he didn't, I certainly felt guilty enough to get the heck out of there."

****

They postponed the search until Monday. "Woods will most likely be deserted on a workday," Guy reasoned. Saturday morning, Guy went for another try at the evidence file.

"The sheriff is off this weekend. I can give the dispatcher some excuse for being there and suggest he go get us some fresh doughnuts." Leaving the cabin, he paused on the step, scanning the woods in every direction while both cats wound around his ankles. "Those pickups parked in front of the lodge are normal for a Saturday morning. Some families will practice on the archery range a little later." Kneeling, he gave both felines the attention they demanded before looking up to add, "But you stay inside, Maggie. And keep the door locked."

She'd slept away most of the previous day's anxieties, but his warning jittered her up again. Glancing around, she saw enough clutter to pitch in and put things to rights. Sweeping the kitchen area, she listened to the host on a talk show expound on the dignity and courage Jacqueline Kennedy showed after losing a baby, her husband, and her position in life in a matter of weeks. Trying to imagine how deeply those losses cut, Maggie felt her own troubles fade.

"Jackie is moving on. You can do the same." Dust flew before her broom. Every room swept, she mopped the bathroom linoleum before settling in beside the stove with a fresh cup of coffee.

Her hands wrapped around the mug gave her a good view of her nails. She screwed up her face in disgust. "Looks like you scrubbed that floor with a pail of water and some of Grandma's lye soap, Maggie." So much had happened in the six days since she reached Alden that she'd scarcely had time to think about grooming. She *had* kept an eye on her diminishing supply of face cleanser. Stopping shipment of her trunk had cut off her supply of ingredients—at least she hoped Scaff Russell had received her message about that.

Anxiety swirling through her midsection, she decided to phone. Scaff didn't answer her call. When Rose didn't pick up either, Maggie heaved a sigh. If the worst had happened, and the trunk had been shipped, she'd simply find an excuse not to open it in Guy's presence. She reverted to more immediate problems, glanced at her nails with a frown, and went to fetch her manicure kit.

Once her nails were cleaned, shaped, and buffed, she pressed her beige silk blouse and teamed it with her brown slacks. Her grandmother's pearl ear studs provided the perfect accessory. Preening a bit before the bathroom mirror, Maggie couldn't suppress a nervous giggle. *Wouldn't Doreen just have a conniption about the earrings?*

"Conniption." Maggie repeated her grandmother's expression for a screaming fit and began to laugh. Out of control, the laughter broke into sobs. Racked with loss she couldn't reason away by the greater losses of others, she clung to the washbasin to stay upright. Beneath the onslaught of childhood memories untainted by all that had come to pass, the bourbon stowed under the kitchen counter called her name.

Howling against temptation, she grasped the sink

until exhaustion drove her to the commode. There she sat, staring at the linoleum's faux tile pattern, seeing only her own weakness. When something finally came into focus, she moaned in dismay at the tear stains on her silk blouse and stripped it off. At the sink, she splashed her face with icy tap water. Makeup tricks learned in Hollywood camouflaged remnants of her tears. Scarcely had she slipped into a sweater when a key rattled at the front door.

She flew to meet Guy and flash-analyzed his grin.

"You found Doreen's letters!" She flung herself into his arms.

"Whoa," he said, giving her a hug before shedding his coat. She hung it beside the door while he warmed his hands over Old Firebelly. "Do you remember an 'Eve' or 'Bill' from your childhood?" he asked, but before she could reply, gave her a long, once-over and grinned again. "Well…aren't you gussied up, then."

Why she felt like he was the first man to look at her with approval, Maggie chose not to consider. Despite the tingle in her private parts, she managed a prim "thank you" before adding in a rush, "Eve and Bill. I don't remember either name—but tell me more."

"Doreen's letters referred several times to the two. I read between the lines and decided Bill might have been her lover."

"Surely she wouldn't have gone on about him if that were the case."

"Maybe Johnny knew the guy, and writing things about him came naturally to her."

Eyes closed, Maggie tried to dredge up faces to fit either name. Failing, she lifted her lids and shrugged. "Maybe if we looked through the phone book and I saw a Bill Wojowski, or some other unusual last name, I could place him among Doreen's circle of friends."

Guy phoned every Bill in town, and an Eve Bradley without finding anyone who claimed friendship with Doreen. Disappointed, she expected the same reaction in Guy. Instead, mischief crept into his eyes.

"I guess you don't want to throw a drunk, then," he said.

He had no way to know of her morning's battle, and so she hid the stab of pain beneath a droll expression. "Since I hit town, not a day has passed that I didn't long to escape into a bottle." A wry laugh slipped out before she added, "Right now I'd settle for a pot of tea and a dozen chocolate brownies."

"You'll have to make the brownies."

She did, and when he declared them delicious, agreed. He'd fussed at her for not putting on an apron in the kitchen, but the light in his hazel eyes held approval. The few smudges of cocoa on her sweater she considered badges of one day's success. Long before nightfall, they went to bed, but not to sleep.

Awaking to an unseasonably warm Sunday, they lounged around the cabin. He read a Zane Grey novel. Maggie napped and then sewed some buttons on one of his flannel shirts. Their only serious moments involved plans for the next day's mission.

****

Monday morning broke cold. Fueled by hot coffee and toast with peanut butter, they set out for the abandoned homesite. Guy carried shovel, pitchfork, and a small tarp. Maggie toted a grass rake, burlap bags. and coiled rope. The closer they got to the trash pit, the more dread weighed down her footsteps. Guy, too, walked heavily and said little. The few words they did exchange avoided mention of the task ahead.

As much as she wanted to learn what happened to Doreen, Maggie shrank from thoughts of what success today would mean. The worst moment struck when they laid their tools beside the planks that covered the pit.

A breeze tinged with smoke from a distant chimney rattled late-clinging pin oak leaves. She shivered. Guy's arm circled her waist. "If we find her," he said, "you'll get no more trouble from Turkeson."

If he meant to comfort her, she remembered that he'd been packed to leave Alden the night the sheriff assigned him to protect her, and Maggie felt anything but comforted by his remark. "And you'll be leaving Alden when I no longer need your help—"

Her words hung, unanswered for too long. Then he said, "You'll be busy fending off reporters. I'd be caught in the glare. That's attention I don't need."

Not for the first time Maggie wondered what ghosts of the past floated close to his heels. Did he really suppose anything he'd done before moving to Alden would matter to her of all people? But then, if *he* leveled with *her*, wouldn't she have to reveal her deepest secret?

She stepped away from his warmth. "There's too much going on in Washington DC and Dallas for anyone outside of Alden to find anything newsworthy here. Anyway, I came seeking home and family, not headlines."

He retrieved the pitchfork. "Maggie Simpson might not want publicity, but Charmaine Dorsey would be a fool to pass up the best break of her career."

In a minute if you'd stay. The thought left unspoken, she spread the canvas tarp around the well's narrow cement apron. Guy poked at the wood that covered the opening, moving the planks more easily than she'd expected—dislodged, perhaps, when she fell on them during her flight from the old Halperin place.

Uncovered the second time, the pit looked more challenging than she remembered. Guy whistled. "Every hunter in three counties must have tossed in his beanie-weenie can and beer bottle at one time or another over the years."

Her distracted, "uh hmm," drew a glance.

"You're sure you want to be here for this, then?"

She managed a tremulous laugh. "See, I'm not so great an actress after all." She gestured for him to continue.

The hole measured about five feet across. It had always been referred to as the old well but could have served another purpose altogether. Maggie grasped a rusty milk bucket by its bail and tossed it aside, wondering if it came from her grandmother's barn. Guy retrieved a tin dollhouse, flattened, bearing only a trace of the lithographed trellis and roses that once brightened it. Maggie's throat tightened.

"I found a dollhouse like that under the tree the Christmas before my parents left for California."

"And they never came back," Guy said. "You went West looking for them?"

"Had no idea where to look. Gran's last letters to their address came back. I guess they didn't want to be found."

"Back in those Depression years things didn't always work out as planned."

True, and while Maggie appreciated his effort to comfort her, the little girl who still occupied a niche in her heart wanted none of it. She used a sleeve to wipe away the tears that stung her eyes. "Who knows," she said, lofting an off-handed gesture that belied the ache in her chest. "Maybe one day our paths will cross again."

When it became hard to reach down into the trash, Guy climbed down into the rubble. It shifted. He sank down as far as his knees. Maggie pointed out a broken beer bottle. "Watch it, just there at your kneecap."

He handed up the jagged pieces, then pulled out a coil of copper tubing. "Your grandpap in the moonshine business?"

"Wouldn't be surprised. Pretty common around here back then, I think."

As the sun rose toward noon, sweat beaded Guy's forehead. He hung his jacket on a nearby cottonwood limb and went back to work. Junk and more junk added to the pile on the canvas left little to see in the hole.

Maggie plunked down on a fallen log. "I must have been wrong. We'd have found something by now—"

Cut short by a sharp exclamation, she walked over to see the cause. He'd uncovered a bundle of some kind. Anxiety crab-walked through her stomach. "Is that an old rug?"

"Deer hide." He dug deeper. "Two of them, actually."

She shrugged in mingled relief and disappointment. "Some poacher probably dumped them here."

He ran his gloved fingers into a ragged cut. "Something caught in the matted fur." He frowned. "Gravel?" He dumped the material into a rusty can and handed it up to her. "Send down the rope, then. Let's have a better look at these hides."

Maggie glanced into the container before setting it aside to give him the rope. "Maybe whoever shot the deer dressed it out in a dry stream bed," she suggested while he secured the bundle. A fetid odor rose from the pit. She wrinkled her nose. "Eeww."

He tossed up the end of the rope. "I don't suppose you know how to tie a half-hitch?"

Gotcha there. He'd find out. She dragged the length of twisted hemp to the nearest tree, looped it around the trunk and with deft movements secured the knot. "Give it a try, then," she said, mimicking his speech pattern.

Laughing, he tugged. The knot tightened. "Impressive. You were a Girl Scout, then."

She nodded, but he had missed the mark. Not only had a man she knew as Old Tex unwittingly aided in her escape from Dr. Xavier, he'd taught her many of life's practicalities as well. She learned every knot in the rodeo cowboy's bag of tricks during their years on the road from a father-figure beyond reproach.

To talk about Tex, however, would open the conversation to the night they met. Dangerous ground to tread.

Silent, Maggie watched Guy walk up the rope. When he pulled up the hides, the stench sent her into retreat. Pinching her nostrils shut, she watched from a distance while he undid the bundle. More gravel-like fragments came to light.

Guy rolled a piece between thumb and forefinger. A frown creased his brow. "Maybe these are the remains of someone's out-of-season deer kills."

Hazarding a closer look, Maggie turned her ankle on a blackened object among the heaped-up trash. The remnant of an old shoe. She kicked it aside and turned her attention back to the deputy, who selected a slightly larger object from the can. "This almost looks like bone."

Some part of Maggie wanted to agree, while another corner of her psyche recoiled at the possibility he held some bit of her sister's remains. Denial found its way from her heart to her lips. "Crunched up bones from the deer, don't you think?"

His sharp glance told her he wasn't fooled by her failure to accept what might be truth, but he said only, "I know a guy in Tulsa who could tell us for sure. Larry writes textbooks on forensic anthropology and does some independent consultations on murder investigations."

"You aren't going to show Turkeson what we found?"

"I'd like a more objective eye on this stuff at first. I doubt Larry knows anything about you or Doreen, so I'd like his opinion before we give Sheriff Turkeson a chance to laugh our ideas down again."

"You won't get into trouble?"

"I probably should, probably will when he finds out I looked at Doreen's letters to Johnny in the evidence file." His grin held a wry note. "In for a penny, in for a pound." He patted her shoulder. "You're due some shore leave anyway. We'll go this afternoon. After we show the stuff to Larry, I'll treat you to dinner at one of the best eateries in Tulsa. Might even spring for a movie." The can set aside, Guy started refilling the pit.

"But I'm not supposed to leave Alden." She hefted a blackened aluminum saucepan into the well and then the flattened dollhouse. They worked fast, refilling the cavity in short order. All the while, Maggie's emotions teetered between relief over what they hadn't found, and sick suspicion that the substance in the can held a sinister secret. When Guy reached for the sheet metal cover, she spotted the old high-heeled pump in a clump of weeds. "Wait," she called out, grabbing up the shoe.

"Too late," he said, dropping the first plank over the metal.

Maggie glanced at the blackened twist of leather in her hand, looked closer at a hint of red trapped in the texture, shrugged, and tossed the shoe away.

In the distance, two long blasts of a diesel locomotive, one short, another long, caught the deputy's attention. He paused, holding her gaze without appearing to see her.

After the last signal expired among the wooded hills, he pulled his timepiece from its tiny pocket at the waist of his chinos. "Noon freight at the crossing in town. Eastbound. Right on time." He smiled and helped her into her coat before slipping into his. "If we're to clean up before leaving for Tulsa, we'd best gather our gear and get moving."

Chapter 18

Late that Monday afternoon, Sheriff Randall Turkeson made a final round of the walled garden behind the Morning Glory Hotel. After receiving confirmation that arsenic had killed Johnny Rice, he'd launched an all-out search for some container that might have held the poison. Maggie could have tossed it anywhere.

He'd scoured every public and private area in the hotel. Outside, neither a bush, nor a clump of winter-brittle zinnia stalks escaped his scrutiny. Increasingly, despair gnawed at him with the thought she'd probably carried the powder in an envelope, which once empty, she'd torn up and flushed down the commode.

He'd paid six boys ten bucks each to hunt through ditches, alleys, and back streets. Heaped into a pickup truck's cargo bed, their finds included beer cans, candy wrappers, dead cats—even a used condom. Despite his discouragement, Turkeson, poking into fallen leaves around the Morning Glory's hybrid tea roses, smiled, remembering how the boys had yucked it up theorizing who might have used the rubber.

Reminded of the unfamiliar aftershave he'd smelled on his wife's coat next to his on the rack that morning, the sheriff's smile slid away. She'd supposedly attended a committee meeting at church the night before. Maybe the boys found the condom so hilarious because they knew something he didn't.

He forced himself back to business, studying the cedar that grew outside the second-floor room that Maggie Simpson had occupied the night someone supposedly tried to suffocate her—if the story held any truth.

She insisted that she'd locked the door before going to bed. The desk clerk claimed the hotel had kept extra keys in the cubbyholes behind the counter for fifty years without a single question about security until now.

Heaving a sigh, Turkeson tossed his Stetson onto one of the wrought-iron garden chairs clustered around the fountain. He pulled on leather gloves while he surveyed a possible route up the cedar. Could someone possibly climb it to gain entrance to that room's window?

Beneath the tree, he peered up into tangled limbs and twigs only a monkey or a ten-year-old boy could navigate. Turkeson tried anyway, grasping the lowest branch, struggling up, reaching for the next handhold. A twig snagged his jacket's sleeve, another poked him on the cheek. One limb higher and five jabs later, he gave it up.

He dropped to the ground.

Laughter from the hotel's back doorstep forced heat to his neck. He hid his embarrassment by glowering at Ed Danby, who stood munching a doughnut.

"Practicing up to put the star on the town Christmas tree this year, are you sheriff?"

Turkeson managed a chuckle. "Actually, I thought I'd try for Chance Halperin's job as Santa Claus in the big parade."

"Think again, Turk. Chance won't relinquish his title this year of all years—not when the mamas and daddies of all those little kiddies he makes so happy can show appreciation at the ballot box next fall."

"Go easy on the man, Ed. The district could do worse for a senator." He'd considered Chance as a possible suspect in Rice's murder but concluded that the man's ambition outweighed risking his career over a property easement.

Danby surveyed the garden. "Still trying to tie the actress to that arsenic, aren't you?"

"I'll find the connection." Under his breath, he cursed his dispatcher, Sam Woods for blabbing about the coroner's report.

The druggist laughed again. "I'd say that if there had been anything to find, you're too late. Your suspect and her keeper have been busy."

His expression sent centipedes on patrol through Turkeson's belly. "I hope you don't plan to stand there 'til suppertime looking like the Speak-No-Evil monkey, Ed. Spill it."

What he spilled about Maggie and Guy Warner snooping around town against his orders knotted Turkenson's stomach. He sat beside the fountain brooding long after the druggist left. Elbows propped on his knees, he stared down at his dusty boots while rotating the Stetson by its brim. Initial anger at his deputy for disobeying a direct order to keep the woman under wraps gave way to bafflement over the search itself. Why would the actress keep pursuing the missing sister angle to explain Johnny's murder, unless he, Turkeson, followed the wrong track in the investigation?

He refused to consider wrong an option.

Did the sister lie somewhere pushing up daisies, as Danby had said Doc Whitsitt figured? Or, as Danby saw it, had Doreen dumped the kid sister with the traveling medicine show so Doreen could skip town with whoever got her pregnant? The sheriff scowled. Could his own wife as easily fly the coop?

The aftershave he'd smelled on Helen's coat that morning flooded his senses anew, overpowering the scent of fallen leaves and winter-dry grasses around him. Should he confront his wife or not? If so, what then?

Torn by the very idea, he swallowed heavily and stood a minute to let his arthritic knee joints settle in before heading to his patrol car in the alley behind the hotel garden. Easier than thinking about facing down Helen; maybe he should just take over for Warner and look after Maggie himself.

That should make the wife sit up and take notice.

He smiled passing beneath the trellis with its overload of winter-dead vines. The smile dropped when he stepped into the alley.

A stranger waited beside his black and white. Hunched into a tweed overcoat and brown fedora, the man might as well have had the words *City Slicker* tattooed on his forehead. Turkeson grunted. City slicker searching out the sheriff of Hicksville during a murder investigation meant complications. Big-time attorney? Reporter?

Tweed Coat leaned away from the car's fender and stuck out his hand. Clasping it in a brief handshake, the sheriff noted how dry and cool the stranger's palm felt against his moist one and felt himself reduced from law officer to clod.

"Alan Rinehart," the man said, *"Los Angeles Blade*. I'd like to talk to you about the Rice case."

L.A.? *Holy shit*. Turkeson fixed him in a *get lost* look. "Anything you need is in the daybook at the office."

"I saw nothing there about the attempt on Charmaine Dorsey's life while she slept in her hotel room."

Turkeson's gut clenched. "Maggie Simpson to us. No highfalutin names like Charmaine Dorsey in this case. And I have nothing more to say about her while this investigation proceeds."

"Don't you, in fact, have absolutely nothing concrete to tie Miss Dorsey to John Rice's murder? Even after today's exhaustive search?'

Damned nosy son-of-a-bitch. Turkeson pushed the man aside and climbed into his vehicle. Rhinehart caught the door and leaned in. He'd eaten something with onions for lunch.

"I understand you're keeping the woman under wraps."

"For her own protection."

"Protection from someone out for vengeance in a friend's death? Or to silence legitimate questions about her missing sister?"

"I'll have more to say about that when I know something more." Turkeson tugged on the door handle.

Rinehart held fast. "I'd like to ask the woman a few questions about that myself, Sheriff. Could you arrange a meeting?"

"Look, Rinehart. I don't want to be rude, but I have

work to do." Turkeson wrenched the door shut and hit the lock.

The reporter tipped his hat, leaned near the window. "Then you'll excuse me while I ask around until I find her on my own." Retreating, he flashed a knowing smile. "By the by, I hear your deputy makes himself scarce these days. If I were to sniff him out, might I find Miss Dorsey as well?"

Turkeson drove away in the opposite direction from the cabin Guy and Maggie occupied at the hunting lodge. If Tweed Coat thought he'd be stupid enough to go warn his deputy of trouble, the jerk had horse hockey for brains.

The reporter tailed him about a block behind. Turkeson drove aimlessly until the man gave up. But it picked at the sheriff's mind how he should have fed Rinehart some mumbo jumbo about her whereabouts that sounded authentic. Now he'd be after Maggie like a beagle with his nose to the ground.

If the jerk found her, he'd likely interview her as a victim, not a suspect.

He considered hustling her off to the Tulsa County Sheriff's department for safekeeping. Parked in front of his office thirty minutes later, he felt a lot more sympathy for the officers in Dallas who had failed to protect Lee Harvey Oswald. The difficulties he faced looking after a two-bit actress suspected of murder in a backwater town boggled his mind.

Chapter 19

His khaki-colored eyes intense, the anthropologist poked through the pebbles in the coffee can. Maggie and Guy watched in silence. She thought the deputy appeared anxious, but for her part, the array of books, journals, bones, and lab equipment in Larry Cole's home office left little doubt that this fellow the deputy called a "bone man" could identify the can's contents.

She'd felt less confident when Cole's wife ushered her into the tiny living room earlier. Cluttered with toddler-sized furnishings and toys for twin daughters, the apartment didn't scream success in the way many people define the word.

Now, as Cole held the container near the high intensity light attached to a shelf at his shoulder, Maggie swallowed drily, her insides shaking while he examined the fragments.

He glanced around at her.

She leaned forward. "Is it—"

"Definitely not your sister," he said, and as if reading how torn she felt between relief and disappointment, gave her a comforting smile.

"But it is bone, isn't it?" Guy asked.

Cole retrieved a hominy-sized fragment and rolled it between his thumb and forefinger. "Not adult. Shattered adult bones would be jagged." He held out his hand for them to look. "See how smooth and rounded these are?"

Guy nodded. "A baby, then."

"A fetus—perhaps." He angled a glance at Maggie. "Your sister was pregnant at the time of her disappearance?"

Her nod sent his gaze to the deputy. "You found the material scattered among some old deer hides in a well. Damp, or dry?"

"Maybe a cistern, really. But dry now. Why?"

"The damper the environment, the more rapid the disintegration." Lines snaked across the scientist's broad forehead. "You found no other remains?"

"None."

Lips pursed, Cole made a humming noise.

Guy said, "We suspect Maggie's sister had an abortion in the early summer of nineteen forty-five. Could this have been her baby?"

An image rose of the infant torn from her sister's womb and discarded in a junk heap. Maggie's throat closed around an involuntary moan. Guy clasped her hand.

Cole's expression saddened. "You found a lot of this material?"

"Quite a lot. Is that significant?"

"Could be." He turned to Maggie. "Significant at three months. Or this could be the remains of an unborn fawn some hunter dumped along with the hides after field dressing the doe."

Her hope that the substance came from a fawn must have been obvious. Cole patted her shoulder. "I'll scope these fragments and run some comparisons." He walked them to the door. "I have a meeting this evening, and a bit more work on my presentation. How about I make this tomorrow morning's priority and give you a call?"

****

Maggie had thought it would be impossible to relax and enjoy dinner with so many questions still unanswered, but she hadn't reckoned with crystal chandeliers, Victorian decor, and her escort's charm. The bond between them strengthened over prime rib and twice-baked potatoes in an intimate corner of Tulsa's popular Louisianne restaurant.

The arrival of coffee and chocolate cheesecake brought a discernable shift in her companion's mood. Did he share her dread of returning to Alden's grim realities?

He consulted his pocket watch. "It's only eight o'clock. We can catch the last showing of that Audrey Hepburn and Cary Grant flick at the Rialto."

"*Charade?*" Maggie uttered a wry chuckle. "The story of our lives."

On the way to his car, she snuggled against his shoulder. A light fog hushed the night and intensified the masculine scents of his aftershave and the wood smoke trapped in his tweed sport jacket.

A figure loomed out of the mist in front of them.

Maggie recoiled and cried out in surprise at the same time her Hollywood-conditioned reflexes focused at once on the camera the man raised. Light ripped open the darkness.

Guy shielded his face with both hands. "Judas H. Priest." His curse rode over the photographer's, "Great shot, Miss Dorsey."

Grasping the man's collar, Guy jerked him forward. "I don't know who the hell you are, mister, or who you think we are, but you've made a mistake. Beat it."

Shocked by what struck her as over-reaction, she tugged at Guy's jacket sleeve. "Let me handle it. You'll only make things worse."

Already the intruder maneuvered for a second shot. "Stow it, Deputy Warner. I already cut through that crap with Sheriff Turkeson." The flash fired again. "What about the attack on Miss Dorsey in her hotel room? What's the real—"

Out, shot Guy's fist.

The man ducked and deflected the blow to return a left hook. He caught Guy squarely in the chin.

Guy staggered, but quickly regained his balance. "Bastard." He swung again.

"No! Guy—" Her warning too late, Maggie heard his fist connect. The other man's lungs whooshed air, and he fell to his knees. His camera crashed to the sidewalk. Film slithered off the roll. The flash attachment bounced away into the darkness.

"Lunatic!" The man scrabbled around on his hands and knees, retrieving his equipment.

Lunging forward to snag the film first, Guy took an uppercut that dumped him at Maggie's feet. Blood poured from his nose.

She fell to her knees beside him, her heart stopping, then galloping double-time. "Guy?" Her breath half-sobs, she swabbed at his injuries with the hem of her skirt. She glanced up at the reporter. "You stupid man—could have killed him."

"He came at me first."

Guy raised himself onto his elbow. "You had it coming for sneaking up on us like some tabloid hack. I should call the police."

Not a real option of course. Having left Alden against the terms of her release from jail, she'd be locked up again, or worse, the deputy could be fired and forced to leave town. Glancing down to see Guy bleeding from a cut on the lip too, she felt guilt heavy as a hair coat. But for the rash trip into town Friday morning that dragged him into her troubles, he'd be safe at home, whittling beside the fire. She swallowed the lump in her throat and dabbed at the blood with a tissue. "I think you broke his nose," she quavered.

"It's just I'm damned sick of these stonewalling hicks around here. Two days of trailing you down and all I got to show for my time is a busted camera and two good shots, probably spoiled. How about it, Miss Dorsey? Have we got the kind of story your agent claims, or are you gonna play cute with me too?"

"I'll give you the story when there *is* a story."

"What about the attack on you at the hotel? That's plenty to go with right now."

Maggie clamped her lips together, shook her head.

"And what about that stop you made over on Peoria? What has that got to do with anything?"

He'd followed them to Larry Cole's house? Shaken that he might go prying there too, she said, "Some friends planned to join us for dinner. Their kids got sick."

A groan from Guy ended the conversation. Maggie and the reporter got him to his feet and into the car, but her legs shook so hard that she stumbled going around to the drivers' side. She reached out, supporting herself on the front fender to stay on her feet.

"You sure you're able to drive back to Alden?"

"Yes," she said, opening the door. "But I'm going to find a doctor for the deputy first."

Guy held up a hand in protest. "No doctor. Home."

He wouldn't be argued down.

Fog shrouded the curves and hills between Tulsa and Alden, turning the short drive into a slow-motion Grand Prix that tested Maggie's endurance. Guy spoke twice: once to give directions and again to ask, "Did you get the film?"

"Ruined, I'm pretty sure." She crossed her fingers.

His whispered, "Thank God," sharpened her guilt. Whatever lay behind his need to avoid publicity, she had to do everything in her power to keep attention away from him.

They reached the cabin after midnight. Shivering, Maggie checked the cold ashes before starting a fire. Guy stood aside, looking like he'd been shot from a cannon and landed on his nose. Blood crusted his nostrils. A cut at the corner of his puffy mouth oozed scarlet.

"I'm so sorry, Guy."

"My fight."

"I feel responsible."

"Forget it, Maggie." He trudged over to the kitchen and retrieved the Jack Daniel's from under the counter. The stiff drink he poured and then put the bottle away left her wondering how some people could do that, and she could not. Involuntarily, her tongue slipped out to moisten her lips.

She dragged her focus from the amber liquid in his glass. "We need to talk about what happened, Guy. That scumbag surprised me as much as he did you. I have no idea how he found out I'm with you, much less where we went yesterday."

After tossing down the drink, he put the glass aside. "Thanks to your sleuthing in town Friday, everyone knows where you are."

To that, she had no defense. She opened her palms in the heat rising from Old Firebelly. "Okay. But I don't understand why you flew off the handle at that reporter. I could have talked him out of that story. I—"

"Maggie. Maggie." He shook his head. "Don't pretend you weren't in on the setup from the beginning."

"You can't really believe that—"

"That your agent sent the man?" Guy cut in, closing the space between them. "I heard him tell you that."

Seen up close, his battered face quelled the surge of anger his accusation had sparked. Quietly, she said, "Yes, the man claimed that Scaff Russell had tipped him, but before going code red when he showed up, you might have noticed my shock. And why don't you try to consider how I feel after learning that the one person I depended upon for help sent a reporter instead of a decent attorney?"

"Chance is a good attorney."

"Yeah, sure."

"Yeah, Maggie. And how do you think I felt, then, staring into a camera and knowing my picture could show up on the front page of some big city rag back East?" Guy raked splayed fingers through his hair.

"Oh Guy…" She trapped his hands between hers and drew them to her heart. "Who are you really? What, or who, are you hiding from?"

The emotions seething in his hazel eyes added to

her confusion, but finally he burst out, "My name is Frank Jackson." He wrested free of her grasp. "And because I have never been able to keep *this*," he touched his nose gingerly and winced, "out of other people's business, I can never again cross a city street anywhere in America without watching over my shoulder for mob retribution."

"Go on." Dry as the last leaves on a pin oak in December, her words rustled into silence broken only by flames crackling in the stove. Pride settled into Guy's expression.

"I held this crazy notion about truth, justice, and the American way," he said, paused, eyes narrowed. "Corny?" He snorted. "You tell me—my maternal grandmother fled Czarist Russia after her husband and parents were shot down in one of those ethnic pogroms petty tyrants are so fond of launching. She hid in a root cellar with my mother, two years old at the time, and an infant boy. Living on raw vegetables and apple cider for days, she nursed both children. When spring came, she escaped across the border, walking most of the way."

Maggie gasped. "With two babies?"

"The baby didn't survive the cellar. Grandmother considered freedom worth the hardships she suffered on a long road to this country. 'Never forget,' she used to say—" A smile ghosted across Guy's swollen lips. "She'd shake her finger under this foolish nose of mine and say, 'never forget how wonderful is America. Never forget how wonderful is the right to take troubles to a judge. To have jury who will listen. Who will make things right.' "

Guy shrugged, his smile bitter now. "Trouble is, juries don't always make things right, Maggie. In

Toledo I learned they don't always serve justice. My wife knew. She kept saying, 'Leave it alone, Frank. Leave it be.'"

The wife. Maggie held her breath, and when he said no more asked, "Leave what alone?"

"Carloads of structural steel shunted off at a siding in the CS&O railyard. Replaced by low grade stuff barged in on Lake Erie. I saw the crooks truck out a load of the good ones late one night."

She remembered him saying he'd been a railroad detective. "And the poor quality stuff?"

"There are some skyscrapers in this country I wouldn't go near on a windy day, much less inside."

Maggie clutched her chest in horror. "Who made the switch?"

"A mobster named Ed Moroni. I testified against him, but he got off with a slap on the wrist."

"This Ed Moroni. He's out to get you, then?"

His smile puzzled her momentarily. "You're picking up my speech patterns, Maggie," he said, his gentle tone easing the stricture in her chest. "Yes, Maggie. Moroni's after me, and probably out of spite, my wife and son as well. Jill divorced me. Took Billy. I don't even trust myself to try and find out where they are."

Aching to hold him close, Maggie had no idea how to breach the despair she saw on his face. "How did you wind up in Alden, Oklahoma, of all places?"

"My attorney and Chance Halperin were buddies in law school. Far as I know, only those two people know my whereabouts." He shrugged. "You get it, then—why I can't afford the kind of attention Charmaine Dorsey the actress can draw."

His words hung in the air a few seconds before Maggie protested. "But I'm not famous."

He snorted. "We both know how Hollywood types at all levels attract publicity the way overripe fruit draws gnats. Seen by the wrong eyes, one paragraph under a picture buried on the obituary page in the right rag could bring a hit man to Alden."

Maggie looked down at her hands, stained yet with Guy's blood, and quailed at the deeper stain that marked her escape from Dr. Xavier. "Go, Guy—" her voice broke. "Get as far away from me as that old Studebaker can carry you. I don't need—" The word "you" stuck in her throat, but she cleared it away and began again. "I've gotten myself out of worse predicaments than you can imagine."

A keen light sprang into his eyes. "Such as?"

"Never mind." Surveying the dried blood on his nose, his cut lip, and the raw scrape on his cheek, she flung a gesture at the kitchen table. "Now sit while I get a cloth and warm water to clean up those battle wounds."

He sat.

After filling a pan at the sink, she examined the cut on his chin. "Do you have peroxide?"

"That linen closet in the hallway. Top shelf."

After she'd patched him up, he stood and gusted a heavy sigh. "Thanks. I suspect that you can handle most anything you set your mind to, but I can't leave you alone in a town itching for an old-fashioned necktie party. Truth, justice, and the American way, you know. Plus—Grandmother would haunt me forever if I ran out on you. I'm also curious about those bone fragments we left with Cole."

That said, he disappeared into his bedroom and shut the door.

****

Alone in the Murphy bed, Maggie lay awake while self-recriminating whispers slithered at her from every dark corner. She acknowledged them. If only she'd insisted they come directly home after meeting with Cole. Now she'd lost Guy's trust. Would he ever believe again that she had no thought for any publicity she might gain through this mess?

If she could go somewhere new, forget Hollywood and Doreen, maybe she'd find relief from guilt, and the nasty man with his hateful camera would lose interest in Alden. Then Guy Warner would feel safe again.

She'd tossed the keys to the Studebaker onto the kitchen table when they came in from Tulsa. She visualized picking them up, heard Beetlebomb's smooth-running engine turn over, felt the wheels take her to the road out of town.

Where, exactly, might she go? Listening to the fire crackle, she summoned the red rose on midnight velvet that would soothe her to sleep. The image shifted into that of the Jack Daniel's bottle stashed under the kitchen counter.

Maggie counted the days. *Five hundred eight*, she'd been sober.

Chapter 20

"One," Guy counted, lifting Maggie from the chair when he found her slumped over on the kitchen table the next morning and snoring loudly. The empty liquor bottle at her elbow told him all he needed to know about himself—boor and hothead—and about a woman pushed past her emotional boundary by last night's dust-up over that damned reporter.

"Day one," he repeated, "you're starting from day one again."

"Ummow." She tried to pull away.

His grip demanded she step forward. "Step one," he counted, and supporting her, kept talking as they circled the room once, twice and a third time, pausing only for him to put yesterday's leftover coffee on the range to warm.

When the brew smelled strong enough to boil the paint off the Studebaker, Guy sat her down, filled a mug with the murky liquid, and set it in front of her. "Careful, it's hot," he warned. She grimaced through the process but looked less bleary-eyed after downing the coffee. "Come now, Maggie. A good shower is in order."

He deposited her under the spray and adjusted the water temperature to a tad under lukewarm. "Day one," he said, making her repeat it after him as he closed the curtain.

Seated on the commode to wait, he ignored her complaints about the cold and when she finished, helped her towel herself dry.

"Bed, then?" he asked when she finally met his gaze with eyes so full of self-loathing he had to look away.

He tucked her into the Murphy bed in the front room and headed to the kitchen to start breakfast. "Could you eat some dry toast?"

Her reply came in a soft snore.

Guy sighed and scrambled himself some eggs. No sooner had he forked in a mouthful when a knock sounded at the door. He opened it to meet Chance Halperin's eyes, glacial blue.

Braced for eviction from the cabin, Guy got a reprieve when the attorney shifted his regard to Guy's nose. Wide-eyed then, he opened his mouth to speak but obviously caught a glimpse of Maggie in his peripheral vision. Slack-jawed, he stared at the tumble of red-gold hair on her pillow, then the pale oval of her face.

"Earth to the Planet Krypton," Guy said drily. "Do you read me Captain Halperin?"

Halperin's cheeks, already flushed from the morning chill, flamed scarlet.

"It's the first time you've seen the grown-up Maggie, then."

The attorney tugged at his buttoned-down collar and adjusted the knot on his narrow black tie. Head tilted toward the slip and bra puddled on the foot of the bed, he said, "Obviously, there isn't much of her that *you* haven't seen."

In a room suddenly and unaccountably too warm,

Guy wondered when Maggie and her paraphernalia had become a comfortable part of his surroundings. He hadn't felt this trapped since, at age eight, he got caught snitching a piece of bubble gum at the grocery store.

This time, he tried to bluster away his embarrassment. "She's a babe all right, but one who spells more trouble than either of us needs in a lifetime."

Halperin shrugged. "And what's with that nose? Looks like a busted walnut. What the hell is going on here, Jackson?"

Guy's real last name on the attorney's lips reminded him how much he owed the man for setting him up, a total stranger, in Alden. Yet, the same man's callous attitude toward Maggie, whom he'd known as a child, warned against revealing too much about her personal search for facts about Doreen's last days in Alden. "A reporter came sniffing at Maggie's heels. He and I had a disagreement." Enough said.

His friend's silvery blond eyebrows shot up. "A reporter came here?"

"No."

In the expanding silence, Halperin shot a troubled glance at Maggie. "I don't want some damned reporter snooping around after some kind of in-depth story on that woman and her keeper in a cozy cabin setting on my property."

Guy shook his head, emphatic. "Over my dead body."

"Make damn certain." Halperin pointed with his chin. "As soon as Sleeping Beauty wakes up, get her out of here."

"That would pretty much put the wraps on our

investigation into her sister's whereabouts...surely you concede that."

Appraising Maggie in slumber, Halperin appeared beyond hearing at the moment. When she stirred and mumbled indecipherable protest against something in her dreams, his gaze softened. "Easy to see why you'd fall for her." Abruptly, he spun, pointing at Guy's nose. "Listen good, my friend. When the trouble she brought to town blows up in your face, you'll look back on that busted-up snout as a mere scratch."

"Blows up?" Guy's thoughts flipped to the booby-trap he'd found in the stove Friday evening. Even though Halperin appeared innocent, distrust prodded Guy to ask, "When I ran into you Friday afternoon—outside the grocery store—I asked if you'd seen Maggie—"

"And I told you I'd picked up some documents at home, took them to the county clerk's office where I also did a title search."

The battle between his desire to trust this friend and knowing how easily the man could have sabotaged the stove kept Guy silent too long.

Halperin looked uneasy. "I also dropped in on Sis, but getting ready for a date she flitted around in such a twit I left her be. I picked up a suit from the cleaner's, after which I stopped off at Fate's store."

"What time was that, then?"

"A bit before I talked to you." He narrowed his eyes in thought. "About five o'clock." He did an eyeroll and sighed. "I don't suppose you'd care to tell me what this is all about."

"You didn't stay long at Fate's store."

"Note on the door said he'd gone to pick up

something from an estate sale."

"Whose estate?"

"The Romines', I suppose." He poked a finger at Guy's chest. "And no more answers until I know why you need a play-by-play of my afternoon."

Friendship and trust won. "While Maggie and I were both out Friday, someone planted a jar of gasoline in Old Firebelly's cold ashes." He gestured at the stove and recounted how narrowly he and Maggie had avoided a disaster.

At his friend's gasp, Guy added, "I can't quite imagine Paula Rice dashing out after her husband's funeral that morning to wreak death and destruction."

"But you have no problem imagining your best friend trying to blow you into the next county?" Winter had returned to the attorney's baby-blues.

"I first thought Ed Moroni," Guy defended himself. "I had to remind myself that Maggie's in my keeping. Or I should say my attempt at keeping. She's pretty independent."

"Talk around Alden is that she had the run of the town during the funeral." Halperin laughed. "A secret is a secret as long as it's held by only two people. Whispered to a third, it becomes news."

Almost overwhelmed with the need to get the attorney's educated opinion about what Maggie and he had learned about Doreen in recent days, Guy opened his mouth to ask, but reconsidered. Even if Halperin had Maggie's best interest at heart, which he clearly didn't, some casual remark of his, overheard at the courthouse, could make its way to the sheriff.

The moment passed. Halperin cast a final, shuttered glance at Maggie. "I still want her off my property as soon as she's able. And I think you shouldn't count out Ed Moroni as the architect of your gasoline bomb."

A chill rippled along the deputy's spine. Hiding his fear, he bid the man goodbye, closed the door firmly at his heels, and went to scrape his cold breakfast into the trash bin along with the empty whiskey bottle.

****

Some time while she slept, gremlins had installed a kettle drum in Maggie's head. She awoke to its beat and to the nauseating odor of bacon frying.

A groan fought its way out her parched throat. She begged the gods of fortune to whisk her back into the fog of sleep but sensed appraisal that coaxed her eyes open. That damned deputy, of course. After the initial rush of irritation, she saw more sympathy than censure and regretted the harsh thought. She sat up.

He offered her a hand. She shook her head. "You've babied me enough. Just catch what's left of my brains when they drop out, will you?"

A rueful chuckle preceded a very grave voice. "I'm sorry I unloaded on you last night. I should have realized the sordid details of my past would scare hell out of even a tough cookie like you."

"Not so tough," she countered, her tone rising into alarm as she took a tentative step only to discover someone had installed a marshmallow floor while she slept. High stepping to the rocking chair beside the stove, she regretted every footfall. Grasping the wooden arms, she levered herself into the chair with a groan. "I've pushed you into such a mess here," she said. "What if that mobster or his cronies finds you because of me?"

Guy had crossed to the kitchen range where he stirred something in a skillet. "I'm responsible for my own troubles, Maggie. I smelled complications the minute you sashayed into that coffee shop. Cautioned by one of the best attorneys in Oklahoma no less than twice before he preached at me again this morning, I should have packed up and left town days ago."

Leaning forward, she clasped her head between her hands in an effort to muffle the drumbeat while his words penetrated the thunder. She glanced up. "So, I *did* hear you talking with someone earlier. Chance Halperin?"

"He ordered us out. I think I bought us some time, but don't count on much."

"God, what a mess I've made of things."

Her lament drew a half-smile from Guy. "Show me any alcoholic who hasn't fallen off the wagon now and then."

"But I'd made it almost five hundred nine days." Heartened by a glance she could only describe as tender, she conceded, "I guess I have to start counting again."

"You already have—day one, isn't this?"

Memory squished into her soggy brain. "You're right." Her right forefinger pressed to her left thumb, she counted, "One."

It sure enough did feel good to make that fresh start, but Guy had goofed on another point. "Alden must have been a nice place before I got off that bus," she moaned. "Now a good man is dead. Everyone is filled with hatred and suspicion. And I'm no closer than ever to finding a place where I really belong."

Before he could reply, she unburdened her heart.

"No wonder this country's in such decline, Guy. People like me bumbling around, screwing up our lives and everyone else's by hanging on to stupid old resentments as if they were heirloom treasures."

"That's it, then?" he asked when she finally ran down. "You really do carry around a load, don't you?" He opened a cabinet door and took out a blue bowl.

The everyday business of watching him serve up scrambled eggs settled her a bit. Hunger rumbled through her stomach. On a wistful sigh, she said, "You have to admit that everything I said is true. I thought making things right with Doreen I could do some little part to make up for what happened in Dallas and—"

How he reached her so quickly without dropping skillet or bowl, Maggie couldn't fathom, but his palm silenced her plaint. "You came here because you felt responsible for the President being shot, then." He rolled his eyes in exaggerated disbelief.

"Mmmphft," she argued against his hand, but when he freed her lips, picked up where she'd left off. "Aren't we all to blame in a sense? You've read the editorials. Heard the news commentators. Do you question the observations of people like that?"

Lofting a defensive wave, he transferred the eggs from the stove to the table with a decisive whack of pottery on Formica. "You need food, Maggie." He poured coffee into two white mugs.

The aftertaste of that earlier brew still bit her tongue. "Spare me the java."

"Fresh pot." He pulled out a chair, staring at it until she dragged herself over to the table. "Kennedy," he said, pushing the chair under her rear, "got shot because some punk couldn't deal with his own hostilities and his inability to handle differences of political opinion." He filled their plates. "I've just come through a period in my life when I considered justice a crock, but I sure as hell didn't go gunning for the judge that let Ed Moroni walk."

Queasy, Maggie eyed the perfectly cooked eggs. To please the cook, she forked in a mouthful, chewed, and swallowed. Getting that bite past the self-blame stuck in her throat proved difficult. When she could speak again, she reopened her argument. "John Rice is dead because I came looking for Doreen. You can't change that."

"Jeez, but you're single-minded." He gestured with his fork. "On the other hand, it's quite possible that a killer has strolled around Alden bold as brass for eighteen years. I have no doubt that Rice died to protect that person. How about we see that justice catches up with him, then."

Emotionally bound by his intense expression, Maggie wanted to reward him by feeling better about herself. "Listen to us," she quavered, "none of it makes sense unless Doreen is really dead, and we don't even know that for sure. Maybe I should be praying that she turns up alive, instead of trying to prove she's not."

His eyes softened, more gray than hazel. He motioned at her plate. "Finish your breakfast. We have work to do to find the truth one way or another. You can pray while we do that."

The eggs tasted better and went down easier on the second try. After she and Guy tidied the cabin, they began poring through Guy's stack of area phone books in a wider search for Eve and Bill. No luck. They talked to every Bill who answered his phone. None claimed a sister named Eve.

****

The following day, Guy cautioned Maggie not to traipse off on her own while he went to talk to Rice's widow again.

Maggie didn't traipse but shuffled in a direct line across town to the high school. Coffee grounds rubbed on her face and stippled with traces of red and a light foundation, added years. Her stash from Fate Halperin's shed provided a long brown coat, a yellow turban, and sensible brown oxfords.

Her pose as an alum putting together a reunion of the class of 1942 got her past the principal's office where a student receptionist directed her to the library. There, Maggie's inquiry befuddled the young woman's male counterpart, whose focus preferred the fuzzy pink sweater that clung to a girl seated at a round table piled with reference books. The pale skin between the youth's fresh crew-cut and protuberant ears reddened. "How can I help you?" he asked and to his credit managed a respectful expression for the dowdy creature looking at him across his work counter.

"Miss Harriet Duvall," Maggie whispered. "Class of nineteen forty-two. I'm planning a reunion and misplaced my yearbook. Perhaps I could peruse that issue in your collection…refresh my memory as to the classmates I hope to locate."

The student wrinkled his forehead and glanced around uncertainly. "I don't know, ma'am. I think you should talk to my supervisor, Mrs. Rand. She teaches social studies this period."

"I spoke to someone in the office." Pausing, Maggie hoped the lie didn't bear unpleasant fruit. She consulted her wristwatch and widened her eyes in astonishment. "Oh my. Is it ten o'clock already? I've an appointment to keep, you see—if you could direct me to the yearbook collection—" Her smile transmitted what a nice, helpful young man he would be, coming to her aid. And although he glanced around again, his attention lingered on Miss Pink Sweater, whose fluttery eyelashes facilitated matters for Maggie without further ado.

Seconds later, she occupied a corner table piled with yearbooks while Crew-cut hung over Pink Sweater's shoulder with earnest concern for her apparent problem with some errant fact.

Maggie felt a poignant tug for the innocence of youth she'd missed, sighed, and pushed aside regret for the matter at hand. Thumbing through the annual for her sister's senior year, she spied Eve Thompson. On the same page, in the bottom corner, a face similar to her own drew a gasp.

Johnny Rice had told her she resembled Doreen. Dr. Whitsitt had remembered her as pretty and quick to laugh. Doreen's image revealed something more—sensitivity. A growing belief strengthened in Maggie—her sister had been neither hard, nor cruel enough to abandon her.

An old, dead weight sighed and shifted in her heart, leaving it lighter. Glancing around to see that no one observed, she tore out the photo and stuffed it into her coat pocket. Her search in the book for a William or Bill who might have been the friend mentioned in Doreen's letters to Johnny, turned up no one. In fact, the scarcity of young men in the photos brought home how many had been away at war at the time—youthful volunteers.

Among candid photos at the back of the book she did find a snapshot of an Eve in a sweetheart pose with a younger-looking boy named Gerald Trent. She had started to tear that one out when a strident buzz from the hallway startled her heart into her throat. Books slammed. All around her, chairs screeched back from tables.

Swept into the corridors with students exciting the library, she dodged flung-open locker doors and a linebacker-sized hall monitor. The man's eyes focused on Maggie a split second before she scurried past him and around a corner. Past the girls' restroom and out the rear exit she sped before stopping to catch a breath.

Twenty minutes later she reached the cabin. Flushing out Maggie the calico and her friend Jiggs as well, she took a moment to stroke their backs and whisper sweet nothings. In return, she got yowls and meows that held a strangely accusatory note.

The cats kept up their tirade outside while Maggie shed the heavy coat and peeled off the sweat-soaked turban. A quick finger-comb of her hat-hair sufficed before she changed into her kimono and settled into the telephone chair beside the door.

"Trent. Trent. Trent," she repeated, searching the local directory. She found an Edgar, whom she dialed and learned that his brother, Gerald and his wife, Eve, lived in a small town near Tulsa.

She'd just cradled the receiver when Guy burst into the room. Up she sprang. Both talking at once, they went on a moment before breaking into laughter. It took a beat for her to digest what he'd said, and when she did so, her knees gave way, dumping her back into the chair.

"My trunk is here?" Words that roared in her head emerged as a hoarse whisper.

Oblivious to her distress, he radiated self-satisfaction. "I slipped the express man ten bucks to bring it out here instead of unloading it at the hotel where the Turk could—" Guy broke off, his eyes narrowed. "What's wrong, Maggie?"

Had she told him, he wouldn't have heard, his eyes harder now, focused on the aging techniques she hadn't taken time to remove from her face.

Scowl lines crept across his brow. "You've been at it again," he said, to which she nodded, and pushing aside her worries about the trunk for the moment, blurted, "I've learned who Eve is and where she lives."

If she expected him to share her joy, the way he marched her to the bathroom indicated something different. "Stay out of sight. The guy with the trunk will be here any minute."

"But—" The door closed in her face.

"Please, Maggie. Just once, stay put."

"Guy?" She jerked open the door. "Listen. Didn't you hear me say I've found Eve? She's in—"

A loud banging on the front door interrupted her. "That'll be the delivery man," said Guy, closing the door in her face.

She heard him greet the man. Heard thumps and bumps. Dry-mouthed and nauseated, she stared through her mirrored image into the stark fear of the thirteen-year-old girl who closed her ears to the thumpings and bumpings of agony on the floor behind her as she fled, the apothecary case in hand.

Would the freedom she sought then continue to

elude her until she lay in her grave? And then, would she exchange the emotional chains of guilt for the physical bonds of hell? Vaguely, she registered sounds of the delivery man's departure.

A rap sounded at the bathroom door. "All clear."

He'd expect her to open the trunk immediately. How might she delay it?

Yet delay she must until after they talked with Eve Trent. Once he'd seen the trunk's contents, trust would die. Frantic to buy time, Maggie stripped off the kimono and stepped into the shower, turning it on full blast and willing the water to cleanse the guilt from her face.

She heard him come in the room. "Maggie?"

Her heart hammered her ribs.

The shower curtain grated open on its rust-streaked rod.

Never had she felt so naked. Showing him her back, she huddled into herself, murmuring, "I thought you'd be overjoyed that I found Doreen's friends."

He said nothing, and after a moment stomped loudly from the room. "Your Eve had damned sure better give us some of the right answers, or you're in hotter water than you'll ever get in that shower."

Hiding her face in her hands, she listened to his retreat until a new thought coalesced out of the familiar, self-accusatory swirl in her head. What had Guy meant by that parting remark?

She dried herself hurriedly and wrapped in the towel, took her kimono off the hook beside the shower and stepped into the living area. Guy still stood near the front door. Afraid that somehow sparing more than a glance at the trunk she might reveal her dread, she tried diversion. "I don't guess you'd care to explain how things could go worse for me if Eve can't tell me more about the 'Bill' my sister mentioned in her letters."

He gave her a wan smile. "I had a conversation with Paula Rice this morning. She's no longer a suspect in her husband's murder as far as I'm concerned."

Maggie wrapped the kimono around herself more tightly and sank into the rocking chair beside the stove. He took off his watch cap, stuffed it into a pocket on his coat, and hung it near the door. He crossed to the stove. "Shortly after your initial meeting with Johnny, he contacted someone in the law firm that handles his business. Paperwork to transfer the Simpson property to Paula is already under way."

"So?"

"I figure Johnny wasn't saint enough to return your share of that land, but he knew how badly his wife wanted to establish that children's camp on the property. He eased his conscience by deeding it to her."

Blood surged hot into Maggie's cheeks, and she shook more violently. The property that had rightly passed to her and to Doreen now belonged to someone with no history in it at all. She found solace in knowing the place would bring joy to lives that struggle to belong, but giving credit for that to the frosty blonde who'd treated her so shabbily the night Johnny Rice died would take some doing. "Why didn't Paula tell you about getting the property when you interviewed her before?"

"I didn't ask the right questions." Pulling over a kitchen chair, he sat facing her. "Admit it Maggie—as a detective, I'm a damned good night watchman." His lips twisted into a wry smile. "As for you, my dear, I wait with bated breath to hear the details of your investigatory accomplishments of the day."

After hearing her account, he congratulated her on her success and had the good grace not to remind her that she'd transgressed again. Abruptly, he slapped his hands on his thighs and popped up from the chair. "Let's get that trunk unpacked for you, then."

Confused and beleaguered by fear, Maggie sprang up and went to the refrigerator. She rummaged for a snack she didn't want. "Let's eat a bite first." In truth, she wanted a slug of whiskey. *Day two*, she told herself.

"Eat? I've heard nothing for days but how you wish you had the stuff to stir up a fresh batch of face cream."

"I'll manage a while longer." She retrieved a package of bologna, the mayonnaise, and a head of lettuce. "Let's have a sandwich and get on our way to interview Eve Trent."

Red crept up his neck. "If you're thinking of going along—" He shook his head and raked both hands through his hair. "Dammit to hell, no!"

Chapter 21

He'd been unable to argue her down. They had to pass through Tulsa on their way to interview Eve Trent, and having heard nothing from Larry Cole regarding the material they left for him to analyze, they stopped at the anthropologist's apartment.

Mrs. Cole told them her husband had been called out of town unexpectedly. It would be several days before he could get back to them. Dark circles under her eyes, the young woman brushed straggles of red hair from her eyes. "I promised Larry I'd call you…the twins came down with stomach flu and I forgot. I'm sorry."

On their way back to the car, Maggie noticed how carefully her companion scrutinized the parking lot and the street in both directions. "You think that reporter might have picked up our trail again?"

His smile reassured her. "I think we outfoxed him."

The dusty green sedan had tailed them out of Alden. She recognized the make as similar to the one parked outside the restaurant the night the man followed them there. This time Guy's knowledge of back roads had helped them elude him. Coupled with a sun-washed November day, anticipation of what Eve Trent might reveal about Doreen's last days in Alden eased Maggie's disappointment over the lack of information from Larry Cole.

They'd gone a couple of blocks when Guy let out a string of curse words. Scowling into the rearview mirror, he struck the steering wheel with the palm of his hand. "Damned hack reporter." He gripped the wheel. "Hang on."

The Studebaker leaped forward, cornered on screeching tires into a side street. Behind them, the green sedan fishtailed around the turn, squared away, and charged toward them.

Guy negotiated another corner. They sped through an intersection.

A car horn blared.

"You just ran a red light," Maggie gasped.

"Damn shame."

Two more turns. Guy glanced into the rearview mirror. "I think we lost him," he muttered, but maintained speed a minute or two before easing the car onto the main thoroughfare toward their destination.

When the jellied contents of Maggie's stomach finally settled, she smoothed her bangs aside. "Sweet car."

"You bet your life, honey."

The rare endearment stirred a pleasurable ember that grew and warmed her until he braked the car at the curb in front of Eve Trent's bungalow. There, Maggie's high dipped precipitously, her thoughts on the trunk back in the cabin. So much depended upon what the woman might be able to tell her that would lead to another suspect in Johnny's murder. Her involuntary shiver drew Guy's hand over hers on the seat between them.

She'd told him how quickly Eve's initial graciousness on the phone segued into coldness when asked if she and Doreen had had a mutual friend named Bill. Eve had denied such a friend, but after careful persuasion, and a bit of Hollywood name-dropping on Maggie's part, the woman had agreed to this meeting.

Guy opted to stay in the car but gave her hand a reassuring squeeze. "Break a leg, Maggie."

The stage jargon to wish her luck put a smile on her lips, but only until Eve opened the door. The woman wore a closed expression. A split-second later, recognition, then pleasure flickered in her dark eyes. "Why, you really *have* been in Hollywood all these years, haven't you? I saw you in a late-night movie not long ago." All aflutter, she ushered Maggie inside and to an overstuffed chair at one end of a matching tweed couch. The furniture faced a large, cabinet-styled television set tuned to *As the World Turns*. At the moment, Eileen Fulton as Lisa held a lip lock with some male actor whose name escaped Maggie.

Eve fluttered over to the television set, lowered the volume, and then at the window next to the set, pushed aside the draperies and peered out.

"Are you sure your friend in the car out there wouldn't like to come in?"

"Thanks, but he's nursing a bad knee." Maggie knew he'd actually wanted to keep a lookout for the green sedan.

While Eve clucked sympathetically, Maggie compared the young matron in black capris and crisp white blouse to the perky brunette pictured in her high school yearbook. Eve had resisted the enticement of "Only her hairdresser knows for sure," allowing prematurely gray locks to have their way in a becoming salt and pepper effect.

She flitted over to the couch. Perched on the end nearest Maggie's she said, "How sad about Johnny. I saw a little write-up in the Tulsa paper."

The uncertainty that flitted through her eyes suggested that the item might have mentioned Maggie as a possible suspect. Good breeding, or perhaps Eve's obvious awe of anything vaguely Hollywood, got both women past the moment. Eve pressed her lips together for a moment, then staring past Maggie's shoulder at the television set, said, "So you're here about Doreen?"

Maggie nodded and was taken aback when the woman bounced to her feet and crossed to the television set. She tapped the screen.

"I'll bet you know all those people, don't you? Is Eileen Fulton really like that in person?" Back on the couch, Eve lowered her voice to a confidential tone. "Does she sleep around?"

Frustration aside, Maggie had to chuckle. "I'm afraid I don't know Miss Fulton that well. Now, about my sister—"

Eve clapped her hand over mouth, sprang up again. "Where are my manners? I stirred up some chocolate chip cookies and made fresh coffee." At the kitchen door, she paused. "You do drink coffee?"

Nodding, Maggie would have preferred getting right to the matter at hand.

"Sugar and cream?"

"Black, please. And thank you."

The woman disappeared and reappeared within seconds. On a tray she had arranged cups and saucers patterned with black and turquoise triangles and dots, and a plate heaped with cookies. "I hope you aren't on a diet—" she said with a laugh. "Aren't actresses always?

But surely, just one little chocolate chip cookie—"

Laughing along, Maggie helped herself. "One teeny cookie can't hurt." The acidic smell wafting from the coffee cup suggested how long the woman had been ready and waiting for her visitor. She sipped carefully, composing her expression as the bitterness bit her tongue. "Now, Mrs. Trent—"

"Oh, please," her hostess broke in, placing the tray on the coffee table before she settled onto the couch, "call me Eve." She lifted her coffee up, holding it aside while her eyes catalogued every detail of Maggie's appearance. "That green suit. How becoming. I hadn't realized how green your eyes…even greener than your sister's, though hers are positively emerald."

Her reference to Doreen in the present tense brought Maggie forward in the chair. "When did you last hear from my sister?"

The woman narrowed her eyes in thought. "I think I saw your first picture. *Jericho Junction*? I first thought you were Doreen, but that made no sense because you looked too young. But of course, those makeup artists do wonderful things." Pausing, she grabbed a breath.

For a moment, Maggie succumbed to vanity. *Someone actually remembered seeing me in a movie.*

"Anyway," Eve continued, "I was so happy when I realized it must be you in the role. I knew how much you wanted to be an actress."

"You're sweet to remember, Eve. Frankly, I'm astonished you noticed me back then." *Whoa, Maggie*, she told herself sternly—remember what's important here. She returned her half-empty cup to the tray. "Please, Eve—have you heard from Doreen since she left Alden?"

The fleck of invisible lint or dust the older woman suddenly found the need to brush off her black trousers could only be evasion. Maggie sat back in her chair, her outward composure belied by the urgency that surged through her veins.

As hoped, the silence bore down until her hostess felt the need to break it. "Your sister wanted you to have a chance on the stage awfully much, to give up as she did, everything dear." Eve's black penciled brows slid together at the bridge of her nose. "To take you so you could perform with that medicine show…but I expected to see you both back in Alden before Johnny returned from overseas."

Maggie dredged up enough patience to explain away the old gossip yet again and watched incredulity set her listener's mouth askew.

"You mean Doreen didn't go with you?" Eve gasped.

"I hoped you knew where Doreen might have gone."

Faint lines creased Eve's forehead. "She'd have no reason to stay in touch with me."

"But she referred to you so often in her letters to Johnny. I assumed you two were very close."

"For a while," Eve said. "But not after she—"

Her protest evaporated and trouble clouded her eyes.

"You and my sister had a falling out?"

"Doreen and I became closer after our guys went off to war."

A pause. "Yes," Maggie coaxed, "go on."

"She and I went to the movies together. Things like that. Then she began coming out to the farm where I lived with my parents and my older brother. Bill got a deferment—"

Abruptly silent, she avoided Maggie's intensity.

"Bill is your brother?"

"Nickname." Eve fidgeted in her seat, glanced off toward the television set. "Edward by birth, he wore this old New York Yankees baseball cap until the bill actually came off. Even then, he wouldn't give up that cap. Dad started calling him Bill. The name stuck." Caution sharpened her eyes. "I'd have thought you'd remember him. You came to our farm with your sister a few times. Most young men were in the service then, but Bill's diabetes kept him home."

Maggie scarcely knew what to say. She hadn't imagined Eve and Bill as siblings. How could she ask flat out if he and Doreen had been lovers? And why hadn't she remembered visiting this woman and her brother?

Half to herself, she said, "I should remember Bill, I guess. I sure had my head in the clouds back then."

A smile played around the corner of Eve's mouth. "You were really star-struck, all right. I remember you telling me once to call you Judy."

"That must have been just after I saw *The Wizard of Oz*," Maggie mused aloud. "Until I returned to Alden, I hadn't realized how much reality I'd missed back then."

"Yes, well—" Eve's amusement faded. "Probably it's best you didn't pay much attention to what went on around you."

Almost afraid to breathe because she suspected what might come, Maggie asked, "What do you mean?"

Eve looked down at her hands twisting in her lap.

"I owe you the truth. If you're determined to find your sister, you need to know she ran around on her husband while he fought overseas. She probably left town with some man."

"Not Bill, then."

Eve glanced up with a tiny smile. "He gave her a fling all right, or maybe it was the other way around."

"Did he father her baby?" Maggie spoke softly.

Eve's mouth fell open. "Baby?"

"You didn't know about her pregnancy?"

"Good heavens, no. Are you sure?"

Maggie nodded and looking down at the tiny ripples in the coffee that remained in her cup, fought down the tremors in her lower arm. Her voice lowered in shame. "I know that she sought an abortion."

A moment passed. Eve cleared her throat. "When was this?"

"June, nineteen forty-five."

The other woman sagged back into the couch, relief in her eyes. "Then the baby couldn't have been Bill's. She'd have been seven months along—too far gone to hide her or abort her pregnancy."

"You're sure?"

"Absolutely. Your sister lost interest in Bill shortly after Christmas that year."

Tears shimmered in Eve's dark eyes. "Bill moved to Kansas City right after they split up. He didn't come home for over a year. By then he'd married. He died a few years ago. Please don't bring his name into this? His widow and three children would be crushed to learn he'd ever stepped out with a married woman."

Still overwhelmed by the extent of her sister's marital unfaithfulness, Maggie could only nod her head in affirmation. She could still see in her mind Johnny's expression when he admitted to saving Doreen's letters. He'd loved her so much.

Maggie's thoughts roamed to the scrapbook Johnny had mentioned. "Did Doreen ever mention a scrapbook she kept?"

Eve puckered her lips and narrowed her eyes. "Yes-s-s," she drew out the word, "Doreen showed me the book one time. Green leatherette cover. I don't remember much of what it held—dance programs, newspaper clippings, and such." Her expression saddened. "As for the notion Doreen found someone to abort the baby, and that person is behind what's been happening lately you're way off-base. Old Lady Winthrop died several years ago."

Maggie's breath caught in her throat. "You know the abortionist's identity?"

Eve's lips tightened, her gaze sliding everywhere to avoid Maggie's. "That woman left me sterile," she whispered. "Only your sister knew about my own pregnancy when Gerald went overseas. The idea of being left alone to raise a child terrified me. I can't believe my selfishness in hiding it from Gerry—" she said on a sob.

When she finally looked at Maggie, the woman's eyes revealed how many ways hearts could be broken, lives shattered. At least only she, Maggie, suffered from her own mistakes.

At least up to now. She couldn't avoid opening the trunk forever.

The smile she gave Eve Trent belied the weight in Maggie's chest. She patted the woman's hand. "Don't worry. I'm good with secrets."

Out in the car again, relating Eve Trent's story, she left out the woman's heartbreaking admission. When she'd finished, she said only half in jest, "Guy Warner, either I have a double scotch on the rocks, or a hot fudge sundae with whipped cream and nuts—or you're going to witness an episode of the screaming meemees."

He drove to the nearest soda fountain, where molten chocolate blended with cold vanilla ice cream worked its magic. After scooping in a few hurried mouthfuls, Maggie rested her elbows on the black marble counter and watching him enjoy his milkshake, smiled. How many such moments had she and her sister shared in the wire-backed chairs around the round tables at Danby Drug in Alden? Countless. Simpler treats back then. Simpler life.

Or so it had seemed to a child.

"I'm afraid Doreen gave little thought to her marriage vows," she reflected aloud, and at her companion's quizzical expression, added, "God only knows who fathered Doreen's baby."

Guy lifted his straw, mouthing a blob of ice cream off the lower end, and then angled a glance her way. "You noticed absolutely nothing of her loose behavior at the time?"

Intense green lights in his soft hazel eyes flashed "go" signals that coaxed her into remembrance. She nodded. "I understand now why I couldn't enter my sister's bedroom at night without knocking, then being told to come in. And why Doreen played her radio until all hours. I suspect now she had a visitor." Maggie finished her sundae, licked the chocolate smear off the back of her spoon, and dropped it into the empty dish.

The handle clinked against heavy crystal. "I don't know, Guy. Maybe Doreen isn't dead but is somewhere living happily ever after in sin."

Guy slurped the last of his shake through his straw and then nodded.

"Even if she made mistakes," Maggie went on, "I hope she's alive." Pausing, she sighed. "I don't suppose I'll ever learn the whole truth."

"Maybe so, maybe not. You said Eve knew about the scrapbook."

"Yeah. But if it held photographs of guys other than Johnny, Eve doesn't remember them."

Though Maggie saw her own discouragement mirrored in the deputy's eyes, he said, "It wouldn't hurt for us to have a look for ourselves." He gave the soda jerk two dollars and told her to keep the change, then turned to Maggie. "First chance I get, I'll pin Fate down about the scrapbook. Least he can do is make an effort to look for it."

On their way out to the car, Guy scanned the street in both directions before lengthening his stride, checking for the green sedan that had followed them from Alden, Maggie guessed. He didn't speak until they were about a block down the road.

"If Doreen slept around," he said, "Folly Halperin almost certainly knew about it. She knows everybody and everything."

"Do you suppose she knew about Doreen's pregnancy?"

"Wouldn't doubt it a bit."

"Then why won't she come forward?"

"Probably for the same reason she didn't mention the trouble between the Rices over the Simpson property. You can bet she knew about it—the woman is a shameless gossip—but I've never heard her utter a single tidbit regarding any of the upper-crust families whose homes she cleans."

"So, you think we should look for Doreen's lover among the households of Folly's present and former employers?"

He nodded.

Maggie gave him two thumbs-up. "Let's do it as soon as we get back to Alden."

He turned onto a street lined with department stores in front of which pedestrians hurried along with Christmas packages under their arms. Warmth crept into her heart. Hardly more than a week ago, she'd thought America would never recover from the trauma of President Kennedy's assassination. "But the system works," she mused aloud. "The country and its people go forward despite talk of conspiracy and defeat."

"Conspiracy?" Warner angled a glance her way, his brow rumpled in confusion.

She laughed. "Sorry. Thinking out loud about the supposed third shot. From the grassy knoll—we're so fortunate to live in America where a transition in leadership goes smoothly no matter the circumstance that brings that change."

Unexpectedly, he swerved into a parking lot beside an imposing bank building.

Maggie grabbed the handhold inside the car door. "What?" She looked around for some threat.

Leaning over, he kissed her on the cheek, then on the lips. Cool and firm at first, tasting of strawberry ice cream, his mouth warmed over hers. Bongo drums pattered in her chest.

She came up for air, gasping, "Well, yes."

Rusty red eyebrows cocked, he asked, "What were you saying a while ago about going to talk to Folly as soon as we get back to Alden?"

"A woman can change her mind. Let's go home."

They'd gone maybe two blocks before thoughts of the trunk awaiting them at the cabin inserted themselves into fantasies his kiss had aroused. Desire's ashes blew out the Studebaker's open window to mingle with smoke spiraling from curbside leaf piles raked from artfully landscaped suburban yards.

The mood changed once on the open road where he kept checking the rearview mirror, his obvious concern about the reporter's sedan weighing Maggie down with guilt for drawing attention to Guy's place of refuge.

Along valleys and over wooded hills, trees waved branches lonely for summer garb. Rocks bared their teeth against the winter to come. Shivering in the Indian Summer breeze that poured through the open windows, Maggie came to a decision. When Guy started to turn onto the boundary road that would carry them around town to the lodge grounds and his cabin, she reached for the wheel. "Take me to the sheriff's office."

He blocked her hand. Tapped the brake. "Are you nuts?"

"The only way to get that news-hound off our back is through Sheriff Turkeson."

"I don't know how you expect him to help. Besides, we'll be seen together."

"You know as well as I do that half the town knows I'm in your custody." At the next corner, she grasped his shoulder. "Please, Guy. Trust me to know what's right in this instance."

Huffing in exasperation, he turned toward Main Street. "You have more than a vague notion how you're going to get the Turk to call off the reporter, then," he declared.

"Slightly more. Do you have any acting talent?"

"I've played one kind of role or another since the day I left Toledo."

"Then stay sharp. Once I get your boss on the defensive, we'll have to ad lib like the dickens to take things the direction we want them to go."

His expression that of a man who needed an antacid, he muttered doubts all the way to the sheriff's office. They found him bent over his desk, shuffling papers.

Glancing up slack-jawed, he slammed the desk with his fists and shot to his feet. "What the hell do you two think—" he sputtered into silence, but fixed Maggie with dark eyes so like Dr. Xavier's that her knees turned to water.

She drew enough Joan Crawford starch into her soul to remain standing. "I think it's time I stopped slinking around like a skunk-shot dog, and you, Sheriff Turkeson, started spending as much time trying to find the real killer in this town as you've spent scapegoating me."

"The hell!" He slammed the desk again, palms open. Papers scattered. "I've followed every lead in this case, from the phony baloney Chance Halperin and Paula Rice are trying to shift off on one another, to the vandalism on Rice's construction site. Old man Halperin, I'd guess—sugarin' them gas tanks at the construction site to get even for little brother over the easement squabble." He grabbed a breath.

Guy's startled, "Old man Halperin did that?" left Maggie seeking some meaning in the exchange while Turkeson barked an ugly laugh.

"I'm telling you this, Warner." Leaning across the desk, the sheriff supported himself on one hand and tapped the badge on his deputy's chest with the other. "Either stay out of my way on this case, or I'll pin that damn star on someone who will."

His lips chiseled stone, Guy unpinned the badge and held it out.

Wait a minute, Maggie wanted to say. *The script is going south here.* A pointed look from the ex-deputy sent her a message of its own. *Your cue, Babe.*

A prompter whispering a reply from stage left would have been welcome. Instead Maggie plucked something doable out of her cartwheeling thoughts, gave herself a couple of beats to steady herself, and then said, "How about this? You could put me in the hotel with a guard on my door. The reporter who's been dogging us around will love that story slant." She stared over his shoulder and plucked a headline from thin air: "*Sheriff Fires Deputy for Seeking Truth in Case Against Actress.*"

Red blotched the sheriff's cheeks. He eyeballed the badge in the deputy's hand as if the shiny metal object had sprouted twitching feet and antennae. After a moment he pushed Guy's hand back. "Keep the damned badge." He turned on Maggie. "As for you— first thing tomorrow I'm taking you over to Tulsa. If you won't show some concern for your own neck, then by Gawd I'll find someone in the sheriff's department over there who will."

Her heart plummeted, but she got her chin up and

issued a counter-threat. "You do that," she blurted before the thought had fully developed, and improvised, "I'll go to Tulsa, but only after I give that reporter the interview he wants."

"You stay away from that damned reporter."

"Only as long as I remain in Deputy Warner's custody."

The staring match that ensued ended on a shrug from Turkeson. "So be it. But you can't go back to Chance Halperin's place."

Guy huffed up. "So that's it! Chance pressured you to get us off his property."

"He made a reasonable request." Turkeson jerked open the center drawer in his desk. "Now this," he said, displaying a sheet of paper, "is what I call pressure."

Bold and black on the page, random-sized letters cut from newspaper headlines shouted an ultimatum: *Get an indictment against the murdering bitch from Hollywood or start looking for another job.*

His blind obsession with her guilt emptied Maggie's lungs in a long sigh. "Why can't you accept what this really means?"

"I'm sure you'll be happy to set me straight."

Hands on her hips, she did just that, concluding with the booby-trap left in Guy's stove. His obvious shock at that news turned him on Guy, who showed Turkeson his palms. "Hear her out."

Maggie shook her head in exasperation. "How can you be so nearsighted. I raise questions about my sister's whereabouts, her former husband dies in a way that makes it look bad for me, and when that doesn't put me out of commission someone tries to kill me—twice."

He snatched the letter from the deputy and shook it at her. "A petition to get me out of office is already circulating. It wouldn't surprise me to find out that whoever sent this warning had no part in that action. This kind, Miss Dorsey—" his tone belittled her stage name. "This kind of man doesn't bother with petitions. This kind plants booby traps."

"But my sister—"

"I know about your sister's baby problem," he said, barking a laugh. "Those who take me for a fool, get fooled. You two have cut some pretty fancy didoes through the middle of my investigation, but it's kinda like the old story about the turtle and the rabbit. I plod along, but I get there."

His forefinger scolded them in turn. "Hear this, now. Until I've got something stronger to go on than your hunch that Doreen Rice met some terrible end in Alden, Maggie remains the chief suspect in Johnny Rice's death." The outthrust digit zeroed in on Guy.

"Move her into the Morning Glory. There's an empty apartment across from Folly's. Has two bedrooms," he sneered, "if you need two. Stay with her, Warner. Any time I check, I'd better see that old Studebaker out front, else I'll assign her to someone who knows how to follow orders."

Maggie would have protested had Guy's hand on her arm not propelled her toward the door.

She glanced back at the sheriff. "I meant what I said about talking to that reporter unless you get him off our backs."

Once outside, she stopped. Guy kept going, tugging her toward the car.

"But Guy, we can't stay at the hotel."

He inserted her into the passenger seat.

"Shut up in that stuffy old place we'll never learn who fathered Doreen's baby."

"You'll be right across from Folly. You can work on her." He closed the door firmly.

Maggie cranked down the window. "Folly won't tell me a thing."

He came around and settled into the driver's seat.

She leaned back, arms crossed over her chest. "I won't go to that hotel."

He swiveled around, raking his fingers through his hair. "Jeez, Maggie. For once will you trust *me* to figure something out?"

Despite his anger, his eyes holding hers quickened her heartbeat. She could not, dare not, fall in love. Dragging her gaze away, she stared down at her hands, twisting them in her lap.

Neither she, nor Guy spoke again until they reached the lodge grounds.

He pulled into the graveled lot that fronted the cedar lodge and the groundskeeper's cabin she'd called home for the past ten days. He stopped and turned off the engine. "I wish I'd had the delivery man take the trunk to the hotel after all. Now I'll have to borrow a pickup to move it."

The trunk. Maggie's heart skipped a beat and then raced ahead. *Word would fly, as it always did in Alden. Turkeson would hear. He'd get a warrant and rifle through her belongings.*

The realization slashed through Maggie's earlier reluctance for Guy to see those things. He had to know the worst about her before they moved into the hotel, but once he did, he'd almost certainly leave town.

Tears burned her eyes as she opened the door and hurried ahead of him.

Chapter 22

Her trunk still sat near the front door. Key in hand, she knelt there, quaking inside, but desperate to learn if she could keep his trust. If he left town, she'd be alone in hostile territory.

She fumbled with the lock, the sound drawing Guy's glance from the stove where he stoked up the fire. He hiked an eyebrow. "You opening that now? Better to get on over to the hotel, don't you think?"

"There's time."

He started emptying the refrigerator while she took out the apothecary kit. Similar to a modern attaché case, but deeper and wider, the satchel opened at the top. Her steps heavy with dread, she carried the case to the table where her icy fingers struggled with the buckles that secured the closure.

Guy unloaded the milk, jam, and pickle jar from the crook of his arm into a box then came over. The case's contents drew him closer, touching the tiny balance scales, the mortar and pestle and then the pill tile. Maggie held her breath.

When his attention turned to the assorted glass containers secured to the inner walls by narrow leather bands, she heard his soft whistle. "What have we here, Maggie?"

"Frontier doctors carried their own prescription labs."

He selected a vial of fine, yellowish granules and studied the label. "Elm Bark Powder?" He made a face. "Like bark from a tree?"

Safe territory, she told herself. Explain everything as matter-of-factly as she could about the old remedies and she'd be all right. The knowledge steadied her voice. "Mixed with hot water, the powder is an effective cough suppressant."

"Hmm," Guy pooched his mouth and nodded his head. "This belonged to Dr. Xavier, then?"

A simple question, but one that opened too many side-roads to the darkest corners of Maggie's past. Dry-mouthed, she went to the sink for a glass of water, chugged it down, and then began to tell him the easiest part. "Xavier's keepsake. He was a snake oil salesman, not a real doctor. The case belonged to his father who practiced medicine in the late nineteenth century."

"The huckster thought well of his budding star to give you a family heirloom," he said, fitting the vial back into its loop and selecting the one next to it. "Adonis Root?" Now what might that have cured?"

Adonis being a legendary Greek lover, of course. No need to comment, her heart pounding too hard to speak anyway as he continued his explorations. He indicated a sizeable brown bottle labeled *Bromide of Potassium*.

Cod Liver Oil," she said.

He grimaced. "Oh yes. Mother spooned that nasty stuff down my gullet every time she thought I 'looked puny,' as she put it."

Maggie tried to smile, but he'd be asking tougher questions soon.

What is it?" he asked. "You look like you'd seen a

ghost."

"Read them all," she whispered, her mouth parched.

The furrows in his forehead deepened. He chose from a row of smaller glass containers. "Sodium Salicylate?"

"For headaches."

"Senna. . ." He chuckled. "This one I know about too—a laxative."

She closed her eyes while he continued in rapid succession: "Alcohol. Hydrobromic Acid. Sulphate of Strychnine—"

Hearing his indrawn breath, she held hers, knowing what remained in the case.

"Belladonna?" he went on. "Digitalis? My God, Maggie. Some of this stuff is poison."

No need to look up—his shock clanged like a bell in her head. When she knew she must respond, doubt sheathed in ice met her gaze. She swallowed hard.

"Like some of the other stuff, Belladonna is deadly only in certain quantities, and most has been used in medicine and cosmetics in the past." She snatched a bottle of jojoba oil from a partitioned corner in the bottom of the case. "This is innocuous, but it is one of the ingredients I use in my face cream."

"Umm," he murmured, continuing his explorations. He withdrew a small bottle. "*Arsenic trioxide?*"

"Not an ingredient I use in anything, but at one time face powder included arsenic to lighten the complexion." Her heart knocking against her rib cage, she said hurriedly, "That container was empty when I took the case from Xavier—"

"*Took* the case?"

Blood drummed in her ears. "I...I...meant to say, 'when Xavier gave me the bag for a keepsake.' You're right, he did think a lot of me." Despite knowing Guy wouldn't be fooled, she couldn't stop herself. "When I went away, he gave me this as a memento of my years with the show."

"In what year?"

"Nineteen forty-seven. I had just turned thirteen. I hid in the back of a rodeo cowboy's pickup and—"

"You ran away? How could he have given you a farewell gift if you ran away?"

Lips clamped tight, Maggie sprang from the floor and reached for the telephone on the nearby student chair. Guy trapped her hand on the receiver.

"Who are you calling?"

"I've been a fool to come this far without an attorney." She tried to twist free of his grip, sobbing, "Please. I have to call my agent. He'll send a lawyer."

He released her wrist, but grasped her shoulders, turning her to meet the accusation in his eyes.

"Did you kill Johnny Rice?"

"No, I did not," she said, her head high, her conscience clear on that one true thing.

"What is it, then? 'Trust you,' you keep saying. For God's sake, Maggie, for once would just level with me?"

She opened her mouth. Closed it.

"Maggie?"

Secrets cloistered in the deepest shadows of her heart for almost nineteen years uncoiled and ripped from her throat. "All right. I poisoned Dr. Xavier. He murdered his supposed wife, and then he...he...and when I couldn't bear it any longer, I dumped what remained of the arsenic, in that case, into his soup. I just meant to make him sick enough so I could get away."

A white line crept around Guy's lips.

Released abruptly, she staggered against the telephone chair, the impact jarring a ding from the instrument. Her hands over her face, she collapsed into the seat and braced for his recriminations.

The silence that ensued bloated into a presence more unbearable than hateful words. The pressure crushed her spirit, and she spoke into her sweaty palms. "Wherever you planned to go before I moved in here, your instincts to run were dead on. I'm the worst possible news you could imagine."

Silence.

She looked up then, using her eyes to plead from the depths of her being: *Trust me, this one time above all, don't leave me.* From the dry cave of her mouth, she rasped, "Please, don't tell Turkeson about this empty vial. He'll never believe I didn't have some of the stuff on me when I came to town. I won't have a prayer of learning what happened to Doreen."

Guy erupted from his frozen silence, flinging his arms wide. "The hell with Doreen. Do you think I've stuck my neck clear out to Christmas in this case because I give a friggin' damn about your round-heeled sister?"

Maggie gasped.

"That's right. I care about you, Maggie. Or at least I care about the real woman that sometimes trickles out around your half-truths and manipulations." He jerked a chair around from the kitchen table and straddled the seat, his knuckles white grasping the padded backrest. She barely heard him say, "Why don't you tell me the whole story and let me decide for myself what to tell Turk?"

A moment's consideration and a dollop of hope convinced her that trust worked both ways, and she began with the bitterest pill she'd ever had to choke down. "I should have run away from the medicine show long before I did—" her voice broke.

Guy waited, expressionless.

"I turned twelve a week after we left Alden. I'd performed with several other children while the show played here. A crowd favorite." The smile Maggie managed felt like a taut rubber band. "Doreen wisely refused when the Xaviers invited me to join them on the road a while. Later, out of the blue when they were ready to move on, she changed her mind. She said she'd come for me on my birthday, July Fourth."

"Doreen didn't show up."

"No. And by August, Xavier had Linette and me doing things in private that I knew must be wrong."

Pain sizzled up into Maggie's wrists, drawing her attention to her fists clenched white between her knees. She tried to relax, but could not, for the mind-stills of herself and the older woman in the trailer's tiny studio where portrait lamps beamed hot on naked flesh. Still staring down at her locked hands, she murmured, "The pictures had started innocently enough—pretty little portraits. Then he told me all the big Hollywood stars included nude photos in their portfolios. He said early experience would help me later—that I'd learn to accept the process—and then Linette began posing with me—"

The guttural sound from Guy drew her attention to the storm in his eyes. Aware that the rest of her story might rip away the last shred of his trust, Maggie could no longer contain the emotional poison that had eaten at her for so long. "Audiences loved me. I loved the applause. Linette played the piano, and after we incorporated my song and dance routine into Xavier's pitch for his vitamin and iron elixir, we couldn't work the crowd fast enough to supply the demand."

Guy stood, pushing aside the chair he'd straddled, the turmoil in his expression softened to compassion. He reached down to her hands, still locked between her knees, and clasping them, lifted her into his arms.

The worst yet to come, she gave way to shame while he stroked her back. "I dreamed of *Stardom*," she sobbed, "so when he demanded different poses—ones that left me feeling dirty—I chose denial."

The gentle hand paused mid-caress. "Did she force you—"

"No!" Maggie caught a breath and steadied her voice. "Linette liked men—especially Xavier with those piercing dark eyes of his." The shudder that raked her loosed another sob. "Most women would consider such a man good-looking I suppose. To this day I can't bear a man with such eyes."

"Odd you picked up on Xavier's character and your older sister didn't."

"In the beginning my excitement over the opportunity to be on stage, blinded me. Anyway, Doreen…we all…thought Xavier and Linette were husband and wife. They certainly acted like it after he started photographing us together and I didn't realize why they became so lovey-dovey after those sessions."

Guy murmured something unintelligible, but decidedly angry. Maggie drew away and wiped her nose with the back of her wrist, anger sparked in her too. "After he killed her, for no reason I could imagine back then, I learned the unpleasant truth. Johnny had already come and gone without me. I'd seen him in the audience, but he hadn't so much as come to me to say hello."

"He did lie, then. Telling everyone in town how he'd failed to find you."

"Xavier told me that Johnny paid him to keep me with the show a while longer, explaining he and Doreen needed privacy to rebuild their relationship after he returned from overseas. The war had been over for some time then, most of the soldiers were back home. I had no idea about such things and believed Xavier's story until I returned to Alden last week. Johnny told me that morning that he'd been persuaded to leave me with the show, 'because I loved performing so much.'" Maggie paused, dreading what remained to be told. A log in Old Firebelly fell apart, causing them both to jump and then to laugh without humor.

After a moment, Guy said, "Go on."

She told him how Linette had loved brandied fruit, which Xavier did not, and that Maggie wouldn't even try. "The bastard made the stuff to please Linette. He didn't know, but I'd seen him add something powdery to the mixture. Months later, I found the apothecary case in the back of his closet. When I saw the arsenic, the bottle, and how little it held, I remembered what I'd seen him do. I knew the stuff had sickened Linette."

Clearly taken aback, Guy said, "You hadn't suspected anything when she died so violently?"

"Linette didn't suffer the way Johnny did. She just wasted away"

"I think that happens with small doses over a long period," put in Guy.

She nodded. "Anyway, we played in a little burg in Texas when she died. People thought she and Xavier were my parents. Everyone made a fuss over us. Turned out for a nice funeral.

"Not long after she died, Xavier began slipping into my bed at night to comfort me, telling me he knew how much I missed her, and I did for the most part because she treated me kindly." Feeling tears hot in her eyes again, Maggie blinked them away and went on. "Xavier had the camera rigged on a tripod so that he could—"

She collapsed into the kitchen chair Guy had turned around earlier.

He whirled and stomped over to the stove. Jerked up the poker. Flung open the door on the firebox and jabbed the flames to a roaring blaze. "Damn, damn, damn the bastard to burn in hell!"

"I should have run away that very night," Maggie said, studying a knot on the varnished pine wall at the far end of the room. "I stayed as long as I did because my love for the stage overpowered shame."

The door on the stove clanged shut. Footsteps approached, and the familiar scent of Old Spice aftershave drew close. Looking at him, she saw tenderness that wrapped her heart in warm mist as he knelt at her feet.

She touched his cheek. "By the time I realized that those photographs had absolutely nothing to do with my future as an actress I didn't know how to stop what Xavier thrived—and profited on."

"He sold the photos?"

"At first only those of me and Linette. Then, the second winter in Springfield, times got hard. The traveling medicine show was becoming a thing of the past. You remember how after the war things changed as people moved around more and became more sophisticated?"

"More worldly than sophisticated, I'd say."

"The innocence that had added to my stage appeal early on had perished. Bookings dropped." Maggie drew a deep breath. "A man who bought one of the photos came to the house. He must have been seventy-five years old at least."

Swearing softly, Guy gathered her from the telephone chair and down into his arms. Seated on the floor, he held her close, his chin rested atop her head.

"I actually heard the old goat ask Xavier to let him pose with me in a photo," she quavered.

"He what?" Drawing back, Guy looked down through eyes that spat fire. "The bastard didn't make you do it?"

"Xavier wanted me all to himself. I'd hated Doreen and Johnny for abandoning me, but no more than I hated what I had become. I meant to escape and make trouble for them any way possible, even if it meant showing the photographs to some preacher or law officer and blaming my sister for abandoning me."

Guy reminded her, "You were actually a prisoner."

"Xavier *did* let me do the grocery shopping while he sat outside in his old gray sedan. I held back a dollar here and there. When I had twenty, I stuffed some clothes into a pillowcase and hid it on the back porch. I intended to put just enough arsenic into his stew to make him sick so I could get away."

She shook her head. "I couldn't *believe* how sick he got—vomiting all over the couch, then clutching his belly and falling on the floor. He begged me to fetch a doctor, but I stood frozen in shock until he started convulsing."

"What did you do then?"

"I ran. Just as I ran out on Johnny when he lay dying. I knew I'd be blamed because of the argument over the property transfer." Maggie lowered her head to Guy's chest. "I'll never get over leaving him so sick."

"You ran from the past," Guy said, stroking her hair.

"I've done that since that night in Springfield."

"But you called the ambulance for Johnny Rice."

"Then I left him alone to die."

She thought everything had been said until Guy remarked, "I find it odd that a girl so young could commit murder and escape as easily as you said you did. You'd have been missed. The police would have put out an APB."

How Tex the cowboy had sheltered, respected, and kept her safe, Maggie felt too exhausted to explain. Wrapped in a sense of homecoming, she listened to the fire crackle and felt the tightness in her throat ease a bit.

After a while, he asked, "Did it ever occur to you that Xavier might not have died?"

Open-mouthed with shock, Maggie considered, discarded, and considered again the possibility that the man had survived. She sat up. "You think maybe—" Simply to dare hope that murder didn't number among her sins in life came too hard to express.

With a little boost up, Guy gave her hand a squeeze. He sprang to his feet. "You start packing your things for our move to the hotel, then. And I'll make some calls to Springfield."

An hour later, they knew Dr. Xavier had not died—at least not in the summer of 1947. Maggie, meanwhile, had stowed the apothecary case in her trunk and locked it. While she retrieved her luggage from the hallway closet and started taking her clothes off the hangers to pack, the idea that her abuser might still be abusing, blazed in her chest. At Guy's pronouncement, she said, "I'm going to find the old bastard, and don't look so flabbergasted—Springfield is less than four hours away. You scrounge up something for me to drive and cover for me here. I'll leave tonight."

Guy, still holding the receiver, dropped it into the phone's cradle and held up both hands, palms out. "Whoa! Not on my watch you'll not sashay off on that kind of wild goose chase."

"Not so wild. He lived in the house that belonged to his father before him. Why wouldn't he still be there?"

As if unable to argue with that logic, he said nothing more, but the firm line of his lips signaled further resistance ahead. She put her suitcases on the bed in his room to pack for their move to the hotel, and when she'd finished, carried everything to the open front door. Guy, feeding the cats on the stoop, glanced up, unsmiling.

He slammed the screen door coming in. "I can't imagine why you'd want to set eyes on that piece of shit ever again."

Maggie dropped her suitcase and cosmetic bag. Grasping his wrist, she said through clenched teeth, "I don't want to share the same air in a room with such filth. But telling you my story a while ago I realized what absolute power Xavier has held over me since my twelfth birthday when Doreen failed to show up. Even believing him dead he controlled my thoughts and my reactions to others." She relaxed her grip. "Until you came along," she whispered over a catch in her throat, "I never knew a man I trusted enough to really give myself to heart and soul—not even Tex Avant."

Standing loose now, his expression open, he asked, "Who is Tex Avant, then?"

"A trick roper who traveled the rodeo circuit. I hid in the back of his truck the night I ran away." A cold breeze puffed through the screen door, making her shiver.

Guy closed the door. "Tell me the rest. I'll wash up the breakfast dishes while you talk."

"I'll dry."

He took the dishpan and one to rinse in from under the kitchen sink and filled both with steaming hot water. "Wasn't your cowboy curious about a runaway girl?" He squirted detergent into one pan and started washing a plate.

"I told Tex my parents were dead. That the aunt I lived with didn't want me."

Guy swished the plate through the second pan and handed it over.

She toweled it dry, rubbing off a speck of egg yolk stuck in the blue leaf design around the plate's border. She held it up. "Cupboard? Or are we packing the dishes?"

"Cupboard. Apartments in the hotel are furnished…so, Tex didn't question your story about the aunt?"

"He was lonely too. Cared for me like a brother until he took a bit part in a western movie. He died in a freak accident on location."

"After that what did you do?"

"Worked as a gofer on the set. Later, I assisted a make-up artist. Eventually, a director took me under his wing."

Scrubbing a spatula, Guy angled a narrow-eyed glance her way. "Everyone knows the reputation directors have when it comes to ambitious young actresses."

Maggie snorted. "Scaff Russell would be a happier, wealthier agent today had I been willing to sleep my way to success. He invested a lot of time in me because he once dreamed I'd win the Oscar for best actress." Maggie uttered a wry chuckle. "I think he must have eaten some bad liverwurst at the studio commissary before he had that dream."

"I'm still afraid I don't get how seeing Xavier will diminish his power over you. Couldn't it make matters worse?"

"Would coming face to face with a tiger be more terrifying than hearing it stalk you in the bushes? Besides—" she dropped the dried spatula into a drawer, "Xavier might know more about my sister's final days in Alden than he told Johnny. Something changed Doreen's mind about letting me accompany the medicine show."

No sooner had she expressed the notion when a possible reason struck her. "Do you suppose he gave her what she couldn't get from the Danbys at the drugstore?"

"An abortive drug?"

She nodded.

"Why would he confide in you if he kept that from Johnny?"

"Maybe if I threaten to show the police one of the photographs he took of me and Linette?"

The casserole dish Guy held above the dishpan almost slipped from his hands. He made a quick save and then glanced at Maggie, wide-eyed. "You still have one of the pictures?"

"No. But Xavier won't know that."

Chapter 23

Loblolly Hill Nursing Center in Springfield stood among spreading oaks to which clung a few brown leaves. Freeze-dried zinnias flanked steps leading up to a veranda, the flowers no more brittle than Maggie felt at sight of the old man whittling in one of the rocking chairs lined up on the porch. Stomach churning, she angled a glance at Guy, thankful for the junkyard dog in him. He'd refused to let her face Xavier alone.

The whittler leaned forward and gave them a snaggle-toothed smile.

Not Xavier, thank goodness. Under the bill of the man's plaid corduroy cap, his eyes peered back, rheumy gray rather than black. He nodded. "Howdy."

Although she tried her best to smile, Maggie's lips trembled instead.

Guy nodded at the old gentleman. "Good morning, sir. Fine one, isn't it, then?"

"Let's get on with this," Maggie whispered.

Already past noon, their day in Springfield had started at a convenience store where the old Xavier house had stood. Best the store manager knew, the man lived in a nursing home. Guy's third phone call located him. "The doctor will be glad of a visitor," they'd been told. "Whom shall I tell him to expect?"

Retribution, Maggie had longed to say, but curbed her response. "I want to surprise him. Just say that an old acquaintance is coming to call."

Leaving the oldster on the porch to his solitary whittling, she and Guy stepped into the home's overheated reception area. An atmosphere heavy with disinfectant didn't mask the urine undertone. To their right, a young woman looked up from her desk.

"We're here to see Dr. Claude Xavier," Maggie said, appalled by how out of breath she sounded. "Mr. Warner here phoned earlier."

The woman nodded and spoke into the intercom. "Yvonne? Dr. Xavier's visitors are here." Moments later rubber soles squeaking on the tiled floor signaled someone's approach. The nurse, a motherly type with heavily permed hair, led them through a living area where several residents sat in wing chairs upholstered in floral plastic. They all glanced up from watching Monte Hall ask some contestant in a clown suit to choose a door, and seeing no one of interest, wilted in disappointment.

Six frail women occupied wheelchairs, one keen eyed, the others slumped in sleep or lost in dementia. The nurse hustled Maggie and Guy through the room into a corridor. She led them past open doors that exhaled fusty odors so thick that Maggie sensed them sucking at her feet. She held Guy's hand more tightly.

Ahead, their chubby escort prattled on—this and that about the weather, the tragic events in Dallas, how Jackie bore up at the funeral, and that precious little John John, saluting the coffin.

In the deepest part of the building, at the last door, she said, "Dr. Xavier's room," her attempt to smile more a grimace.

So, the old man hasn't changed. Maggie had made

it this far on automatic pilot. Now, her reflexes pulled her back. Outside the door, her feet stone, she thought her heart would knock a hole in her chest.

A gentle push from her companion, and a murmured, "A tiger in the bush, Babe," got her going.

The man in the wheelchair pinioned her with eyes dark as hell's basement in a cherub-shaped face.

The deepest whiskey glass had never shaken that lecherous gaze from her memory.

Shrunken, his Einstein hair white and limned by winter sun pouring through an unshaded window, he appeared downright saintly. Except for the eyes.

"You have company," the nurse intoned, her hands dragonflies alighting, flying away to smooth the velvet lapels of his maroon robe, and finally the patchwork lap robe over his knees.

Then the woman hustled from the room.

Her haste told Maggie that despite his years, Claude Xavier remained an unsavory piece of humankind. At least he no longer remained a threat to the young.

The man's penetrating gaze flitted after the nurse, ratcheted to Maggie. She advanced a few steps. He nodded, as if in recognition.

For the first time in her life, Maggie felt the empty head other actors had described to her as stage fright. "Break a leg," she said under her breath, then drew a ragged, deep breath.

"Hello, you old bastard."

His eyes darted about in their sockets. All the while, he nodded, and under the lap robe, his hands shook with tremors. Drool hung on his lower lip.

"Who…are…you, and what…do…you want of

me?"

He hadn't nodded but suffered with palsy. *Divine justice.*

But if Xavier's body had failed him, his mind clearly hadn't. Onyx pupils burned with suspicion. "Who…are you?"

"Maggie Simpson," she quavered, paused, and drew a breath. "I'm here to show you that not only did I survive your filthy influence, I've figured out how much stronger and better a human being I am that you could ever dream I might become."

His trembling hands appeared to skip a beat before he, too, visibly regrouped. "Maggie." The utterance slid over her, oily, clinging. For the space of several minutes, mutual hatred crackled in the room.

Shattering in their clarity, a thousand ugly scenes leaped from Maggie's burial ground of ugly memories.

His eyes, reading her, plundered her shame.

The blood that scorched her cheeks jerked her to the present where she donned indifference. Guy nudged her shoulder.

"Doreen. Remember?"

"Yes," she began, "about my sister—" seeing the old man nod, she faltered.

His gnarled hand snaked from beneath the lap robe and pointed a crooked finger at Guy. "Your husband…there…how does…he…like the…things I…uh…taught—"

Maggie saw Guy's fist knot at his side. He stepped forward.

She touched his shoulder. "This old piece of shit isn't worth the trouble you'd get if you knocked his face down." She curled her lips in disgust. "He's nothing. A round. Empty. Zero."

Muttering something about the devil's shit, Guy retreated.

The old man narrowed his gaze on Maggie. "Murdering…bitch. Almost…got…job done, but I ne…ver…told."

"Of course not." Maggie wondered why she'd never considered before, that telling on her he'd have risked exposure, even jail—the worst fate a child molester can experience. The realization unraveled the knot inside her. Years of guilt soared up, out through the window toward the trash dumpster there, self-recrimination one more discard among cardboard boxes, empty milk cartons, and rotund garbage bags. She met the old man's regard head-on and found her voice.

"And you," she said, "will do well to cooperate now. Tell me what you know of my sister's situation when she turned me over to you."

Lower, his head bobbed, settled lower and lower until his chin rested on his chest. "Be damned."

"You be damned," she fired back. "It isn't too late for me to ruin what little life you have left. I know you poisoned Linette."

The old man's palms, dancing on his knees knocked the little quilt to the floor. Scrawny fingers fluttered, flew, until he dropped them into his lap where his hands twitched like dying rats. Staring down at them, he began to speak.

Doreen, he told her haltingly, came to him for an abortive after the show's opening night in Alden. He refused her, but Maggie had been one of the first children coming forward to audition for a skit in the next night's show. Two days later he gave Doreen what she wanted and bragged up Maggie's performances, saying how well the customers liked her and how she deserved the opportunity to hone her skills by traveling with the show for a few days.

To his surprise, Doreen hadn't used the drug after all. The day the show left town, she told him her lover wanted her to have the baby, and that they planned a short trip together to work out how they might eventually marry.

Doreen had said she hoped Maggie wouldn't be too much trouble for the Xaviers to look after for a week or so.

At this point in his story, the old man lifted cruel eyes. Clearly intended to gouge her soul, the look merely reaffirmed her triumph over his evil.

She glanced at Guy, who stared at the other man as if he were a pile of rotted offal. "Come on, Guy." She tugged him toward the door. "There's no tiger after all—just the droppings one left behind."

Turned to go, she glanced at his bureau beside the door. Seated on the chest, her back to the wall, the doll in the pink net tutu released memories that trapped Maggie's breath in her lungs. She whooshed it out and pointed. "The doll." In a cheap, black plastic frame beside the ballerina, the black and white image of a young girl holding the doll prickled the hair on Maggie's arms.

Guy stepped over, peering at the image. "You?"

She nodded. "Get me out of here." *One step. Two.* Maggie hesitated, pivoted, snatched the photograph, and clasped it to her chest.

"No!" Xavier's cry nipped at her heels as she

marched from the door and down the corridor. "Mine!" He bleated the word again and again until she and Guy rounded a corner into blessed silence. Still, she couldn't stop shaking and staggered against Guy. He wrapped one arm around her waist. On jellied legs, she made it with him past the watching eyes in the front gathering area and out onto the veranda.

She filled her lungs with crisp, pure air, the inhalation a shudder.

"You okay?" Guy asked, his eyes soft as morning mist.

She nodded.

The old man on the porch looked up from his whittling. This time, she acknowledged him with a smile and gestured at the wooden object in his hands.

"Pretty good work," she observed. "A dog?"

He beamed with pleasure. "Pointer."

Maggie stepped closer. "My friend here, is a wood carver too."

"That so?" Rheumy eyes appraised her companion. "What's your specialty, son?"

"Miniature cars and trucks."

"And he's pretty good at it," Maggie said.

"I haven't whittled much lately," said Guy, giving her a grin. "Busy with other things."

The glint in his eyes warmed her right down to her toes in the black suede pumps. He too, must have been thinking about their first night together, him whittling while they sat near the fire, and the lovemaking that followed.

"You two sweethearts?"

Maggie stifled a peal of laughter. *Leave it to the little ones and the old folks not to beat around the bush.*

"Just good friends," she said as they moved away. Guy cast the old man an exaggerated wink.

"Traitor," she whispered, falling into step beside him. He chuckled off and on until they reached the asphalt parking lot where he boosted her into the cab of the old pickup he'd borrowed. The springs shrieked, the upholstery exhaling dust and the rancid odor of old cigarette smoke. After he'd climbed into the driver's side, she relinquished the photo.

"This belongs to a time I'm not going to let matter any longer, except maybe as a way to help us learn what really became of my sister."

He rumpled his brow. "And how might it help?"

"That doll was a gift from someone—Doreen wouldn't say who—that last spring we spent together."

"You were eleven years old."

"Almost twelve."

He placed the faded black and white photo on the dashboard and then started the old Ford's engine.

"I'd really outgrown dolls," Maggie reflected. "I loved it anyway, because a ballerina seemed almost the same as an actress. Plus, what could be more exciting than an Easter gift from a secret admirer?" She cast the scene in her mind—her sister beautiful in new finery. "Doreen pranced around in a fancy outfit from the same mysterious friend. A peplum dress." Seeing his perplexed expression, she laughed and said, "A peplum is a flounce attached to a belt and is worn over a slim skirt."

The engine coughed and tried to expire, but Guy finessed the accelerator. The old heap jerked forward, jarring the photo off the dashboard. Maggie caught it midair.

"A flounce," he said then.

She gave him an eyeroll.

He grinned.

"Okay. A length of gathered material shorter than the skirt."

Another grin—better than any tonic Maggie remembered from the medicine show's inventory.

"I'm glad you came here with me," she told him, then mused aloud. "The style would have disguised Doreen's pregnancy for a time. The navy-blue fabric had white polka dots. She dolled it up with a white straw hat, red shoes, and a matching handbag. Impressed an eleven-year-old, I can tell you."

"A rich lover, then."

"I don't know. Nothing she said then gave me that impression. I didn't even realize the gifts came from a man, but they must have."

Maggie studied the photograph of herself as a child, innocent in gingham. "Xavier shot this soon after we left Alden. Later, I despised the doll because it reminded me of Doreen's betrayal."

The old truck coughed and sputtered onto the street. Brakes squealed at the first stoplight.

Maggie tilted an eyebrow. "This old piece of junk won't conk out on us before we get back to Alden, I hope."

His unrestrained laughter at that delighted her as always, but he didn't promise they'd get home. The light turned green. Once Guy had coaxed the pickup forward again, he shot Maggie a glance. "Does Xavier's story make you wonder if Doreen and her lover might simply have gone away together and decided to stay?"

It was the kind of happily-ever-after ending

Maggie hoped might yet put the wrap on the drama of her life, and Doreen's, but she'd not fallen for sweet music and soft laughter. "You're forgetting about Doreen's pearl ear studs from old Halperin's shed. She wouldn't have left town without them. Xavier's story only makes me wonder who fathered Doreen's baby, and if he had murder in mind, rather than matrimony."

"Maybe Johnny subconsciously linked his wife to some guy through that scrapbook. Otherwise, why did he mention it to you?"

"The needle in the proverbial haystack."

They approached the turn onto their highway back to Alden.

Maggie caught a glance from gray-green eyes reckless as a teenager's locked on a drag strip. He said, "Whatever cock-and-bull story Xavier told to explain his illness, there'll be no record of your part in it. We could just turn the other way. Start fresh somewhere far from Alden." Irony touched his smile. "It isn't as if fresh starts are new to either of us, and sooner or later I'm going to have to make one again, with or without you."

For a couple of heartbeats, Maggie dreamed the impossible dream, then heaved a sigh. "It wouldn't work, Guy. I could run again, but unanswered questions about Doreen would haunt my life forever."

They jolted through a pothole in the road, rattling a fender. "Damn," Guy swore and then said, "You're assuming there is a clear answer, Maggie. You've already risked more than you've gotten out of this crusade of yours."

Her crusade? Resentment prickled in her throat, or was it wounded pride? "I couldn't hope for a bigger reward than staring down Xavier as I did."

Guy nodded, his expression chastened.

"What's more," she continued, "consider all I've learned about my sister. Rather than a distant someone to blame for all my troubles, she has become a real woman again—one who laughed and loved—loved not always wisely or well, but deeply. And best of all, she didn't discard her unborn child, or toss me aside. She meant to fetch me from *The Health and Happiness Revue* as she'd promised. I feel it here." Maggie touched her chest over her heart.

"Only you don't really know that, do you?" The reckless glint had faded from his eyes. "You won't know for sure until you prove someone killed her. And every day you spend searching for that proof puts you at risk of being charged in Rice's death."

****

Sheriff Turkeson figured his deputy and the actress had been gone a good six hours when he discovered their absence. Halfway through his first cup of coffee of the day, he'd received a call from Ray Evans, who expressed second thoughts about lending the deputy his pickup truck. Warner had come asking to borrow the old Ford about eleven o'clock the previous night.

The deputy had told Evans the Studebaker needed a valve job, and that he had important business over in Missouri. Had left some earnest money in an envelope in case something happened that he didn't get back on Friday as promised.

"Hell, Turk," Evans said hotly, "I didn't know nothing about that stuff between your deputy and that actress woman until Irene got home from work at the hospital over in Tulsa this morning and told me what she heard at the beauty shop the other day. I always figured Warner for an ace sort of fella, you know? Kept mum about the good fishing hole over on Turkey Creek I'd told him about."

Turkeson bit back the damns and hells that nudged his lips, thanked the man, and hung up.

Evans would understand his abrupt response when word got out about Helen.

When he'd called, Helen had just placed a plate of perfectly cooked bacon and eggs on the table in front of Turkeson. On his way to answer the phone, he'd heard her say that she'd filed for divorce. He'd hardly been able to talk to Evans over the knot in his throat.

By the time he hung up the receiver, the knot strained with accusations he wanted to hurl at Helen, but did not. In the kitchen he found her washing breakfast utensils in the kitchen sink. Noting how gracefully her neck curved beneath the long, smooth coil of dark hair at its nape, he couldn't speak for wanting to tell her how much he loved her and begging her to stay.

Pride turned him around. He stalked through the living room with its Early American furnishings to the coat rack near the door. As if observing someone else's hand, he noticed how the fingers shook retrieving the brown jacket to his uniform, and then his Stetson.

The lawman in him finally took charge, leapfrogging his thoughts to the work cut out for him by his deputy's foolish disregard for authority.

Maybe Randall Turkeson couldn't handle his wife, but by God he'll show 'em he can handle the sheriff's department.

Leaving the house, he checked his watch. Seven-thirty a.m. At the hotel he found Deputy Warner's Studebaker parked and probably mechanically sound. He held little doubt that the man would be back for that car. As for the woman, Turkeson figured she had caught the bus out of town.

He rang up Judge Roller and persuaded him that Maggie's things were fair game for a warrant to search both the apartment in the hotel, as well as the groundskeeper's cabin at Halperin's lodge. At five past eleven he emerged from the hotel, wearing a smile and carrying the damning evidence he'd found in the woman's trunk.

What's more, he thought he might find the right words to convince his wife to stay. After issuing an APB for Evans's pickup and its occupants, he started practicing what he'd say to Helen and headed home for an early lunch.

The house echoed with emptiness. Lingering scents of the bacon she'd cooked earlier, and her flowery perfume in the bedroom, taunted him. Sheriff Turkeson sat down on the edge of their neatly made bed and wept.

Chapter 24

On the drive back to Alden, Maggie had pondered Guy's remark about the need for proof of Doreen's death. She couldn't decide if the greater pain would be to know her sister died in some ugly way or to go on believing she lived and had, in fact, abandoned Maggie all those years ago.

She stared into the light that sliced the darkness ahead, the truck's headlamps illuminating only asphalt and a sliver of roadside ditch. On the curves, the beam shot into the woods, revealing the occasional abandoned house whose sagging front porches and empty windows intrigued her with questions about people gone away.

The effect brought to mind how she and Guy caught glimpses of the truth about Doreen through the thicket of deception nurtured around her through the years, and the frustration Maggie felt about the unknown that remained.

When the steady glimmer of Alden's streetlights appeared through breaks in the trees, they met a vehicle that bypassed them, then swung across the roadway to follow. Red and blue lights flashed in the pickup's rearview mirror. Maggie glanced at Guy his face eerie in the green glow from the speedometer.

"Shit." Guy's rare invective tightened the noose around her heart. He guided the truck to a stop on the bumpy shoulder, the patrol car behind them. Guy's fatigue settled deeper into worry lines on his brow.

"Maybe it's nothing, Guy. Maybe you were speeding."

"In this heap?" He clasped her hand, his palm sweaty while they watched a flashlight beam dance toward them through frost-browned weeds.

"Not a word about Xavier," Guy warned, cranking down his window.

As if she could have forced a sound past the stone in her throat.

Thirty minutes later, standing opposite Turkeson at his desk, she saw the open apothecary case among scattered papers, dirty coffee mugs and sandwich wrappers. He held the empty arsenic bottle, triumph hot in his smile.

"I can explain—" she choked out.

Guy applied gentle pressure to her arm. "Not without an attorney, Maggie." Dizzied by blood rushing into her head, she nodded. The sheriff's face darkened. He pointed at the deputy.

"Warner, you cocky bastard. I don't know where the hell Chance Halperin found the likes of you, but I'd bet my last nickel you'd been kicked off a police force somewhere."

"Don't bet what you can't afford to lose." Despite his calm reply, the white ring around Warner's mouth warned Maggie that an eruption boiled in his chest. She flung him a cautionary glance.

Turkeson turned on her.

"And you—" he said.

Heart in her throat, she retreated a step.

"—you made a pretty picture, swearing before the

D. A. last week, how you'd abide by whatever conditions he set on that stolen vehicle charge if he'd let you out of jail. You didn't have the slightest notion you'd keep your word, did you?"

The sigh she barely managed, brightened his eyes with satisfaction. He said, "I should have known. Hell, you're a damned actress." He leaned back in his chair. "I'll not waste breath asking why you chased off to Missouri. You couldn't say a word I'd believe."

Guy his target now, Turkeson glared. "What kind of lawman, even a rogue, would carry a murder suspect across state lines and be stupid enough to come back?"

"One smart enough to realize everything about Rice's murder shouts 'cover-up killing.' One curious enough about how and why Doreen Rice vanished without a trace that I can see through the idle gossip this hick town feeds on." Both hands planted on the desk, leaning across, he added, "Let me remind you Maggie hasn't been charged with murder, which means she can go any damn where she pleases. And at best, the evidence you claim in that empty bottle is circumstantial."

At that lengthy indictment of the Turk's case against her, Maggie stifled the desire to give Guy a big hug. She took satisfaction in the purple that crept up from beneath the older man's knotted brown tie into his cheeks, and finally his forehead.

He stood, eye to eye with Guy. "Are your pants so damned hot for the damned woman that they've fogged your damned brain? She carries around a poison lab and you still—"

"I don't carry it around," Maggie wedged into his diatribe, her cheeks burning now. "And some of the stuff, I use to make my own face creams and the like." She withdrew a small bottle. "Some of this benzoin, for instance, mixed with pure alcohol, distilled water and glycerin is the recipe for a lotion that's older than your grandmother, but still effective for clarifying the skin."

Turkeson thrust the arsenic container under her nose. "And this?"

Her heart thudded. "Victorian ladies swore by that for creating the perfect pale skin so in vogue back then." Pausing, she flapped her hand dismissively. "Besides, that bottle has been empty for—"

Guy saved her from herself. "You damned well know you're out of line here, Turk. She needn't say another word without legal counsel."

"Then you'd best get a lawyer in here, pronto. Miss Dorsey has some tough questions to answer."

"Chance Halperin, then?" said Guy, glancing her way.

She shook her head.

He lifted his shoulders, hands open. "Should we call your agent again?"

The resignation she heard matched what she felt, but Scaff Russell could probably come up with a decent attorney, which seemed wiser than choosing someone at random. Guy's hesitancy made it plain that he feared Russell would sic the reporter on them again.

"Well?" Sheriff Turkeson exclaimed.

Maggie flinched and drew a shaky breath. "I'll find someone out of Tulsa."

****

One o'clock on a December morning left much to be desired for a man alone in a cabin so recently filled with the scents, smiles, and sheer audacity of a woman on a mission that had captivated Guy Warner as completely as it had Maggie Simpson.

He retrieved the pink silk kimono puddled on the hallway floor where someone, probably Turkeson, had dropped it while searching the cabin. Why had she left it here when they moved their things to the Morning Glory? Had she felt some premonition? Guy had never imagined this depth of failure—her jailed, he, stripped of his badge, ordered to stay away from her.

He crumpled the robe's soft silk against his face, inhaled her fragrance, and felt his last ounce of strength evaporate. More than thirty-six hours without sleep muddled his thoughts, and with heavy steps, he plodded to the bedroom. He fell, fully clothed, across the bare mattress.

Why hadn't he argued down her decision to pick an attorney from the phone directory? What kind of pansy would abandon the woman he loved out of fear for himself?

The question plagued him but exhaustion won what remained of the night. His uneasy slumber tortured him with visions of her before a jury.

****

Attorney Robert Jamison didn't impress Maggie at first glance. All feet, elbows, and Adams apple in his cheap gabardine suit, he lacked only a placard around his neck: *Fresh Out of Law School.*

To his credit he showed up within hours after she called. The toast and coffee she'd managed to eat off her breakfast tray roiled in her stomach, but she offered her hand and smiled as if the sight of him renewed her confidence. "Thank you for coming so quickly."

His firm handshake heartened her.

He said, "From what I've learned about your situation here, I considered time of the essence."

A moment's silent appraisal followed, during which Maggie heard papers rattle from the direction of Turkeson's desk.

Jamison glanced toward the chest high room divider that separated the cell from his office space. "Sheriff." Authority rang in his tone.

Turkeson stood.

The attorney said, "If you would step outside, please."

"But the radio—"

"I know the codes. Should an emergency call come in, I'll apprise you." He spun around then, leaving the sheriff to scowl at his back.

"Now, Miss Dorsey, or if you prefer, Miss Simpson?"

"Maggie is fine."

He patted the cot, lofting a musty smell from the old army blanket. "Sit beside me here while you bring me up to speed so I can determine how best I can assist you."

She sat, every muscle taut with dread of all she must reveal. "You need to know I haven't much money, not enough for bail, or for a retainer."

Although a bit thin, his respondent smile made her feel better. "At this point in my career I need clients more than I need money," he said, withdrawing a notebook and pen from his shiny black briefcase.

"There's so much to tell—"

"The beginning is always a good place to start."

Maggie began there, telling him how she left Alden in 1945 and what followed through the subsequent turning points in her life. Her account ended with her visit to the nursing home.

If any sordid detail shocked Jamison, he didn't show it. He asked a few questions, nodded occasionally, jotted notes on a yellow legal pad.

"So you see," she said, watching him write, "why I can't explain the empty arsenic—"

"But that's exactly what you must do at the right time."

Fear's icy fingers tightened around her throat.

The lawyer's keen blue eyes probed her fears. "Your reluctance is justified, Maggie. And while it sounds absurd to feed a pig corn when he's content with table scraps, that empty container represents a mere thread of circumstantial evidence against you in Mr. Rice's death. I can't think of a judge in this district who won't be fair-minded about the circumstances you describe. In any event, I'm glad you're locked up."

Stunned, Maggie leaped to her feet and pointed at the cell door. "I think you'd better leave, Mr. Jamison. I obviously made a mistake believing anyone in this part of the world might care about my welfare. I need to get out of this place. Continue my search for the truth."

Jamison remained seated. "Need I remind you of the two attempts on your life? Once people know Sheriff Turkeson has no real case against you, whoever killed your brother-in-law, and very probably your sister as well, will be even more determined to stop your meddling."

"I'm not even sure Doreen is dead."

"Let's assume that for the moment."

Wilted by his calm demeanor, she plunked down onto the cot again.

He nodded. "If you are as near as you think to finding some answers, this is the safest place for you right now."

"But how can I just stay here and do nothing?"

"Think of it as staying here to help your friend."

A lean-faced young man, the attorney's features softened at the bewilderment she couldn't hide.

"Don't you think Mr. Warner holds a better chance of finding the murderer if he isn't hampered by the need to protect you as well?"

****

An insistent pounding at the door dragged Guy Warner from the deep sleep he'd finally achieved. One eye open, he peered at the bedside clock. *Eight a.m.?* He blinked the haze from his vision and glanced out into the hallway while the knocking and yowling of cats persisted.

"Yeah. Yeah." He muttered curses all the way to the front door, which he jerked open to a sight no man should face before at least two cups of coffee. The hungry cats flanked the tallest, gawkiest young man Guy had seen anywhere off a high school basketball court.

The beanstalk wore a gray fedora. When he introduced himself as Maggie's attorney, Guy groaned inwardly.

Ten minutes later at the same threshold, the cats sated on tuna, slept in the sun, and Guy's attitude had taken a one hundred and eighty-degree turn. The rawboned young man in the ill-fitting gray suit seated across from him at the chrome dinette had made his case that Maggie in jail was safer than in the hotel apartment they'd moved into before leaving for

Springfield.

Guy had laughed outright at Jamison's description of Sheriff Turkeson trying to decipher his prisoner's newfound contentment. "I'll bet old Turk is still leaning back in his chair sucking his teeth over that one," he remarked. "As for Maggie, you have a golden tongue for sure, persuading her to stay put."

"She didn't easily concede."

"Promised you she'd go straight to the apartment, stay there if you could get her out of jail, didn't she?"

"I didn't let her get as far as a promise I doubted she'd keep."

Unable to suppress an eyeroll, Guy said, "Means well, Maggie does, but has little patience with legal process. Goes off on these tangents."

Jamison chuckled. "For all her meddling, she places a lot of confidence in you, sir."

"I'm afraid I failed her this morning," said Guy, shaking his head. "I promised to search Fate Halperin's house for that scrapbook, first thing—and it's almost eleven o'clock."

The lawyer pushed back in his chair and retrieved his fedora from the end of the table. "She told me about the memento. Frankly, I think if you find it at all, it won't likely provide a substantial lead."

"I hope you didn't tell Maggie that. She's about out of hope." Rising, Guy extended his hand across the table. The attorney gave it a firm shake and, donning his fedora, started for the front door.

He turned, adding, "I suggested she concentrate on memories surrounding the photograph she took from Xavier. Anything she can recall about the doll or the gifts to Doreen, or the woman's emotional state at the time might prove helpful."

"After more than eighteen years?"

Jamison opened the door. "Twenty-two years ago, at age six, I received a Red Ryder BB gun for Christmas. I can close my eyes today and see the holly design on the wrapping paper."

****

The confrontation outside Maggie's cell pitted Sheriff Turkeson against the nasty little man Maggie remembered as Case Murray. Again, she became the bone gnawed over in the heat of anger. A petition Murray delivered called for the sheriff's resignation for his inefficient handling of the John Rice murder case. That the town's favorite candidate for Rice's poisoning sat not fifteen feet away on the cot in her cell, did nothing to temper Murray's ire.

"I hear you've got her goddamned poison case there, and that empty bottle that held the stuff. Why the hell haven't you filed murder charges?"

Turkeson all but chortled. "You're behind the curve, Murray. It's done."

Maggie watched the other man grapple with the knowledge he'd somehow missed the juiciest tidbit served up for Aldenites to chew on since she hit town.

"Now," said Turkeson, slapping the desk "some of you smart guys come up with something more than circumstantial evidence."

"You have the poison bottle."

"Two thousand miles away when Johnny died."

"She probably carried the stuff here in an aspirin box," argued Murray.

"Find me the box." Disinterest droned in the sheriff's remark.

"Okay, so she wrapped the stuff in a piece of paper, dumped it into Johnny's decanter, then flushed the paper down the crapper."

"That's exactly what I think happened. And that, Murray, is assumption. I need evidence."

"Get off your ass and find it then," Murray growled, reaching into his coat pocket and whipping out a folded sheet of paper. He thrust it at the sheriff. "I'm supposed to deliver this." Empathy had crept into his tone. "Hell, folks like you in this town, Turk. We all feel bad that Helen ran out. Don't make us petition for a recall."

After the man left, Maggie heard Turkeson phone Chance Halperin to arrange a meeting. The part of her that respected the attorney for helping Guy gave thanks that Halperin had never come here. He'd also advised Guy against participating in her efforts to find out what happened to Doreen—going so far as to suggest he leave town.

Sam, the dispatcher, arrived to relieve Sheriff Turkeson for lunch and bring Maggie a tray. Even the Morning Glory's excellent ham and beans over cornbread stuck in her throat like old peanut butter. When she'd swallowed as much of it as she could, she lay back on the cot and stared at the bars on the window above her bed. Slumberous after a night without sleep, she tried in vain to concentrate on Jamison's recommendations, but her thoughts spun back to her arrival in Alden and how she'd changed in eleven days.

She had found a measure of relief from guilt, but the greater focus had become obsession to find justice for Doreen. She'd been able to forgive Johnny at least. Wouldn't any reasonable person expect a man who hadn't seen his wife in a decade or more to seek legal closure so he could at least remarry?

She wished she could tell him what she'd learned and apologize for misjudging him.

****

Guy emerged from the woods path. Through the horizontal boards that formed the corral, he could see Fate Halperin's red bicycle on his front porch, but the old man's van was nowhere in sight. Barnyard smells drifted from the corral where a swaybacked cow stood munching her cud. She mooed at Guy as he walked through her domain.

Approaching the house, he hallooed.

Nothing stirred, except the light breeze that worried the bare branches of a lilac bush in the back yard. He hallooed again. Silence.

No one in rural Oklahoma locked their doors. Anyway, on his earlier visit Guy had seen nothing in the house that anyone would want to carry off. He did wish he felt less guilty about snooping through Halperin's things though. After telling himself the old man could've avoided the need for this if he'd shown the slightest interest in helping find the scrapbook, Guy opened the door to the enclosed back porch.

Air soupy with the stench of dust, clutter, and barnyard shoes engulfed him. Kitchen cabinets were visible beyond the window in the connecting door. At the end of the counter, a ribbon of brown paper studded with dead flies spiraled down from the ceiling. Old-fashioned flypaper? Guy had no idea the sticky strips remained on the market.

About to step inside, he heard a chuckle beyond the closed door. Frozen mid-step, his mouth as dry as ancient parchment, he cast about for an explanation for his visit until a scratching sound made him laugh. He went in. "Well good afternoon, Jefferson Davis," he greeted the Fate's pet racoon, which rose to its haunches, his tiny paws propped on the leg of Guy's chinos.

Kneeling, he stroked the animal's back. The critter's beady-eyed stare held reproach. "Sorry old buddy. I'm fresh out of peppermint sticks. Didn't expect to find you home." Guy toed him gently aside and stood. "You surely committed some serious infraction for Fate to leave you behind today. Raid the henhouse again, did you, Jeff?" Halperin complained often about his pet's taste for eggs fresh from the nest. The crime usually earned the animal a few days in the old home slammer.

The raccoon followed Guy into the living room. Clutter ruled as it had on his earlier visit. Big cartons still overflowed with faded draperies and other auction odd-lot goods. On the couch, newspapers teetered in a higher pile, and when the raccoon scrambled up to perch there, shed a few advertising inserts.

How much easier it would have been had the old man troubled himself to look for the scrapbook. Obviously too busy reading Barry Goldwater's *The Conscience of a Conservative*, open upside down on the lamp table beside the sofa. A dry orange peel curled beside the book.

Guy tackled the big cartons first, finding nothing under the linens but stained plastic storage containers and assorted ash trays. He checked a bookcase and lifted the curved top on a trunk crammed with old photos. Time and people preserved for posterity turned up in the layers, but no scrapbook. "Shit." He closed the lid on posterity's discards.

The raccoon twitched his whiskers as if to say, "You expected gold and jewels?" Guy snatched up the orange peel and threw it at him.

"Here, chew on this."

It obviously needed more flavor to occupy the animal. Jeff dogged Guy's heels at every step.

In one of the bedrooms, Jeff displayed a talent for the hunt by sniffling along the linoleum toward the closet. Inside, clothing drooped on hangers or mounded on the floor beneath hangers empty on the rod. At Guy's every turn, there sat the raccoon watching through the bandit-like black fur around his eyes.

After stepping on the critter's tail for the third time, Guy snatched him up with a snort of exasperation and carried him into the kitchen. "I need to get you involved with something tasty." On the counter along with a shredded wheat box, empty milk bottle and of all things, a shoe box full of seashells, lay an empty box that once held peppermint sticks. Shreds of cellophane clung to the carton's edges. "Here," Guy swept the carton onto the floor with his free arm, "enjoy the smell." The box fell open at the end of the counter. Guy set the animal on the floor, aiming to dash into the living room and close the connecting door, but turning, knocked down the flypaper that coiled down from the ceiling.

The raccoon pounced. Sniffed. He grabbed the strip, which stuck to his paws.

"Okay, then. Can't hurt you to get involved with that," Guy said and chuckled. He spied the box of unopened coils on a shelf above the refrigerator and tossed down a couple more before replacing the one that had fallen. Flies buzzing around dirty dishes piled in the sink assured him the strip wouldn't look brand new for long. He escaped into the living room and closed the door firmly.

The search went better without the pesky raccoon's help. A quick toss through a hallway closet yielded nothing that resembled Doreen's scrapbook. Same in the bathroom, where stacks of magazines beside the commode indicated that the old man might benefit from an occasional dose of Milk of Magnesia.

Sometime later, on his knees to look under a bed, Guy heard a commotion in the kitchen. *The old man home?* Heart pounding, he considered whether to beat it out the front door, or sit down in the living room and pretend he'd been awaiting Fate's arrival. Pretty brassy, that would be. Besides, there remained the matter of the closed door to the kitchen, and the flypaper scattered on the floor. Halperin would know that even his highly intelligent and wily pet couldn't have gotten that down.

Frozen with indecision, he recognized only animal sounds in the racket and whooshed out a long breath. An investigation revealed Jeff ensnared in the sticky flypaper, brown scraps clinging to his ears, his nose, even his tail.

"I'll bet that's the first thing you've tried to eat that fought back."

The remark earned Guy a wounded look.

Kneeling, he unwound the paper and picked off the pieces. "Sticky damn stuff," he said, gathering the mess into the semblance of a ball. He rammed it into his coat pocket to dispose of later. The wad stuck to his hand. He picked it free with his other hand, thrust it down again with his fingers. It took three tries to get the stuff into his pocket.

At three o'clock by the clock on Fate's kitchen wall, Guy had had enough of raccoons and dust bunnies and the search for an elusive old scrapbook. Outside, he paused on the back step to pull fresh, cool air into his lungs. Clouds had rolled in. Sleet peppered his cheeks. Something brushed past his leg. That quickly, a black-ringed tail and mottled black rump marked Jefferson Davis's escape.

"Damn!" Too late, Guy realized he'd stood holding open the screen door.

The raccoon was halfway to the barnyard.

Guy gave chase. "Wait," he shouted, wishing he'd brought a supply of peppermint sticks to coax him back "Here, Jeffy." Clucking his tongue didn't work any better than his pleas.

Jefferson Davis disappeared into a stand of sumac.

Chapter 25

Maggie shivered beneath a gale that blew her umbrella inside out. Startled awake from the nightmare that hadn't visited her since someone tried to smother her in her room at the Morning Glory, she studied a water stain on the ceiling. Safe in jail. She eased out a breath.

"Maggie?"

Unseen, but heard beyond the low wall that divided the cells from the sheriff's office, Sam the dispatcher snored.

"Sssst. Maggie."

The icy draft that had triggered her dream bore the whisper down from the window above her bed. The air carried the scent of Old Spice aftershave. Maggie's heart did a handspring.

"Guy?" she murmured, and boosted herself to her feet on the cot. She propped her hands against the wall, about a shoebox length away, to peer out the opening. In the gloom, his face appeared as a ghostly blur on the other side of the bars. How he had removed the pane without rousing the dispatcher didn't matter nor did the possibility of disaster in the making.

She tiptoed up to kiss him through the bars. "You're cold."

"Cold nose, warm heart." He kissed her again.

When they reluctantly moved apart, Maggie cast a

furtive glance at Sam. Tilted back in his chair, his denim-clad legs crossed at the ankles on his desk, he snored as loudly as before.

On a tight little breath, she whispered. "Did you find it? Doreen's scrapbook?"

"Sorry."

He sounded as drained as she felt. "You looked everywhere?"

"I figure he threw it away."

"Not hardly, Guy. If Fate's like his sister, he hasn't discarded as much as an empty matchbook in his entire life."

"I don't know…you'd best take your attorney's advice, then. Concentrate on the gifts you and your sister received at Easter that last year you were together…if you can dredge up any hint about who gave them."

As if she hadn't fallen asleep trying to remember. "All I can come up with is the impression of a man's voice coming from her bedroom at night."

"A gravelly voice? A wimpy one? Basso?"

After a moment's consideration with her eyes closed, Maggie came up with, "Well-modulated." Sighing, she leaned forward again, her forehead against the narrow ledge beneath the bars. She'd counted so much on finding something in the scrapbook to go on.

"Maybe Fate has the memento in his store and doesn't know it," Guy said softly, his breath warm.

She pushed herself upright and shrugged. "You could ask him again."

"Nothing doing. I accidentally let his pet raccoon run off into the woods today. He'll figure out that someone gave his house a toss and put two and two together—"

"You could maybe get a look inside his store," Maggie cut in, desperate and almost out of ideas.

The dispatcher snorted, then broke into a fit of coughing. Maggie dropped to a crouch then rolled under the blanket. The glass grated softly back into the opening as feet thudded to the floor beyond the room divider.

"Miss Dorsey?" The dispatcher sounded very near.

"Mmmpft." She peered out from under the covers, said "Ummm?" then fell back onto her pillow. It whooshed air that smelled of old chicken feathers.

Through an eyelash on the half-open lid, she saw the dispatcher outside her cell, unmoving, silent so long she feared he might hear her heart pounding. Only when he moved away did she dare draw a deep breath.

****

Sunday afternoon wasn't the optimal time for breaking and entering, Deputy Warner discovered once he set out to search Fate Halperin's second-hand store. On the walk across town, he'd seen three carloads of teenagers dragging Main. Now he confronted the large padlock on the back entrance to Halperin's junk store and wished he'd waited until dark. But that would have required a flashlight, which would've attracted attention.

He cast a final glance up and down the alleyway, shook his head in disbelief at the typical Fate Halperin array of rusted auto parts, washtubs and other oddments scattered around the shop, then set to work. By the time he'd jimmied the lock, his palms were wet inside his gloves. Motor scooters putt-putting close by ticked up his pulse. Glancing around, he stepped quickly into the moldy-smelling storeroom and put his ear against the closed door. The scooters sounded like the Cushmans that belonged to Chance Halperin's son Kent and his pal, Art Collins. They came close and fell silent.

No doubt the two were out back. Would either of them notice the open padlock?

The clink and clank of metal indicated scavenging activity and a voice, probably the Collins kid's, declared, "If there's a radiator hose in this mess, I'll eat my gym socks."

Loud puking sounds and a guffaw erupted. "You'd better be glad Uncle Fate is always right," Kent said. "If he claimed to have a hose for that old Chevy here, we'll find one." More clanking. Kent spoke again. "Too bad about old Jefferson Davis. Uncle Fate'd have come found us a hose 'cept he's so bummed out about his pet."

His pulse ticking, Guy pressed closer against the door. Jefferson Davis? What about Jefferson Davis?

"Hey, over here!" A rattle, the tinkle of glass. "I told you we'd find it." What sounded like an avalanche followed, feet crashed through the weeds around the junk and the scooters popped to life.

After the clatter receded, Guy pushed away his concern for the raccoon and asked himself what the heck he thought anyway, breaking and entering. Tomorrow he could walk into the store seeking some doodad or another and have a good look around without arousing the old man's suspicions.

The answer, of course, lay all around him in the jam-packed storeroom where a customer wouldn't ordinarily wander. He'd found Old Jeff dogging his heels in Halperin's house a nuisance, but the guilty conscience that nipped and prodded him this afternoon bothered him more. Turned out that the 'public' Fate ruled his storeroom as well as in the well-organized display areas out front. All the shelved boxes were labeled with their contents. He left, convinced that the old man knew his inventory as well as he claimed, and that it did not include Doreen's old scrapbook.

Dusk threw long shadows beneath the oaks and pines around his cabin when he returned to find two hungry cats and Chance Halperin on his front step. Eyes hard as blue marbles perused Guy's dusty clothes. "I see you've been out shaking the bushes for clues on your lady friend's behalf."

"Someone has to help her." Maggie the calico meowed and rubbed against his pants leg.

"Yes, the woman is in a real fix," the attorney said, drily, "And you hate being her knight in shining armor, don't you?"

With nothing to say in his own defense, Guy let the silence lengthen until Halperin decided to fill it. The man lowered his head and fiddled with the zipper on his gray sweatshirt. "I've been with Fate most of the afternoon. He buried Jefferson Davis yesterday."

Guy's memory served up the raccoon's escape he'd allowed and with it dread of learning what might have been the result. He knelt to scratch the calico's head. "What happened to old Jeff, then?"

"He ran off into the woods Friday. Fate searched yesterday and again this morning. He found only fur, stripped bones, and old Jeff's red leather collar."

Regret tightened Guy's throat. "How awful." He knelt, stroking the cat to hide the guilt he felt stamped on his face. He told the calico, "The fridge is bare, old girl, but I think there's a can of Puss 'n Boots left under the cabinet." Still avoiding his friend's regard, he stood and unlocked the door. He stepped aside for Halperin to enter.

The big man shivered and hugged himself. "Damn, you keep it cold in here." Nodding, Guy found the cat food, scraped it into the bowl, and tossed the empty can into the trash.

Meanwhile Halperin had a fire started in the old potbellied stove and had settled into the wooden rocker nearby. "It's especially hard on Brother because he let Jeff get away."

Guy, stepping in after feeding the cats, did a double take. Had the animal returned after he, Guy, let him get away, and escaped a second time? He hadn't sorted things out when the attorney spoke again.

"I guess Fate and Jeff were down at the barn Friday evening. Fate milked old Bessie. One minute, his pet nosed around nearby, the next minute—gone."

His bullshit antennae extended for no reason he could fathom. Guy dragged a kitchen chair close to the fire and sat forward while his friend continued.

"You can imagine Fate's grief. Those two were pals for eight years."

"That long, then."

"That long. Sister and I spent yesterday afternoon trying to perk up the poor old fellow. He loves meatloaf, and she made up a dandy one, and some scalloped potatoes. We stayed for supper."

"When you see Fate again, offer my regrets. I'll drop in on him one day soon."

The attorney narrowed his gaze. "By the way, you look like hell. Too much Maggie Simpson, I'd guess."

The remark called for a buzz-off look, to which the attorney tilted an eyebrow. "That reporter came to my house today."

Enough said, Guy figured, but of course the attorney in Chance probed.

"He had talked to Maggie."

A chill wind blew out of the Ohio mob, right into Guy's veins. He shivered. "Oh, God. What did Maggie tell him?"

****

The reporter had been gone no longer than fifteen minutes before Maggie realized her dreadful mistake. Sick at heart, she glanced at the window above her cot. How could she face Guy when he returned to report on what he turned up searching old man Halperin's store? Had her rash promise to give Alan Rinehart an exclusive interview after she'd been cleared of murder, stemmed from a subconscious need for publicity? She'd used it to rid herself of the reporter. Hadn't she?

She sat on the edge of the cot long after he'd gone, her face in her hands that sickened her with their smells of old wool from the blanket. How could she not tell Guy what she'd done? His life might depend on his leaving Alden before another day dawned. She owed him that option.

No longer able to sit, she paced. Once Guy left town, she'd have no one except Jamison on her side.

Turkeson brought her supper tray.

He eyed her from head to toe, the derision in his regard reminding her that her gray wool slacks had gone baggy in the knees and that lint speckled her black sweater. She brushed herself off and swept her bangs to the side. "I'm not hungry."

"Better eat somethin' this time."

She waved him away.

After he'd gone, Sam the dispatcher came in for his shift. Maggie tried to read one of the *Life* magazines Turkeson had brought in earlier that day. All the photo coverage of the drama around President Kennedy's assassination made her heart heavier. She turned to the few personal items she'd been allowed in her cell. A raveling on the beige sweater folded at the bottom of the bag snagged a fingernail. For lack of scissors or an emery board, much less a file, she let one of the tears that burned in her eyes, slide free. Another escaped, and then another. Silent, she wiped them away with the back of her hand.

That night, Guy appeared at the window above her cot far later than on Friday. She'd fallen into an uneasy sleep. Again, her name whispered and a cold draft from above roused her while the dispatcher snoozed undisturbed. She couldn't imagine sleeping that soundly while seated at a desk.

She stood but didn't lean near the opening for Guy's kiss as before. The accusation in his eyes twisted a dagger in her heart. "You know about the reporter." Her voice quavered.

"If you hope for a big career boost out of a story about how you've been wrongly charged, I wouldn't advise you to pose for a new set of publicity stills if I were you," he murmured. "There is no scrapbook."

No scrapbook meant no clues that might point to the identity of Doreen's lover. And little hope of learning if her sister had gone away with him or died at his hand.

Maggie's tongue lay frozen in her mouth.

"You're back to square one, then." Guy sounded as weary as she felt. She waited for him to continue, and to say he wouldn't be back. His eyes glittered green in the half-light. "I had this crazy notion you were starting to see me as something more than the cavalry."

"I do."

"We could have been a thousand miles away from here by now. I wanted to take that other highway out of Springfield."

And leave your precious Studebaker in Alden? she'd wanted to ask. "I have to know what happened to Doreen." True.

"Let your attorney find out, after which you can land that big movie role your agent is dangling."

She trapped and held his gaze. "You don't really want me to care about you, do you? You'd rather be the victim of your dedication to truth, justice, and the American way."

"If you think that, I've wasted my time this past two weeks." He disappeared from sight.

Maggie rested her head against the bottom of the window ledge, shivering, waiting to hear the glass pane grate back into place. A random absurdity floated into her mind—why glass on the outside? Inside, she could break it and slit her wrists.

At a soft rustle she looked up to see him back at the opening, resignation in his expression. "If you have any fresh ideas that might help you, I'll pass them along to Jamison. I won't promise more."

Chapter 26

Guy kept his promise to Maggie first thing Monday morning. The classified ad he placed in the local weekly requested information about a green scrapbook from the 1940s, possibly purchased at a secondhand store in Alden. The contact number reached Maggie's attorney, Robert Jamison.

Guy meant to be long gone before the ad appeared.

First, he felt bound to visit Fate Halperin's farm. The man deserved an apology of some kind. How to manage that without opening himself to suspicion in the raccoon's escape washed around in his gut as he turned into the man's driveway the next morning.

The old man, on his knees beside the lilac bush in his backyard, stacked stones into a small mound. He didn't look up when Guy drove in. Over his usual crisp overalls and shirt, Fate wore a herringbone tweed jacket. A wheelbarrow sat at his side.

The care he took in transferring stones from the barrow to his pet's resting place tightened Guy's throat. He'd helped his son Billy construct a similar monument to a pet turtle.

When Halperin finally noticed he had company, he scrambled to his feet with astonishing agility for a man well into his sixties. Thunder in his expression, and in his voice, he unleashed a torrent of obscenities. Every word a whiplash on Guy's guilt-ridden conscience, he stopped where he stood, still holding the car door open.

As the words "...stray dogs..." and "John Rankin" sorted themselves out of the tirade, Guy eased out a breath. He approached the man with his hand extended. Halperin grasped it, but his fingers trembled and he appeared drained of his fury.

"I regret my foul language," he said, "but I have warned Rankin a dozen times about those mongrels. The next time they come around my place that blue tick bitch who leads the pack gets an arrow through her heart. Anyone who shows such total lack of regard of another man's property deserves treatment in kind."

The uneasy sense that Fate wished the same treatment for Rankin pestered Guy. And what transpired here? Again, he couldn't understand why the old man hadn't told Chance about coming home to find the raccoon outside the first time. He must have realized someone had been inside the house in his absence that day.

The old man's scrutiny now made Guy feel squirmy inside. Did those eyes hold an accusatory edge?

Unexpectedly then, a rueful smile twisted Halperin's lips. He clasped Guy's hand, more warmly than the first time. "I failed to thank you for coming. How boorish." Studying the rock structure at his feet, he shook his head. "I'm afraid I'm not myself right now." He lifted a cigar-box-size rock with irregular edges from the wheelbarrow. Dozens of tiny circles covered the limestone's surface.

Guy touched the stone, curious.

Fate said, "Crinoids. Some call them sea lilies. They first appeared in the Cambrian age and became extinct during the Permian. The sections were connected then and grew from the ancient seabed. The fan-like growth on the top gives them that name. It is rare to find the extension intact in fossil form."

Interested, but more caught up in the memory of him and Billy burying the turtle, Guy crouched on his heel to help Fate cover his pet. He had to clear a burr from his throat before he could speak again. "Some people go through a lifetime without knowing what a special friend a pet can be."

An utterance that sounded as if it came from his heart escaped the old man's lips as he placed the last stone. Gnarled hands on the grave, he bowed his head.

Guy stood, unable to speak. He brushed dirt and bits of winter-dead grass from the front of his chinos. When Halperin's eyes finally met his, they brimmed with tears.

"I anticipate a sharp lapse in demand for peppermint sticks around Alden," Fate said, his voice tremulous.

A kid whistling in the dark? Guy knew the feeling and patted the man's shoulder, old age's bones there sharp through his tweed jacket. An impulse to reveal how well he understood Fate's loss passed without expression. It would open too many doors to his past.

Halperin walked with him to the Studebaker.

Its chrome trim winked in the sunlight—familiar, everyday moment that broke through Guy's sadness with a smile.

The old man caught the edge of the open door and leaned in. "I say, Deputy, Sister Folly mentioned to me that that actress woman got herself put back into jail. I regret the difficulties she created for you as well, and trust that you have learned the error of your ways for falling for her lies. Someone broke into my storage shed the day after Thanksgiving and snooped through my house Friday. I strongly suspect that woman."

"That so?"

"I assume that you finally figured out she is bad news," said Halperin.

A nod his reply, Guy drove away feeling like a heel for letting the old man drop another black ball in Maggie's box of accusations. However, what he might have said in her defense had escaped him then, and still did.

That night he stayed resolutely away from the window of her cell, and Tuesday morning rose at first light. He swept the floors with short, angry strokes that scattered more dust than they vanquished. The telephone shrilled. He almost tripped over the broom getting to it.

Larry Cole, the anthropologist in Tulsa apologized for being slow to get back to Guy. "You sure enough found yourself some human fetal remains in that well, buddy. And—" excitement crept into his voice, "you have also a proximal phalange from an adult female. Young. Early twenties, I'd say."

Guy blinked and rubbed his forehead in an effort to grasp that last remark. "Now in plain English—what the hell is a proximal phalange?"

"That part of your finger nearest your palm. Are you sure there were no longer bones among those deer hides?"

"I'm sure. Only more of that pebbly stuff."

"Think hard. It would have been small specimens—finger and toe phalanges, teeth. Material separated from remains when they were moved. And by the way, that happened recently."

As if the man at the other end of the line could see, Guy shook his head. He could think of nothing, except to wonder who might have moved the skeleton.

"You still there?"

"You threw me for a loop, Cole. Someone moved the bones?"

"It makes sense from this end. You're asking a lot of questions around Alden. If the material came from your friend's sister, her killer probably panicked. Figured someone as familiar with the neighborhood as you two would think to look in the well or cistern, whatever purpose that pit originally served. I'm guessing cistern because—"

"Why would he leave the hides behind?" Guy interjected.

"Too bulky maybe? I don't know. But when you find the rest of the bones, you'll likely find deer hair with them. You're on the downhill run, buddy."

He felt more like a man on a cliff with invisible hands at his back. How could he abandon Maggie at this point?

"Warner?" Cole said in his ear.

"I worry how Maggie will take this, and what comes next."

"Well, get cracking, man."

"I'm afraid I'll have to leave that up to her lawyer. I'm leaving town."

"You have to be kidding."

"Sick folks back at home."

"Oh?"

So, the explanation sounded phony. Guy let it ride,

thanked the anthropologist, and rang off.

After phoning Jamison with the news, he finished cleaning house. Most of his stuff remained in boxes after his move to the hotel apartment—and back—after Turkeson jailed Maggie. Guy stacked the cartons near the open door, where the cats rubbed against the screen and yowled urgent requests of an indeterminate nature. He eyed the calico's belly and sighed. "You've been reckless again." He shook his finger at Jiggs. "You horny old rascal."

"*Yeow-r-r-r,*" Jiggs boasted.

Did feline intuition warn them of his planned departure? Who would look after them once he'd gone? He thought about the kittens running wild in the woods and heaved another sigh. "I suppose I could take you both with me."

"*Meow-r-r-r,*" both cats agreed.

Once he'd set the cabin to rights, Guy fled to the coffee shop in the Morning Glory Hotel for a good lunch and some idle conversation. He hoped the latter would ease his conscience for not bidding Maggie goodbye.

He kept a sharp eye out for the reporter's old green sedan but saw nothing of it. Arriving at the coffee shop after the usual noon crowd had drifted away, he found a counter stool beside a pint-sized man who introduced himself as a door-to-door encyclopedia salesman out of St. Louis. The waitress took Guy's order for the fried chicken special, turned to the pass-through, and spiked the ticket. The soap opera on the television mounted behind the counter reclaimed her attention.

The salesman waved his fork at the TV set. "Every day I lose two or three hours because of the darned soaps. A herd of white elephants could stampede down the street, and women don't want to hear about it until their program is over."

After Guy clucked his sympathy, conversation settled onto the Kennedy assassination—in particular the theory that there'd been a second shooter on a grassy knoll. The salesman found the theory plausible. Guy voiced disagreement, mostly to keep the conversation flowing so he didn't have to think about Maggie sitting alone in her cell.

At three o'clock, the salesman picked up his sample case and left. Guy went to fill the Studebaker's gas tank and check the oil. A domino game in progress in the filling station drew him in for the rest of the afternoon.

He got home to find Chance Halperin on his doorstep again.

Coatless in the gathering darkness, the attorney shivered in the cold.

"Jeezus Priest, Chance!" He hustled his friend inside. "You have a key. Why don't you ever just come in and stoke up the fire?"

"Tried that. Too hollow feeling in there with all those packing boxes around."

Guy poked life back into the coals in Old Firebelly and added wood. He rummaged in a packing box for the coffee pot he'd meant to use in the hotel apartment in case the scant kitchen items provided there lacked one.

When he had the brew going, his friend nodded approval. "Smells good and strong—just what I need."

"Un huh. I went to see your brother this morning."

"He told me. Thanks for thinking of him." Sadness

touched Chance's smile. "He lost family, you know."

Guy nodded.

After a moment's silence, his friend's blue eyes caught regard. "You weren't going to tell me you were leaving?"

"It's hard to tell a friend goodbye over and over." Guy filled two cups and placed them on the dinette. "Sorry not even a stale donut in the house." He sat at one end of the table, Chance at the other.

"This time you're really going." The attorney sounded pleased. Idly, he stirred his coffee, the spoon clinking in his cup. "You're smart to get out. The woman isn't worth the tenuous position you're in for sticking by her this long."

Despite his effort to stay cool, Guy felt a defensive prickle in his gut. "You assume a lot for someone who has yet to exchange a word with her as far as I know."

"I've seen enough of Maggie Simpson to know she's her sister's kind."

"I didn't think you knew Doreen well, either—"

Halperin inspected a hangnail. "I know the facts."

Guy waited to hear the man's version of truth.

"Everyone in Alden knows her fickle nature. Left the man who loved her without giving him a thought."

To waylay everything that he could reveal about that old fable, Guy took a swig of java. The scalding liquid brought tears to his eyes. He blinked and rebutted his friend without detail. "How could a man of your reputation at the bar totally accept such hearsay? You were off to learn lawyering when Doreen disappeared."

Mild as the rebuke had been, the attorney gave Guy a pointed look. "True," he finally admitted. But those who tell the story are people whose word I have no reason to doubt." He paused, lifted his coffee, and narrowed his eyes. "You've based your judgment on the testimony of a total stranger practiced at convincing others what is staged, is real." He blew into his cup, lofting the brew's aroma, sipped, and then said, "Do you blame me for celebrating your decision to move on before you step out onto your porch some morning and into the arms of one of Ed Moroni's thugs? That, my friend, would be reality."

A loud pop from the stove released a resinous fragrance. Even those heart-warming atmospherics left Guy feeling empty and wondering why. "If I need to contact you sometime in the future, it'll be all right, then," he said.

"Absolutely."

The conversation turned to where he might go, and Chance asked if he'd have financial resources enough to manage while he looked for work. Loath to admit he'd be pinched, Guy turned the topic to Sheriff Turkeson's marital problems. Halperin, as circumspect as usual when it came to matters concerning one of his clients, had nothing interesting to offer.

They shook hands across the table. "Chance said, I do appreciate you visiting Fate. Believe it or not, that's what I came here to tell you…sorry I got too busy trying to run your business to attend to my own."

Guy insisted that the attorney take his peacoat against an evening that had turned sharply colder. "I think I'll head to warmer climes. Won't need such a warm coat." They stepped out onto the porch. "You saw the little monument Fate built over old Jeff's grave, I guess."

A self-conscious grin crooked in one side of the

attorney's mouth. "Sis and I helped gather stones for it Sunday afternoon. I felt like an ass at the time, but I hoped to make Fate feel better—"

After they'd said goodbye, Guy reheated the coffee and wished he had a sibling to share his good times—and his bad. Very late that night, he woke with a start. Bolt upright on the edge of the bed, he stared into the darkness. Dreamworld and reality coalesced, a porous mesh woven of things witnessed and words spoken over the past two weeks. He flung back the covers. Moments later, layered up in warm clothes, he pulled on his Wellingtons and went to find a lantern.

Chapter 27

By Wednesday noon without word from Guy, Maggie knew she'd driven him away. She alternately castigated herself and gave thanks that out of her life, he faced less risk of discovery by Ed Moroni's thugs.

Sheriff Turkeson had spent the weekend moving into the cell next to Maggie's. His clothing rack afforded each occupant some privacy.

He'd gone out often only to return in a short while, stomping about in frustration and muttering things about the damn Monday morning quarterbacks telling him how they'd have handled "that murdering she-devil."

Maggie received her share of unwanted attention. An inordinate number of citizens stopped in to lodge complaints over barking dogs, petty thefts, and vandalism as serious as writing the "F" word in yellow chalk on the sidewalk in front of the post office. Every complainant craned his or her neck for a glimpse of Alden's notorious prisoner.

Oddly, she and her jailer started behaving like soldiers from opposing armies lost on the battlefield in a blizzard and hunkered in the same trench for warmth. The phenomenon manifested itself in small ways. He afforded her the privacy of the shower room for increasing lengths of time without standing guard outside the door. She no longer found his swarthy complexion and dark eyes, so like Dr. Xavier's, a sign she welcomed as proof that her showdown with Xavier would eventually free her of his power to control her thoughts.

Late Wednesday afternoon, a small but vicious tornado named Paula Rice swept through the office's front entrance. Her Jackie Kennedy hairdo in disarray, sans lipstick and wearing a rumpled black suit, the petite blonde stood facing the sheriff across his desk. She daggered a look at Maggie before hammering Turkeson with curses worthy a longshoreman.

Apparently, she'd returned that morning from a visit with her in Colorado and learned about the apothecary case. She pointed at the sheriff's nose. "And why haven't you called in help from the state? Someone who knows how to investigate a murder."

"You're out of line here, Mrs. Rice."

"Johnny would turn over in his grave if he knew what a joke of a sheriff his campaign donation got the county."

A loud bang indicated he'd slammed his desktop to lever himself to his feet. Maggie flinched.

The blood that suffused Turkeson's face and neck suggested an impending stroke. His reply, however, held more sadness than anger. "The John Rice I knew and admired would spin in his grave if he knew you condemned his former sister-in-law on the basis of circumstantial evidence. What's more, I'd be the laughingstock of my profession if I brought in outside help."

"Laughingstock?" Paula's giggle teetered on the edge of hysteria. "What do you think you are already? From what Folly tells me, Helen has run off with some itinerant peddler of pots and pans."

Maggie watched Turkeson's bravado leak away. He sat down heavily, the loss she glimpsed in his expression another chip in her enmity toward him. Empathy fell from her lips unbidden. "Paula is just out of her head with grief, Sheriff."

If the woman had temporarily forgotten the original object of her visit, Maggie's remark produced instant recall. Wild-eyed, the woman rounded the room divider, her boxy black handbag clutched as if ready to become a weapon. Maggie withdrew, glad of the bars that protected her. The other woman stood outside the cell, her gray eyes marbles.

For the first time Maggie entertained the probability that it had been she, Paula, who pressed that plastic bag over Maggie's face that night in her hotel room.

But that made no sense. She'd have been too distraught by grief. *Wouldn't she*? And it strained belief that she'd planted the jar of gasoline in the cabin's heating stove. Ed Moroni inserted himself into her thoughts.

Maggie wondered if she and Guy Warner were both targets, but from different threats?

Sheriff Turkeson's chair squeaked. He stood again, fatigue in every line of his body.

Maggie said, "Paula—I am truly sorry about Johnny's death. But if you would just listen to some things I've learned about Doreen—"

"Don't mention that tramp sister to me," Paula said through clenched teeth. "I'll never forgive her for breaking Johnny's heart, and I'll never forgive you for what you did to him." She burst into tears and reached into her handbag.

Maggie expected her to withdraw a tissue. Instead, a gun flashed into view. "Gun!" Maggie shouted and dropped to the cement floor. She tried to weasel under her cot, but couldn't manage.

Paula aimed the weapon and squinched her eyes shut. She hesitated an eye-blink too long. Turkeson darted to her side and struck down her arm.

The gun clattered to the floor and spun against the cell. Maggie crawled over and pulled it between the bars, her head abuzz with contradictory thoughts. She leaped to her feet.

Paula screamed and fainted. Maggie glanced down at her shaking hand. She still held the pistol, its business end pointed at the spot the woman had just vacated.

White around the mouth, Turkeson reached in and pried the gun from Maggie's grasp. She retreated to the cot and sat trembling while the sheriff locked the weapon into a desk drawer. He walked to the cell that adjoined hers. She heard water splashing in his lavatory.

A wet towel in hand, he came back and kneeling beside Johnny Rice's widow, gently bathed her face.

Maggie drew her feet up on the cot, knees clasped to her chest lest flesh and bones shake apart. Why had she listened to Robert Jamison's advice? How could anything outside these walls be more dangerous than what she had just experienced?

Paula moaned, roused, and with the sheriff's help made it to a chair opposite his desk. She collapsed, sobbing into her hands.

Too nauseated to move, Maggie couldn't summon

guilt with Jamison still trapped in her thoughts. Why hadn't she heard from him? Had either he or Guy placed the classified ad for the scrapbook? And if either had received any word from the forensics man in Tulsa, why had she received no word?

****

After an exhausting night in the woods, Guy Warner rang Larry Cole's doorbell shortly after eight a.m. The bone man came to the door blinking with sleep. One whiff from the brown grocery sack Guy handed him widened the khaki-tan eyes.

He peeked inside, wrinkled his nose, squeezed the top of the bag shut and held it aside. "Holy cow." He emphasized the *ow* in cow. "You're going to explain this, I suppose?"

After doing so, Guy withdrew the blackened old shoe from the pocket of his mackinaw. "Could you give this a look, then? It came from the same place we found the bone fragments."

Cole took it, examined the material, the shape. "A high heeled pump."

"Can you determine the original color?"

"Sure." He sidled a quizzical glance at Guy. "Do I report to you, or to the girlfriend's attorney."

"She isn't my girlfriend."

Scratching his belly, Cole yawned widely, then laughed.

****

Sheriff Turkeson, at his desk early Thursday morning, sat reading the paper. "What's this about a green scrapbook?" he called out to Maggie.

Her stomach had knotted with anticipation the moment he walked into the office with the paper folded under his arm. She'd paced to keep her anxiety in check while he read the local weekly.

"Scrapbook?" Innocence breathed out with the word.

Upon reaching her cell, Turkeson thrust the paper at her, its inky smell reaching out. He'd folded the classified section to the outside. He poked at one of the ads. "This is your Robert Jamison, isn't it?"

"My attorney, yes. What does the ad say?"

"Enough to tell me this scrapbook with its mementoes of the World War Two years, possibly purchased at a secondhand store in Alden, connects to your half-baked theories about what happened to your sister."

Half-baked had become synonymous with rejection, of which Maggie had had more than enough in her life. She turned away.

"And—" he said, "the damned scrapbook is something that might hold a lead that could get both our necks out of a noose and you're too goddamned stubborn to give yourself that kind of break because you and that goddamned Guy Warner decided I'm too stupid to be of any use." His lecture expired into a whisper.

Maggie sighed and faced him again. "I haven't seen you show much interest in saving my neck."

"I'm a fair man, Miss Dorsey. All I ask is one scrap of solid evidence that points to a second suspect in Johnny's death. If you think there's somethin' in that old scrapbook, I need to know. Locked up here and without Warner to run defense for you, you're in a hell of a tight position."

His sour expression suggested the same level of

frustration that roiled in Maggie's chest.

All that day she hoped against hope for some input from Jamison. When Turkeson brought her supper tray, she held both hands up in refusal. "I'm really not hungry. Could I call my attorney?"

"Why should I do you any favors?"

"Because you're as curious as I am whether the classified ad turned up anything."

He acquiesced. Beside him at his desk, she dialed her agent in California instead of the attorney.

She'd no more than said the word, "Scaff," when the sheriff knotted his brow.

"It's Charmaine," she blurted into the receiver, "Please, Scaff, get a competent attorney out here. I'll do whatever you—"

Turkeson tried to hit the disconnect button in the receiver's cradle. "Be damned!"

Maggie blocked his reach.

He pried the receiver from her hand.

She leaned forward, shouted into the mouthpiece, "I'm out of rope here, Scaff. If I don't get out—"

Slammed into its cradle, the receiver jostled the phone off the desk. The instrument crashed to the floor. Turkeson retrieved the base with one hand and held the receiver to his ear with the other, scowling and then slamming both parts of the phone onto the desk.

"Now you have no phone, I'd guess."

"It'll fix. But I can't fix the stupid thing you've just pulled." He marched her to her cell.

"I'm entitled to a competent lawyer." The door squawked on rusty hinges, clanged shut.

Sheriff Turkeson thrust his face so close to the bars she could tell he'd eaten the same kind of supper she declined—tuna on rye. His eyes cast daggers. "You think I want a damned city sharpster throwing his weight around my jurisdiction?"

A skimpy canvas curtain stretched from corner to corner in front of the commode afforded little privacy, but Maggie needed somewhere to escape. She sat on the cold stainless steel and listened to him bellow, "See if I do you any more favors." Murmured curses followed, after which he radioed a highway patrol trooper named Al to send a telephone repairman.

Unsure whether Scaff Russell would even respond to her appeal for help, Maggie tried all the next day to keep an open mind about Jamison. She avoided Turkeson by curling up in her blankets with a copy of *Gone with the Wind*. Never before had she felt as much empathy for Scarlett O'Hara's desperate battle to survive no matter the cost to her character.

The imposing man who swept into the sheriff's office with Scaff Russell at half-past eight that night did much to restore her faith in the male gender. Through horn-rimmed glasses, Edward Arthur Brewster's sharp blue eyes picked her over from head to toe.

"You're right, Russell. She's got great cheekbones."

Hope fell to shards at her feet. Justice might not wear gray worsted wool after all. Russell, meanwhile, bestowed his father-knows-best regard from beneath caterpillar eyebrows grayer than she'd remembered.

"All she needs," he said, "is a decent script and some good press. Both are lined up for her once you get her out of this little spot of trouble she's gotten herself into in this jerkwater town."

Maggie's confidence sank to colder depths. Had

she not been so desperate for help, she'd have demanded Turkeson show her agent and his slick lawyer the door. Her cheeks hot, a harsh rebuttal on her tongue, she managed a reasonable comeback instead. "When you hear my story, Mr. Brewster, I think you'll see that the spot of trouble I'm in isn't all that insignificant."

He fluttered a hand in dismissal. "All I need to know right now is whether or not you killed—" He glanced down at a notebook she hadn't noticed before. "John Frederick Rice."

Her heart took wing when she could say without the slightest implication of doubt, "I have never, ever in my life, killed anyone, or wanted to."

Although he appeared somewhat taken aback by her emphatic response, the attorney nodded, then glanced at Turkeson, who stood looking on through the bars. "On what charges are you holding Miss Dorsey?"

"Murder…and larceny of an automobile…and—"

"Has bail been set?"

"She doesn't want out."

"Oh, but I do," Maggie cringed inwardly at the appeal in her glance at the sheriff. Scaff withdrew a checkbook from the inside pocket of his suit coat.

Turkeson did an eyeroll. "I'll arrange a hearing. If she's freed, the judge will hold you responsible for her safety."

Maggie wondered if matters could get much worse.

How the sheriff got her a hearing in the middle of the night she attributed to his eagerness to get rid of her. For once in her life, feeling unwanted felt good.

At midnight she entered the hotel apartment in which she and Guy had originally planned to set up housekeeping before their fateful trip to Springfield. Identical in layout to Folly's across the hall, her quarters lacked only her neighbor's wealth of personal possessions. Rose-patterned chintz covered the overstuffed chairs and couch. Otherwise, the room offered little in the way of hominess.

The place even smelled empty with a gaseous undertone that drew her to the tiny cookstove in a closet-sized kitchenette where she found a crusted-over pilot light. After cleaning it, she lit the burner to heat water for tea.

A quick check of all the windows reassured her they were too far off the ground to permit entry, and well-screened. She raised a sash in both the living, and bedroom, where her things remained scattered after the sheriff's search while she and Guy were in Springfield.

The room's cell-like dimensions got little relief from the Blue Boy print that hung above the bedside table. She'd have preferred the equally famous print of the guardian angel overlooking two children.

She didn't spare a glance into the tiny, adjoining bedroom. The cot and closet Guy had briefly claimed would be as empty as her heart without his easy smile and gentle touch.

No time for mourning. Nearly two decades of surviving on her own had taught Maggie to pick up whatever broken dreams life left behind and move on.

Scarcely had the thought formed when a knock at the door challenged her resilience, setting her heart aflutter with the hope that she'd find Guy standing there.

Hope died when she opened the door on her new lawyer and Scaff Russell. Russell pushed Brewster aside and stepped into the room. His glance ricocheted from corner to corner. "We wanted to make sure you'd be safe here." His restless eyes settled their focus on the windows, the sheer panels billowing in the pine-scented night breeze.

Maggie motioned. "I'll close them in a minute. I'm fine, really."

But the men were obviously on a greater mission than securing her safety. Brewster settled into an easy chair at the far end of the couch, which angled across one corner near the windows. He rested his leather briefcase on his lap and leaned his head against the chair's back. A weary sigh gusted from his lips. He closed his eyes.

Russell glanced around once more and then plunked onto the sofa. Air whooshed from the cushions. "It does seem safe as in church," he conceded. "And God knows Eddie and I could use the sleep. Jet lag is murder."

Unable to suppress a smile at the image of the citified attorney as an "Eddie," Maggie tried to imagine even his mother calling such a stuffed shirt anything but Arthur. When he began to snore, the Eddie image clicked.

Maggie sat facing her visitors. She picked at the worn fabric on her armchair and wondered how she'd overlooked the weakness around Brewster's mouth earlier.

Her throat tightened with the fear she'd erred again, firing Jamison.

Eddie snorted awake. He blinked and straightened in the chair. Maggie faked a cough to cover a smile. Chameleon-like, the man donned arrogance. "Weary as we all are," he said, retrieving his notebook from his briefcase, "I require details about the events and your movements of the past three weeks in Alden."

Maggie complied, leaving most of Guy Warner's involvement on the cutting room floor.

The attorney jotted notes without comment. When she'd finished, he stood.

Yawning widely, Scaff Russell pushed himself up off the couch. "Let's see if this flophouse has a couple more rooms, Brewster. I wanted to tell Charmaine all about this great new role I'm lining up for her, but..." His voice trailed away on a glance at his wristwatch. "Almost one o'clock. I'm beat.

Seeing them out, Maggie felt suddenly drained. Might Arthur Edward Brewster be nothing more than an actor?

Chapter 28

Maggie awoke to distant strains of Christmas music. Wayne Newton singing about seeing his mama kissing Santa Claus? Gradually she separated snippets of nearby voices from Newton's lyrics. Disoriented, she looked for the stain on the ceiling above her cot and recognized old, yellowed ceiling paper instead. Her gaze drifted to the wall beside her bed to the Blue Boy print.

Freed, she'd slept between sheets fragrant with sunshine and fresh air. Contentment curled through her chest. The conversation she'd heard came from the hallways outside her room. After a moment she recognized the woman's voice as that of Folly Halperin.

"Thanks for mending this, Sis," a man put in, his golden tone vaguely familiar.

Chance? The attorney brother?

Folly said, "We couldn't have had Santa Claus strolling among Alden's children with a rip in the seat of his trousers, could we?" Laughter rolled, hers bright and bubbling, his low-pitched and golden.

"I'm more concerned," he remarked after their amusement subsided, "about how shocked the younger set's parents might be upon learning that the man who wants to represent them in the Oklahoma senate wears bright blue silk boxers."

More laughter.

Blood surged into Maggie's ears, drumming, impelling her from the bed. She grabbed something to wear from the tiny closet, wrinkled her nose at the gray flannel slacks that had trapped scents of old concrete and despair from her cell. They'd do. The beige sweater smelled as bad, but she pulled it on with the slacks and walking into her loafers, hurried through the living room.

Her hand lingered at the door to the hallway, the porcelain knob cold in her palm. She'd heard that smooth voice before in the cabin while Chance talked to Guy with her half-asleep nearby. *And years ago, beyond the wall that separated her bedroom from Doreen's.*

Maggie turned the knob but hesitated again. What if she were mistaken? Added to Chance's already low opinion of her, a rash and false accusation would only add to her humiliation.

But he had to be the one. Why else had Folly and Fate stymied every effort Maggie and Guy had made to get information that might reveal the identity of Doreen's lover?

She turned the knob, hesitated briefly, then looked out into the corridor. That second's delay cost her heavily. No one there.

Final indecision gone, she dashed across the hall and knocked on Folly's door.

Probably thinking that Chance had returned for some reason, Folly smiled opening the door, and then open-mouthed with surprise, stepped back reflexively.

Maggie pushed into the room. "I don't think you want to hear what I have to say where someone might eavesdrop…it's about Chance and Doreen."

The woman's pinched expression belied any possible denial. Her work-roughened hands fluttered up to her leopard-print housecoat's shawl collar, picking at it, her gaze averted.

"Chance and my sister were lovers, weren't they?"

"No!" Folly twisted her hands, tears bright in her eyes. "You're wrong, Maggie. Doreen cheated with some stranger. The photograph. I told you."

"Johnny knew nothing of such a photograph, but *you* knew something he didn't—that Doreen was pregnant that summer she disappeared."

"That's ridiculous," Folly bleated. "Why would she confide such a shameful thing to me? We were never close."

"You clean for old Doc Whitsitt now and probably did back then as well. You could have snooped through the doctor's files."

Folly glanced around as if seeking a way to make a break for it, and then, defiant, declared, "Even if I did know about her pregnancy, I couldn't identify the father."

"Don't try to tell me you didn't know about her affair with Chance. You Halperins are as close as peas in a pod." She waited a beat, then asked, "Where's the handbag, Folly?"

Eyes wide in surprise, Folly opened her mouth, then snapped it shut.

"The red alligator bag you carry. I think that's the one Chance gave Doreen at Easter that last year, when he gave me the ballerina doll. What did he do, give you the purse after he killed my sister?"

"You're insane, Maggie. I found that handbag among your sister's things when I helped Fate empty the house. He gave it to me."

Maggie blinked. What else had the older Halperin given his sister? "Did you see a scrapbook? It had a green cover. Has anyone asked you about it?"

Folly shook her head, her hands shooting out, grasping Maggie's shoulder with claw-like fingers. "Why would Chance kill your sister? He blanched white as a sheet when he heard she had gone away with that medicine show man."

Heart thudding, Maggie pushed the woman away. "Your brother gave Doreen shoes that matched the bag. Did you find them?"

"There were no shoes."

"So there. She would never have worn the shoes anywhere unless she carried the matching handbag too. What's more, I found our grandmother's earrings too, in—" She bit back what amounted to admission of trespass on Fate's property. After a moment, she said, "Doreen wore those pearl ear studs everywhere."

Sorrow added years to the older woman's face. Now focused on the red velvet mules she wore, she murmured, "Chance would never have harmed your sister, no matter how badly she wounded his heart."

"You know better. So does Fate, I'm sure. That's why the two of you panicked when it came out that my sister and I hadn't left Alden together at all."

"We only have your word on that."

"Bullfeath—" before she got the word out, Maggie remembered how easily she might have fallen victim to the poisoned bourbon. She edged back into the hallway. "Maybe the three of you conspired to kill Johnny and hoped to quiet me as well. You heard our argument. You had access to that decanter."

"You're wrong."

Her words rang true, but the woman's color rose.

"I think I'll have a chat with Sheriff Turkeson," said Maggie, and left the woman standing in the doorway, wide-eyed with dismay.

More shaken than she'd realized, Maggie fumbled with the lock on her apartment door then stood looking around for a telephone that hadn't been installed yet. She could use the pay phone in the lobby, but would Turkeson take her call?

Her feet made the decision, carrying her from the apartment at a run, through the Morning Glory's back entrance and along the stone-paved path through the garden gate into the alleyway.

Buoyed by the morning chill, she dashed down alleys remembered from childhood and sprinted through unfenced backyards.

****

Folly slammed the door behind Maggie and stared at it for several minutes. Fraught with indecision, she paced the room until she heard Maggie leave her apartment across the hall, then decided to call Fate. He picked up on the second ring.

"It's Sis." She held one hand over her ratcheting heart. "Fate—" She cleared her throat. "you won't believe this, but—"

He didn't interrupt her breathless account of Maggie's accusations. She concluded in dismay, "She thinks he killed Doreen."

His groan shook Folly to the core. Never had she heard such defeat from the Rock of the Halperin clan. He struggled to speak, blurting, "But…of course…that must be…dear God in Heaven."

Tears controlled with such effort slid hot down Folly's cheeks. Her throat closed around a sob, but she managed to choke out the rest of her horror. "He must have killed Johnny too. And tried to kill Maggie and that deputy. Oh, Brother…she intends to tell Turkeson."

She waited through another brief silence, then, "Enough tears, Sister." The family bulwark stood firm once more, giving her pause enough to hear him explain that he'd warn Chance away before the sheriff could get to him. "Now listen carefully," he said at the last, "here is what you can do to help."

****

Maggie, breathless from her sprint to the sheriff's office stared at the dispatcher in disbelief. "What do…you…mean…he isn't here?"

Sam leaned forward, elbows propped on the desk. "I mean, he's laying out traffic patterns for the Christmas parade this afternoon."

"When do you…expect him back?"

"Ma'am, we're short handed without that deputy. The Turk is gonna be busier than a three-legged dog in a chicken yard until after the parade."

Her knees buckled. She grasped the curved wooden arm on one of the chairs that faced the desk and sat down hard. At a burst of static from the dispatcher's radio, she learned forward. "You can radio him."

"Only in an emergency. Otherwise he would be mean as a cornered badger."

"This is an emergency. Don't you get it? I know who killed my sister. Chance Halperin is who! And he must have poisoned Johnny Rice and tried twice to get rid of me."

Silence. Outside, a car horn blared. Somewhere in

the distance, snare drums beat a brisk tattoo. Finally, a sideways grin slid across Sam's face. He slapped the desk and whooped with laughter. "Chance Halperin, a killer? That's the most ridiculous charge I ever heard."

All through her explanation, his closed expression signaled his interest level. When she finally gave it up, he ramped up her frustration with an eyeroll. "So, where's the *corpus delecti*? Your sister's remains?"

Her inability to answer the question left him looking smug. Out of nowhere then, Edward Arthur Brewster leaped into her thoughts. How had she forgotten she had a new lawyer, and that he and her agent had planned to take rooms in the hotel? Maggie leaped up and sprinted out into the street.

Again, she took all the shortcuts, avoided streets where she saw people carrying band uniforms or festooning flat-bed trailers with red and green crepe paper. She used the Morning Glory's front entrance and ran past the archway to the coffee shop without glancing inside.

At the reception desk, she wheezed, "I need to talk to Mr. Brewster or Mr. Russell."

The clerk blinked a few times before finding his voice. "I sent them to the Willow Inn over at Sand Springs. I'm full—a train derailed a few miles up the track from here, and I had a repair crew come in."

Checking her pockets for stray change, Maggie asked for the inn's phone number. The man rummaged in a desk drawer but glanced up to say, "By the way, a call came in for you. Guy Warner had important information about the sister you say you're in town looking for. He said to meet him in the amphitheater." His expression quizzical, the clerk added, "He said you'd know the place."

Maggie gasped. *Guy hadn't abandoned her after all.* On wings of joy, she wheeled around and dashed from the lobby. Fresh adrenaline spurred her to the woods at a fast clip, but upon entering the silent ranks of winter-bare trees, she slowed lest she trip on a root hidden on the leaf-strewn path.

She reached the abandoned homestead, averting her gaze from the once-loved wishing well that had held the deer hides. Whether or not the material in the hides had anything to do with Doreen, the spot had been reduced to a pit of discards haunted by her loss. Approaching the cedars near the old house foundation, she began to feel another human presence. The idea that Guy knew she'd pass this way and wait here instead of in the hollow crossed her mind before she remembered other times she'd sensed a watcher in these woods.

Maggie stepped more softly, every sense fine tuned.

Lines from the children's song about the Teddy bears' picnic frolicked into her head, chiding her megrims. *And me, caught for once without a disguise,* she teased herself—a whistle in the dark.

Snap. Ear-shattering, the twig broken under an unseen foot paralyzed Maggie. She faltered and almost fell. Every nerve ending electric, she tried to picture the danger—a man whose face she couldn't recall, but one whose words flowed like molten gold.

Guy hadn't left her a message at all. She'd been lured here by Chance Halperin.

Terror pushed her ahead, her thoughts on the wicked steel arrow points she'd seen in the hunting lodge. A tingle leaped into her back. She imagined a drawn bow, the missile's impact between her shoulder blades.

Her feet recognized the trail down into the bowl-like hollow, moving her forward while she scanned ahead for hiding places. Rock outcrops and winter-bare bushes dotted the natural amphitheater's floor, and on the opposite slope Folly Halperin sat upon their stone, once-upon-a-time stage.

Sister in league with the devil?

Confused, Maggie slackened her pace, stumbled, and fell to her knees. Something jabbed her knee, drawing her hand to a tear in her slacks. Even so, she kept moving, rolling off the path and behind a nearby bush. Her heart hammered. Through bare branches, she saw the other woman leap from the once-upon-a-time, make-believe stage. "What are you running from?"

"Don't...play games," Maggie panted. "I know you and Chance set me up for him to settle his problem with the Simpson women once and for all."

Folly reached out. "You're wrong. I'm just supposed to keep you here so—"

"Not...staying." Maggie scanned the hollow's slope to her right for an escape route. At the three o'clock position, tangled vines on the rim promised good cover. Hesitant, she glanced back the way she'd come, thinking her stalker might be there. No one.

Had she imagined him?

Or had he circled around to those vines, waiting for her to expose herself so he could carry out whatever plan fevered his brain. Did the danger lie up there, or behind her?

The lesser threat lay ahead. Crouched, Maggie dashed for a boulder near Folly, who, stood at the foot of the flat stone ledge.

The woman wrung her hands, her blue eyes pleaded. "Please, can't we talk? I've felt so bad about all this, but Chance has such a bright future."

"A future he denied my sister. Are you so blinded by love for your brother that you'd overlook—"

Startled by the whine of a missile past her ear, Maggie dropped onto her stomach. The object struck the boulder above her and clattered to the stony ground.

An arrow? Upon sight of the metal point, honed razor-sharp and glinting in the sun, Maggie felt her heart stutter, stop, and then gallop. The light dimmed, her world reduced to the throbbing of pulse in her ears.

"Chance?" Folly's wail scattered the darkness that threatened to engulf Maggie. She shook the cobwebs from her head and looked down to see Folly at her knees. Their gazes locked, wild disbelief in the blue eyes holding Maggie's.

"Oh, honey," Folly moaned on tremulous lips that wilted over a sob. "Are you all right? I had no idea—"

Footsteps hammered the pathway down into the hollow. Maggie glanced there, cried out, and curled down closer to the boulder

Folly leaped to her feet.

A shout rang out from above and to their left, "For the love of God, Sister, get down."

Maggie looked up at the tangled vines.

"Brother?" Folly dropped to her knees a split-second before a second arrow swished down.

Slow to realize the whimpering she thought came from Folly had crept from her own throat, Maggie crawled around the boulder for deeper cover. Sheltered on the far side of the rock, she glimpsed the man running down on the path

He wore a Santa Claus costume.

Folly scrambled around the boulder too. Shot a bewildered glance at the costumed man. "Chance?" Her confusion disintegrated into hysteria. "Oh no. What are you and our brother thinking? This is madness. *Madness.*"

Chapter 29

To Maggie's surprise, Guy Warner's off-key rendition of the Teddy bear song fell from Santa's lips. No lyrics had ever sounded more beautiful. "Guy," she cried, half-sobbing with joy and relief as she flung herself into his arms.

He hugged her tightly. "Chance and I knew that if I wore the Santa suit, Fate would mistake me for him, whatever the old man meant to do here." He touched Maggie's cheek. "You're all right, then."

She nodded, but nothing made sense. "But isn't Chance the one who—"

Folly moaned, the sound as taxed with confusion as Maggie's thoughts.

Guy said hastily, "Thank God I made it in time." He looked up at the rim. "Where is the old devil?"

"Old Devil."

"Yes, Fate Halperin."

Maggie touched her forehead to try and settle her spinning thoughts.

"But I thought…isn't it Chance who—"

"Yes, and no. He'll be along. But where's the old man?"

She pointed at the tangled vines, now above and to the left of her position opposite the path down into the hollow. "But how did you know to find me?"

"Heard you'd received a message from me. I didn't

send one and had learned enough about the Halperins to suspect a trap for you."

"But the costume...how did you—"

"Chance Halperin is clean in this nasty business...at least the current nastiness. I went looking for him after I heard you'd been summoned here. I pinned him down about a tag I found in Doreen's scrapbook—"

"You found it!"

"—the tag came off a handbag. Genuine alligator. Same as the shoe we found in the pit. I connected it to the red bag Folly carries, the one she says turned up when she helped Fate clean out Johnny's house. I figured the old man knew nothing about those gifts from his brother to Doreen, or he wouldn't have given it to his sister."

"Who had the scrapbook?" Maggie remained hung up on the fact that he'd found the scrapbook. "Why didn't you let me know you'd found it?"

He didn't reply but put his finger to her lips. "I couldn't imagine Fate and Doreen as a couple, even after finding out he had access to arsenic, and I'd just seen Chance in costume where the floats line up for the parade."

Maggie caught up with the story. "Fate set me up?" She angled another glance up at the vines.

Folly covered her ears. "No. No. No. No. No."

"He's bringing Sheriff Turkeson," said Guy.

"Oh nooo—" Folly sprang to her feet.

Guy pulled her down by the hem of her coat.

"Brother wouldn't hurt me," she blubbered.

"You can't know," said Guy. "He's operating on something deep and cold."

Her face hidden in her hands, Folly poured out her grief, her keen echoing up the hollow's slopes to haunt the woods above. Maggie gave the gooseflesh on her arms a quick rub and then drew her old friend down beside her while Guy hazarded a cautious glance around the boulder.

Maggie asked, "Do you think he's gone?"

"I think the costume rattled the old man as much as it did you two. He's still processing. It's the advantage I hoped to gain."

Praise for his cleverness teetered on the tip of Maggie's tongue when crashing sounds from above drew their attention. Fate emerged from the thicket, his old-fashioned recurved bow drawn, the arrow nocked.

He called down "Chance? I have no idea why you are here, but I am happy to see you. We must not let the bitch get away."

"Must be befuddled by the costume, then," Guy murmured.

Folly jerked free of Maggie's embrace, and leaping up waved both arms. "You're mistaken, Fate. It isn't—"

Maggie pulled the woman down and clamped a hand over her mouth.

From somewhere in his voluminous scarlet velveteen jacket, Guy produced a revolver. He knelt and peeked around the rock, his weapon trained on Halperin.

Eyelids squeezed shut, Maggie flinched at the shot. Her eyes flew open to see dust and leaves settle around the old man's feet.

Fate lowered his bow. "Brother?" He darted behind the brush.

Maggie held her breath while Guy, crouched, advanced up the slope. "Fate Halperin, Chance is bringing Sheriff Turkeson to take you in on suspicion in the deaths of Doreen and Johnny Rice, and attempts on Maggie's life."

"*Chance?*" He called again, "Brother?"

"Brother!" The word repeated, shouted now from the pathway Maggie had taken down into the hollow. There stood the younger Halperin brother with Sheriff Turkeson. The two angled off the trail to the right across the slope toward Fate's position.

The old man held his threatening stance. "Stay away Chance. This is my affair."

"Put your weapon down, Fate."

"Why didn't you stay out of this, you fool? I would have dealt with this snoopy woman—have I not always cared for you and Sister to the extent humanly possible?"

"Yes. Yes." The affirmations ripped from Folly, who darted from shelter, eluding Maggie's grasp. She struggled upslope toward Fate.

Guy and Maggie followed, their path bisecting that of the sheriff as he came puffing after Chance. The three stood together a short distance from the Halperin siblings united near the vines.

Fate's eyes were locked with those of his younger brother. "I thought my ears had failed me when you came to visit that summer and spoke of your plans to divorce Elizabeth and marry Doreen." He wilted visibly. "You had it all, Chance—the intelligence, the beautiful wife, and her influential father. And you, almost an attorney already, would have discarded everything for that nobody?"

That nobody? The words struck Maggie like hammer blows. Heat flared into her chest. A hateful rebuttal sprang into her thoughts, but Fate Halperin's crumpled expression stayed her tongue. Toppled from the family pedestal, he'd been broken into as many pieces as her life had been fractured by his actions those many years ago.

Fate addressed his brother again. "You were the first Halperin to graduate high school. We were—" His voice cracked. "Sister and I were…are…so proud of your accomplishments."

The two men stared at one another for a heartbeat before the younger shook his head, tears glistening in his eyes. "And so you…killed her?" The golden, orator's voice rattled and rent like tin in a windstorm.

Chance reached for the bow. Fate relinquished it. Tears on his cheeks, Chance tossed it into the tangled underbrush.

Maggie stepped forward to touch the grieving attorney's arm. "You truly loved my sister, didn't you?"

"More than life. When I believed she had gone away with the medicine show, I wanted to die." He gave her a tremulous smile. "You bear a strong resemblance to Doreen. I noticed it the morning I saw you asleep in the cabin."

He referred to the morning after Thanksgiving, when he'd learned that she'd been put into Guy's protective custody. "Not fully asleep," she said.

"To this day I don't know how I kept from waking you right then, begging you to tell me everything you knew about where she went."

"You'd have asked the wrong person. Doreen had promised to come for me in a couple of weeks. I never saw or heard from her after the day I left with the medicine show."

"Even when I believed she'd thrown me over for another, I loved her." Chance turned to his brother. "But I had betrayed her, telling you of our plans, and that she and I would meet to discuss them further."

Malice in his tone, Fate said, "And I sent her a note in your name, asking her to meet you much earlier. And I waited."

Maggie had been snared in the distant past by the web of deceit Fate had spun around her sister. She broke free at the word, "note."

"You forged her name on a note to Johnny, too," she blurted, the shred of empathy she'd felt for him earlier caught back into the cold knot in her chest.

Fate, chin up, relentless, opened his mouth.

Chance spoke first. "How could you kill someone so beautiful?"

"With the same weapon that took care of you with the game I put on our table. Deer are beautiful animals too."

Chance winced, as if the arrow had missed Doreen and sliced into his heart. He turned and started down the slope, his stalwart frame diminished.

Slipping and sliding in pebbles and loose earth, Maggie hastened after him. "Don't beat yourself up. Your friend Guy taught me a lot about the fallacy of borrowed guilt. You and Doreen broke wedding vows. *He*—" she flung a gesture "—defied God's law to the fullest extent possible."

Folly, who'd followed the exchange with the expression of an accident victim trying to decide whether she might live or die, covered her ears and fled down into the hollow.

Turkeson had watched open mouthed with disbelief, but the woman's flight startled him to life. He fumbled the handcuffs from the leather pocket on his belt.

"Fate Edward Halperin," he said, cuffing him as he pronounced the charge and informed him of his rights.

The sheriff took Fate by one arm, Chance by the other, and they continued down toward the wide limestone outcrop. She shouted after them. "Did you stalk my sister like the animal you are?"

No reply.

The quaver moved from her stomach into her arms and legs as she imagined Doreen's joy shattered by terror like that she, Maggie, experienced when he stalked her to the amphitheater minutes earlier. Or had Doreen sensed nothing, the arrow flying out unseen to pierce her heart?

Tears sprang hot into her eyes. Vision clouded, she stumbled, and would have fallen had not Guy wrapped his arm around her waist. "Come along then," he said. "You, alone, never failed your sister. But for you, justice would not have been possible." He hugged Maggie close. "But for you, my belief in justice might never have been restored."

She shuddered. "I hope Doreen died quickly—how much worse if she had felt someone watching."

At the bottom of the slope, the old man staggered. He made it to the rock ledge with help from his siblings and the sheriff, and there, sat gasping. Focused on him, Maggie wondered how his mind became so twisted.

A flash of insight knotted her stomach. Her gasp drew a glance from Guy. "There but for the grace of

God, go I."

Guy drew her to a stop, his hazel eyes soft. "I know you're thinking about the means you used to escape Xavier, but you were a child, desperate to escape a predator. Fate Halperin *is* a predator."

She nodded, her heart full of love for his goodness. "I'm working on forgiving myself, but it's hard."

He nodded. "You don't know this yet, Maggie, but the deer hides in your old wishing well had held human remains. Larry Cole confirmed the gravel-like material as fetal bone, and the longer bone as adult. Fate probably spied on us there Thanksgiving Day and felt pressed to move what remained of his victims."

Fresh loss sharp in her heart, she clutched the pain with her free hand. "Will we ever find her? Will my sister ever rest in peace?"

"Come along, then," Guy said. "The old bastard will tell us everything. He wants to flaunt how clever he is."

"You're more clever, Guy. You figured out enough of the story to suspect him."

Color stained his cheeks. "Didn't take a Sherlock Holmes to see unfulfilled ambition in Fate's appetite for knowledge, or complex character in someone so outwardly fastidious who lives in a pigsty."

They reached the ledge. Fate's stare scourged Maggie's companion at every step.

Guy told him, "I regret letting your pet escape when I searched the house for Doreen's scrapbook."

The poison in the old man's eyes intensified. "I suspected that someone had snooped. Did you suppose I am too stupid to know when someone disturbs my belongings?"

Turkeson turned on his former deputy. "That warrantless search can get you fired, Warner."

"You'd already fired me, remember? Besides, no one made a legal complaint." Shaking his head in dismay, he added, "Sadly, I didn't find Doreen's scrapbook that day. I regret, even more, distracting that raccoon with flypaper."

Maggie tilted her head at Guy. "Flypaper?"

His eyes never shifted from the hatred that burned in Fate's glare. "You went on to me about how that neighbor's dogs tore Old Jeff to pieces. But when I dug up the raccoon's carcass, I didn't find a scratch on it."

Fate struggled to rise. "Dug up my friend?" Cuffed to the seated sheriff, he sat down hard.

"Well, I guess I should say that I moved the rocks—and put them back. Probably not exactly as they'd been arranged before." A half-smile crossed Guy's lips. "Clever you should have noticed something different about the monument."

Obscenities and spittle flew from the old man's lips. He tugged at his restraints. "When Jefferson Davis came home Friday night, near death, I suspected whoever let him escape into the woods had deliberately given him the flypaper. I'd read up on the old stuff and knew the sticky coating contained arsenic."

A stricken expression on his face, Guy murmured, "I had no idea…"

Fate curled his lip. "Did you believe that I would not notice how the coil in the kitchen no longer held a single insect? Did you believe that I did not know how many coils I had used from the box? How stupid are you?"

"Stupid enough to give some of the stuff to your

pet to play with so he'd quit dogging my tracks, but when he got tangled up in it, not stupid enough to leave the scraps around. Those I stuck in my pocket. I had them analyzed after hearing your cock-and-bull story about some neighbor's dogs killing Jeff. Too late for poor Jeff, I learned that arsenic coated flypaper in the early days. But I wasn't too stupid to figure out that you had it in for Johnny for some reason, and—"

The old man snorted. "That property easement nonsense cost John Rice plenty in construction equipment repairs after I sugared the gas tanks. When Maggie came to town asking questions about her sister, I did what I knew best for the Halperin name. I slipped in the back door while Johnny and Paula ate supper. And Old Jeff—" Fate's voice cracked. He cleared his throat. "My old friend enjoyed the outing."

"And left a mess my foot slipped in when I watched him and Maggie outside that window!" Guy exclaimed. No one reacted, all eyes on Chance.

He'd studied the tassels on his loafers for much of his brother's confession. Now slumped lower, he hid his face behind his hands. Folly burst into a fresh spate of tears.

Maggie expected Fate to say something to comfort his siblings, but madness leaped into his eyes. "I purchased that old flypaper at an estate auction last year. The ingredients were different in the early days. I soaked some of the stuff in a bottle of the Jim Beam that Johnny Rice favored. The right time to use it arrived with Maggie."

His smile raised goosebumps along Maggie's spine.

Purple rushed up into the sheriff's neck. He stood,

the old man cuffed to his wrist jerked up with him. Turkeson led the way across the hollow's floor to the trail opposite the make-believe stage. Maggie followed and never looked back.

Fate tossed a few words over his shoulder. "You are ruined, Brother. And for nothing."

Chance, his arm around Folly's waist, glanced down at her and got a watery smile in return. He directed his attention to his brother again. "Say no more. You need counsel. Doreen Rice was a kind-hearted, beautiful woman guilty of nothing but being lonely and loving unwisely." Despair settled over his features as he and Folly fell in behind the sheriff and Fate. "When Guy showed me her scrapbook this morning—" Chance fell silent.

The scrapbook again! Maggie stepped away from Guy, her arms akimbo. "You might have told me some of this. I thought you'd left the country, and me in jail."

Apology settled into Guy's expression. "It seemed better this way. Jamison and I—"

Like a flashbulb going off, highlighting all the day's madness and grief, Maggie realized how petty she sounded, and how silly Guy looked in the baggy red velveteen Santa suit. A giggle tickled her throat. She restrained it but yanked at his straggly beard, white cotton gray with age and sprinkled with what resembled bits of gold tinsel. "And take that fool thing off, will you?"

He complied, only his eyes smiling. He stuffed the beard into the front of his jacket.

The group started up the path. She asked, "So what else in the scrapbook clued you in?"

"Raffle tickets for a free Easter ham at Merkison's

Grocery." He inclined his head toward the attorney.

Had Guy lost his mind? She considered and then dropped her jaw and stared open-mouthed for a beat or two. "Chances?" She rolled her eyes and nodded. "Of course. We used to call raffle tickets 'chances.' Spend a quarter, get a chance to win something of value." How silly of her adult sister to symbolize her lover and the giver of those red accessories in such a girlish way. With her next breath, Maggie chastised herself. Hadn't she just gained a deeper insight on the sibling she'd lost too soon? "What a sentimental and clever woman, my sister."

"Hey, down there!" The shout from above drew everyone's attention. At the head of the trail stood Scaff Russell, his attorney friend, Edward Arnold Brewster, and the reporter who'd dogged Maggie's and Guy's tracks days earlier. Sick at heart, she looked away, only to see Guy shoot a glance at the newshound, then at his bulky camera.

He turned on her, steel in his gray-green eyes.

"Guy, I didn't—"

He'd wheeled, striding back down the trail and into the hollow.

"Hey, Santa," the reporter shouted. "Wait up." He ran after Guy, who had already neared the rock ledge at the bottom of the opposite slope.

Chance Halperin released his sister's waist and blocked the man's way.

"Leave him alone. He has a parade to catch."

Hollowed out, Maggie watched Guy walk away. The rigid line his back presented paralyzed her. He bypassed the flat stone outcropping and climbed upslope. On the far rim, he pushed aside winter-bare undergrowth.

She watched the red-clothed figure until the woods swallowed him.

Chapter 30

Maggie shivered beneath the morning breeze. She stood among several observers on what had been her grandmother's farm. Fate remained in his cell but had directed them to this spot on what would become Paula Rice's camp for disabled children.

Missing too, the deputy who deserved so much credit for exposing the evil that killed Doreen and Johnny. Maggie had heard nothing of Guy since he stalked from the natural amphitheater the previous day.

Turkeson stood nearby, unable yet to meet Maggie's eyes without looking away and adjusting his collar. Imagining his embarrassment over being bested by a fired deputy, she knew he shared her desperate wish that Scaff Russell and his camera crew would buzz off.

For the umpteenth time she told herself how wisely Guy Warner had done exactly that. If only the telling could make her feel less lonely in his absence.

She wanted to scream at the workmen to dig faster, yet dreaded the last turn of the shovel. The smell of damp, loamy earth she and Doreen had grown up associating with promise of new life, a fine corn crop, now bespoke death.

Maggie shivered again, the wool slacks, black sweater set, and her cloth coat little good against nerves and winter chill. Her young lawyer stood at her side.

He'd accepted her apology, and her thanks, for helping Guy find the scrapbook and figure out the clues it held.

His more seasoned counterpart represented the Halperin clan in the silent group. The shame that weighed down Chance's handsome features showed clear evidence of the borrowed guilt Maggie knew so well.

His and his sister Folly's apologies had earned Maggie's forgiveness, but how long would they carry the burden of their brother's treachery?

For her part, Maggie saw madness in the old man's decision to move the remains by night after realizing she'd eventually think to look in the old trash pit.

"Here, easy now!" The workman's exclamation drew her nearer the ditch. In the bottom of the hole, the corner of a black garbage bag stuck up in the loose dirt.

Maggie clamped her hand over the nausea that boiled up in her stomach. The sickness continued to rise and lodged in her throat. She blinked back the tears that stung her eyes to no avail. The droplets rolled hot down her icy cheeks.

Turkeson's gaze finally met and held hers, his once frightening eyes, sheep eyes this morning. "You oughtta go get in the car."

She forced words past the bile in her throat. "I came to Alden to find my sister. I'll wait."

But when the pitifully small bag that held Doreen's bones lay exposed, Maggie looked away. She heard the bundle lifted onto the ground beside the grave. Plastic rustled, exhaled the stench Maggie remembered from the old deer hides in the pit.

"Is…is it…?" She covered her mouth to hold back what little breakfast she'd managed to swallow.

"Must be," Turkeson said. Plastic rustled again. "Bigod!" Turkeson exclaimed. "The old bastard bundled the other shoe up with her and didn't even realize what he'd done."

****

Crouched nearby behind a stack of old lumber, Guy Warner shivered in his thin, khaki jacket. Every lick of common sense he'd ever claimed told him he should be far away.

Twin diesel locomotives couldn't have dragged him from Maggie until he knew for sure her quest would end among the ditches and piles of dirt destined to become a place for mentally disadvantaged children to romp and play. He'd heard of the widow Rice's breakdown. He hoped the project would continue without her to oversee progress.

Doreen had wanted her child and Chance's to live. Maybe she rested in peace here on the old Simpson home place, and Maggie might arrange for her return to some private corner of the property once the authorities released her remains.

Through a break in the haphazardly piled boards, Guy studied the determination on Maggie's mouth. Often exasperating, the look always tempted him to kiss it away. He held little doubt she'd make it just fine and have a happy career back in Hollywood.

Why didn't he feel better about leaving, then?

The thought shoved aside, he watched the workers remove the black plastic bag from the earth. Turkeson checked the contents. Guy leaned closer to his peep hole. Something sharp poked his knee, but he didn't flinch, too fixed on the object the sheriff retrieved from the bag and handed to Maggie.

She clutched it to her heart and closed her eyes. Her lips moved.

Guy, watching closely, thought she said, "Forgive me for doubting you, Doreen."

Chance Halperin lowered his head and stumbled away. His wife, who stood near Folly, watched him go.

Maybe in time she'd forgive too.

At noon that same day Guy drove past the city limits in Ray Evans's old pickup truck. Selling his Studebaker to buy the truck pained him, but not nearly like leaving Maggie behind.

On the dashboard, the highway map lay as crisply folded as new. He could think of nowhere he wanted to go, except to the Morning Glory Hotel, where he suspected Maggie would welcome him with as much joy as she would a pimple on her pretty little nose.

He switched on the radio. "HELL, brothers and sisters. This country is headed for hell in a handbasket unless we repent." The voice soared a notch. "Repent…repent…"

Guy clicked the off switch. No use, he knew, trying another station, not on Sunday in the Bible Belt. His stomach felt sour enough from too much black coffee and Chance's sermon about how foolish he, Guy, had been for not at least phoning Maggie before skipping town.

He fumbled what felt like a roll of antacid tablets from the his peacoat's side pocket. Stared down at the object in surprise. A tube of lipstick? Then he remembered that she'd run out of the kind she made herself and brushed on. He returned the tube to this pocket and patted the bump it made.

Two miles beyond the city limits, he glanced into

his rearview mirror and swore. Would the man never give up?

He let the Ford drift onto the shoulder and braked. He cranked down the window and leaned into the opening on one elbow with his forehead propped in his hand while he watched in the side mirror. The attorney climbed from the white Corvette, circled around to open the passenger door.

Gaze narrowed, Guy twisted in his seat to look over his shoulder.

The old woman who got out, hobbled on a cane. Bent almost double, she stepped, stopped, stepped, stopped, as if any inch of ground might suddenly open beneath her sturdy black oxfords.

Her gray-streaked hair knotted at the nape of her neck, she topped it off with an electric-blue hat that sported a tall green feather. Despite a steadily rising temperature, she wore a heavy brown coat that dragged at her heels.

A grin tickled Guy's throat before he felt it twist his mouth. He climbed out of the pickup to wait for her. At first, he thought she was mumbling at him.

When he caught a familiar tune, and the word disguise, his grin widened.

She sang a few more lines.

Guy burst out laughing.

Eyes clear as emeralds slanted up beneath the blue hat brim. "Going my way, Sonny?"

"Have I any choice?" He tilted his head toward Chance Halperin, just putting her luggage next to the cat carrier in the pickup's cargo bed.

Tears bright in his blue eyes, Chance saluted and turned quickly away.

Guy helped Maggie into the truck, the little boost he gave her rump anything but polite. She slapped at his hand, but laughed.

"Wardrobe by Folly Halperin?" he guessed. "I've seen her wear the hat."

"It helped get me through the hotel lobby without a second glance from the camera crew waiting there with Scaff Russell."

"You'll have to teach me some of your tricks."

Her smile queried exactly what tricks Guy had in mind and agreed to almost anything.

Neither spoke again for the space of several deep and satisfying kisses, after which he cranked up the old pickup and eased it back onto the tarmac.

"You'll miss old Beetlebomb," she said, patting his leg.

"She brought enough that I can trade up. Easier to disappear from Ed Moroni's thugs without her."

"I'll have to check with Chance Halperin later about final disposition of Doreen's remains," she said, and then appraised him carefully. "I hate to tell you, but the peacoat is too identifiable. Moroni's guys will be on you like a crow on a grasshopper."

He hated to give up the coat, he'd had it since Korea—had reclaimed it that morning from Chance, who'd worn it home that night he told Guy about the raccoon's death.

But what the heck. "I could let go of the coat too. Play vacuum cleaner salesman. Cheap suit. Old fedora."

"And I could play the farmer's daughter." Giggling, Maggie gave his leg another pat, higher up.

A word about the author…

Raymona Marie Anderson loved writing for newspapers and magazines, but more loves making-up stories. Her *Two Hearts in Time* from The Wild Rose Press drew from travel writing experiences to concoct a steamy romance set in Yucatan. *Bitter Pills and Deadly Potions* cools down to chilling suspense in small-town America. Native to such a place, the author, like the story's main character, played a brief role onstage when a traveling medicine show came to town in the late forties. Unlike that character, she suffered no ill consequences. An Oklahoma resident for most of her life, she now lives in Arkansas.

Thank you for purchasing
this publication of The Wild Rose Press, Inc.

For questions or more information
contact us at
info@thewildrosepress.com.

The Wild Rose Press, Inc.
www.thewildrosepress.com

To visit with authors of
The Wild Rose Press, Inc.
join our yahoo loop at
http://groups.yahoo.com/group/thewildrosepress/

Milton Keynes UK
Ingram Content Group UK Ltd.
UKHW031833300124
436988UK00013B/837